CARA DION

Print ISBN: 979-8-9882826-6-2
Ebook ISBN:979-8-9882826-5-5
Imprint: Independently published

First edition

Cover designed by Stephanie Anderson at Alt 19 Creative.

Also by Cara Dion

Love Song Series

Irreplaceable

Indiscreet

Undeniable

Aster Bay Series

Whisking It All

Just For Show

Visit my website to learn more and download free bonus content:

*For every woman who has been told to make herself smaller:
May we all learn to unapologetically take up space.*

Prologue

16 months ago

On a Wednesday in June, Kyla Mitchell made the biggest mistake of her life.

The Williston University art gallery was housed in a sand-colored stone building on the edge of the main campus, across the quad from a glass and ivy-covered building that housed the library. Every Wednesday afternoon, Kyla skipped buying a sandwich from the cart outside the library and instead spent her break staring at her favorite painting. It was her small oasis in the midst of the chaos of her senior year, a moment she made for herself to gather the strength to face the uncertainty of her impending graduation.

Everything was coming together: she was graduating a year early, she had a job she loved working as a bakery assistant for a farmstand in town while she decided what type of photography she'd like to pursue professionally, and she'd even met a guy a few weeks back who was cute and funny and didn't stare at the way her jeans dug into her belly when she sat down.

So what if the guy didn't give her butterflies or the job didn't challenge her creatively or her parents wouldn't be attending her graduation? Kyla was happy.

Happy enough.

That particular Wednesday, she was one of the only people in the gallery, which wasn't unusual. At the end of a long hall, the building opened up in a small gallery space with art arranged around the perimeter. She didn't need to look at the pieces—she knew each one in this room by heart.

First on the left would be the marble carving of a snowy owl, its knowing eyes staring down anyone who dared to meet its gaze. Next the bronze casting of a woman in a 1950s swimsuit building a sandcastle, sand dripping from her fingers onto the tallest spire. The sculptures eventually gave way to sketches—mostly woodland creatures with the occasional landscape—and then, on the other side of the room, the oil paintings. Kyla's favorite.

She checked her phone. Brodie, the guy she'd been seeing, was supposed to meet her. They'd only been dating a few weeks, but she wanted to introduce him to this place she loved, to see how he'd react to the oil painting of a run-down dinghy bobbing in a sea of gray—gray water, gray sky, the only color the faded red of the boat. She loved that painting, though she couldn't explain why. Over the last three years she'd spent hours studying it, trying to uncover why it made her throat feel tight and her eyes water, but she never uncovered its secrets.

As she approached the oil paintings, she came to a startled stop. For the first time in three years, someone else was seated on the wide bench in front of her favorite painting. Not just any someone, but the most handsome man she'd ever laid eyes on.

Though he was sitting, he was obviously tall, his broad back and large biceps straining the seams of his tweed blazer. His hands were folded in the lap of his jeans, a brown briefcase on the floor beside his Oxfords. From here, she could see the way his sandy-colored hair was too long on top, flopping into his eyes, giving him a boyish appearance despite the hint of gray at his temples. A carefully sculpted five o'clock shadow defined his strong jaw and framed full lips.

Kyla shook herself and continued on towards the bench. It was large enough for them both to sit, even if she suspected it would be harder to focus on the painting with this Thor of a man sitting next to her.

What is wrong with you? It's not like you've never seen an attractive man before.

"May I?" she asked, gesturing to the empty place on the bench.

He smiled, his eyes warming and crinkling at the edges. She felt that warmth down to her toes. "Please." He scooted over slightly to give her more room.

Kyla settled on the bench, placing her bag on the floor beside her, and checked her phone again. Brodie was already five minutes late. This new guy might be funny but he certainly wasn't punctual.

"I love this painting," the man said, inclining his head towards the dinghy. "There's something so defiant about it."

"Defiant?" She turned to look at the painting herself. "I would have said serene."

There was that smile again. "That too. But that boat is holding its ground. You can tell."

"What do you mean?"

"It's the only boat in the water. It's battered and beaten but still floating. There's a storm coming in." He pointed to wisps of gray clouds at the edges of the frame. "But it's still bobbing along. Dinged and weathered but still bright red." He turned towards her, lowering his voice as though telling her a grave secret, his expression growing serious. "It's a survivor." He smiled with just the slightest curve of his lips and straightened up again.

She turned back to the painting, her nose tingling with warning of oncoming tears and she blinked them away. What a silly thing to cry about.

"Someone should be caring for it," the man continued, oblivious to her impending illogical breakdown. "But still it persists. It takes care of itself."

"Maybe it doesn't have a choice."

He turned to look at her then, his eyes roaming her face, and she had the strangest sensation that she'd said more than she meant to. He opened his mouth as though about to speak, but she cut him off, afraid that if she let him keep talking, she'd reveal too much of herself.

"Are you an art history professor or something?" she chuckled, hoping to dispel the uncomfortable tangle of emotion knotting itself in her belly.

"Or something." He ran his gaze over her, his eyes crackling with mischief and heat when he returned to meet her eyes, and held out his hand. "I'm Gavin."

She shook his hand, telling herself to ignore the zing of electricity that shot up her arm at his touch. *Probably just static.* "Kyla."

"I've seen you before. Here. Admiring this painting."

"I come every Wednesday."

He hummed and dug into the briefcase at his feet, producing a giant chocolate chip cookie. He broke it in half and held part of it out to her. "So do I."

She laughed incredulously, staring at the proffered pastry. "What is this?"

"It's a cookie."

"You're going to get us in trouble. I don't think we're supposed to have food in here." She bit her lip to suppress her smile. Why was talking to this guy so much fun? When was the last time she'd been so tempted to bend the rules.

"It'll be our secret." Her skin tingled at the words in his smooth, gravelly voice. Suddenly she wanted all his secrets, and to share all of hers in return, to craft secrets of their own. When she still didn't take the cookie, he shrugged. "Suit yourself." He pulled her piece back and took a giant bite out of it.

"Hey!" she laughed. "That was my half."

"I thought you didn't want it," he teased.

"Who doesn't want a cookie?" She took the unbitten half from him and sank her teeth into it.

He watched her eat, his eyes tracing the movement when her tongue darted out to lick the chocolate from her lips, and her stomach flipped.

She felt a momentary twinge of guilt—she was meant to be meeting Brodie, after all—but he was late, again, if he was coming at all, and they'd only been dating a few weeks. She'd let him down gently. Tell him it wasn't working out. She didn't want to be the girl who was waiting for the guy who may or may not remember they were supposed to meet; she wanted to be the girl who shared secret pastries in art galleries with handsome men that shared her love of art.

Stop getting ahead of yourself, Kyla. This guy's just a flirt, and he's probably twice your age. You can't go breaking up with Brodie just because some older guy with a movie star smile paid attention to you for a few minutes.

"If you come every Wednesday, how come I've never seen you before?" she asked.

"I usually come just before closing, when I'm done for the day. But last week I came on my lunch break."

"And you decided it was the superior time to visit the art gallery?" she asked.

"If it meant I might get to talk to you, then yes."

This guy was too charming, too smooth. She knew she should brush it off and go about her day but there was something disarming about his smile, a quiet swagger that said he could break your heart but wouldn't. An intriguing confidence that promised he might just ruin you for other men. For the first time in a long time, Kyla found herself wondering if that might be exactly what she needed.

If he asked her to leave with him, she would say yes without hesitation.

Ask me.

"Besides," he said, turning back towards the painting as he popped the last of his cookie half into his mouth, "anyone who loves this painting as much as I do is worth getting to know."

"It's my favorite."

"Mine too." He lowered his voice, his eyes narrowing as he stared at the painting, as though he expected the boat to actually bob up and down on the canvas. "Sometimes I dream about that boat, about who might have left it all alone like that. About who will come find it."

"You mean who will rescue it?" she asked.

"I don't think it needs rescuing. But I'm sure it wouldn't mind the company." He glanced at her and this conversation suddenly felt so much heavier than talking about a painting.

"I'm sure it wouldn't."

As though he knew, somehow, that she needed a reprieve from the intensity of their conversation, he gestured to the corner of the room. "That's my second favorite piece."

She turned to look. "The Klimt knock off?" she asked, wrinkling her nose.

"No, the sculpture."

"What sculpture?" She glanced around, following the direction of his gesture. "Do you mean the trash can?"

"The sculpture," he confirmed. "What do you think it's called? Homage to modern consumerism? Decay and Discard?"

"I think it's a trash can, just like every other trash can on campus," she said with an incredulous laugh.

"And here I thought you were an artist," he teased, nudging her shoulder with his own.

"In fact, I am. A photographer."

"Really?" His smile lit up his face and she had the strangest urge to press her lips against that gentle curve. "Anything I might have seen?"

She turned on the bench so she was facing the opposite wall and gestured towards a small arrangement of three photographs. He took her hand, pulling her up after him and leading her across the room, ignoring her laughing protests.

"These are yours?" he asked, not releasing her hand even once they'd reached their destination.

"Mmhmm. My senior thesis."

The first photo was of her boss, Cheryl, her hands dug into a mound of dough as she kneaded it, half her face bathed in shadow and the light highlighting the strength in her hands as it worked the dough into submission. The second was of her boss' husband, Ricky, triumphantly holding a bunch of beets above the earth where they'd been growing only moments before the photo was snapped, speckles of dirt still falling from the purple orbs, dirt caked in the creases of his hand and streaked across his face. The final photo was Cheryl and Ricky together, her stirring a pot on the stove as he stood behind her, hands on her hips and face nestled into her shoulder, a quiet contentment on both their faces illuminated by the sun streaming through the window to their right.

"Simple pleasures," she said. He turned to look at her, an unreadable look on his face. "That's what I call it."

"They're beautiful." He swallowed, the bob of his Adam's apple a tempting distraction, and turned back to the photos. "You really captured their relationship."

"That's my boss, Cheryl, and her husband—"

"Ricky," he finished. She turned questioning eyes his way. "I know the DaSilvas quite well. I didn't know Cheryl had an employee, though."

"I help with the baking for the farm stand."

He nodded, his eyes running over her as though he were seeing her for the first time all over again. He shuffled closer, rolling his lips through his teeth in a way that made her wonder what those lips and teeth would feel like on her skin.

Ask me.

His eyes held hers and she tried to trace the shimmering flecks of gold in his green irises, the way they danced like flames.

"Kyla, would you—"

"Babe!"

Kyla exhaled sharply, shaking herself from whatever magic spell Gavin had been weaving around her, and turned to find Brodie marching across the gallery towards her. His sneakers squeaked on the polished floor and she forced herself to smile as he approached.

"I wasn't sure if you were coming," she said.

"Sorry about that. I'm awful at keeping track of time." He came to a halt beside her and slung an arm over her shoulder, its weight heavy across her neck, but when he spoke, he addressed Gavin. "What are you doing here, old man?"

Kyla turned to Gavin, confusion creasing her brow. His mouth opened and then closed without speaking. Again he swallowed, ducked his head and ran his fingers through his hair, before he met Brodie's eyes again. "Just admiring the art."

"Do you two know each other?" Kyla asked, glancing between them.

Brodie gestured to Gavin. "Babe, this is my dad."

Chapter One

A good father wasn't supposed to lust after his son's girlfriend.

But Gavin West did. More than a year after Kyla had started dating his son, and somehow he fantasized about her even more now than he had that first day.

It made him a shitty father and at least ten kinds of asshole, but Christ, he wanted her more than he'd wanted anyone in over a decade. He wanted her bright smiles and her brilliant mind, lazy mornings discussing her art and hazy midnights tangled in each other's arms—fuck, he wanted it all.

Figures that the only woman you want is the one woman you absolutely cannot have.

He'd passed a sleepless night, knowing Kyla Mitchell was under his roof with his son. He supposed that was why he only half heard them as they shuffled down the stairs into the kitchen in the morning, not giving him enough time to make himself scarce. He was still fumbling with the coffee maker when Kyla appeared around the corner, the sunlight streaming through the window over the kitchen sink making her blonde hair shine like silver. He immediately clocked the tight set of Kyla's lips, the way she fiddled with the strap of the tote bag slung over her shoulder, though Brodie seemed oblivious to his girlfriend's mood.

"Move out of the way, old man," Brodie laughed as he sidled up next to him at the kitchen counter. He took the little plastic piece that Gavin could never fit into the coffee maker properly from his hands. "I've got this."

"Thanks," Gavin mumbled. He focused on getting juice from the fridge and pouring a glass. He set it on the kitchen table in front of Kyla and she flashed him a shy smile as she accepted the juice, the apples of her cheeks growing pink. He swallowed down all the things he wanted to tell her, none of which he was allowed to say to his son's girlfriend.

You're beautiful, and *you deserve better than my son,* and *I could make you happy.*

"You two are up early," he said instead.

Brodie used his teeth to rip into a package of pop tarts, taking a bite out of the corner of one of the overly sweet pastries as the coffee maker finally started working. Brodie tilted his chin towards Kyla. "Ky needs to be at the bakery early today. 'Swhy we stayed here last night—it's closer. Probably stay here tonight too." He held out the second pop tart to Kyla. "You want one, babe?"

She blinked away from where she'd been watching Gavin as he brought out the creamer and refilled the sugar bowl, anything to keep his hands busy.

"No, thanks."

"I was about to make eggs for myself," Gavin said. He wasn't. "I can make you some too. Both of you."

"That'd be really nice. Thank you," she said with a soft smile.

"Your eggs are shit," Brodie said around a mouthful of pop tart. He threw a wink at Kyla. "I'll make 'em."

Brodie grabbed the non-stick pan and a large metal spatula from the rack over the stove, a spatula that would scrape the hell out of the non-stick coating and destroy the pan. For all his time spent working in the kitchen at Lemon and Thyme, Brodie still hadn't learned how to take care of his things. Gavin pulled the spatula from his hand and replaced it with a silicone one.

"Actually, I'm glad we caught you this morning," Kyla said, and Gavin tried not to let that stupid flutter in his chest read anything into her words. *This is a reading-free zone.* "I have those photos you wanted," she continued. Gavin turned to find her digging into her bag, her gaze darting between Gavin and Brodie. "The ones for the Travel Network proposal." She pulled out a tablet in a black leather case and placed it on the kitchen table, watching Gavin expectantly.

"Great." He hoped his heart wasn't beating loudly enough for her to hear. He took the seat opposite Kyla and picked up the tablet. "May I?" he asked, his fingers poised to flip open the case.

She smiled. "Please."

The screen blinked to life on a stunning photograph. In it, Kyla's willowy blonde roommate Jo stood on the sidewalk in front of Aster Place in a floor length gown, complete with puffy sleeves and a glittering skirt made from layers of tulle. She wore a tiara that Gavin recognized as the one Aster Bay High gave each year to its homecoming queen. Jo looked back over her shoulder at the white, Federal-style mansion, an expression of beatific longing on her face. The historic house museum and its famous rose bushes were limned with rose-gold light as the sun set behind them, making the entire picture seem to glow.

Gavin had known Kyla was an excellent photographer—certainly the best in Aster Bay—when he'd asked for her help with this proposal, but he hadn't expected this level of detail.

"Where did you find a powder blue ballgown?" Gavin asked, staring at the expertly staged photograph.

"Never underestimate Tessa's thrifting skills." Kyla pointed to the glittering silver pump peeking out from beneath the hem of the ballgown. "And it's amazing what some spray glitter can do to an old pair of shoes."

"That glitter got everywhere," Brodie said over his shoulder as he whisked the eggs. "Her apartment looks like a stripper bomb went off."

"This is perfect," Gavin gaped as he swiped to the next photo, ignoring his son's comment.

This time Jo wore a long, form-fitting pink dress, her hair pinned up at her temples. The hem of the dress brushed the grass of Longfield Farm as she stood in the open doorway to the barn. One side of the shot displayed the endless, sun-kissed fields of the farm, sheep grazing freely and the sleepy, modest farmhouse off in the distance, a plume of smoke rising from the chimney. The other side was dark, the dimly lit main room of the barn beyond the open door, the floor covered with piles of hay and the rafters hung with drying herbs and dyed wool in various muted shades. At the far edge of the frame, a single spinning wheel sat amidst a pile of hay, a mysterious light shining on it so that the polished wood gleamed, drawing the attention of Jo's Sleeping Beauty as she moved from the daylight into the barn.

"It's easy when there are so many beautiful places to shoot." Kyla blushed, as though she wanted to brush away his praise.

There was another of Jo in a Rapunzel wig, her braided locks studded with flowers and her arms stretched wide as she twirled on the town common, her dress fanning out around her knees. Another had her donning a simple blue dress and apron, a basket looped over her arm with a baguette peeking out of the top, as she walked down Main Street, the storefronts all looking charming and quaint with their window boxes of fresh flowers. And another of her in a red wig and skimpy teal bathing suit as she walked along the beach, bare feet sinking into wet sand.

"If these don't convince the Travel Network that Aster Bay is the perfect place to film their new show, nothing will," Gavin said. "You've made the town look like someone painted it."

"You said to make it look like a fairytale. Princesses and all."

"And you delivered. You'll have the tourism board banging down your door once they see these."

Kyla laughed, a self-effacing chuckle as she brushed off the compliment. "I have a good camera."

"You have an *expensive* camera," Brodie said.

"You're talented," Gavin corrected them both.

Why did she keep deflecting? It was something he'd noticed ever since he'd started hiring her as the photographer on his marketing jobs for the town—Kyla Mitchell didn't know how to take a compliment.

But Gavin wasn't just placating her. Kyla was an exceptional photographer. He'd hired her on several occasions over the last ten months since the Food and Wine Festival when her photographs of their friends Jamie and Tessa had gone viral locally and helped the festival draw in larger crowds than ever before. It had been her idea, as well, to change their marketing strategy, to target a younger demographic with packages that showed off their small Rhode Island town. They were using that same strategy again this year, and even a month before opening day, the festival was nearly sold out.

Gavin may have been the marketing professor, and the Merchants' Association's de facto marketing consultant, but Kyla was innovative and naturally gifted in a way he never would be. He knew how to optimize internet ads, how to use email marketing to nurture customers, when to buy billboards and when to get op-eds printed in the local paper, but he wasn't coming up with anything new. Everything Gavin did could be learned in a book—like the ones he used to teach his students at Williston University so they, too, could be textbook-perfect marketing machines.

But Kyla saw things in new ways. Pride bloomed in his chest each time she rose to the challenge, but it was complicated by something else—a tinge of envy, of longing. He knew the mechanics but she knew how to turn them into art. He wanted to understand how her brain worked, how she shifted the lens of her camera and changed the narrative, how she knew that angle and that light and that shadow would combine to take a person's breath away.

The next shot featured Jo in the same red wig and a Princess Diana style white wedding dress on the steps of St. Anthony's, her arm linked with a smug-looking Brodie in what was, obviously, a Halloween store Prince Eric costume. The church was lit from within, the stained-glass windows shimmering like gems in the stone façade against a cloudless blue sky.

"I see you got in on the act," Gavin said to his son.

"Jamie gave me the day off work to help." Brodie poured the beaten eggs into the hot pan on the stove. "Since it was for the town."

Gavin was surprised Kyla had convinced his son to dress up, even if it did mean he'd gotten a day off work. Then again, women were often able to convince their boyfriends to do things they might not otherwise do. Or so he gathered. It had been a long time since Gavin had been anyone's significant other.

Kyla lowered her voice, as though she was sharing a secret with Gavin. "A case of beer and a pizza and he's pretty amenable to most things."

"Right," Gavin said.

He didn't want to know what else Kyla might have done to bribe his son. And he really didn't want to examine why that was. The more he worked with Kyla, the more he got to know her, the less he understood why she was giving his son the time of day. His throat tightened with a twist of guilt at the thought. *Just another thing to feel guilty about.*

Gavin swiped to the next image and his breath caught in his chest. This one was dimly light, lush velvets and soft leathers emerging from the shadows. There, at the center of the photograph, lying flat on her back on the wood floor, was Kyla. Her back was arched, her knees bent, a hand dug into her hair, more silver than blonde in the stark lighting. And she was practically naked.

He knew he should hand the tablet back, turn it over, put it down—*anything* other than keep staring at it. But he couldn't tear his eyes away. She wore a black lace bra, the cups not nearly large enough for her generous chest. The dusky circles of her nipples furled against the fabric, the light drawn to those hard peaks the same way his eyes were. Her abdomen was a swath of bare skin, smooth and pale, lushly curved and pillowy soft, only interrupted by the thin strap of her panties. It indented her skin and he wanted to push the string away, soothe the red mark he was almost certain it had left behind.

Fuck.

But there was something more than just the bare skin and unapologetic sexuality. Somehow the picture had captured something he'd never seen before in a photograph—a vulnerability, an open-hearted offering up of herself. Almost as if she were being reborn of those shadows, washed clean by the light. A raw, unabashed embracing of not just how goddamn sexy she was, but of her strength. This wasn't a woman who demurred when she was offered a compliment. This was a woman who knew her worth, who demanded the things she wanted. It was like seeing some private moment of awakening not meant for him.

"Which one—" She leaned across the table to see which photo had him so riveted.

He snapped the tablet case shut and pushed it back across the table towards her, his lungs burning, his mouth gone dry. "Sorry. That one's not—"

She cursed under her breath, her cheeks turning pink as she shoved the tablet back in her bag. "It must have skipped to the next album. So stupid," she mumbled under her breath. "Not even a good shot."

"It's stunning," he said. *Shut up.*

That pink traveled down her throat and her eyes locked with his.

"They all are," he said.

"Thanks." Her voice was a barely-there whisper of sound that he felt down to his toes.

Stop. She's your son's girlfriend.

Kyla studied him for a moment and he watched in fascination as the blush cleared from her skin, just the barest hints of it still lingering on her cheeks. She squared her shoulders, meeting his gaze with a confidence he felt sure she had rehearsed. "I've decided to open my own photography studio."

"That's great—"

"A boudoir photography studio," she continued, cutting him off.

"Not this again," Brodie groaned as he set three plates of eggs on the table and moved back to dig through the dishwasher for clean forks. Over the clatter of silverware, he continued. "Babe, I thought we talked about this. Why would anyone pay you to take their dirty pictures when they can just take naked selfies like everyone else does?" He dropped the silverware onto the table in a pile, keeping one fork for himself as he took the chair between Gavin and Kyla.

"Lots of people pay for boudoir photography," she said, her voice smaller somehow.

Brodie snorted as he stabbed a forkful of eggs. "Nah, babe. No one pays for porn anymore." He gestured with his fork towards her untouched plate, a smug smile curving his lips and, for the first time in his life, Gavin seriously considered punching someone. "Don't let those eggs I made for you get cold."

"I think it sounds like a great idea." Gavin's fingers dug into his coffee cup. He didn't know anything about boudoir photography, but if that photograph in her portfolio was it, it was hardly porn. It was sexy as hell, sure, but it was also artistic, evocative. "Have you thought about where you'd like to open the studio?"

Kyla looked down, pushing her eggs around her plate. "I've already talked with Natalia. She's been looking for ways to expand her lingerie shop and appeal to more of the brides who come to town for wedding season. She's willing to partner with me. I just need to get together the capital to renovate the empty unit next-door to her shop with changing rooms and furniture, replace the windows, upgrade the heating system. That kind of thing." She spoke softly, glancing up at Gavin every few words.

She never once looked at Brodie, a fact that made Gavin both immeasurably grateful and infinitely angry. She should be able to share her excitement with her boyfriend, and instead his son was being a dismissive ass.

Gavin's brain was struggling to process it all, his mind unhelpfully repeating the thought that there might be more photos like the one he'd glimpsed. He forced himself to focus on what she'd said, about the mechanics of opening the business. "That sounds like a big investment."

"It is. I have a meeting next week with the bank—"

"You know what you should do." Brodie gestured with his fork, bits of egg falling off the tines onto the table. "You should see if you can be one of those photographers that goes into schools and takes all the kids' pictures for the yearbooks and shit."

Kyla's brow furrowed as she stared at Brodie in disbelief. "You want me to take school pictures?"

"Why not? There's a hell of a lot more school kids who need their picture taken than people who are gonna pay for that other stuff." He slid his empty plate away from him, shaking his head like she just didn't understand. "It's not even *good* porn, Ky."

"Brodie," Gavin warned, the sharp edge to his voice the same one he'd used when his son was a kid and had thought it would be funny to tell scatological jokes at Thanksgiving dinner.

"What?" Brodie asked. "You saw it." He frowned. "That's weird as fuck, by the way." The frown turned to a disbelieving laugh at the sheer ridiculousness of Gavin having seen Kyla's photograph.

But Brodie was wrong—not about Gavin having seen the photograph; that was objectively weird, though he supposed no weirder than him lying awake at night imagining what could have been if he was twenty years younger. *Add it to the list of unconfessed sins.* That photograph wasn't porn, and it wasn't just *good.* It was so painfully beautiful it belonged in a museum, and the fact that Kyla didn't seem to know that, that his son had the power to make her doubt it, was more than Gavin could take.

"I have to go." Gavin pushed away from the table and his uneaten plate of eggs. "I have papers to grade before my first class."

"I'll send you the files," Kyla said with a weak smile, "for the proposal."

"Thank you." He hoped he could imbue those two words with so many things— *you're an amazing photographer,* and *I'm sorry my son is a jerk,* and *I wish I'd met you first.*

Gavin grabbed his briefcase from its place by the door and shrugged on his coat, pretending he couldn't hear Kyla and Brodie's whispered argument at the kitchen table. Once in the safety of his car, he gripped the steering wheel with both hands and leaned his forehead against the cool leather, squeezing his eyes shut. But the image of Kyla burned behind his eyelids, her back bowed, a look of surrender on her face as the light kissed her curves.

Chapter Two

"Just arch your back a little more," Kyla said between snapping shots with her camera.

Jo, seated on the floor of their living room with her head resting on the seat of their secondhand couch, which had been artfully draped with a fuzzy teal blanket to hide the rips in the fabric, complied with the direction.

"Perfect." Kyla hovered above her, balancing precariously on a dining room chair that she'd dragged into the living room, and snapped another shot. "Now, put your left hand in your hair. No, your other left."

"I only have one left." Jo smirked as she switched hands.

"Relax your mouth. That's it. Don't move."

The sound of her shutter clicking in rapid fire filled the room. Kyla lowered her camera, glanced at the image on the screen, and then hopped off the chair. "I think we got it."

Jo sat up and adjusted the strap of her lacy bodysuit. "Let me see." She lifted herself up onto the couch and patted the spot next to her for Kyla to sit.

Kyla held the camera's screen out towards her roommate, clicking through to show the last few images they'd captured.

"Damn, my ass looks good," Jo said. "You are so good at this."

"Your butt looks good all the time."

"True. But you are also really good at this."

"Thanks." Kyla hugged her camera to her chest and leaned back on the couch. "Natalia wants to blow up a few shots and hang them in the dressing room at her shop."

"It's a good idea," Jo said, pulling on the strap again. "And once you get your studio opened next door, it'll be good advertising for you too."

"That's the idea. Cross promotion. If I can ever get a loan."

"You will. I have a good feeling about your next appointment." Jo got to her feet and disappeared down the hall.

"I hope you're right," Kyla called after her. "This is the last bank in the area. If they turn me down too—"

"They won't," came Jo's answering shout. "Remember, eye on the prize. This is your year." She reappeared in the doorway to the living room wearing a fuzzy bathrobe and, Kyla suspected, not much else. She struck a dramatic pose in the doorway. "The Year of Kyla." Kyla hurled a throw pillow at her with a laugh. "Besides, you've already checked one item off your list for the year."

Number one: stop settling for happy enough. Break up with Brodie once and for all.

Kyla had been surprised how easy it was to end things with Brodie. They'd been together—off and on—for over a year. Though, if she was honest with herself, for the last six months he'd felt more like a friend who regularly borrowed her car and who she'd have mediocre sex with after a glass or two of wine. There was no spark. Lately she wondered if there'd ever been one, or if she'd just convinced herself that he was nice enough, cute enough, interested in her enough. He hadn't cringed at the faint stretch marks on her stomach and never made her feel bad when she had an irrational meltdown in the ice cream aisle (though that happened less and less—therapy for the win, thank you very much), so what did it matter if he didn't set her heart racing or get her all hot and bothered?

At least, that's what she'd been telling herself. But for the last several months she couldn't help wondering: what would it be like if someone *did* make her weak in the knees? What would it be like to date someone where there wasn't just a spark, but a whole damn bonfire?

She didn't know. But she intended to find out.

The Year of Kyla.

"I'm proud of you, by the way. For finally kicking Brodie to the curb. You deserve so much more," Jo said.

"It wasn't all bad." Kyla fiddled with her camera. "In the beginning... He was the first guy who didn't make me feel like he was doing me a favor, taking the fat girl out on a date."

Jo stared at her in disbelief. "Showing the bare minimum of human decency doesn't earn him a pass on all the other ways he made you feel shitty about yourself. And fuck those other guys."

Kyla sighed, straightening her shoulders, adopting a posture of more confidence than she felt. That's what her therapist had said to do, right? Fake it until it felt natural. "I don't want to talk about Brodie anymore. I've spent enough time talking about him."

Jo nodded and plopped down on the couch next to Kyla again. She flipped on the television, cycling through the channels until she found the evening news. "I hope it's not going to rain tomorrow."

"Big plans?" Kyla asked.

"I picked up an extra shift at The Bay Breeze and horny frat boys are less likely to come out in the rain, which means fewer tips for their smoking hot bartender." Jo gestured to herself as though she were on display.

"It's official," the chipper host on the local news said on the television screen. "The Travel Network's newest production, *Once Upon A Town*, has just announced that it will film its first season in Aster Bay."

"Isn't that the show we took those fairytale pictures for?" Jo asked.

"Did they just say what I think they said?" Kyla grabbed the remote and turned up the volume.

The host on screen continued, "Producers describe *Once Upon A Town* as a cross between *The Bachelor* and the network's popular *Small Town America* series with a unique fairytale twist. One 'Prince Charming' will be chosen from amongst Aster Bay's male residents to join the show, where single women, known as 'eligible ladies,' will vie for his heart and a chance at a happily-ever-after worthy of royalty, complete with a cash prize."

"Oh my God, Ky, that's perfect!" Jo chirped, sitting up straighter.

"What is?"

"Shhh!" Jo waved a hurried hand to silence her friend as the prepared video for the segment began to air.

"You're the one—"

"Hush!"

A tall, attractive, middle-aged man with hardly any hair and wire-framed glasses appeared on the screen. Text across the bottom of the screen identified him as Patrick Kemp, Executive Producer. "In traditional reality dating shows, the couples fall in love while isolated from their real lives: their friends, families, careers—even the places they live. It's only at the very end that those elements are introduced, like a final test of their relationship. But relationships don't happen in a vacuum. In *Once Upon A Town*, the cast will live in Aster Bay during filming, with our Prince Charming being chosen from Aster Bay, so our show is completely immersed in this sense of place from the beginning. Of course, we also believe that love should be a fairytale and there is no place better for a modern fairytale than America's small towns."

Jo hit Kyla's arm excitedly. "That's exactly what you need!"

"A bruise?" Kyla asked, rubbing the spot on her bicep.

"A modern fairytale!"

The voiceover on the screen told viewers that Patrick Kemp was the nephew of local resident, Judy Kemp, and he'd spent his summers visiting Aster Bay as a child. "I was thrilled when the town put forth a proposal to host the first season of *Once Upon A Town*. Aster Bay was one of the only towns to fully embrace the fairytale theme in their proposal," the producer said. "Dr. West and Ms. Mitchell put together a very impressive proposal. Ms. Mitchell's photographs really helped our creative team envision how our show could work here, and we are excited to revisit many of the locations featured."

"Holy shit," Kyla breathed, leaning forward at the same time Jo sprang into the air whooping.

"You just got a shout out on the *news*!" Jo cried. "Fuck, yeah!"

"He liked my photos," Kyla said, hardly believing any of it was real. "Holy shit. Our proposal won."

It had been seven months since they'd submitted their proposal. She'd begun to give up on the idea that they might be chosen, had wondered if she should have found a way to represent Aladdin and Snow White and whatever other fairytale would have convinced the people at The Travel Network to come here.

But now they had. They'd chosen Aster Bay. She and Gavin had done it.

Did Gavin know yet? She reached for her phone, itching to text him and ask, but her finger hovered over his name on her screen without clicking. Was it weird to text him, now that she'd broken up with his son? Sure, they'd worked together on a few projects, but he'd only been throwing her a bone since she was dating Brodie, right? Would he even want to hear from her, or did he hate her now?

"Hell yeah, it did!" Jo said, still celebrating. "If that bank doesn't give you your loan now, they are a bunch of morons.

You're basically a celebrity!" She turned back to Kyla and, registering the tension in her posture, the way her lips pulled down into a slight frown, planted her hands on her hips. "Kyla Georgette Mitchell."

"My middle name's not Georgette."

"What could possibly be wrong?"

Kyla lowered her phone and looked up at her friend. "Do you think Gavin knows?"

Jo shrugged. "If he didn't before, I'm sure he does now." Her lips tipped up in a knowing smirk. "Of course, you could always text him and find out. Maybe invite him out for a drink to celebrate." She bobbed her eyebrows in a comically suggestive way.

Kyla nearly choked on her tongue. "I can't—I couldn't ask him to—He's Brodie's *father*," she sputtered.

"Methinks the lady doth protest too much." Jo's smirk grew into a full-blown smile. "Besides, it's not like you and Brodie are still together. Daddy's fair game."

Kyla scrambled off the couch, needing to move, to shake off the nervous energy suddenly flowing through her veins at the mere idea of what Jo was suggesting.

"There's a reason Gavin West is always voted the hottest professor at Williston. I'd let him teach me a thing or two any day," Jo said.

"Jo!"

"You can't honestly tell me you haven't thought about what it would be like."

Of course she'd thought about it. She'd thought about it way too often since they'd met, wondering what might have happened if she'd met Gavin before she met his son.

Nothing, you weirdo. He's twice your age and, even if he wasn't, everyone knows Gavin West doesn't date.

Brodie had told her about his father's lack of a love life, how he never brought any women home, had never even mentioned a woman since his divorce.

But that didn't stop her from fantasizing about Gavin`. In the last few months, she couldn't help but think about him more and more. With each unsatisfying night spent in Brodie's bed, with each new project she and Gavin worked on together, she wondered—what would it be like to be with Gavin? And if she hadn't been dating Brodie, would she have had the chance to find out?

Stop being ridiculous. Even if he did date, he'd never date you.

Kyla clicked off the television as the news anchor read off a web address where interested candidates could apply to be a part of the show. She pushed the coffee table across the room, clearing space for the next set of poses.

"Are you ready to do the next outfit?" she asked, reaching for her camera.

Jo laughed, untying the robe and tossing it on the armchair in the corner of the room. Dressed only in a high cut thong and a cropped, ribbed, white tank top that didn't even cover the bottom curve of her breasts, Jo strutted to the now-cleared space in the center of the room.

"I'll let you dodge the conversation this time, but only because we have work to do. Where do you want me?"

"On your back," Kyla said, turning on her camera and gesturing towards the floor.

Jo arched an amused eyebrow at Kyla and they both burst out laughing before Jo lay back on the hardwood and let Kyla guide her into the next series of poses. And if Kyla focused hard enough on making sure Jo tilted her chin just right, that she pointed her toes and bent her legs, that the light highlighted her cheekbones and the shadows enhanced the definition in her abs, well, then there wouldn't be any room left for thoughts about Gavin West.

Chapter Three

"We are so fucked," Baz grumbled into his Scotch. "Why do we even bother playing every week? We always lose."

"Because it's fun." Gavin scanned the answer card they'd been handed when they arrived at The Rookery for their weekly trivia game.

"Losing is not my idea of fun," Baz said.

"Don't listen to him." Ethan placed a plate of chicken wings on the table and took his seat between Baz and Gavin. "He's just annoyed that Jamie and Tessa aren't here."

"They're on their honeymoon," Gavin said, as if his friends didn't know that already. "They'll be back in a few days."

"And while they're off honeymooning, we're about to get creamed by the granny squad." Baz selected a chicken wing and placed it on one of the small plates Ethan had brought over. "Where's the silverware?"

"What silverware? It's a chicken wing." Ethan tore off a piece of the bright orange sauce-coated meat with his teeth.

Baz sighed and got to his feet. "I don't want to get sauce all over my hands," he said as he went off in search of a fork and knife.

"Is he grouchier than usual or is it just me?" Ethan asked.

"Mrs. White set him up on a date with Trisha last night,"

Gavin said, waving off Ethan's offer of a chicken wing. "It did not go well."

"Of course it didn't. They don't have anything in common. Why'd he even agree to go?"

"You try saying no to Mrs. White," Baz said as he returned to the table with a plastic fork and knife.

"Thankfully she doesn't seem interested in setting *me* up with her granddaughter," Ethan said. "Wait, should I be offended by that?"

"You're just not Trisha's type, I'm afraid," Mrs. White said as she and Mrs. Kemp appeared at their table, a cloud of Chanel accompanying their arrival. "My niece, Penny, on the other hand—"

"That's okay, Mrs. White. Thanks," Ethan said, wiping his hands on his napkin.

"Of course, you boys could always apply to be on that new show since you're so unsatisfied with my matchmaking." Mrs. White grinned. "Judy's nephew is one of the executive producers, you know. We could put in a good word."

"Patrick has excellent taste," Mrs. Kemp chimed in, her chest puffing up with pride. "His partner looks just like Harrison Ford."

Gavin glanced between his friends, who both looked as horrified as he was at the idea of appearing on a reality dating show. "I think we're all set, Mrs. Kemp, but thanks for the offer."

"Gavin West, one of these days you're going to put your mother out of her misery and bring a woman home to meet her again," Mrs. Kemp said, a look of pity in her eyes.

Baz snorted. "Unlikely."

"I already had my one great love," Gavin said, repeating the line he'd been telling himself for years. If he had learned anything from his failed marriage it was to trust his gut, and his gut hadn't been interested in anyone for more than a few nights of meaningless sex in years.

That's not entirely true. You're interested in Kyla…

Fine. He hadn't been interested in anyone *he could actually have*.

"Nonsense. You and Jessica divorced over a decade ago. Time to get back in the saddle," Mrs. White said. Gavin nearly spit out his drink at the suggestive eyebrow bob that accompanied her words, the shock on his face met with a laugh from Baz.

"And what about you, Sebastian?" Mrs. White asked.

Aside from Baz's mother, Mrs. White and her friends were the only ones who could get away with calling him by his full name. The retired elementary school teachers had taught Gavin and his friends when they were just kids, and sometimes he was sure the elderly women still saw them as a group of sticky six-year-olds.

Baz lifted his Scotch in a mock toast, a grim smirk twisting his lip up at the edge. "My mother long ago made her peace with my bachelorhood."

Mrs. White hummed in a way that always made Gavin suspect she knew more than she let on. But if Gavin thought he had secrets to keep, Baz had even more, and there was no way Mrs. White could know about either of them. At least, he hoped not.

"If you change your minds, you know how to find me. Patrick is just a phone call away and I'm sure he owes me a favor or two." Mrs. Kemp waved as she and Mrs. White headed back towards their table.

"This is your fault, you know." Ethan pointed a half-eaten chicken wing at Gavin.

"My fault?"

"Yeah. You're the one who got this show to come to Aster Bay in the first place."

"It's going to be great for tourism," Gavin said defensively. "The whole thing is basically an advertisement for the town."

"Unless they choose some asshole as the star," Baz said.

"Prince Charming," Gavin corrected. "They're calling the guy 'Prince Charming.'"

"I'm not saying that," Baz said as he cut off another piece of his chicken.

"Not saying what?" Brodie asked. He slid into the empty chair beside Gavin and grabbed the last chicken wing. "What are we talking about?"

"The new reality show your dad brought to town," Ethan said.

"Crazy, right? Who'd want to film a show here?" Brodie asked around a mouthful of chicken.

"Where's Kyla?" Gavin glanced towards the door.

Brodie shook his head with a rueful laugh. "Who knows? She's not talking to me."

"What happened?" Gavin asked at the same time Ethan said, "Again?"

Brodie shrugged, but the tight set of his jaw belied the casual gesture. Gavin balled his fist on his knee. He shouldn't care, shouldn't want to know the details of their argument. It shouldn't matter.

He hated himself that it did.

"So much for reinforcements," Baz grumbled.

"Maybe I should apply to be on that show," Brodie said. "I'm basically twenty-six."

"You're twenty-three," Gavin said.

"Close enough."

"Alright, who's ready to play some trivia?" Mike Greenhall called from the front of the bar as he rang an old school bell to get everyone's attention. "Tonight's featured category is romantic comedies of the 80s and 90s."

Baz threw back the rest of his Scotch. "Like I said, we're fucked."

Gavin and Brodie drove away from The Rookery without speaking, the radio playing softly in the background, but inside Gavin was dying to ask about the breakup. To make sure Brodie was alright. Not because he wanted to know about Kyla.

Keep telling yourself that.

"Are you coming home tonight?" Gavin asked as they pulled out onto Main Street.

"Nah. I left my car at mom's," Brodie replied. Gavin glanced in his rear view and made a left turn, heading in the opposite direction of his house towards the small ranch where his ex-wife and her second husband lived.

"You want to talk about what happened with Kyla?"

A good father would ask his son about his fight with his girlfriend, right?

Maybe, but a good father didn't hope that girlfriend had broken up with his son for good this time.

And even if she had, what good would that do him? Alleviate his guilt when he jerked off thinking about her, or when he picked up a woman at the club and imagined he was with Kyla instead? No, his Catholic upbringing made sure there was no end in sight to that particular brand of guilt.

Brodie reached forward and turned up the radio. "Same thing that always happens."

Gavin waited for him to continue, his chest aching with the restraint of giving his son time to collect his thoughts.

"I don't think she's gonna take me back this time." Brodie turned his face out the window, and Gavin's heart clenched at the sadness in his son's voice.

Everyone in town could see that Kyla and Brodie weren't a

good fit. Gavin loved his son more than anything in the world, but even he had been surprised when Brodie's relationship with Kyla had lasted more than a few weeks. Kyla dreamed big. She had plans for her future, ambition, and Brodie…didn't. He flitted from pipe dream to pipe dream, one day declaring he wanted to be a chef (though he had no interest in culinary school) and the next talking about creating an internet start-up (not that he knew what *kind* of start-up he wanted to create). His plans were always half-baked and discarded before they'd even begun to take shape. Even worse, he didn't seem to know how to support Kyla as she pursued her own goals.

"What's different this time?" Gavin asked.

"She didn't seem mad when she said it was over. She just seemed…done."

"I'm sorry."

And he was—though there was also a not-so-small part of him that was relieved. Kyla got under Gavin's skin in ways he couldn't quite explain, lingering in his thoughts long after they'd last spoken. It wouldn't be the worst thing if their interactions were limited to the work they did together for the Merchants' Association, if he no longer ran into her in the hallway outside the bathroom in the early hours of the morning when she slept over with Brodie. If he could stop hoping/dreading that he'd get a few minutes alone with her, that she'd look at him the way she had that first time they'd met before she knew he was Brodie's father…

That relief quickly turned to disgust with himself. His son's heartache shouldn't bring Gavin any measure of relief, no matter the reason.

"Whatever." Brodie stretched out his neck side to side like he could shake off the ending of a long-term relationship. "Nick wants to go to a club in Providence this weekend. Kyla never wanted to go and gave me shit if I went without her, but now I can do whatever I want. Nick's always talking about the cute

Rhode Island College girls."

Nick was Brodie's stepbrother. One year younger than Brodie, he'd be done with his degree in public relations in just a few weeks, and he partied as hard as he studied.

"You're going to try to pick up someone new already?" Gavin couldn't believe it. Brodie put on a brave face, but he was clearly taking this breakup harder than he wanted to admit.

"No better way to get over someone, right?" Brodie's smile was more of a grimace. He sniffed and turned back to the window.

"Are you sure you're ready for that? You and Kyla were together a long time."

"Are you offering me dating advice?" Brodie asked with a snort. "Dad, I can hardly get you to open the Windr app, and I spent so long setting up your profile."

"I don't think I'm cut out for online dating."

"You don't date at all. I can't remember the last time I saw you with a woman."

That was by design. When Gavin and Jessica had divorced eleven years ago, after twelve years of marriage, Gavin had found himself thirty-two years old and with no clue how to even start trying to date. He and Jessica had met freshman year of college; he hadn't picked up a woman he actually wanted to date since he was a teenager.

And there was Brodie to consider. While the divorce had been unusually civil—Gavin and Jessica had held each other and cried the day their divorce was finalized—it was still an adjustment for their son. Gavin had promised himself he wouldn't bring another person into Brodie's life unless he was sure that person was sticking around. Which had, unintentionally, translated into not dating at all.

After a while, Gavin got used to being alone. There had been a few women over the years, adjuncts or visiting professors at the university with whom he had developed long-term friends-with-benefits arrangements, or women he met at the club, but it was never anything more than sex. Now, all these years later, the idea of starting over, of first dates and meeting the parents (or children), just seemed too hard.

Besides, the only woman he was actually interested in was not an option.

"Maybe *you* should apply to be on that show," Brodie said.

Gavin glanced at his son as they turned onto Jessica's street. "Since when do you care so much about my love life?"

Brodie shrugged noncommittally. "I don't know, Dad. I don't like the idea of you being alone. Being lonely."

Gavin's heart squeezed in his chest. Was Brodie lonely?

"Good thing I have you then," he said as he pulled into the driveway and put the car in park.

Brodie turned in his seat so he was facing his father, his expression more serious than Gavin had seen it in a long time. "I've decided to move out West."

Gavin blinked. "This is the first I'm hearing of it."

"Yeah, well… Nick's planning on moving to LA after graduation. He's got an internship with some talent agency starting next fall and he's going to head out this summer."

Gavin nodded, his heart racing. "Good for him."

"I want to go with him."

"And do what?"

Brodie fiddled with his seatbelt, avoiding Gavin's eyes. "I don't know. I've been thinking about trying to get a job as a PA." He glanced up and, at Gavin's encouraging nod, continued, his words tumbling out faster, excitement sparking in his eyes. "About the only thing I never get sick of is watching movies, ya know? I never really thought about it before but there are all these people who work in Hollywood making movies, so why not me?"

Gavin couldn't help but smile, even as his heart clenched at the idea of his son moving so far away, of all the things that could go wrong without Gavin there to fix them. He'd been the one to get Brodie every job he'd ever had, calling on his own friends and connections to take a chance on his son. He'd been the one to pick him up on the side of the road when his car broke down because he forgot to put gas in the tank. If Brodie was halfway across the country, who would do that for him? Who would make sure he was alright?

"But most directors and producers and shit start as PAs. Nick says it's all about who you know, so if I want to get that kind of job, I gotta be where the people hiring those jobs are. I gotta start to meet them. And when Nick starts his internship, he'll be meeting all kinds of people and he said he could introduce me."

Gavin didn't think he'd ever heard Brodie so excited about the idea of a job before. Maybe this would be the dream that stuck. Maybe if he wanted it badly enough, he'd figure out the other things. He knew Jessica thought he babied their son, made things too easy for him, but was Brodie really ready to stand on his own?

He swallowed. "It sounds great, B. Really. I had no idea you were thinking about any of this."

"Well, I am." Brodie straightened his shoulders. "So, you should, you know, make plans or whatever. So you're not alone when I leave."

Gavin gripped Brodie's shoulder, squeezing. "Son, I—"

"Nope." Brodie unbuckled his seatbelt and practically threw himself at the door to shove it open with his shoulder. "That's enough feelings talk for one night."

Gavin chuckled. "We hardly talked about our feelings at all."

"I'll be home tomorrow after my shift at the restaurant." Brodie shut the car door and bent down to speak to his father through the open window, resting his elbows on the edge of the car frame with a smirk. "If you want, I can help you fill out that show's application. Or show you how to find your matches on Windr…again."

Gavin shook his head, throwing the car into reverse as Brodie straightened up and stepped away from the car. "Good night!"

Brodie waved and then trotted up the driveway to his mother's house as Gavin backed out of the driveway and headed home. Alone.

Chapter Four

"How are we feeling tonight? Red or white?" Jo asked, holding up a bottle of Nuthatch wine in each hand.

Kyla grimaced. "Neither."

"What's wrong with wine?" Jo asked. Molly made grabby hands for the bottle of red. Jo laughed and handed it to her.

Kyla held up her glass, half full with a pink concoction she'd put together when she got back from the bank. "I'll stick to my bay breeze, thanks."

"More for us then," Jo said, pouring herself a glass of the white wine before flopping down on the couch next to Molly. Jo leaned back against the armrest of the couch and folded her long legs over Molly's lap. "Now will you tell us why we're day drinking?"

Kyla took her drink and sat cross-legged on the floor, leaning back against the scarred leg of the second-hand wingback chair. She didn't want to be eye-level with her roommates for this, didn't want to see the pity bloom in their eyes. "I had my meeting at the bank."

Molly sat up straighter on the couch, the movement jostling Jo, wine sloshing precariously in her glass. "And?" Kyla shook her head. Molly slumped back on the couch. "I'm sorry, Ky. No wonder you broke into the hard stuff."

"Malibu is hardly the hard stuff," Kyla replied.

"She's right. When Kyla starts drinking the Captain, that's when we have to worry," Jo said.

"What'd they say?" Molly asked.

"The same thing all the other banks said. I don't have enough equity and my income from the bakery isn't high enough to get the loan without a co-signer."

"Did you ever actually ask your parents if they'd do it?" Molly asked. "Maybe they've changed their mind. Maybe they—"

"My parents have been very clear about how they feel about my choices. If they had their way, I wouldn't have any say in anything that happened in my life. Besides, they know how to find me if they wanted to. They're not going to co-sign a loan for me when they can't even be bothered to pick up the phone on my birthday." Kyla took a sip of her drink to stop herself from talking and set it down on the coffee table with a final-sounding clunk.

"Motherfuckers," Jo grumbled under her breath.

Molly leaned forward, throwing Jo's legs off her lap, and slid a coaster under Kyla's glass, wiping away the thin ring of moisture that was left behind on the second-hand table. "So what's next?" she asked, ever the pragmatist.

"Nothing's next. That's the last bank in town."

"You're not giving up," Jo said. "You are a fucking amazing photographer, Kyla Bernadette Mitchell."

"My middle name isn't Bernadette."

"There has to be someone else who can co-sign for you. What about Tessa?" Jo continued, ignoring Kyla's interjection.

"I can't ask her to do that. She's my boss."

"She's also your friend," Molly said.

"No. I can't ask anyone else."

Molly stood and disappeared into the kitchen, calling over her shoulder, "This calls for greasy takeout. What'll it be: pizza or Chinese?"

"Pizza," Jo and Kyla called back in unison.

"Anything else?" Molly asked as she returned with the takeout menu for The Pizza Stone. "I could go pick up a few pints of our good friends Ben and Jerry."

"No, thanks. Pizza's good," Kyla said.

"One Aster Bay special coming up." Molly wandered back into the kitchen, already dialing to place their order.

"You alright?" Jo asked when they were alone.

"I'll be fine."

Jo set her wine glass down on the coffee table and slid onto the floor across from Kyla, their knees brushing. She placed a hand on top of Kyla's to stop her from picking at the skin around the edges of her thumbnail. She hadn't even realized she was doing it. "Not what I asked, Ky. Are you alright?"

Kyla avoided meeting Jo's eyes. They'd been friends for years, having met in their writing class on the first day of fall semester freshman year. Jo knew Kyla better than anyone. She'd been there that last horrible time Kyla's parents had visited and every time Kyla and Brodie broke up—if there was anyone who knew when Kyla was lying, it was Jo.

"What if my parents are right?" Kyla asked, staring at her hands in her lap. "What if I can't actually run my own business?"

"Your parents are the biggest motherfuckers—" Jo broke off at Kyla's wince. She rolled her eyes. "They don't know what the hell they're talking about, and they're manipulative jerks who think they can make all the decisions about your life without ever telling you a damn thing."

"They did eventually tell me." Kyla hated that the betrayal still stung.

"Yeah, after they thought they had the right to bargain you away like you were a literal object. They tried to arrange a marriage for you without your knowledge or input. In the twenty-first century!" Jo exclaimed.

Kyla knew it wasn't what she wanted, but she couldn't help

thinking about what that life might have been like. It certainly would have been easier than pleading with bored businessmen for a loan they had no intention of giving her. In her parents' world, all she'd had to do was comply. Be silent, don't think too hard about what she wanted, and just do as she was told. Why had that been so hard? Sure, she'd have to shut down the parts of herself that didn't fit, the things that sparked inside her chest, but—

"Stop. You are letting them get in your head and they aren't even here," Jo said. "They think they can make you go crawling back if they tell you that you aren't capable of making it on your own. But they are *wrong*, Kyla. Not getting a loan has nothing to do with whether or not you can run a business."

"There's no business to run without the loan."

"We'll find another way." Jo squeezed Kyla's hands.

"What if Brodie's right and no one wants boudoir photography anyway?"

Jo snorted. "Brodie doesn't know shit. You are a badass photography genius, and he is the king of the motherfuckers." Kyla shot her an exasperated look. "I'm not apologizing for that one."

"Pizza will be here in thirty minutes," Molly said as she came back into the room. She took one look at her friends on the floor and sat down beside them. "I think it's time we revisited your list."

Kyla groaned. "I never should have told you guys about that."

"But you did, so too late now. Get it out." Jo twirled her finger in a 'hurry-up' motion.

Kyla dug her phone out of her pocket and brought up her notes app. She scanned the screen and then dropped the phone on the floor. "This is ridiculous. I can't do this."

Jo grabbed the phone. "You can. We'll help." She cleared her throat with theatrical flair and flashed a grin at her friends before she began reading from the phone screen. "The Year of Kyla."

"And inspired idea," Molly said.

"I stole it from a Sarah MacLean novel," Kyla said.

"Inspired all the same," Molly replied.

"*Number one: stop settling for happy enough. Break up with Brodie once and for all,*" Jo read.

"Done and done," Molly said. "Proud of you for that, by the way."

"*Number two: Do something that pushes me outside of my comfort zone.*" Jo paused thoughtfully. "What's something that makes you uncomfortable?"

"This conversation," Kyla muttered before taking another sip of her drink.

"Keep going," Molly urged.

"*Number three: Have amazing, toe-curling, life-changing, scream-your-lungs-out sex.*"

"That's not what it says!" Kyla protested, reaching for her phone.

"It does now," Jo laughed, keying in her addition to Kyla's list.

"It certainly couldn't hurt," Molly said.

"*Number four: Open my own boudoir photography studio like the badass business babe I am so I can help other women feel like badass babes too.*"

"You're editorializing," Kyla said.

"I'm just adding the things you forgot to write," Jo replied.

"You've already taken the first step by breaking up with Brodie, and that's arguably the scariest," Molly said.

"You know, it wasn't though," Kyla replied, leaning in. "I mean, I'm going to miss him, but I honestly think we were only still together because neither of us wanted to rock the boat."

"Because he didn't want to give up his free rides and reliable sex, you mean," Jo said.

"The sex wasn't even that good," Kyla reminded her.

"Doesn't matter. To a twenty-three-year-old guy, sex is sex, and guaranteed sex is infinitely better than no sex at all,"

Molly said.

"Besides, that's exactly why you need my revised item number three. Those toys in your bedside table are only going to get you so far," Jo said.

"You're not supposed to know about those!"

"Ignore her," Molly said. "Not that she's wrong, but ignore her. You are going to check off every item on that list, Ky. Even the ones Jo added."

"Especially the ones I added," Jo chimed in.

"So, what's next? The photography studio? Sounds like it's time for plan B," Molly said.

"There is no plan B." Kyla reached for her drink. "I can't open unless I can renovate the space and I can't renovate without a loan. Where am I supposed to get $50,000?"

Molly smiled, her eyes sparkling. "You could go on that new show they're filming in town."

Kyla nearly did a spit take as Molly's suggestion hit her. "You've got to be kidding. I can't go on a reality dating show."

"Why not?" Molly asked. "It's being filmed right here in Aster Bay, you're within the age range, and you're single—"

"Barely," Kyla protested. "Brodie and I only broke up a few days ago."

"You two have been breaking up for months," Jo said. "Just because you finally stopped resuscitating it, doesn't mean your relationship wasn't dead a long time ago."

Ouch. It was true, but it still hurt to hear.

"The final couple gets $100,000 at the end. Even if it's not your perfect love match, you could split the money with Prince Charming and still walk away with fifty grand," Molly said.

"You're assuming I'm going to make it to the end. What if I get eliminated in the first week? Then all I will have done is make a fool of myself."

Jo scoffed. "No one in their right mind would eliminate you. You are a total babe."

Kyla shrank under the compliment. Even if she had never felt more confident in her body—thanks to nearly two years of therapy—she still had trouble believing other people thought she was attractive. Her experiments with boudoir self-portraits had helped her feel sexier, it was true, but she also knew that so much of the photographs was about lighting and just the right angle, an exaggerated arch in her spine and the perfect outfit. It was one thing to do that for a single image and another thing entirely to do it for a reality show with multiple cameras capturing every unflattering angle for weeks on end.

"Stop that." Jo frowned. "Whatever story you're telling yourself right now, just stop." She reached behind her and pulled Kyla's tablet from the little shelf at the bottom of the coffee table. She flipped open the black leather case, swiping through Kyla's countless boudoir self-portraits and stabbed a finger at the screen. "You are smart and funny and gorgeous and just the fucking best, Ky. If the *Prince Charming* they pick for this thing can't see that, he doesn't deserve you. If you don't want to do the show because you have some kind of moral objection to the premise of one guy dating like twenty women at once, then fine, don't do the show. But don't count yourself out because you don't think you're worthy of winning."

"They probably won't even pick me to be on the show," Kyla said, her defenses weakening in the face of her friends' outpouring of support.

"Then you won't have lost anything by applying," Molly said. "And even if Prince Charming has horrible taste and you don't win, it would still be amazing exposure for your business. Think how many people would want to come have a boudoir session with the girl they saw on TV."

"I guess it couldn't hurt. The bank did say that if I had clients lined up, it would be easier to get a loan." Was she really going to do this?

"See! You can't afford *not* to apply," Jo said.

Molly grabbed her laptop from where it sat on the end table by the couch. "We can help you fill out the application. It'll be fun. Oo! It could even count as your 'outside your comfort zone' thing!"

"Nuh uh—the application alone doesn't count. Going on the show would, though," Jo said. "And who knows, maybe being on the show would also help you cross off item number three. The people on those shows are always banging."

Kyla thought about it for a moment. It wasn't the craziest idea her friends had had. If she got cast, and if she won, she'd have enough money to renovate the space for her studio. And if she didn't win, maybe she could parlay her fifteen minutes of fame into a waitlist of clients. But maybe Jo was right—maybe she'd even meet someone capable of curling her toes.

That's an awful lot of ifs and maybes.

Jo laughed, pointing to the laptop in Molly's lap. "Start typing before she changes her mind!"

Kyla got to her feet, gathering her glass. "I need a refill if we're going to do this."

When she returned to the living room, her roommates were huddled around Molly's laptop, giggling like children as Molly typed.

"How's this?" Molly read from the screen. "*A bakery assistant by day and a boudoir photographer by night, Kyla is newly single and looking for a fresh start.*"

"You spelled 'big dick' wrong," Jo said, pointing at the screen.

"What?" Kyla sputtered, her panic subsiding when she caught Jo's grin. "Jerk."

"So you *don't* want a guy with a big dick?" Jo asked.

"I'm pretty confident that's not one of the questions on the applications," Kyla said.

Jo shrugged. "You never know."

"I guess technically that could go under 'what you look for in a partner,'" Molly said with a thoughtful narrowing of her eyes.

"Don't even think about it," Kyla warned.

"Don't worry. It's just a series of checkboxes anyway. Yes to someone who has a job. No to someone who still lives with their parents," Molly read as she clicked.

"You two don't even need me to be here for this, do you?" Kyla asked as she sat down in the wingback.

"Nope," Jo said as Molly continued to click.

"There's a statement you have to confirm, though. *I am willing to date, on camera, a man between the ages of twenty-six and forty-five.*"

"Click yes," Jo said, pointing at the screen.

"Shouldn't I be the one to tell her to click yes?" Kyla asked. Jo and Molly looked at her expectantly, a challenge arching one of Jo's eyebrows as she waited for Kyla to give in. "I mean, forty-five is a lot older than me."

"And there's no one you can think of who's a lot older than you that you'd be willing to date?" Jo asked with a knowing smirk.

Kyla rolled her lips between her teeth as a blush colored her cheeks and she pictured it—an older man, maybe just barely into his forties, maybe with shaggy, dirty-blonde hair that fell into his eyes when he laughed and a smile so wide and white it belonged in a toothpaste commercial. Someone who wore glasses when he graded papers and smelled like orange and sandalwood. Someone who always defended her, believed in her, who wanted to hear about her work and valued her opinion. Someone who, based on the way he filled out a pair of gray sweatpants, even checked off Jo's 'big dick' requirement.

Not that Gavin West would ever apply to be on a reality dating show. She'd never seen him date *anyone* so she couldn't imagine he was likely to start by dating multiple women at once on television.

Jo barked out a laugh. "That's a yes. Click yes, Mol."

Kyla took another sip of her drink and willed the heat that was gathering low in her belly to dissipate. It didn't matter that she and Brodie had broken up—it was still inappropriate to think about his father that way.

That was part of why you had to break up with him for good this time. What kind of person can't stop fantasizing about their boyfriend's father?

"Dating history?" Molly asked.

"That's easy. Just Brodie, right?" Jo chimed in.

"Right," Kyla confirmed.

"All that's left to do is upload some photos." Jo reached for the tablet again.

Kyla lunged, grabbing the leather case from her friend's hand. "No way. You are not submitting these with my application."

"Why not? If you get chosen to be on the show and they put those pictures up on their website or on the screen, it'll be great advertising for your business," Jo said.

"I'm in my underwear," Kyla hissed.

Jo's brow furrowed in confusion. "So? There are pictures of me in my underwear all over the internet."

"That's different. You're a model."

"And so are you," Jo said, pointing to the tablet.

"I'm a photographer." She turned to Molly, desperation in her eyes. "You wouldn't send in pictures of yourself in your underwear."

"True, but I'm a high school teacher, not a boudoir photographer," Molly said.

"Just one," Jo bargained. "We'll send in the one of you at the Food and Wine Festival last year, too, to balance it out."

"I bet no one else will be sending in professional boudoir photographs," Molly said. "It could help you stand out."

Kyla closed her eyes, her grip on the tablet loosening. "I cannot believe I'm letting you talk me into this."

Jo opened the tablet and began swiping through it. "Trust us, Ky."

Chapter Five

"And then I said to Ricky—'Ricky,' I said, 'the baby and I need more of those cake pops.' And the poor man just couldn't help himself. He bought a whole dozen!" Cheryl exclaimed, laughing, as she bounced her toddler on her hip and watched Kyla fill her order at The Corner Bakeshop. "But you know that. What you don't know is that my Ricky is a bit of a clumsy duck. Can't help it. Comes from his father. One day he just slipped and fell on the sidewalk and lay there like a fish out of water, flopping around, until someone came home and found him."

"When did Ricky fall?" Kyla asked as she put the last honeycomb and lime cake pop in the box with the rest of Cheryl's order.

"Not Ricky—his father. Though, I suppose Ricky did fall, this afternoon when he came home with the pops. Slipped on a wet patch on the porch and fell flat on his butt, right on top of the box of cake pops he'd just collected for us."

"Papa fall!" the toddler said, clapping.

"That's right, sugar bear," Cheryl cooed.

Kyla handed the box over the counter to Cheryl. "I hope you can keep these ones away from Ricky. They're the last ones we have today."

"I'm so glad I got here before you closed!"

Tessa pushed through the swinging doors that led to the kitchen, dusting flour off her hands as she entered the bakery. "You just snuck in under the wire."

"I'll let you two go," Cheryl said. "I've got to make sure Ricky's icing his behind anyway." She waved goodbye and left the shop, the bells over the door tinkling in her wake.

Kyla followed after her, flipping the sign on the door to closed. "I love Cheryl. I swear I do. But sometimes—"

"You wish she'd take a breath?" Tessa asked with a knowing smile. "I know the feeling. What were we talking about before she got here?"

"Your honeymoon. I still can't believe you skipped Small World. It's a classic," Kyla said, shaking her head.

"Tell that to my husband," Tessa laughed. "But we did ride Pirates of the Caribbean four times."

"Four times?"

Tessa grinned. "Jamie said it was research." Kyla cast a questioning glance her way as she resumed wiping down the counter. "He's very into role play lately."

"Oh," Kyla said, blushing.

"I bought him an eye patch in the gift shop and everything."

"Okay!" Kyla threw her towel at Tessa. "I don't need the details."

Tessa caught the towel and laughed. "Someday, you are going to meet a man who makes you *feel* things, K. All the way down to your toes. Dirty, filthy, wonderful things."

"My toes are just fine, thank you," she said, moving on to pre-folding cardboard boxes for the next day's order.

Tessa sighed like she didn't really believe her, and Kyla wasn't sure how she felt about the fact that somehow Tessa could tell that Kyla had no experience with 'dirty, filthy, wonderful things.' She wasn't a virgin, but sex with Brodie had always been more perfunctory than *wonderful.* It certainly didn't inspire the kind of giddy grin that Tessa wore whenever she talked about her husband, or the heated looks between the newlyweds that were so heavy with lust they could change the temperature in a room.

But maybe some women couldn't get to *wonderful*. Maybe some women were so inside their own heads, so preoccupied with how their bodies must look from every awkward angle, that *wonderful* wasn't even on the table. What if she was never able to check off number three on her list, no matter who her partner was?

"What are you still doing here anyway?" Tessa glanced at the clock. "Your shift ended half an hour ago. I know you didn't stick around just so I could embarrass you with my honeymoon stories."

Kyla shrugged, focused on keeping her folds precise along the scored lines, lining up the edges. Never mind that she'd been wearing her coat for the last twenty minutes, certain that Brodie would show up any minute to make the exchange so she could go. She'd worked another ten-hour day, trying to save up as much cash as possible to put towards the renovations, and all she wanted to do was go home and take a bath, but her ex-boyfriend couldn't even manage to show up on time to pick up his own stuff.

Tessa's lips settled into a pursed line as she glanced at the box of Brodie's stuff that still sat behind the counter, waiting for its owner. "Do you want to come to The Rookery with me and the guys? I think we might actually win tonight."

Kyla smirked. "Is Mrs. White out of town?"

Tessa batted Kyla's arm playfully. "No, but tonight's trivia theme is 'Hollywood sweethearts.' No one knows a Meg Ryan movie like I do."

"You haven't even seen *French Kiss*," a familiar, deep voice said with a chuckle.

Kyla and Tessa turned to see Gavin standing in the doorway, his hair wind-tousled and falling into his eyes more than usual.

"I miss one movie and this guy will never let me live it down. You want your usual?" Tessa asked, already moving to fill a box with Gavin's favorite cupcakes.

"Sure. Actually, Kyla, I was hoping I'd catch you."

He moved around the counter to where Kyla was still stacking empty cardboard boxes.

"Is everything okay?" she asked.

Maybe Brodie had gotten hung up at the restaurant and was running late? But then why send his dad to tell her? Why not just text her?

He smiled sheepishly and ran his hand over the back of his neck. "Everything's fine." He grimaced and lowered his voice. "But Brodie's not coming."

Kyla blew out a frustrated breath and leaned back against the counter. "What's his excuse this time? Did his car break down again? Or, no, don't tell me, he just plain forgot?"

Gavin shifted uncomfortably on his feet, his lips pressing into a flat line. "I'm not sure. But I didn't want you to wait for him."

She nodded. "I appreciate that. Thanks."

"Come out with us." Tessa looped an arm through Kyla's as she handed the now-full box of baked goods to Gavin. "It'll cheer you up."

Kyla gave her friend a tight smile. "Another time."

"You can join in on our pool to see how long it takes my dad to get uncomfortable and shut down the honeymoon stories." Tessa had married her father's best friend and, now that they'd all figured out how to navigate their new normal, she delighted in pushing his buttons about it.

"Tell him that pirate story and my bet is on ten seconds," Kyla said.

"Pirate story?" Gavin glanced between the two women with a confused smile.

"You don't want to know," Kyla said at the same time Tessa said, with a wink, "I'll tell you later."

Gavin chuckled. "I take it you and Jamie enjoyed your week with the mouse, then?"

"More than I expected. I have to admit, I didn't think Jamie was going to get into it like he did, but by the end, he was a total convert. He's already talking about all the things he wants to do when we go back."

"I'm so envious. I haven't been in years," Kyla said.

"I didn't take you for a theme park fan," Gavin said with a soft smile, his warm eyes landing on hers so full of interest that she found herself talking before she'd really thought about her answer.

"We went every year when I was kid. It was my reward for getting good grades. At least until junior year of high school."

"What happened then?" he asked.

She froze, the explanation dying in her throat as he waited for an explanation. *I got fat. Mom was embarrassed to have to buy me a new bathing suit in the plus size section of the store, so I told her I didn't want to go anyway. My parents went on vacation without me and I stayed home and ate Ben & Jerry's for dinner every night for a week.* But she couldn't say any of that to Gavin.

She blinked away the memory even as it ached in her gut, like an old wound acting up with the weather. She knew it was just the echo of old hurts, but they still scraped at her skin, scrabbling for purchase she refused to give them. Instead, she smiled too brightly. "You know, I don't really remember."

His smile faltered, as though he detected the lie. When he looked away, she missed the warmth of his gaze. *What the hell is wrong with you?*

"When are they going to announce the Prince Charming for this reality show thing?" Tessa asked, adding a second box of baked goods to Gavin's pile.

He cleared his throat and turned his attention to Tessa, his smile strained. "I don't know. They've been going through the applications but Mrs. Kemp says they're having a harder time casting it than they expected."

Tessa's eyes gleamed. "Think we can convince Baz to apply?"

Gavin barked out a laugh. "Not when he's sober."

"Challenge accepted." Tessa glanced between Kyla and Gavin, her mischievous grin fading as her brows narrowed and she took a hesitant step back towards the kitchen. "I'm just going to go double check that I turned all the ovens off. Never can be too careful," she said before disappearing into the kitchen.

They stood in uncomfortable silence for a beat before Gavin took a halting step towards Kyla, setting his boxes of pastries on the counter. "Actually, I didn't just come here to tell you about Brodie."

"Oh?"

Her heart fluttered in her chest, her pulse picking up speed as he shuffled even closer, the hint of a smile pulling at the corner of his lips.

"I have good news. The Travel Network is going to use your photos to promote the show."

"They are?" she gasped.

He nodded, his eyes sparking to life again. "I'm not sure how many of them, but the option to use the proposal images as part of the show's marketing was built into the contract, and my contact at the network says planning to use at least a few. They promised me that you'll get full photography credit and—"

Kyla squealed, launching herself into his arms. "Oh my God! That's amazing!"

After the barest moment of hesitation, he wrapped his arms around her waist, large hands pressed flat to her back. When he laughed, the sound vibrated through her chest.

"*You're* amazing, Ky." Gavin's voice was low, like the words were just for her, and she melted into the heat of his hands on her back, the orange and sandalwood scent of him. She dipped her head, biting her lip and breathing him in, this man who always believed in her.

As the excitement bubbling beneath her skin slowed to a simmering warmth, she became increasingly aware of exactly whose arms she was in, and exactly how much she should not like the way it felt to be wrapped in his embrace. It was weird to want to keep hugging your ex-boyfriend's dad, right? Still, she couldn't suppress the smile stretching across her face. It was the first bit of good news she'd had in months.

His hands flexed against the small of her back and then he cleared his throat and stepped away from her, gesturing with a tilt of his stubbled jaw to the box on the floor with Brodie's faded New England Patriots hat peeking out of the top. "I can take that stuff back to him. If you want."

"That'd be great. Thanks." Kyla bent to pick up the box at the exact same time that Gavin did.

Their foreheads bumped against each other, and they both took a step back, mumbling apologies. When they stood back up to their full heights, each pressing a hand to their foreheads, she couldn't help the snort of laughter that escaped between her clamped lips. He dropped his hands to his hips and looked down at the floor, shaking his head, loose strands of hair falling into his eyes as he laughed.

"Are you okay?" he asked, glancing up at her.

"I'm fine," she assured him.

"I don't just mean because of that," he said, gesturing to his forehead. "I mean with everything… With the breakup."

"Yeah." A slow smile spread across her lips that was matched by one of his own. "I think I am."

"I'm glad."

Tessa poked her head back out from the kitchen. "We've got to get going if we're going to make it to The Rookery in time for the first round."

"Right." Gavin swept up the box of Brodie's things, his coat pulling taut around his back and biceps as his muscles bunched with the movement.

Kyla's eyes caught on his powerful thighs straining against his dress pants, the way his body changed beneath the weight of the box, and heat crawled up her throat. She had the strongest urge to drag her nails over those thighs, to dig them into his backside, to push his coat from his shoulders and feel the corded muscles of his arms with her fingertips. To trail her fingers further down, to slide her hands over—*No.*

She spun away, putting her back to Gavin as she pulled her own coat tighter around herself even though she was suddenly plenty warm.

"Are you sure we can't convince you to come?" Tessa asked.

"I'm sure." Kyla turned back to Tessa and Gavin, hoping they wouldn't be able to tell what she was thinking. "I really just want to go home and take a bath."

Gavin's eyes changed, just for a second, a flash of heat, of hunger.

You're imagining things.

"Next time then," he said.

"Sure. Next time."

Alone in her apartment, submerged beneath a mountain of bubbles, Kyla finally let her mind wander to the way Gavin's biceps and forearms had flexed and tensed. To the way his eyes had flashed hot and hungry, dangerous, briefly glimmering with heat when she'd met his gaze.

She slid a hand beneath the bubbles and circled her clit, fast and hard, as she imagined those deep hazel eyes that burned in her memory, her toes curling and her back arching away from the cold porcelain of the bathtub, her climax sparking through her.

She collapsed back in the bath, keeping her eyes closed, as though she could hold on to the memory for a moment longer if she didn't open her eyes. She could pretend she hadn't walked away with Brodie the night she and Gavin had met, hadn't spent the last year wondering what if.

Chapter Six

Gavin leaned against the front of his desk, crossing his legs at the ankles, and leaning back on his hands. "So given what you know about consumer behavior at this event last year, who would you target your advertising towards next year?"

A few hands shot into the air. He nodded at a young guy in the front row in a Williston University sweatshirt. "Forget teenagers and college students. Focus on families with young kids."

Gavin nodded, encouragingly. "And what could you do to make it clear this is a family friendly event?"

A woman with a crown of bantu knots halfway back in the lecture hall answered, "Change the branding. Swap the neutrals and pastels for bright, saturated colors and pictures of children and families at the event."

Gavin smiled. "Very good, Lex." He pushed off from the desk and made his way behind it, gathering his papers. "We're out of time for today. For next class, I want you to take a stab at creating an advertising piece for this event. It can be a billboard, a poster, a newspaper ad—whatever you'd like. Remember, it's just a concept piece, so I won't be judging you on your graphic design abilities."

He watched as his students gathered their belongings and shuffled out of the classroom. It was his last class of the day and he was looking forward to heading home and kicking back with a beer and a good book. The latest in the romantic suspense series he was reading waited for him in his mailbox, ready for him to uncover who the serial killer was that had been terrorizing the small mountain town, and whether or not the feisty, young detective and her grouchy, older partner would finally get together. (He knew they would. It was his favorite part of romantic suspense—the couple always ended up together.)

"Knock, knock, anyone home?" Judy Kemp's voice rang out through the lecture hall as the door at the top of the stairs opened.

"Aunt Judy, there's no point in saying 'knock, knock' if you're not actually going to wait to be invited in." A tall, mostly bald man wearing wire-frame glasses came through the door after her, followed by a short man with an orange tan.

"There you are!" Mrs. Kemp said, as though she'd been hunting all over for him.

Gavin set his briefcase back down on his desk. "Here I am."

"You must be Gavin West," the tall man said, turning his attention to Gavin and holding out his hand. "The architect of Aster Bay's revitalized marketing plans."

Gavin shook his hand. "I can't take all the credit."

"He's modest, too," the tall man said to Mrs. Kemp with a nod of approval.

"And you are?" Gavin asked, crossing his arms over his chest and leaning back against his desk again.

"My nephew, Patrick." Mrs. Kemp fondly patted the man's shoulder. "And his friend."

"Zayne Porter. Executive Producer." The shorter man extended his hand towards Gavin.

Mrs. Kemp lowered herself into an empty seat in the front row of the classroom. "I heard about Brodie and Kyla. What a shame. His loss will be another man's gain."

Every muscle in Gavin's back and shoulders tightened at the idea. He couldn't think about Kyla being with another man, though he also didn't want to think about her being with Brodie.

Just don't think about her at all.

"Does this Brodie want to be on the show?" Zayne asked.

The hair on the back of Gavin's neck prickled at the predatory gleam in Zayne's eye. "He's moving to California," Gavin said at the same time Mrs. Kemp snorted and said, "Brodie's just a child."

"What can I do for you, Mr. Kemp, Mr. Porter?" Gavin asked, hoping to steer the conversation away from his son.

"We have a proposal for you," Patrick said, with a glance at his aunt. "And I'd appreciate it if you'd hear us out before you shoot it down."

"Of course." Gavin inclined his head to indicate that Patrick should continue.

"I think you should be our Prince Charming," Patrick said. Mrs. Kemp squealed in delight as Gavin coughed, choking on air. "No one knows Aster Bay as well as you and certainly no one is a bigger advocate for the town. The network wants to be sure we don't lose the travel and tourism aspect of the show amidst all the dating fanfare, and I've had a few calls from Norm over at the Merchants' Association already wanting assurances that we'll choose someone who will represent the town well. My aunt tells me you're the man for the job."

Gavin shot a panicked glance at Mrs. Kemp whose look of unrestrained glee would have been comical if she hadn't just set him up to be so thoroughly ambushed.

"I'm not sure—"

"She also said you wouldn't want to do it," Patrick said. Gavin nodded tightly.

"This isn't going to work," Zayne muttered.

"You're single, attractive, within the window of our acceptable age range, and frankly, if I can't convince you to sign on, I'm not positive if the production will even go forward." Patrick held up his hands in a gesture of surrender.

"What are you talking about?" Gavin asked.

"The applications for Prince Charming have been…less than stellar," Patrick hedged.

"He means they're dreadful!" Mrs. Kemp chimed in.

"We have a large pool of female applicants—all ages and walks of life, and all of them attractive, accomplished women. But if we can't find a Prince Charming that the audience will root for, this thing is dead in the water before we even start shooting. And this isn't just about this season. If we don't knock it out of the park in Aster Bay, *Once Upon A Town* will be canceled before it ever sees the light of day."

They couldn't pull out of the production, could they? There were contracts that had been signed, memoranda of understanding…all of which likely had escape clauses for this very scenario. The Merchants' Association had already started planning the premiere party. They were building their entire winter tourism campaign around the fact the show would be shot in Aster Bay—billboards had already been reserved, media spots purchased across the country.

"I can't just stop my life for however long you're filming." Gavin ignored Mrs. Kemp's snort of disbelief.

But she's right. What life?

He'd be on summer break before filming began and would be on sabbatical next semester, so work wasn't a concern.

Then what life *are you unable to put on hold? Weekly trivia at The Rookery with the guys? Drunken Scrabble matches with Baz? Making sure Brodie eats a vegetable every once in a while?*

"We understand how challenging that can be," Patrick answered, oblivious to Gavin's silent argument with himself, "so we'll be filming on an accelerated timeline. Just five weeks."

When had his life become so predictable? There was a time he had thought of himself as spontaneous, adventurous but, fuck, how long had it been since he'd done anything outside of his routine?

"I don't date," Gavin said.

The memory of Kyla jumping into his arms the day before flashed through him, unbidden, and his hands clenched at his sides, as though his skin remembered the heat of her through her shirt.

"Yes, my aunt mentioned something about that." Patrick smiled.

"Audiences will eat that shit up—the lonely divorcé who put his own love life on hold to be a father. It practically sells itself," Zayne said. "And if you don't find someone you want to choose at the end of all this, we can choose for you. It can all be just for show."

Gavin scrubbed his hand over his eyes, suddenly exhausted. "There has to be someone else."

"If there is, we haven't found him yet," Patrick said. "Look, we'll coach you through the entire process. You don't have to do anything you don't want to do."

"There are worse ways to spend a few weeks than with a bunch of beautiful women vying for your attention," Zayne said. "Pick one you like, or hell, pick 'em all. Some kissing is always good for ratings and, if you hook up with more than one woman, the drama is reality TV gold."

Gavin shot up from the desk and walked around to the other side, needing to put some distance between himself and the producers.

Patrick shot a glare at Zayne. "The winning couple will receive $100,000 to split between themselves as they see fit. Even if you don't find your true love match on the show, think of what you could do with an extra $50,000. Think of all the good you could do for Aster Bay by ensuring the town is shown in the best possible light."

Patrick reached into his pocket and pulled out a business

card, extending it to Gavin. Gavin stared at the little rectangle of paper as though it might grow fangs and bite him. When he didn't take it, Patrick sighed and set it down on the desk.

"Take a few days and think it over. You can call or text me and let me know what you decide, but if we don't find our Prince Charming by the end of the week, we'll have to move on to other projects."

"You really should do it, dear," Mrs. Kemp said, getting to her feet. "Who knows? You might be surprised by how things work out."

Chapter Seven

"How did you even find this place? I thought sex clubs only existed in romance novels." Kyla stared up at the simple sign above the nondescript doorway. Olympus was, according to Jo, one of the most exclusive sex clubs in the Northeast. Not that you'd know it from where they stood on the sidewalk.

Jo shrugged. "That hedge fund guy I was dating a while back brought me. Or maybe it was the stock broker? One of the finance bros."

"I can't believe I let you talk me into this."

"You're the one who wanted to do something outside your comfort zone."

"Yeah, something like try the calamari pizza at The Pizza Stone or sing karaoke at The Rookery."

"What happened to crossing off number three on your list?"

Kyla glanced at the door again. Could she do it? Could she meet a random guy at a *sex club* and have hot, anonymous sex? She tugged on the leather pencil skirt she'd bought for the occasion. When she'd purchased it, she'd felt sexy, daring. Now she just felt silly.

"Stop. You look perfect." Jo batted Kyla's hands away from the hem of her skirt and straightened the straps of her lacy bodysuit.

"I'm wearing lingerie. In public," Kyla hissed.

"Then we better get inside so you're not *in public* anymore," Jo said with a wink.

Kyla followed Jo through the heavy metal door into a dimly lit lobby. The narrow vestibule was outfitted with textured wallpaper in a dark green and a high tin ceiling, a large mahogany reception desk at the opposite end blocking off double doors draped with deep velvet curtains. Even to get a day pass to accompany Jo, Kyla had had to submit test records proving a clean bill of health, but despite the shopping and medical tests, none of their preparations had truly made it feel real that she was about to enter a sex club.

And yet, there she was. About to take a page from Jo's book and find a guy for a no-strings night of hot sex. She could do this. *The Year of Kyla.*

Jo greeted the man behind the desk like a long-lost friend, planting a kiss on each cheek as though there was nothing at all intimidating about him. He had to be well over six feet tall and looked nearly as broad, a crooked nose speaking to past injuries and his biceps straining the fabric of his suit jacket, the tendrils of a tattoo snaking up the side of his neck from beneath his starched shirt collar. After a few minutes of chatting, and flashing their IDs, Jo and Kyla were waved through the double doors.

"Welcome to Olympus," Jo said, spreading her arms wide.

Kyla hardly knew where to look first. The club resembled a cabaret club, with a long bar along one wall and a low stage at the other. In between, café tables covered the main floor, with sleek, leather booths lining the outer walls. Everything was black and chrome, leather and velvet, with large crystal chandeliers lending pockets of light to the otherwise dimly lit space. One wall was entirely covered in mirrors above the chair rail and white, ionic columns flanked the stage, where a single black chair sat vacant under a spotlight.

As Kyla scanned the room, little details began to emerge,

making it clear that Olympus was not like any other club she'd ever been in. The bowl on the bar top was filled with condoms, not peanuts, for one thing, and the high shelf behind the bar was lined with crystal and metal sex toys of every size and shape imaginable, not bottles of booze.

"Holy shit," she breathed.

"It's great, isn't it?" Jo asked, adjusting her cleavage in her own lacy lingerie top. "I'm telling you, all you need is to find a hot guy to make you come so hard you see stars and you'll feel like a new woman. Comfort zone obliterated by multiple orgasms."

Kyla wasn't entirely sure that was true, but she had to admit, she was excited about trying Jo's plan. She glanced around, adrenaline flowing through her veins, making her feel fizzy and light, like she could float right out of the impractical heels she'd borrowed from Jo.

"Where do we start?" Kyla asked.

Jo laughed. "We start with a drink."

She guided her to the bar where she ordered them each a Captain and Coke.

"What's back there?" Kyla asked, indicating a hallway that disappeared around the corner.

"The private playrooms. But that's the three-hundred-level experience. Let's stick to the main floor tonight." Jo led her to a booth at the edge of the room with a clear view of the stage. "The floor show will start in just a few minutes."

Kyla hardly heard what Jo said next, however, as her eyes snagged on a familiar form across the room. There, in a booth by himself, sat Gavin West. Their eyes locked and Kyla forgot how to breathe, how to form words. She couldn't be sure in the dim light, but she thought she saw his jaw clench, his hand ball into a fist on the table. His eyes flicked over her outfit before he gave her a tight nod, lifting his drink slightly in her direction before throwing back the brown liquid.

"Kyla Meriweather Mitchell—"

"That's not my middle name."

"—are you even listening to me?" Jo asked.

"Gavin's here." Kyla turned to face her friend, her heart pounding in her chest and that fizzy feeling suddenly feeling more like she was a soda bottle that had been shaken up and was able to explode.

"*Gavin* Gavin? Your ex-boyfriend's *father*, Gavin?" Jo asked. "Where?"

"Don't look!" Kyla hissed.

"I always knew Daddy West had a kinky side."

She only had a moment to register Jo's laughter before a familiar, deep voice broke over her. "Ladies." Kyla looked up into Gavin's eyes, noting the slight strain to his smile, the tension in his shoulders. He wore a dark suit jacket, the top button on his shirt undone and Kyla's gaze snagged on the way the dim light cast shadows in the hollow of his throat.

"Gavin!" Jo exclaimed, as though she had been unaware he was there. "I didn't know you were a member here."

He shifted uneasily on his feet, fidgeting with his cuffs. He cleared his throat. "It's not something I advertise."

"Of course," Jo said smoothly, smiling. "This place is known for its discretion, after all. I've only been a member myself for a few months. And this is Kyla's first time."

His gaze fell on her like a physical touch, even if his eyes were still guarded. "I just wanted to say hi. I don't want to interrupt your girls' night out."

"Nonsense!" Jo exclaimed, sliding over in the booth and pulling Kyla with her to make room on the circular bench. "Join us."

Kyla could hardly hear over the blood rushing in her ears. Gavin glanced around the room, as though weighing his options, before giving a tight nod and sliding into the booth beside her. Immediately she was hit with his orange and sandalwood scent, the smell wrapping around her, taunting her.

No sooner had Gavin slid into the booth than Jo got to her feet. "Oh, I see someone I need to say hello to. I'll be right back." She shot a wink in Kyla's direction before disappearing in the crowd at the bar.

"Real subtle, Jo," Kyla muttered under her breath.

They sat in awkward silence for a few moments, Kyla sipping rum and Coke through a cocktail straw and doing her best to avoid looking at her ex-boyfriend's father. Finally, Gavin leaned back in the booth, his thighs spreading slightly, and folded his hands in his lap.

"How about we make a deal?" he asked. She set her drink down and drew her bottom lip between her teeth. His eyes tracked the movement, but then he blew out a breath and glanced away again. "I won't tell anyone I saw you here, and you don't tell anyone you saw me."

"What happens in Olympus stays in Olympus?" she offered.

He grinned, some of the tension in his shoulders easing. God, he was gorgeous. "Exactly."

"Deal." She held out her hand to shake his and immediately recognized her error. His large hand closed around hers, the electricity of his touch shooting up her arm and setting her skin tingling.

"How about we go one step further?" she asked.

The Year of Kyla.

He arched an eyebrow at her in question. Kyla lay her hand on Gavin's thigh and his eyes snapped to hers, darkening as his jaw clenched. She fought the urge to pull her hand away, to shrink back into the little bubble of safety she'd occupied most of her life. But she was tired of playing it safe.

"Tonight, I'm not me and you're not you." She hoped he couldn't feel the slight tremble in her hand. "We're just two people who are both here to have a good time."

Again, his eyes dropped to her lips. "Deal."

The lights around them dimmed even further as the

spotlight on the stage grew bright, the flickering candle on their table sending dancing shadows across Gavin's stubbled jaw. As one, they turned to the stage just in time to see a tall woman with electric pink hair take the stage. She wore a full bodysuit of fishnet, the netting cutting patterns into her generously curved stomach and thighs and Kyla sucked in a breath. All around them, every eye was on this gorgeous woman, her large body an object of desire, not derision. She glanced around at the other patrons, the rising lust in the room palpable. Power pulsed through her veins at seeing her own body type be the object of desire in such a space.

As the woman settled onto the chair in the center of the stage, a man followed her, his polished dress shoes clicking as he walked. He wore a dark suit with a slim tie, the picture of propriety. He discarded his suit jacket at the edge of the stage and undid his cuffs, rolling up his sleeves as he approached the woman in fishnet. As all eyes in the room watched, he took her chin in a bruising grip, turning her face to his and kissing her.

"She's beautiful," Kyla breathed.

"She is," Gavin said, cutting a glance in her direction.

Her skin heated under his gaze, and she noted the way his eyes darted around her face, dipping to trace the edge of her lingerie top, before he returned his attention to the stage. Kyla swallowed the last of her drink and watched as the man on stage moved to his knees and sucked on the woman's nipples through the netting.

Kyla couldn't look away, her own nipples curling into tight peaks as she watched. It should have been awkward, watching the couple on stage while surrounded by a crowd of other people, all equally turned on. She'd watched porn before but that was always a furtive thing, two-minute clips on Reddit with the sound on her phone turned off, and as soon as she'd come, she'd always been washed with shame. But this—this was intoxicating, even more so because of the man sitting beside her.

We're just two people who are both here to have a good time.

Could that be true? For one night, could they forget about the Brodie of it all?

The man on stage knelt between the woman's legs, holding her open for everyone to see, and licked a hot stripe over her center. Kyla felt her own breath knock from her lungs, heat pooling between her legs. She shifted in her seat, seeking a friction she couldn't achieve on her own. Not fully clothed anyway. She hadn't known what to expect, but she certainly hadn't expected *this*, to be so turned on just by watching somebody else. But it wasn't *just* that. It was also the orange and sandalwood scent invading her senses, the heat of the man beside her, the feel of his gaze turning to take in her reaction with each escalation on stage.

She turned to meet his eyes, tearing herself away from the display on stage as the woman in fishnet moaned her pleasure and bucked against the man's mouth, and felt a new heat creep into her cheeks. Gavin stared at her, and she had the strangest sense that he hadn't watched the performance at all. That instead he'd been watching *her*.

"Just two people?" he murmured, brushing a lock of her hair behind her ear.

She nodded, her mouth gone dry, and let her fingers dig into the hard muscle of his thigh just a little.

"Tell me, Kyla. Do you like watching?"

"Yes," she breathed. "You?"

He nodded. With a single finger, he traced her collarbone, drawing his fingertip back and forth over the ridge. The simple touch drew goosebumps across her skin.

On stage, the woman's moans reached a crescendo as she shivered and shook in the chair, and Kyla hardly noticed. Her entire world had narrowed to the slide of that single finger over her skin, the heat of Gavin's gaze, the sharp line of stubble on his jaw, the thousands of things she wanted him to do to her here in the darkness of the club.

She shifted towards him, but he stilled his hand. "Keep watching the show."

She scanned his eyes, wanting to memorize this new glimmer she saw there, the way the gold flecks in his irises seemed to gleam with heat. Biting her bottom lip, she nodded and turned her attention back to the stage, as if that could distract her from the hot knots coiling low in her belly when she inhaled Gavin's orange and sandalwood scent.

"Why'd you come here tonight?" he asked, his finger resuming its path to brush against the lace cupping the tops of her breasts.

The man on stage growled, "again," and buried his face between the woman's legs again, her cries piercing the heavy blanket of lust that lay over the crowd. Kyla shivered, pressing her thighs together.

Gavin smiled wryly as her hand slid higher on his thigh, closer to the prominent bulge behind the placket of his pants.

"If we really were just two people…" He shook his head, huffing out a breath with a sardonic chuckle.

One finger slipped beneath the edge of her top, skating over her nipple. She whimpered at the contact, her nipple painfully tight beneath the slow glide of his finger. Would he put his mouth on her the way the man on stage had done? She slid her hand higher, her pinky grazing his erection. His cock jumped in response to the small touch, so she did it again, wishing there weren't layers of clothing between them.

"The things I'd do to you," he muttered so softly she almost didn't hear him.

"Do them," she said, breathless.

His eyes snapped to hers, wide and wild.

The sound of her phone ringing in her purse broke over them but Kyla hardly noticed she was so busy watching the fascinating way the gold in his eyes glinted hungrily. It wasn't until the woman at the next table cleared her throat loudly and shot them a withering glare that Kyla registered the robotic music.

Blinking out of her trance, she dug her phone out of her purse, all the blood rushing from her face at the sight of the name on the screen. She quickly silenced the phone and dropped it face down on the table.

"Everything alright?" Gavin asked, his voice so gravelly and deep it rasped against her skin.

"Fine," she said too brightly.

Her phone began to ring again and she cursed as she fumbled to silence it. This time, Gavin's eyes landed on the screen a moment before it darkened, reading Brodie's name in flashing letters.

"He probably just locked himself out of his car again," she mumbled.

Gavin cleared his throat and leaned back in the booth. Cold air rushed into the space between them. "I didn't realize you two were still—"

"We're not. We're not anything. But at least once a week he gets drunk and he calls. I always let it go to voicemail."

Gavin studied her, as though he was trying to determine if she was lying, and she hated the tendril of shame that curled in her stomach.

"Brodie and I are over," she said firmly, noting the way Gavin flinched at the mention of his son's name. "We should have been over a long time ago."

"But he still calls you when he's drunk," Gavin said, all gravel cleared from his tone.

"He does." She deflated. Whatever magic spell they'd been under just a moment ago had been broken and she couldn't help but feel like she'd never get that chance back.

Gavin blew out a breath and flashed her a pained smile. "Enjoy your night, Kyla."

She watched helplessly as he got to his feet and left the club, never once glancing back.

That night, Gavin lay alone in bed and read the same sentence in his book over and over again. With a frustrated sigh, he set the book aside. It was no use trying to read when his thoughts were back in Olympus, still in that booth with Kyla.

Christ, he'd come so close to crossing so many lines, to doing things he could never take back, things his son would never forgive him for.

She'd been so unbelievably beautiful—not just because of the sexy little skirt and the nearly see-through lingerie. Watching her had been better than watching the show, seeing the pink bloom in her cheeks and across her chest as she realized what was happening on stage, watching as her nipples furled into tight peaks beneath her lacy top, and the way she'd squirmed in her seat. He'd wanted nothing more than to lay her out on that table and bury his face between her legs, to find out just how wet she was, his little voyeur.

He cursed under his breath as heat rushed to his groin, his cock kicking in his sweatpants. The thoughts had plagued him nonstop since he'd caught a glimpse of her boudoir photograph months ago, but now—now he could hardly stop imagining the sounds she'd make, the way she'd taste if he tongued her clit. He had to stop thinking of her this way.

But tonight wouldn't be that night. Tonight he was lonely and still a little tipsy and tired of this need that pounded through his veins every time she was near. Going to Olympus was meant to be a distraction, a way to work out some of this inconvenient lust with a willing stranger, just as he'd done ever since his divorce. Meaningless sex, nothing more. It was *not* meant to be the closest he'd ever come to destroying his relationship with his son. What he'd almost done with Kyla, what he'd wanted to do—Brodie would never forgive him.

He slid his hand into his pants, wrapping his fist around his aching erection. He squeezed his eyes shut and let his pants drop further down his hips, the length of his cock springing free.

A groan fell from his lips as he stroked his length, hard and rough, images of Kyla swimming before his eyes. The way her softness would give beneath his touch, how her eyelashes would flutter when he found just the right spot to tease her. How he'd make her come over and over, a hundred times, a thousand, with his fingers and tongue and cock, until she knew just how glorious her own pleasure could be. Until he'd worshipped every curve the way the light in her photograph had.

His hand flew faster, roughly tugging as his hips rocked into his own fist, his breathing coming harder with each image that he had no right to. Kyla spread before him on his Egyptian cotton sheets. Kyla on her knees, her hot, wet mouth waiting for him. Sliding his hand between her thighs as she watched a performance at the club, feeling her swell and break beneath his touch. Kyla, Kyla, Kyla.

He squeezed and jerked himself closer to orgasm and he imagined she was there, watching him the way she'd watched the performance at Olympus, that she looked on as he worked himself. He moved faster, imagining her eyes growing darker as she drew her bottom lip between her teeth, just as she had earlier that night. He recalled her little whimper of need when his finger had brushed her nipple, a sound he was sure she hadn't even realized she'd made, and—*fuck*.

He came with a grunt, his head thrown back and his eyes squeezed shut. The orgasm seemed never-ending, pulsing as he imagined her blue eyes fixed on his cock. Hot ribbons of cum coated his fist and he imagined driving into her instead, filling her, as though he had any right to. As though doing so wouldn't betray his son.

At last, it was finished, and he drew his hand over the oversensitive length of his erection another time or two before he opened his eyes again, keeping his gaze focused on the ceiling as the scent of his misdeeds brought him back to reality.

Fuck, what is wrong with me?

This had to stop. He couldn't keep doing this, couldn't keep thinking about *her* like *that*.

Patrick's card on his bedside table caught his eye. Maybe it wouldn't be the worst idea to start dating again—actually dating, not just fucking random women he met at Olympus. Maybe then he could think about someone other than his son's ex-girlfriend.

Before he could change his mind, he shot off a text message.

Gavin: I'm in. What now?

Chapter Eight

Gavin's shoes were too tight.

And his mouth was dry.

And this had all been a horrible mistake.

He stood on the circular gravel drive outside Aster Place, the weeping willows that framed the grand entrance strung with fairy lights that twinkled as though something magical was about to happen.

Ryan Harris, the overly coiffed host of *Once Upon A Town*, came to stand next to Gavin. As he adjusted the cuffs of his jacket and the precise knot of his tie, he shot a skeptical glance in Gavin's direction. "You turned down the mascara?" Ryan tutted.

Gavin's face already itched with the powder and concealer the show's makeup artist had insisted on applying before filming began. He was absolutely not about to add mascara as well, no matter how much Ryan swore that it would make his eyes "pop," whatever that meant.

"Have you done this before?" Gavin asked, turning his panicked gaze towards the host.

Ryan rolled his shoulders, as though he were warming up for an athletic event and not just hours upon hours of standing around under the obscenely bright lights. "This is my first time with the Travel Network, but I hosted three seasons of Love

Asylum." At Gavin's blank expression, Ryan rolled his eyes and explained. "Contestants are locked in an abandoned insane asylum for a week to see if they can find love while fighting the ghosts of the former inmates. Have you seriously not heard of this? It was huge in Germany."

"I've never been," Gavin muttered, turning his attention back to the empty driveway.

"To an insane asylum?"

"To Germany," Gavin said. "Or an asylum."

Ryan nodded, and shot a grin Gavin's way, inclining his head towards the Federal-style mansion behind them. "This place is way nicer."

"Than an asylum?"

"Than Germany." At Gavin's confused look, Ryan threw his head back and laughed, his blindingly white teeth glinting in the lights. "Loosen up, man. This is supposed to be fun."

"Is it?"

"There are seven single women headed here as we speak, and all of them are dying to get into your bed. Yeah, I'd say that's supposed to be fun."

"I'm not going to sleep with them," Gavin said, horrified at the idea that he would have sex with the women on the show during filming.

"That's what they all say. Oh, look, here comes the first *eligible lady*." Ryan winked as a limousine pulled into the driveway.

Gavin's stomach dropped as the limo rolled to a stop. While the vehicle idled, cameramen appeared from out of nowhere, taking up positions surrounding the limo so they'd capture the first woman's entrance.

"We rolling?" Ryan asked, shielding his eyes as he looked towards the bank of crew members who had set up to the side of the driveway. Davis Locantore, a young man who had been introduced to Gavin as the director and who, even now in the dark of evening, seemed to always be wearing sunglasses, flashed a thumbs up. "Let's do this."

A moment later, Ryan's entire demeanor was transformed. He shifted his stance, all the frenetic energy transformed into a calm steadfastness, and adopted a friendly, open smile, resting his hand on Gavin's shoulder.

"Are you ready to meet the eligible ladies, Gavin?" he asked.

Gavin gawked at the change in Ryan but only for a moment, before he remembered what was expected of him. "As ready as I'll ever be, Ryan."

Ryan's smile widened and he clapped him on the back, taking a step away. The man practically faded into the darkness outside of the circle of arranged lights.

A long, perfectly tanned leg wearing sky-high heels emerged from the limo's open door and paused as the cameras adjusted their positioning, taking in every second of suspense. A moment later, the rest of the woman appeared. She was tall with an hourglass figure and her long blonde hair was swept up in some kind of fancy up-do, loose tendrils falling around her face. Beneath the layers of makeup, her smile seemed genuine, somehow already putting him at ease.

As she approached him, the gravel crunching beneath her impractical heels, her legs flashed in and out of view through the unbelievably high slit in her floor length dress, the hem of which was dragging through the dust of the driveway. The sky-blue gown perfectly complimented her eyes and highlighted her tiny waist. A simple cross necklace swung against her chest, drawing attention to her ample cleavage. As she drew closer, she spread her arms out to the side, silver bangles clanking on her wrist.

"I'm a hugger!" She laughed as she wrapped her arms around his waist, the hint of a Southern accent coloring her words. Even with heels, she only came up to his shoulders, and it took him a beat too long to hug her back with an awkward chuckle.

When she pulled away, Gavin fought the urge to glance down

and see if any of her makeup had rubbed off on his black suit. He assumed it hadn't or the crew would have paused to fix it. Only a few hours on set and he'd already learned that the crew was heavily invested in making sure he always looked perfect.

"I'm Gavin. And you are?"

"Becca. And I know I only have two minutes to—"

"Go again!" Davis shouted from the sidelines.

Becca and Gavin turned confused faces in the direction of the voice and they were momentarily blinded by the lights.

Patrick appeared at the edge of their vision with a reassuring smile. "We don't want to say how long you two have here," he explained. "It takes away some of the magic for the viewers."

"Shoot, I'm sorry," Becca said.

"Not at all. You can just pick up right where you left off." Patrick stepped back into the darkness.

It was hard to concentrate on the woman in front of him, talking a mile a minute about teaching kindergarten and competing in beauty pageants across the South, when there were twenty or more crew members standing just outside of the circle of light, watching every move they made. A camera shifted into Gavin's line of sight, just over Becca's shoulder, no doubt capturing his every reaction, and he reminded himself to smile.

"Don't you think?" Becca asked.

Shit. What was she talking about?

"Absolutely," he said. "I'm looking forward to getting to know you better, Becca."

She beamed, reached forward to squeeze his bicep, and then walked past him, up the steps to Aster Place, and disappeared into the mansion.

Ryan reappeared at Gavin's side. "What did you think of Becca?" he prodded.

"She seems nice." Gavin wasn't sure how else to assess a woman he'd spoken with for only a few minutes. "And beautiful."

Ryan's smile stayed firmly in place but his eyes seemed to say, *Really? That's the best you got?* "Here comes the next eligible lady now," he said, backing away again.

The next woman practically jumped out of the limo. She wore a short, skintight red dress that left nothing to the imagination, cut outs revealing flashes of skin at her waist and a long silver chain around her neck disappearing down the front of her dress. Her dark brown hair was pulled back into an updo, her makeup more dramatic than Becca's had been, making her brown eyes seem overly large and her features more severe.

"Well, hello, Prince Charming," she said with a sing-song tone as she crossed the driveway towards him. Like Becca, she wore ridiculously high heels, and for a moment, Gavin wondered if that had been a requirement of the contestants.

"I'm Gavin." He held out a hand to her.

She clasped his hand with both of hers, pressing his palm to her chest just above her breast. He swallowed down a surprised laugh. "I'm Amanda, but my friends call me Mandy. I'm a Scorpio, proud puppy mama, and a massage therapist. So you know what that means."

She paused for him to respond, as though of course he should know what that string of random facts said about a person. He blinked, forcing the smile to stay on his face. "No, I'm afraid I don't."

She rolled her eyes with a playful smile. "It *means* I'm passionate, I value loyalty, and I'm great with my hands." She gave an exaggerated wink.

Gavin nearly choked on his own tongue and carefully extracted his hand from her grasp. "Thank you for being here, Mandy."

She gave a little shimmy of her shoulders and made her way into the mansion.

"Sounds like Mandy would be happy to help you deal with

some of the tension you're carrying in your shoulders." Ryan grinned, his hand landing on Gavin's shoulder as if to highlight the way they'd crept towards his ears. "Two down, five to go."

Erika was next, a single mother and nurse from Boston. Her dark skin shimmered with some kind of glitter powder across her cheekbones, glinting in the light, and her long box braids were pulled into a high ponytail, the ends of the braids hanging down between her shoulders. She was stunning in a dress of rose-gold silk that shimmered over her skin like water and dipped low on her back, highlighting her strong frame, no doubt toned from years of working on her feet.

"How old is your daughter?" Gavin asked, relieved to talk for a moment about something he understood.

Erika's eyes lit up. "Shelby's ten and she's a little firecracker. She wants to be a scientist and solve climate change."

Gavin chuckled. "Ambitious."

"She is!"

"That's a wonderful thing. You're obviously doing a great job with her."

Erika's smile faltered for a fraction of a second. "I hope so." Her eyes darted to the side, catching a signal that Gavin had obviously missed. "I'll see you in there."

The next limo held a short redhead with bright green eyes and proportions that would make even Barbie jealous. She marched across the driveway, the laces that ran up her calves from her stilettos swinging with each step. She wore a sheer black dress embellished with carefully placed lace appliques, her bra and panties visible through the fabric.

She gripped his hand in hers and slapped it against her ass as she crushed her lips against his. Gavin froze, unsure how to react, but only for a moment before he stepped away, laughing uncomfortably. He tugged his hand out of her grip and held his hands up in front of him as he stumbled back to put some distance between them.

What the hell just happened?

"I'm Christina," she purred. "And now I'm certain you won't forget me."

"You and me both," he said, doing his best to keep his humor about him even as indignation began to flood in. In what universe was it okay to march up to someone you'd never met and kiss them? In the universe of reality television, apparently.

"There's more where that came from." She flashed her eyes down to her chest suggestively.

Gavin cleared his throat and kept his eyes on her face. "Where are *you* from, Christina?"

She blinked, as though the question were unusual. With a grin, she cocked a hip and twirled a loose lock of red hair around her finger. "Maine. So I know exactly how to keep my man warm."

"Okay," Gavin said a little too loudly. "I'll see you in there."

She blew him a kiss before following the path into the mansion.

"She's a real *handful*, don't you think?" Ryan asked, leaning on the innuendo.

Gavin breathed hard through his nose. He wasn't sure how much more of this he could take.

"Just three more. You're doing great."

Veronica was the next to arrive. She was a short woman with narrow hips and few curves beneath her long emerald green dress. Her hair was cut into a shoulder-length bob and dyed with a pink-purple-blue ombre effect. Somehow the multicolored cut complemented her golden skin tone perfectly.

"Woah, this place is gorgeous." She grinned as she crossed the driveway, careful not to step on the hem of her dress. Unlike the other women, she seemed less accustomed to the gowns and heels, and immediately Gavin liked her. "I'm Veronica. Roni for short." She extended a hand in his direction.

"Nice to meet you, Roni. I'm Gavin."

"And here I thought you were Prince Charming."

He chuckled. "Nope. Just plain ol' Gavin."

"That's good," Roni said with an approving smile. "I think I'll probably like plain ol' Gavin better than some stuffy prince anyway."

"What do you do, Roni?" Gavin asked. For the first time, he found himself genuinely wanting to know.

"I'm the Executive Director for a food waste recovery organization in Miami." Gavin had no idea what that meant, but he was impressed. Thankfully, she let him off the hook. "We reclaim unexpired food that will be discarded from grocery stores or restaurants, mostly because it's not pretty enough or it's just not selling, and we distribute it to food pantries and soup kitchens across the region."

"That's amazing. What's it called?"

"Go again!" Davis shouted again.

"What is it this time?" Gavin asked, turning towards the voice with a hand across his forehead, as though that would help him see the director through the glare of the lights.

"You can't ask for the name of the organization," Patrick said, stepping just into the circle of light. "We aren't allowed to endorse any organization or company that isn't under contract with the Travel Network."

"But it's a nonprofit," Gavin protested.

Patrick shrugged and flashed an apologetic smile. "Sorry, Roni."

She waved away the apology. "It's cool. We won't be hard to find with a Google search."

They chatted for another few seconds about Miami's beaches and her love for her mother's Puerto Rican food before Roni, too, was shuffled into the mansion.

Gavin had hardly turned back to the driveway, his head swimming as he tried to recite all the names to himself, when another limo arrived. This time, the woman who emerged wore little more than the requisite heels. Instead of a gown, she stood before Gavin in a shimmery purple bikini, the top barely large enough to cover her chest and the strings across her hips drawn up high to accent her toned thighs and abs.

She laughed, a practiced, grating sound, as she approached him. "Don't tell me I've left you speechless already?" She turned directly to the camera. "I think that means he'll remember me."

"Again!" Davis' voice rang out.

"You can't address the cameras directly unless you're in a confessional interview," Patrick explained from the sidelines.

"Right. Sorry."

"I'm Gavin." He held out his hand to her.

She gave him an incredulous look, then pulled him into a hug, pressing her nearly naked curves against him. "I think we're going to be too well acquainted for a handshake." Finally, pulling away, she gestured to herself in a sweeping motion. "I'm Lauren. I'm from Los Angeles, and, if you couldn't tell, I'm a model."

"Oh." He wasn't sure how to respond to that. "Have you been in any campaigns I might have seen?"

Her smile tightened, her eyes growing colder. "Right now I'm mostly modeling on my Instagram page but I've been contacted by several companies for future endorsement deals."

"That's—that's great. Good for you." He mentally recategorized her occupation to *unemployed*.

"I was Miss Los Angeles three years in a row and—"

"What was your talent?" he asked, hoping beyond hope that it would be something he could file away for future discussion.

Again, her eyes grew colder by a few degrees. "Ribbon dancing."

He forced himself to keep smiling even as he wondered how it was possible that they still had any time left. Weren't these intros only supposed to last two minutes?

"But I'm more than just a pretty face. I'm very into fitness—

yoga, pilates, running—and I really love juicing."

"Juicing? As in, making juice?"

"You'd be surprised how good a juice cleanse can make you feel. Especially if you use Pure Sexxy Juice Enhancer. That's 'sexxy' with two exes."

Gavin glanced off camera, waiting for the production crew to shut down the blatant product endorsement. When they didn't, he turned back to Lauren.

"Well, sure. Two exes means twice the…sexy."

She laughed. "You're going to be fun. I can tell." With a little wave, she sauntered into the house.

Ryan appeared at his side again, his eyes darting back over his shoulder to watch as the bikini-clad blonde walked away.

"I'm sorry," Gavin said, turning back to where he knew the production crew was gathered. "Why was that name dropping okay but we couldn't say the name of Roni's charity?"

"Because Pure Sexxy is a sponsor of the show," Zayne said. He bit into an apple with an obnoxious crunch and continued speaking through the mouthful of fruit. "There's a shit ton of the stuff in all the rooms if you want to try it out."

"I'm good, thanks."

"Just one more eligible lady to meet." Ryan drew Gavin back to the matter at hand. "What do you think so far?"

"I think," Gavin said, choosing his words carefully, "that all of the women have been beautiful and much more…interesting than I expected."

And none of them are for me.

Ryan flashed a weaselly smirk and gestured to the final limo as it pulled into the driveway. "I think you'll find they've saved the most interesting for last."

Dear God, let's hope so.

Chapter Nine

Kyla's dress was too tight.

And her hands trembled as they twisted in the fabric of her dress.

And this had all been a horrible mistake.

Jeannie, the associate producer tasked with escorting her, tapped the back of her hand. "Stop that or you'll be all wrinkled when you get out of the limo."

Kyla released her grasp and fought the urge to pick at the skin around her fingernails. She wouldn't want to ruin the manicure the production crew had sent her for that morning, or have all of America see her ragged cuticles on national television. Her mother would be horrified. Not that her mother even knew she was on this show, or would ever watch something as gauche as reality television. But still.

"You have two minutes to introduce yourself and then you'll go into the mansion with the other girls. You'll be the last to arrive. After Prince Charming does his first impression interview with Ryan, he'll join you all for a brief cocktail party," Jeannie said, consulting her iPad.

"How did the other introductions go?" Kyla asked, more to have something else to think about than anything.

Jeannie shrugged. "Wouldn't know. Once I drop a girl off,

I loop back around with the limo to pick up the next one." She ran an assessing gaze over Kyla, her dark eyes narrowing behind the thick, black frames of her glasses. "You've practiced walking in the shoes?" She gestured to the heels Kyla had been encouraged to wear by Megan, the wardrobe consultant.

"Mmhmm," Kyla said, looking out the window as the limo turned into the driveway of Aster Place.

She *had* practiced, but that didn't mean she was good at walking in them. These shoes were at least two inches taller than any others she owned and the heels were much narrower, but Megan had taken one look at Kyla's old, scuffed, sensible heels and dove head first into her closet of "emergency" supplies. From what Kyla could tell, the closet consisted entirely of high heels, bikinis, thongs, and double-sided tape.

"Just be yourself," Jeannie said. The limo rolled to a stop at the edge of the circular drive. "And stop scrunching up your dress."

With that, Jeannie reached around Kyla and opened the door to the limo. Immediately, the opening was flooded with unnaturally bright light from the filming set up, the fuzzy shapes of two cameras appearing on either side of the open door. Kyla slid to the edge of the seat and carefully swung her feet out the way her mother had always taught her, keeping her legs together so as not to accidentally flash anyone. She kept her eyes focused on the ground, willing her ankles to stop wobbling, as she climbed out of the car and smoothed her hands over her skirt.

The dress was a simple, A-line cocktail dress of navy satin that ended mid-thigh. It was shorter than she would have picked for herself, but Jo had insisted that it made her legs look long and, given that they weren't that long to begin with, she'd take the help of every optical illusion she could get. Besides, there were only so many formal dresses in her size at the mall in Providence and production had insisted that each contestant bring seven—*seven*—different formal dresses. Apparently their gowns for the fairytale balls would be provided, but introduction and elimination ceremony dresses were up to the contestant.

As she righted herself and began picking her way across the gravel driveway, still keeping her eyes locked on the ground, she heard a sharp intake of breath and a distinctly male exhale. She hoped that was a good thing, that he liked what he saw and wasn't put off by the fact that, unlike the other girls, she didn't wear a single-digit dress size. She needed Prince Charming to at least be willing to give her a chance if she had any hope of winning the money to open her photography studio. And who knows? Maybe she could even find love, or at the very least, that mind-altering sex Jo had promised her was possible. After their night at Olympus, she was even more determined than ever to check that particular item off her list.

A pair of large, shiny black, men's dress shoes appeared at the edge of her vision and she breathed a sigh of relief. She'd made it across the driveway without breaking her neck. She smiled the way Jeannie had coached her to—lots of teeth, but not in a scary way—and raised her eyes to take in the man whose heart she would be trying to win.

Her gaze swept over the familiar frame, the close-cropped facial hair she fantasized about, the full lips and dark hazel eyes she knew so well, and her breath caught in her chest. "Gavin?" she asked in disbelief, taking a step forward too quickly.

She lost her footing, stumbling into his arms. He caught her before she came anywhere near hitting the ground and his touch seared her skin.

"What are you doing here?" Her panicked gaze darting between his eyes.

"What are *you* doing here?" He set her back on her feet but still didn't release her, his hands gripping her waist.

Out of the shadows near the entrance to the mansion, Ryan Harris appeared. His slicked-back, black hair glinted in the lights, his thin lips spread into a satisfied smirk. "Surprise!" he clapped his hands together as he approached. "Gavin, I assume you recognize this woman?"

"Of course, I recognize her. She's—" He broke off, as if he suddenly realized he was still touching her, and dropped his hands, clenching his fists.

"In a town as small as Aster Bay, it would hardly be surprising for two people as attractive as Gavin and Kyla to know each other," Ryan said directly into a camera that was hovering nearby. "Why don't you tell us how *else* you know each other?" he asked, turning a shark-like grin their way.

"We've worked together," Gavin said with a meaningful eyebrow raise in Kyla's direction. "Many times. Kyla is a talented photographer and she's helped promote many of the town's events over the last few years."

Ryan smirked. "It's all right, Gavin. We're all friends here." He held his arms out wide as if to indicate the rest of the crew. When neither of them spoke, Ryan's already-thin lips pressed together into a flat line. "Alright. If you'd like, you can save that particular revelation for a bit later," he said with a wink at the camera.

Kyla's head pounded, her heart slamming against her rib cage. She should be mortified by the very thought of doing this show with Gavin, should walk away right now, get back in that limo, go back to her apartment and forget any of this ever happened, list be damned. But she couldn't stop watching the way Gavin's fists clenched and released, couldn't help but feel the heat of his gaze boring into her. The memory of the last time he'd looked at her with such intensity washed over her and she nearly stumbled again, wobbling precariously on her high heels.

She *should* be disgusted by the idea of dating her ex-boyfriend's father. So why wasn't she? Why did she instead have this odd burst of adrenaline coursing through her veins, this giddy anticipation?

Her gaze locked with his again. "You look great." Her voice

was breathy in a way she didn't recognize.

His eyes darkened ever so slightly and he let his gaze linger over her curves before meeting her eyes again. "So do you." He swallowed and she was momentarily distracted by the working of his throat. "We should talk."

Before Kyla could respond, Ryan clapped a hand on Gavin's shoulder hard enough to shake him. "You'll have plenty of time to catch up later, but for now, Kyla, I must ask you to go inside with the other eligible ladies."

"Of course," she said, never taking her eyes off Gavin.

Was he as mixed up as she was about this? Had he known she'd be there? And what did he want to talk about? Brodie? That night at Olympus? Or something else entirely?

Oh, God, what if he tells me to go home?

As she took a step past him, she faltered again, reaching out and grasping his forearm to steady herself. He stared at her grip on his arm for a moment and then looped her arm through his.

"Let me," he said.

He led her to the door and up the steps to Aster Place, allowing her to lean into him a bit as she went and walking slowly enough to let her choose her steps carefully. At the top of the stairs, she turned to face him.

"Thank you." She did her best not to breathe in his orange and sandalwood scent, not to linger over the strands of gray threaded through the hair at his temples and how unfairly sexy they made him look, and failed on both accounts.

He squeezed her hand where it lay on his forearm and then took another step back with a quiet nod, watching as she entered the mansion and closed the door softly behind her.

First impression Interview
Official Transcript

Ryan Harris: Wow, Gavin. Those were seven lovely ladies. How are you feeling right now?

Gavin West: Honestly, I'm a little overwhelmed.

Ryan: Who made the biggest first impression?

Gavin: That's hard to say, Ryan. They each made an impression in their own way. I wasn't expecting Lauren to arrive wearing a bikini, and I certainly wasn't expecting Christina to kiss me.

Ryan: [laughter] You'll need to be careful with that one. Did anyone stand out as someone you want to get to know better?

Gavin: I want to get to know them all better.

Ryan: Of course you do. But who piqued your interest the most.

Gavin: [pause] I'm interested in learning more about Roni and the work she's doing in her community. Giving back is something that's really important to me.

Ryan: A common interest.

Gavin: Exactly.

Ryan: You also have something in common with Erika. You're both parents.

Gavin: I'm sure we'll bond over the trials of parenthood.

Ryan: Though your son is a bit older than Erika's daughter.

Gavin: [chuckles] Just a bit. He's more than twice her age.

Ryan: Speaking of your son, there is another eligible lady here tonight that shares an interesting history with your family.

[Long pause]

Ryan: Can you tell us how you know Kyla?

Gavin: I think you already know how Kyla and I know each other.

Ryan: For the viewers at home, then.

Gavin: As I said earlier, Kyla is a very talented photographer. I've hired her several times over the last few years to take photographs to promote town events, like our popular winter Food and Wine Festival. She took the photographs that helped bring *Once Upon A Town* to Aster Bay.

Ryan: Right. But that's not your only connection, is it?

[Long pause]

Gavin: No. It's not.

Ryan: Kyla used to date your son, isn't that right?

[Pause]

Gavin: She did.

Ryan: Tell us what you're thinking. Will you be keeping her around to see if maybe she chose the wrong West the first time around?

[Long pause]

Gavin: I think she and I have a lot to talk about.

Chapter Ten

Jo had warned Kyla to keep her guard up around the other women. She and Molly had wanted to watch a marathon of *The Bachelor* to help Kyla prepare for her time on *Once Upon A Town*, but after thirty minutes of the first episode, Kyla had begged off. She couldn't watch all those women with their perfect bodies and their perfect hair and their perfect makeup without thinking about all the ways she wasn't perfect. But she had allowed Jo and Molly to share the highlights of what they'd learned from watching:

One: The other women were *not* her friends, no matter how friendly they might seem.

Two: There would be cameras everywhere except the bathroom, but there would probably still be a microphone in there.

Three: Whoever Prince Charming was, he was likely going to be making out with everyone. A lot. Like, right in front of the other women. According to reality television rules, this was perfectly acceptable behavior.

Great, and now you're thinking about making out with Gavin.

Kyla paused in the hallway just outside the double doors that would lead to the drawing room where the other women were waiting for the cocktail party to begin. She steadied herself against the wall with one hand and slid off her heels, breathing a sigh of relief as her arches lowered to the plush carpet. Jo and Molly had told her to be herself, and Kyla would never wear heels that made her feet hurt for hours on end. Besides, if she was just going to get sent home week one anyway—which she absolutely was, because there was no way Gavin was going to keep his son's ex-girlfriend on the show—she might as well be comfortable.

Glancing around the cameramen who dogged her every step, she spotted a nervous-looking young woman with a headset and a clipboard. Kyla held the shoes out to her.

"Can you make sure these get back to Megan?" she asked.

The young woman glanced around as though Kyla might be speaking to someone else. "I'm really not supposed to—aren't you going to wear them?" she stammered.

"Nope."

When the woman still didn't take the shoes, Kyla relented and set them down on the side of the hall, confident that a member of production would retrieve them later.

With a final steadying breath, she pushed open the double doors. The drawing room was lavishly decorated in hardwoods and plush carpet, antique fabric wallpaper in imitation of gilded age fashion lining the walls, and decorative moldings on the high ceiling. And, if Kyla remembered correctly, there was the softest ottoman known to man in the far corner by the French doors that led to the garden. Last winter, the town's Food and Wine Festival had held a Cocktails and Cupcakes party in this room and Kyla had retreated to the ottoman to rest her tired feet once all the pastries had been served.

She made a beeline for the ottoman now, hoping to avoid conversation with the gathered group of model-esque women sipping champagne and assessing her every move. A blonde in a bikini snort-laughed into her champagne flute and turned her back on Kyla, whispering something to a dark-haired woman who was trying to flag down a server for a refill. From the group, a tall woman in a sky-blue dress stepped forward with an expression of pity in her eyes.

"Oh, honey, what happened to your shoes?" she asked, pointing at Kyla's bare feet.

A server with a tray of full champagne flutes offered one to Kyla as he passed and she gratefully accepted, downing a large sip before she returned her attention to the woman in front of her. "Nothing happened to them. I'm just more comfortable without them."

The woman's brows drew together as she considered the concept that someone might forgo one of the trappings of beauty in favor of comfort.

"I'm Kyla."

Her face instantly brightened. "I'm Becca and I'm so happy to meet you, Kyla. Come." She looped her arm through Kyla's and steered her towards the others, "I'll introduce you around."

It didn't take more than a few minutes for Kyla to clock that the bikini woman (also known as Lauren) was going to be the house mean girl and that Becca was too nice to notice her snipes, or that Mandy was well on her way to sloppy drunk while Erika, the mother of the group, was doing her best to slow her pace. Christina, a redhead in a see-through dress, was mostly quiet, while Roni, the oldest amongst them with the kind of multicolored dye job that Kyla wished she had the confidence to pull off, was quick with a witty remark. By the time they were all settling in to hear about Erika's daughter and Roni was openly debating joining Kyla in the barefoot club, the double doors opened and Ryan and Gavin appeared.

The women immediately got to their feet, straightening their skirts and plastering on camera-ready smiles, as though they weren't being filmed the entire time. But Kyla didn't care about them—she was too busy watching Gavin, the way his eyes scanned the group and locked on her, and the strange flip in her stomach that followed.

"Ladies," Ryan said, his eyes sweeping over them, "I hope you've had a chance to get acquainted. Welcome to the beautiful Aster Place. Built in the early 1800s as the summer cottage for a wealthy New York family, today, Aster Place is a historic house museum, preserving the history of the property, family, and region for future generations."

Kyla glanced around, finally locating the teleprompter that Ryan was reading from. No doubt his little speech would run over footage of the mansion, or maybe the photograph she'd taken of Jo as Cinderella on the sidewalk out front. She caught Gavin's gaze again and he bit back an amused smile as Ryan continued waxing poetic about the antiques and artwork housed in the mansion. When he started in on the statuary and landscaping, Kyla barely contained the laughter bubbling up behind her lips, Gavin's eyes dancing with his own amusement at the blatant sales pitch. Kyla shook her head slightly, as if to say, *Who wrote this crap?* and Gavin stifled a laugh with a cough.

Ryan continued, "We are grateful to Aster Place for hosting the fairytale balls this season." The women clapped politely. "Now, ladies, Gavin will choose one woman who made the biggest impression during introductions to spend a few minutes with one-on-one before we end our evening together. Gavin, who will it be?"

He hesitated for only the barest of moments. "Kyla." Her heart jumped into her throat.

"Kyla, if you would accompany Prince Charming out to the gardens," Ryan said, gesturing to the French doors that had magically opened during Ryan's monologue about the mansion.

Gavin crossed the room towards her and she was once again struck by how goddamn handsome he was. His suit had been tailored to show off his muscular arms and powerful thighs, to highlight the strength of his back and his narrow waist. He looked like a movie star and yet he also looked like himself, like the man who had sat across from her at the breakfast table so many times, who came into the bakery looking for blackberry cupcakes, and who never missed a trivia night at The Rookery. How could someone so familiar feel so different?

He held out his arm for her and she took it, letting him lead her through the double doors onto the marble patio as invisible crew members swept the French doors closed behind them. The gardens at Aster Place were always beautiful, but tonight they had been strung with fairy lights, just like the weeping willow out front, and for a moment, it really did feel like she had stepped into a fairytale.

"You're barefoot." Gavin frowned down at her toes, the expression emphasizing the faint lines at the corners of his eyes.

"Oh, that," Kyla said, wishing she hadn't rushed the nail tech through her pedicure. "I'm fine."

"The path is gravel."

Kyla arched an eyebrow at him and stepped off the patio into the lush grass on the side of the path. "Problem solved." She dug her toes into the cool grass.

He smiled, a boyish grin that made him look so much younger than his forty-three years, and toed off his own dress shoes. He tucked his socks into the shoes and shoved them aside, stepping down to join her in the grass. "It kind of tickles," he said, staring down at the grass beneath his feet.

They walked a bit through the garden, each trying to pretend they weren't surrounded by cameras on every side. Jo had assured her she would eventually get used to them, would hardly notice them by the end of filming, but it was hard to imagine she wouldn't always be self-conscious with so many cameras pointed in her direction.

A small marble bench was set amongst the rose bushes, an ice bucket with a bottle of champagne beside it. They exchanged a look, a silent acknowledgment of how weird this whole thing was, but they obliged the crew, sitting on the bench and popping the champagne.

Finally, there was nothing to do but talk. But how much would Gavin want to reveal on television?

"Does Brodie know you're here?" His voice was soft, as if they weren't surrounded by microphones.

She shook her head. "We don't talk anymore. He used to call sometimes when he was drunk but I never answered, and I haven't heard from him at all since he left for California." She glanced at the camera in front of her for a moment, before turning her attention back to Gavin. *You're going to have to get used to the cameras,* she reminded herself. "Does he know *you're* here?"

"It was his idea." Gavin ran his hand over the back of his neck, glancing at the cameras, a frown pulling at the edges of his lips. He braced his elbows on his thighs, clasping his hands between his knees. "Do you remember the first time we met?" he asked, his eyes locked on his own hands.

Of course she remembered.

She swallowed down the fluttery feeling in her chest, the torrent of butterflies trying to break free just as they'd done that day. When he'd told her he loved that painting, too. That he sometimes dreamed about that little boat, about who might have left it all alone.

"You tried to convince me that the trash can was one of the pieces on display," she said, choosing to recall the other parts of their conversation that day, the ones that hadn't made her feel like he could see directly into her soul.

His chuckle felt like a gift, releasing some of the tension between them. He glanced at her, arching an eyebrow and flashing a crooked grin. "Maybe it was."

"Maybe it was just a trash can," she teased, bumping her shoulder lightly against his.

"Maybe I just wanted to talk to you."

She sucked in a breath and as he straightened beside her, taking her hand in his. Kyla was distracted by how soft his hand was, how large it felt closed around her own. She met his eyes, unreadable even in the bright lights of the surrounding production crew, though she caught a flicker of what she thought might be nerves. She wanted to run her hand over his cheek, to reassure him—of what, she wasn't entirely sure.

"Why?" she asked.

He dropped his gaze to their hands, running his thumb over the knobs of her knuckles as he spoke, his voice soft and his face cast in shadow in the dim light. "I can't explain it, but I saw you and I knew I had to talk to you. And then you were funny, and smart, and so…*you*."

Her chest burned as she forgot to breathe. But, really, how could she be expected to do something as banal as breathe when he was saying such beautiful things to her?

He squeezed her hand, a sadness creeping into his smile and she heard the words he didn't say. *Then Brodie showed up.* He had been late meeting her, something that she'd learned to expect in later months, and he'd laughed when he saw them together, proudly slinging an arm over her shoulder and introducing her to his father. Gavin had excused himself pretty quickly, then, mumbling excuses about needing to catch up on his grading, but not before he and Kyla had exchanged a mortified glance.

If Brodie hadn't shown up that day, would Gavin have asked to see her again? Would she have wanted to?

Yes. She didn't even need to think about it. She would have broken things off with Brodie that very night.

In retrospect, perhaps she should have done so anyway. But it had seemed pointless at the time. She couldn't very well break up with Brodie and then casually see if his father wanted to date her instead. He was twenty years older than her, an accomplished professor, and too handsome for words. And besides, Brodie had told her all about his dad—Gavin West was the picture perfect father, always putting his son first. And he didn't date. Ever.

"Do you remember during the Food and Wine Festival when Tessa wanted to build the gingerbread sandcastles?" Gavin asked, the question pulling Kyla from her memories.

"Of course," she said, not sure what this had to do with anything. Maybe she'd been lost in her own thoughts longer than she realized.

"And do you remember how Jamie made her set up the staging area in a very specific location?" His eyes locked on hers as though what he was saying was vitally important.

"Yeah, he wanted them to—"

"Sometimes I think about that," he said, cutting her off. "About how important it was that she be in that spot."

Kyla's eyes clouded with confusion as she tried to figure out what the hell he was talking about. She didn't remember Jamie particularly caring where they'd set up the sandcastles. "It was the perfect staging area," she said slowly. "No one on the beach could see—"

"Exactly."

"Oh!" It suddenly hit her what he was trying to say. "Right. Yeah, I think about that sometimes, too," she lied, doing her best not to look guilty.

No one on the beach could see that little cove where the shoreline dipped back behind the rocks…and the cast and crew weren't scheduled to be anywhere near that stretch of beach for days. Meaning they could meet there and talk without the cameras.

He swept his thumb over the spot on her wrist where her pulse pounded.

"Sometimes I think about that after my roommates have gone to bed," she said slowly, a hint of a question in her voice. That's what he wanted, right? To set a meeting time and place.

He lifted his eyes to meet hers, looking up at her through

that stubborn wisp of hair that was always falling across his forehead.

"Uh, hey, guys?" Zayne appeared at the edge of the circle of cameras. "As fascinating as this trip down memory lane is, can we move along to something a little more interesting for the viewers at home? Something to help them get to know you both better?"

Gavin flashed him an easy smile. "Happy to." He turned back to her, releasing her hand, and she told herself she wasn't disappointed to lose his touch. "So, Kyla, where are you from?"

She laughed, looking around like it was a practical joke. "Here."

"No," he chuckled, "I mean, I know, but before Aster Bay. I don't think I know where you're from originally."

"New Jersey. Princeton area."

"And you didn't want to go home after you graduated?"

Her smile faltered at the thought. There had been a time when she'd planned to go back to New Jersey after graduation, back to the house she grew up in, where her mother and father still held brunch every Sunday after church and managed not to speak to each other once during the entire meal. But that was before, back when she couldn't imagine a life that didn't include daily weigh-ins and shapewear and endless diets. Before she'd met Jo and Molly and Tessa, people who looked at her like she was more than the size of her body, who helped her realize she didn't need to lose weight to be happy.

"My life is here now. My friends and my job…and my future. Aster Bay took me in and made me one of their own, and now I can't imagine living anywhere else."

"This town has a way of doing that." he searched her eyes as though he could tell there was more that she wasn't saying but he wasn't going to push her.

Above the camera directly in front of them, Zayne made a walking motion with his fingers and then pointed in the direction of the sculpture garden at the edge of the property.

"Walk with me." Gavin got to his feet and held out his arm to her. Her stomach flipped as the full strength of his smile landed on her. She took his arm and let him lead her through the garden beds towards the sculpture garden, and when he lay his other hand over hers, she let herself imagine it was because he wanted to touch her and not because he was making sure she didn't trip over the uneven ground.

"Did you always know you'd stay in Aster Bay?" she asked as they walked.

"Pretty much. When I was still in high school, my brother decided he wanted to join the priesthood. He's a year older than me and back then, I idolized him, but I couldn't understand why he would do that."

"You don't share his faith?"

"No," Gavin said with a chuckle. "But the funny thing was, he wasn't particularly devout either. At least, I didn't think he was. Anyway, he left for seminary and my mother was crushed—proud, but crushed. They'd likely never live in the same place again. He'd never give her grandchildren."

"Is that why you had Brodie so young?"

"Yes and no. I knew it would make my mom happy, and Caleb was off making this lifetime commitment. I guess I wanted to feel like my decisions were as important as his. And Jessica didn't have the best home life. She wanted a family, and we were in love. Love will make you do some crazy things."

"Like get married before you can legally drink?" she teased.

He laughed. "Exactly like that." He slowed his step as they entered the circle of bronze sculptures, turned green with age.

"Do you ever wish you hadn't?"

"Gotten married?" he asked. She nodded. "No. Jessica and I were married for twelve years. We grew up together, and we grew apart, but I wouldn't change it." He glanced at the place where his hand rested over hers, his thumb stroking across the back of her hand, before he continued softly. "It gave me Brodie. I would do anything for my son."

Her stomach dropped and she slid her hand from the crook of his arm, masking the sudden pit in her stomach with a feigned desire to examine the statue of Pan up close. What was she doing? Touching Gavin like she had any right to, like any of this would be happening at all if the cameras weren't there. What was she thinking?

She glanced at Gavin to find him watching her, his hands dug into the pockets of his suit jacket and his eyes haunted. He would do anything for his son, including summon her to a midnight rendezvous on the beach, far away from the cameras, so he could let her down gently, tell her that he would have to send her home at the first elimination ceremony. Because that was the only logical reason for Gavin West to invite her to a clandestine meeting that violated both of their contracts.

It didn't matter that she'd always been drawn to him, even though he was the last person she should be drawn to, because Gavin was the kind of guy who put other people first. He wasn't the kind of guy who would have a relationship with his son's ex-girlfriend, least of all on national television.

If only that didn't make her like him even more.

Chapter Eleven

It had been surprisingly easy to ditch the cameras once Gavin retired to his suite at The Barclay for the night.

Gavin had never been in the honeymoon suite before and, while it had the same gauzy white curtains and textured wallpaper in soft grays and blues as the other rooms in the hotel, it also had a separate sitting room, outfitted with plush sofas large enough to seat an army. The cameras mounted throughout the sitting room were more obvious than the ones in the bedroom, where he'd only located two small lenses in the corners trained on the king-size bed with its pile of decorative throw pillows. The bathroom gleamed in marble and gold, a giant soaker tub in the center of the room and a walk-in shower in one corner with glass walls and river rock flooring. *No cameras in here,* he noted—at least none that he could see.

It was the balcony off the bathroom, however, that made his escape so easy. The frosted glass double doors on one end of the room opened onto a small private balcony overlooking the ocean, presumably so newlyweds could enjoy the view while soaking in the two-person bathtub. It also happened to have a sturdy fire escape.

Gavin lowered himself to the ground and, under cover of darkness, made his way down the grassy lawn and rocky shoreline to the little cove at the edge of The Barclay's property. He wasn't sure how long he'd have to wait for Kyla to arrive, so he settled in on a wide, flat rock and pulled out his cell phone.

He wasn't supposed to talk to anyone about the show while it was filming, and he certainly wasn't supposed to put anything in writing. He felt a momentary burst of guilt at violating the trust the production had placed in him, but they hadn't exactly been acting above board themselves when they decided to bring his son's ex-girlfriend onto the show without warning him.

Gavin: Kyla's here.

Jamie: Where? How are you texting us right now? I thought you were filming all night.

Ethan: Brodie's Kyla?

Baz: Do you know any other Kyla?

Jamie: She told Tessa she needed a few weeks off from the bakery, but she didn't say why.

Ethan: And Tessa didn't ask?

Jamie: Guess she didn't see a need to.

Baz: Does Brodie know?

Gavin: I don't think so. I haven't told him yet.

Ethan: But you're going to.

Baz: Don't be an idiot. Of course he's not going to tell Brodie.

Gavin: Why wouldn't I?

Baz: It's none of his business.

Jamie: It violates your contract.

Gavin: So does this text.

Baz: Yeah, but none of us are stupid enough to rat you out.

Gavin paused. Baz had a point. If Brodie told anyone else that Kyla was on the show and word got back to The Travel Network, Gavin would be found in breach of contract, and they could call in those massive fines to penalize him for it. More than that, though, he realized he was afraid of Brodie confronting Kyla, making her uncomfortable about being on the show. Or worse, trying to win her back.

Ethan: I guess if you send her home in the first week, you don't have to tell Brodie anything until after the show airs.

Gavin: I wish I knew why she was here. Tessa really didn't say anything else?

Ethan: It doesn't matter why she's there. You can't seriously be considering keeping her around.

Jamie: Oh shit. You are, aren't you? I don't know if that's a good idea.

Baz: Says the guy who married his friend's daughter.

"Gavin?" Kyla's whispered words broke through the stillness on the beach as she rounded the pile of rocks that hid the cove from view.

He quickly slid his phone into his jeans pocket before she could see it and stood up. "You came." Until that moment he hadn't realized how afraid he was that she might not.

"I hope you haven't been waiting long."

"Not long." He gestured for her to join him on the rock.

She stepped into a shaft of moonlight and Gavin forgot how to breathe. She wore some kind of thin pajama pants, pink covered in black hearts, and an oversized Williston University sweatshirt that he recognized all too well. He knew without looking that there would be a small tear under the left armpit and an even smaller ink stain on the hem.

"Where did you get that?" he asked.

"Get what?" she asked, looking around in confusion.

"That sweatshirt."

"Oh." She pulled the material away from her body by the hem, glancing down at it as if to confirm which shirt she was wearing. "This? I know I probably should have given it back but it's so soft and I've honestly been sleeping it in for so long now… It was Bro—"

"Not Brodie's," Gavin said, cutting her off, his mouth suddenly dry. "Mine."

She met his eyes, the pink coloring her cheeks evident even in the low light of the moon reflecting off the water. "I didn't know."

He wasn't sure if that made it better or worse. It certainly didn't change the fact that his body was having a rather inconvenient reaction to seeing her wearing his clothing, knowing she was *sleeping* in his clothing. He dragged a hand over his face and tried to think of the least sexy things he could—pollution, Chewbacca, that time he was twelve and overheard his grandparents talking dirty to each other through their bedroom wall.

"I can give it back." She reached to pull the sweatshirt over her head.

"No," he said too sharply. If seeing her wearing his sweatshirt had gotten him half hard, watching her take the damn thing off would kill him. "Keep it."

There was a moment of silence while she did that maddening thing where she chewed on her bottom lip, the abused flesh growing redder with each pass of her tooth until it was shiny and somehow fuller.

That's how she'd look after she's been kissed.

Fucking hell. Public bathrooms, tarantulas, nuclear war. He forced his eyes away from Kyla and her tempting curves and soft lips.

"I didn't know you were going to be here," she said at last. "On the show, I mean. Obviously, I knew you were going to be *here* on the beach."

He huffed out a laugh. "Likewise." Then, chancing a glance in her direction, "Why *are* you here?"

"The truth?"

"Please."

She planted her hands behind her on the rock and leaned back, looking out over the ocean. "I can't get a loan to do the renovations on my photography studio. Every bank in the area has turned me down, and without a loan, I can't open. So, I need to get enough exposure to prove I will have plenty of clients, and when my roommates saw that the winning couple gets a payout…" She shrugged. "It's stupid, I know. But I have this list of things I want to do to make this year different."

"Different how?"

"Different…better. Happier."

His heart clenched in his chest. How long had she been unhappy?

"And opening the studio is part of that list," he said carefully.

"But now my whole plan hinges on being able to beat out six other women, all of whom look like freaking movie stars, and I'm…"

"You're what?" He hated the way her lips tilted down into a frown, the way she averted her eyes from him.

"I'm just me," she said with a sad smile.

He wanted to tell her that there wasn't anything "just" about it—she was magnificent. Talented and smart, funny and beautiful. He wanted to tell her that the idea that anyone would choose one of those other women over her was laughable, that the idea that *he* would choose—

Though, of course, he couldn't choose her. No matter how badly he might want to. Only a terrible father would publicly humiliate his son by starting a relationship with that son's ex-girlfriend on national television. And there was the matter of that little clause in his contract that gave Patrick and Zayne the power to override his choices, to effectively choose the winning woman themselves if they wanted to. Patrick had said the clause was only there to protect the network in case he decided to choose someone who turned out to be a liability to the network, but Zayne had implied—and the language allowed—a much broader interpretation.

Bottom line: he couldn't promise to choose her, couldn't promise her the money she needed to make her dreams come true, and thanks to his NDA, he couldn't even tell her why.

Unaware of his racing thoughts, Kyla continued, her voice soft. "And I thought, who knows, maybe for once I'll get the fairy tale ending."

The longing in her voice was a sharp pain between his ribs.

"Kyla—"

"I didn't know it would be you," she repeated, as though she wanted to be sure he knew she wasn't implying that *they* might fall in love.

Fuck, why did that sting so badly?

"But you knew it would be someone from town," he said, a familiar jealousy turning in his gut. "Who did you want it to be?"

Her eyes went wide with surprise at his question, but only for a second before her gaze flickered to his lips and then away.

"Kyla," he said again, gentling his voice this time. When she didn't turn back to face him, he cupped her cheek, turning her towards him and doing his best to ignore the hitch in her breathing when their skin made contact. "Who did you want it to be?"

She met his gaze, eyes pleading with him to stop asking. He dropped his hand back into his lap, telling himself it didn't matter, that she didn't owe him an answer, even if he wanted it more than his next breath. Maybe if she told him who she had hoped for, it would be easier to stop thinking about her.

"Are you going to send me home?" she asked, her eyes locked on his hands.

He blew out a breath. "I should. But if I do, then you won't get your waiting list of clients and you won't be able to open your studio."

"That's not—"

"I want you to open your studio, Kyla."

"Why?"

"Because you're talented and hardworking. Because your business would be a valuable asset to the town." His throat tightened as he gave her his final reason—the most important reason. "Because you deserve to be happy. You deserve to win."

"You can't just let me win for the money," she said, her eyes wary. "What if you like one of those women? What if you fall in love with one of them?"

"I won't."

"You can't know that," she scoffed.

"I won't," he insisted.

She studied him, and for a moment he was tempted to tell her how he could be so sure that he wouldn't fall for one of the other women.

"You deserve to be happy too." Her voice was barely a whisper over the crashing of the waves.

Something in his chest loosened at the idea that she cared if he was happy, that she thought about him at all.

"I'd like you to stay," he said softly. "Maybe we could try to be…"

"Just two people?"

He nodded, his heart in his throat.

Her eyes dropped to his lips again, slower this time. "I think I can do that," she said with a shy smile.

Was she implying they could be like they'd been that night at Olympus? But that had been a dark club in Providence, where anonymity and a collective understanding allowed for them to forget all the reasons they could never just be two people who were attracted to each other—and she *had* been attracted to him. That night at least. Maybe she still was…

It didn't matter. Maybe they could be "just two people" at Olympus, but they'd always be Brodie's father and ex-girlfriend here in Aster Bay, and especially on camera.

He turned away, running his hands through his hair as warning prickled over his skin. This conversation was turning dangerous. "You should get back before your roommate realizes you're gone."

They still hadn't talked about Brodie or how he would feel once he found out they were on this show together, but his son was on the other side of the country now and he wasn't Kyla's problem anymore. Gavin would figure out how to handle Brodie on his own and, in the meantime, if he couldn't give Kyla the fairytale ending she deserved, he could at least do his damnedest to make sure she was able to open her business.

"Gavin?" He turned to face her, finding her already on her feet and preparing to leave, though she still watched him with eyes that saw too much. "I'm glad it's you," she said, though her brows were drawn together, the corners of her mouth downturned.

He opened his mouth to return the sentiment, to tell her he was glad she was there, too, even if it was complicated and impossible, but before he could say anything, she turned and disappeared around the wall of rocks, leaving him alone with his guilt and his fantasies as the waves crashed on the shore.

Chapter Twelve

"So, what's your deal?" Mandy asked the next morning as she plopped into a lounge chair next to Kyla on the back patio of The Barclay. She took a sip of her mimosa and arched an eyebrow at Kyla. "You're from here?"

Kyla blew out a breath. She'd had this conversation at least four times in the last hour alone as the women had gathered on the patio for breakfast. She should just round them all up and tell them all at once. Not the part about being Gavin's son's ex-girlfriend, or the part about all the times she'd thought inappropriate thoughts about Gavin, but the part about living in Aster Bay, about knowing him before she arrived on set.

"There's always someone who's the blast from the past on these shows." Roni took the lounge chair on Kyla's other side, crossing her legs and digging into the pile of scrambled eggs on her plate.

"What do you mean?" Kyla asked.

"All these reality dating shows are similar." Roni took a bite of her bacon. She frowned at her plate and dropped the strip. "Who eats turkey bacon?"

"Similar how?" Kyla asked.

"There are always certain archetypes in the cast." She gestured with her fork to where Lauren stood sipping a water and sucking on lemon wedges. "The blonde bombshell," she said at the same time that Mandy said, "The mean girl."

Roni smirked. "That too." She shifted her fork to point at Christina, who stood piling a plate high with cut fruit, her butt cheeks hanging out of the back of her short shorts. "The sex-crazy one." Next came Becca, who lay on a lounge chair across the patio in a pose that was too perfect not to be rehearsed, an oversized, floppy hat shielding her pale skin from the sun. "The virgin." Ignoring the other women, she turned her attention back to Kyla and Mandy. "You're the blast from the past," she said with a satisfied smile before she popped a grape in her mouth.

"What about you?" Kyla asked. "What's your archetype?"

Roni winked. "I'm the wildcard."

"What about me?" Mandy asked, swapping her empty mimosa for a fresh one as a waiter passed by.

"The drama queen."

Mandy waved off Roni's assessment, turning her attention back to Kyla. "But seriously, you're from here, right? So you know Prince Charming already?"

"This town has about a hundred people in it. Of course she knows him," Christina said, appearing at Roni's side and sitting on the other end of the lounge chair. "Tell us everything."

"Ladies, good morning!" Ryan Harris' booming call to order broke through the conversation, saving Kyla from having to answer. The women dutifully got to their feet and assembled in a line across from Ryan facing the wall of cameras that had accompanied him out onto the patio. "You all look lovely this morning," he said with a plastic smile. "Welcome to your *Cinderella* dates!"

Becca clapped, her smile growing wider, until Lauren shot her a scathing look.

"Our Prince Charming will be taking you all on a group date to historic Longfield Farm where you will compete in a relay race based on the classic fairy tale, *Cinderella.* The two women with the fastest times for their legs of the race will win a shared date with Gavin tonight."

"Are all the dates in groups?" Kyla whispered to Roni beside her.

"Most of them. Though on these shows there's usually more one-on-one dates as you move on," Roni whispered back.

After a few more vague instructions, the women were dismissed to their rooms to get dressed for their "date." Kyla wasn't convinced you could really call it a date when there were seven women all vying for one man's attention. But that didn't stop the little rush of adrenaline at knowing she was about to see Gavin, to spend time with him, even if she'd be sharing that time with the others.

The eligible ladies were housed in one wing of The Barclay, two to a room, except Lauren who had somehow managed to score a room to herself. The rooms were all clustered around a lounge area that had been outfitted with a line of makeup and hair stations on one wall and an arrangement of oversized sofas and loveseats on the other wall. That morning, a hair and makeup artist stood behind each chair, waiting to help each woman primp before they headed out on their date…at a farm.

Nearly an hour and a half of curling irons and eyelash glue mixed with a healthy dose of debate about wedges versus heels, and the ladies were ready to go. Only Kyla, Roni, and Ericka opted for flat shoes and jeans.

"Your ass would look so much better if you wore heels," Christina said to Kyla as she wiped lipstick from the corners of her mouth using the reflective wall of the elevator as her mirror.

"We're going to a farm. It's all grass and mud and hay."

"Suit yourself." Christina adjusted her boobs in her cropped tube top.

"Why are you trying to help her?" Lauren asked with an accusatory narrowing of her eyes. "She already got alone time with him yesterday."

"Someone had to be first," Christina said.

"And he already knows her," Lauren shot back as the elevator doors opened and they headed for the van parked outside The Barclay's lobby. "So, what's the deal? Have you two banged before?"

"Lauren!" Becca exclaimed, pressing a manicured hand to her scandalized chest.

"It's a fair question," Lauren said. "So? Have you?"

"Not that it's any of your business—" Kyla began.

"Anything to do with Prince Charming absolutely is our business. I am not about to let you get in the way of me winning," Lauren said, looming over Kyla.

"Winning, or falling in love?" Roni asked with a pointed glare.

"You know what I mean." Lauren backed away and fluffed her hair. "I'm not here to make friends."

"That was clear," Erika mumbled.

Longfield Farm was only a short drive from The Barclay and thank God for that. The large white van production had rented to transport the cast around town was stifling, a cloud of mingled perfumes and Lauren's suspicious glare making it difficult to breathe.

"Don't worry about her," Roni said to Kyla when Lauren pushed past her as she exited the van. "It's like I said, we've each got a role to fill, and Lauren's the resident mean girl."

Kyla nodded and allowed herself to be herded by a haggard-looking PA towards the path that led up to the main barnyard. *Just like Jo said. These women aren't my friends.*

As they walked up the hill at Longfield Farm, several cameramen arranged just over the crest of the hill to capture their backlit appearance in all its bucolic glory, Gavin came into view. He stood next to Ryan in the center of the barnyard, a handful of chickens and the occasional wild turkey roaming around them. But it wasn't the farmyard fowl that captured

Kyla's attention—it was the way the mid-morning sun gleamed off of Gavin's hair, turning his sandy blonde strands to gold and caramel. His eyes shone with warmth, though she thought the bags beneath his eyes were a bit more pronounced than usual, his stubble-dusted jaw more tense than it was most mornings.

None of it detracted from how handsome he was, however. He wore dark jeans that clung to his thighs and a fitted t-shirt bearing Lemon and Thyme's logo over the chest pocket. She bit back a smile, wondering what other businesses he was going to subtly promote with his clothing during filming.

She was once again struck by how different he was from his son. They may have shared the same sandy blonde hair, but Brodie wore his close-cropped and styled with gel whereas Gavin's was always a little too long, a little windswept. They both had hazel eyes but where Brodie's were mostly brown, Gavin's were primarily green mixed with flecks of gold. They were both tall, but where Brodie still retained the lankiness of his teenage years, Gavin was broad and solid.

And that smile—the one that lit up Gavin's eyes and made them shimmer with warmth, the one that Kyla felt all the way down to her toes each time he turned its radiance her way— that was all Gavin.

"Ladies, welcome to Longfield Farm!" Ryan launched into his prepared monologue about the eighteenth-century farmhouse and its historical significance to Aster Bay. Kyla hardly heard a word, though, because while Ryan talked about tenant farming and the original outbuildings scattered around the property, Gavin was avoiding looking at her.

At first, she thought she was imagining things, but when his eyes traveled down the line of women assembled before him, his gaze never turned her way. He smiled at Roni and Erika, nodded in acknowledgement of Becca's wave and suppressed a grimace when Christina blew him a kiss, but he hardly let his eyes pause in her direction. The realization settled in Kyla's stomach like a ball of lead.

He doesn't want you here. He tried to tell you as much last night, and then you went and made him feel responsible for your money problems.

She barely registered Ryan's instructions for the relay race—something about rolling pumpkins down the hill, hitching horses to a wagon, and finding a tiara hidden in a pile of hay. Instead, her head pounded, and her stomach roiled.

He just feels sorry for you. Did you really think he'd want his son's ex-girlfriend?

But that night at Olympus…he'd wanted her then. And there was a moment last night on the beach when he'd looked at her like he saw *her.* Not the girl who used to date his son, just her.

Maybe she had it all wrong. Maybe it was all in her head after all.

Ryan finished his speech and Gavin turned his picture-perfect smile towards the camera, wishing the women luck.

Was it all just for show? Did she even know him at all?

Confessional Interviews
Recorded individually, edited together into one clip

Lauren: Of course I wanted more time with Gavin, but I'll be honest, I'm not very good at sharing, so I'm just not sure that a date with another woman would be the right time for me to get to know him better.

Patrick: [off screen] Are you saying you threw the race?

Lauren: No! I just maybe didn't run as hard as I could have.

Becca: I didn't mind running, but there were so many bugs. They were everywhere.

Kyla: It's a farm. Of course there's bugs.

Mandy: I knew I needed to win this race. Anyone who has ever watched a show like this knows that it is so important to get one of the early dates. And for a minute there, I really didn't think I was going to win.

Roni: Erika was in the lead by a mile before the rest of us had even cleared the first obstacle. I knew she was going to win. So it was really a race for second place.

Erika: Kyla was right behind me for most of the race.

Christina: I'm not sure what happened. Kyla was ahead of me and then, all of a sudden, she was on the ground.

Kyla: I tripped. Uneven ground, you know?

Mandy: I'm glad she's okay, but I'm even more glad that she fell because it means I get to go on the date with Gavin!

Chapter Thirteen

Gavin stood on his mark in the Aster Place ballroom and rubbed the exhaustion from his eyes. His "date" with Mandy and Erika had lasted until nearly midnight, with production insisting on all kinds of reshoots to make sure they'd captured the trio from every angle in every location. The private wood-fired pizza making class at The Pizza Stone had been fun, he would admit, and would be great publicity for one of Aster Bay's hidden gem businesses, but once he'd realized that an entire bottle of wine had disappeared into Mandy's glass before they'd even gotten the pizza in the oven, he'd been ready to tap out.

Erika, at least, was good company, even as Mandy had continued to get increasingly drunk throughout the evening. But Gavin hadn't been able to stop thinking about Kyla. She'd thrown the relay. He couldn't prove it, but he felt certain. She was so close to winning when she'd stumbled over her own feet in the final leg of the pumpkin race, allowing Mandy to overtake her. Kyla was many things, but he'd never known her to be clumsy.

She didn't want to go on a date with you. You're old enough to be her father.

"Gavin West, you are about to dance with seven beautiful women. What could possibly put that frown on your face?"

Gavin turned into the cloud of Chanel perfume to face Mrs. White. Dressed in form-fitting, all black clothing with a pale pink flutter of chiffon tied around her waist and a pair of black high heels, she looked nothing like his former first grade teacher. She placed her hands on her waist and cocked a hip, smiling at his surprise.

"Well? How do I look?"

"You look great, Mrs. White."

"Darn tootin' we do!" Mrs. Kemp floated into the ballroom in her own all black and fluttery pink get-up. "And aren't you a sight for sore eyes!" She made a spinning motion with her hand and waited expectantly until Gavin finally huffed out a laugh and obliged her with a slow spin.

Mrs. White sucked her teeth. "Those are some excellent jeans."

Gavin felt a blush rising in his cheeks under the octogenarians' sly smiles.

"So, give us the scoop," Mrs. Kemp said. "Any early front runners?"

"Not as such," Gavin hedged, glancing over his shoulder at Ryan as he entered the room, adjusting his cufflinks and straightening his tie as he made his way to his mark. "But I should warn you, you already know one—"

"Mrs. Kemp, Mrs. White, you both look lovely," Ryan said in his most sugary-sweet tone. "Thank you for joining us today."

"Always happy to help out my nephew." Mrs. Kemp beamed at Patrick as he and Zayne made their way into the ballroom, deep in a heated conversation.

"And it's about time this one settled down again." Mrs. White indicated Gavin with a sharp tilt of her head.

Ryan laughed. "The camera is going to love you both. Did Patrick go over the schedule with you?"

"He sure did," Mrs. Kemp said proudly.

"Don't worry about us, young man. You just do your part

and stay off my dance floor," Mrs. White said.

"Yes, ma'am," Ryan replied with a wink. If only he knew how serious Mrs. White was.

It wasn't long before the women filed into the ballroom, each dressed in their own versions of work-out clothes and a pair of heels. Except Kyla. She'd opted for plain white sneakers paired with dark leggings and his Williston sweatshirt. His heart leapt into his throat as he took her in, knowing that this time she'd put on that shirt knowing it belonged to him, and he was hit with the irrational desire to see her wear other articles of his clothing, to peel them off of her, to know how she'd look wrapped in his sheets.

That's your son's ex-girlfriend—the one he still calls when he's drunk, you asshole.

"Ladies, good morning," Ryan chimed as cameramen moved into position. "As you know, *Once Upon A Town* believes that in order for you to really know Gavin, you need to understand where he's from. In Aster Bay, like so many small towns across the United States, that means getting to know the people in town who are important to our Prince Charming. Each week, someone from Aster Bay, someone important to Gavin, will join us to get to know you all a bit and help advise him about which eligible ladies should stay, and who should go home."

A murmur of nervous excitement moved through the group, but Gavin caught Mrs. White shooting Kyla a wink and a smile, as though she weren't at all surprised to find her amongst the women, despite Mrs. Kemp's scandalized, wide-eyed expression. He didn't know how, but somehow Mrs. White always knew everything that was going on in town before anyone else.

"Today, we are joined by two of Aster Bay's matriarchs: Judy Kemp and Helen White. Both Mrs. Kemp and Mrs. White have known Gavin his whole life, having taught him in elementary school and being friends with his mother. And I understand there is a rather cut-throat weekly bar trivia game where you two compete against Gavin and his friends," Ryan said.

"You better believe it," Mrs. Kemp said.

"And we always win," Mrs. White added.

Ryan and several of the women laughed as Gavin shook his head, once again blushing. "Well, today, Mrs. White and Mrs. Kemp are here to teach you all how to waltz so you'll be prepared for tonight's masquerade ball. Mrs. White, I understand that you've won several ballroom dancing trophies, is that right?"

"You know it is," Mrs. White replied. "But stop yammering. No one cares about me. Let's dance!"

With a few more platitudes for the camera, Ryan moved away, disappearing out of frame to join the producers and turning the cast over to Mrs. White and Mrs. Kemp's instruction.

First, Mrs. White divided them into two groups, arranging them in two, large, concentric circles around the edges of the ballroom. "You'll dance with the person across from you as we learn the basic steps. Those of us on the inside circle will lead. When Judy rings her bell." Mrs. White paused as Mrs. Kemp demonstrated by ringing the old school bell that was usually used to call trivia night to order. "The outer circle will move one person to your right, and so on, until you find yourself back where you started."

Gavin glanced around at the inner circle, where he, Mrs. White, Mrs. Kemp, Mandy, and Becca stood waiting for their partners.

Becca's hand shot into the air. "Mrs. White, doesn't that mean Mandy and I won't get a chance to dance with Gavin?"

"That's right."

"But—"

Mrs. White clapped her hands, cutting off Becca's protests and began instructing them all in where to place their hands. Roni, who stood across from Gavin, stepped towards him and dutifully placed her left hand on his shoulder and her right hand in his. Gavin placed his hand on her waist and stepped closer, still leaving a respectful distance between them as Mrs. White reminded them all to keep their dance frame locked.

"Why do I feel like I stumbled into one of those classes from *Dirty Dancing*?" Roni asked as she checked how far apart their feet were from each other.

Gavin smiled. "I can promise you I do not have half the skills Patrick Swayze does."

Roni sighed theatrically, a smile tugging at the corners of her mouth. "Well, what good are you then?"

They stumbled through the steps, Gavin proud of himself when he managed not to step on Roni's feet. He was surprised by how much he enjoyed dancing with her. Roni was easy to talk to, with a razor-sharp wit that kept him on his toes. She was objectively beautiful, with her sun-kissed skin and big brown eyes, the pastel ends of her hair sweeping around her exposed shoulders in her loose-fitting turquoise tank-top.

She was exactly the kind of woman his mother would love to see him with.

But no matter how many times she made him laugh, there was no spark. It felt like spending time with a good friend, or a cousin. And given the way she easily handed him off to the next woman in line without so much as a second glance, he was confident she felt the same way.

His next partner was Lauren. Despite being over six-feet tall himself, Gavin found himself having to look up to meet her eyes when she strutted into place in her sky-high stilettos. Lauren adopted the dance position with a wide, bright smile. "I'm so glad we have a minute alone."

Gavin glanced around. They were literally surrounded by other people, a camera hovering just over her right shoulder, her microphone pack making her expensive, matching Lycra ensemble bulge at her lower back. "Me too," he said uncertainly. "Are you having fun?"

"I am, but I know lots of ways we could have even more fun," she said with a giggle and suggestive smile.

Why does everything she says sound rehearsed?

"Look, Gavin, I probably shouldn't be telling you this—" Her eyes went wide in a comical approximation of innocence. "—but I just really think you need to know."

"Know what?"

She glanced over her shoulder, flashing that innocent look at the camera, before she met his eyes again and took a small step closer to him, despite Mrs. White's explicit instruction to keep their arms locked. "Some of the girls have been talking. I just wouldn't be able to live with myself if I didn't say something and the wrong girl went home tonight."

Gavin worked to keep his face neutral. It was clear that Lauren wanted to be the center of attention and she was willing to do whatever it took—including selling out the other women on the show—to get there. He was all too familiar with people like Lauren, the kind of people who'd say one thing to your face and another thing behind your back, who pretended to be everyone's friend but had loyalty to no one. He had no intention of letting that kind of drama into his life.

Lauren continued, unaware of Gavin's hardening resolve that she be the first woman eliminated from the show. "It's just something Erika said last night after your date, about how being here was harder than she expected. About how much she still misses her ex-husband."

"Her *deceased* husband, you mean?"

Lauren's eyes flickered with annoyance but she locked it away behind the innocent veneer. *Oh, she's good.*

"It's so tragic," Lauren said. "But I would hate to see you keep someone who's still in love with someone else."

"Got it," Gavin said, his tone icy.

"I'm so glad you agree." That wide, plastic smile returned to her face. "It's for the best."

Chapter Fourteen

Sweat dripped down Kyla's chest, a slow drop sliding between her breasts, and she cursed under her breath. They'd been dancing for hours and the ballroom was poorly ventilated. What had she been thinking wearing a sweatshirt in June to a dance lesson?

You wanted him to see you in it. You wanted him to want you.

Stupid. He'd hardly looked at her the entire day yesterday and then, as if that wasn't bad enough, Erika and Mandy had been out on their date until well after midnight. When Erika had slipped into their room, she couldn't stop smiling, gushing about how much of a gentleman Gavin was, how funny he was, how gorgeous his smile was. She was smitten. And Kyla had felt nauseous ever since. She *liked* Erika. She wanted Erika to find her prince charming and get her happily ever after—just not with Gavin.

Finally, it was Kyla's turn to dance with Gavin. She'd been both excited and dreading it since she'd set foot in the ballroom. Now, as she stepped up to him, she regretted her decision not to wear heels. In her sneakers, he was a full head taller than her. She kept her eyes straight ahead, focused on the bob of his Adam's apple and the sharp line of his stubble on his jaw. His hand closed around her waist, gently tugging her towards him, and her eyes fell shut of their own accord as the heat of him seeped through the sweatshirt.

"You're wearing my shirt," he murmured as they began moving through the steps to Mrs. White's chanted counting.

"I think the fact that I'm wearing it makes it *my* shirt." She kept her voice low so the others around them wouldn't hear. "And you said you didn't want it back."

"I don't."

He was surprisingly light on his feet, his arms firm as he spun her around the ballroom. It was so easy to let him guide her around the floor, to gently turn her in whatever direction he wanted to go, to let him take charge. To imagine him taking charge in other times, in other places, with his hands beneath her clothing instead of innocently resting on her rib cage.

"Why did you throw the race yesterday?" he asked.

"I didn't." *How did he know?*

"You did."

"I tripped."

"You didn't."

"Why wouldn't you look at me?"

He stumbled, ever so slightly, recovering quickly enough that no one else noticed. His eyes darted down to meet hers before they both looked away, her gaze once again locking on his throat.

"I looked at you."

She scoffed, her stomach lurching at what she was about to say. "If you don't want me here, you should send me home tonight."

His hand tightened on her rib cage. "I looked at you," he said, his voice rougher. "You're the one who was avoiding me."

"I tri—"

"You didn't want to go on the date with me."

He swallowed, his throat working in mesmerizing ways, his jaw ticking as he clenched his teeth. From this angle she could see every tendon, every muscle, the tiny red mark on the underside of his jaw where he'd nicked himself shaving. She had the strongest urge to press her lips to that mark.

"I didn't want to *share* a date with you," she said carefully.

His eyes dropped to hers again, the color in his irises shifting, like water in a stream, green and gold and tempting her to drown.

"I looked at you," he repeated, his voice soft. The deep timbre of it vibrated in the air between them. "I'm always looking at you. Kyla—" He broke off, his hand tightening around hers, fingers digging into her rib cage. "I can't *stop* looking at you."

Her breathing grew shallow, caught painfully in her chest as she studied his eyes. "But yesterday…"

"When the sun reflects off your hair, it looks like silver. Like you are crowned with sunlight itself. Did you know that?"

She swallowed, nodded. She did know that. She'd played with that effect in some of her self-portrait photography, though she'd never been able to adequately capture the effect or describe it. But the fact that *he* knew that, that he'd noticed— surely that meant something, right?

Warmth washed over her, a dangerous, fuzzy glow that felt like he'd captured that sunlight and slipped it beneath her skin, like she could feel it flowing through her veins.

They'd stopped moving and one of his hands slid into her hair, dragging the strands through his fingers. His eyes darkened dangerously as he huffed out a hot breath through his nose. For one blissful, terrifying moment, she thought he might kiss her. Her lips tingled with desire for it.

His hand fell back to her waist, softly resting against her side, and some of that warmth retreated, disappointment pinging painfully off her bones.

His eyes darted up over her shoulder and she turned to see Patrick approaching them with a furrowed brow. "Hey, guys," Patrick said as he reached them. "Something's up with your mics. We're not getting any audio from either of you."

"That's strange." Gavin dropped his hold on her and took a step back.

"May I?" Patrick gestured to Gavin's t-shirt. Gavin nodded his consent and Patrick lifted the back of his shirt, a flash of hard muscle and tan skin winking into view as the fabric shifted. "The wire's come out of the mic pack," Patrick said as he plugged the wire back in. "That's unusual."

Kyla lifted the hem of her sweatshirt and the wire for her microphone also swung free, the loose end hanging lightly against her rib cage. Right where Gavin's hand had been. She glanced at him, at those sharp eyes watching her. Patrick, done reconnecting Gavin's microphone, moved to Kyla and did the same, reattaching the dangling wire to the pack hooked onto the back of her leggings.

"I'll check with Davis, but he may want to reshoot that last dance," Patrick said. "What were you two talking about?"

"Just about how Kyla chose the locations to shoot for the town's application package for the show," Gavin lied.

Patrick looked relieved. "He probably won't want to reshoot that. No one wants to see behind the curtain on these things, you know?"

"Patrick! Get out of the shot!" Zayne shouted from behind the bank of screens in the corner of the room as Ryan moved back into the center of the ballroom.

"You all looked wonderful out there. Thank you for joining us this morning. I'm sure these dance lessons will be put to good use tonight at the ball. Ladies, I'm sure you have a full day of preparation ahead of you."

A full day of preparation? For a dance?

Kyla glanced around at the other women, some of whom were already chattering excitedly about the beauty routine that would occupy the remainder of their day until the ball that evening.

When she looked back at Gavin, he was still watching her, his gaze hot on her skin like a physical touch. She shouldn't want him—she'd told herself over and over again that she *didn't* want him—but when he looked at her with that fire in his eyes…well, for that look, she was tempted to admit she'd been lying.

Hometown Helper Interview
Official Transcript

Ryan Harris: Mrs. White, Mrs. Kemp, thank you for joining us today. You looked good out there!

Helen White: You say that like it's a surprise.

Ryan: No, no, not a surprise at all!

Helen: I'll have you know, young man, that I have been ballroom dancing since before you were born.

Ryan: And it shows! I mean, you were wonderful.

Judy Kemp: Oh, Helen, let the boy breathe. Go on, dear.

Ryan: Thank you, Mrs. Kemp. You both had a chance to spend a little time with our eligible ladies. What did you think?

Judy: They're all so beautiful! And so poised! Except for that one girl—you know the one, Helen. Dark hair, pretty eyes, wouldn't stop talking about her dog.

Ryan: Mandy.

Judy: That's right. Mandy. That girl had a few too many mimosas if you ask me.

Ryan: So safe to assume you don't think she'd be a good match for Gavin?

Helen: She's not really Gavin's type.

Ryan: And what *is* Gavin's type?

Helen: Someone with a bit more…

Judy: Gumption!

Ryan: Did anyone in particular strike you as a good match?

Helen: Yes.

[Long pause]

Ryan: Would you care to expand on that?

Helen: No.

Ryan: [Nervous laughter] If you don't see Mandy as a good match for Gavin, what about Becca?

Judy: Becca is lovely and so put together. Is it true she was a beauty queen?

Ryan: She did win several beauty pageants, yes. As did Lauren. Do you think one of them would be a good fit for Gavin?

Helen: There are really only three women here who would be good matches for Gavin.

Ryan: Let me see if I can guess who you think would be right for our Prince Charming.

Helen: By all means. You're batting a thousand so far.

Ryan: Roni?

Helen: Perhaps.

Ryan: Erika?

Judy: Oh, yes. I liked her.

Helen: We've told Gavin who we think should go home this evening. Who he ends up with in the end is, of course, entirely up to him. But if I know Gavin West, and I think I do, then I have a good idea who he will choose.

Ryan: Care to enlighten us?

Helen: No, I don't think I do.

Ryan: Who did you tell Gavin to send home?

Judy: That's easy. The drunk one.

Chapter Fifteen

"I just don't understand," Mandy said through her tears, her speech slightly slurred. "We were dancing, and you had this *look* in your eyes—"

"What look?" Gavin asked for at least the third time.

"The look! The look! You know what look." She deflated. "I know I'm not as tall as Erika or as thin as Roni or as blonde as—as any of the blondes. I *know* I'm just the average-looking girl from Vegas and I didn't want to be the girl who cried all the time and got all insecure but…but…" She broke off on a fresh wave of sobs, hiccupping as she buried her face in Gavin's shirt.

He glared at Patrick, just out of frame, and ran a soothing hand over Mandy's back. "Why don't we go get you some water and take a break?"

"I don't need a break!" Mandy stood up suddenly. She stumbled sideways and Gavin reached out to steady her. "I know you think I'm being dramatic but there was a *look*, Gavin. I saw it."

"I believe you, but I swear, Mandy, I don't know what look you're talking about."

She sobbed loudly, pressing her hand to her lips as though that could possibly quiet her wails and dropping her head back onto Gavin's shoulder. Another cameraman joined the circle of vultures already surrounding them and Gavin did his best not to look directly into the lens. Patrick and Zayne had both already spoken to him about being less aware of the cameras, though how the hell they expected him to do that was beyond him.

Erika appeared at the edge of his vision, sidling her way past one of the cameramen. She looped an arm around Mandy's waist and lifted the drunk woman's head from Gavin's shoulder onto her own with an ease that spoke of years of repositioning sleeping children. "Mandy, hon, why don't you come with me, alright?" she asked in a soothing voice.

"He *looked* at me," Mandy sniffled.

"I know, hon. I know." Erika shot a sympathetic smile and a wink at Gavin as she guided Mandy out of the circle of cameras, one of the cameramen breaking off from the pack to follow the two women as they left the ballroom.

Gavin scrubbed his hands over his face and leaned back against the wall, closing his eyes with a groan. *Will this night never end?*

"Is she alright?"

Gavin opened his eyes and met Kyla's curious stare. She wore a floor length ballgown with a full, tulle skirt and a form-fitting bodice that drew his attention to the deep shadow between her breasts. Her blonde hair had been piled on top of her head, winding around a sparkling silver tiara, just like all the other girls wore tonight. Somehow it didn't look silly on her, though. It looked like it belonged there, this tangle of silver and rhinestones glittering under the lights. He'd hardly been able to stop staring at her all night.

Maybe that's what Mandy noticed.

"Are *you* alright?" Kyla asked, eyeing him like maybe he was ill.

Say something.

Over Kyla's shoulder, he spotted Lauren winding her way

towards him, two glasses of champagne in her hands. Patrick and Zayne had been very clear that if one of the eligible ladies requested to "steal" him, he was required to oblige them. The last thing he wanted to do was be pulled away by Lauren when he'd only just gotten a moment to talk to Kyla.

"Dance with me," he said, holding out his hand.

She glanced at his outstretched palm, hesitating only a fraction of a second, before she accepted the invitation, letting him lead her onto the dance floor, right past a frowning Lauren. He pulled her into his arms and began leading her about the room. She followed him so effortlessly, fit in his arms so perfectly, it was like the dance had been made just for them. Like no one had ever waltzed as well as they two waltzed.

Kyla looked up at him. "*Are* you alright?" she repeated.

"I am now," he said with a tired smile.

And he meant it, but what did that mean? He'd spent over a year keeping his feelings for Kyla at bay, making sure his gaze never lingered on her too long, that their conversations were professional or polite but never too personal. Aside from that one night at Olympus—a night he thought about way more than was healthy and that he honestly had started to think might have been a dream—he'd kept his attraction to her under control. What had changed?

She wasn't single before. She wasn't looking at you like…

He wasn't even sure how to compare it. Like he was important to her, yes, but it was more than that. Like she trusted him. Like she wanted him.

Or maybe that was just wishful thinking, getting caught up in the fairytale of the show. Maybe she was just playing the part.

He cleared his throat, forcing his thoughts back to calmer waters. "When did you learn to dance?"

"Cotillion."

"People still do that?"

She chuckled. "They do. It's a right of passage for the children of my parents' social circle. While other kids went to church school or gymnastics, I went to cotillion."

"What does one learn in cotillion?" he asked, smiling despite himself.

"How to set a formal table, to always cross my legs at the ankles, and the foxtrot and waltz. You know, very practical skills for a seventh grader."

He laughed. "I didn't take you for a society girl."

"I'm not, despite my parents' best efforts. But some things are just muscle memory."

He hummed as he spun her around the dance floor. "Your parents must be proud of you, opening your own business."

Her smile slipped for a moment before she asked, "Where did you learn to dance?"

Her deflection prickled at the back of his neck, but now was not the time to push, not with a gaggle of cameramen watching their every move.

Later, he promised himself, allowing her to change the subject.

"Mrs. White taught me."

"Please. There's no way you learned to dance this morning."

He smirked. "You're right. Mrs. White teaches a ballroom dancing class on Tuesday nights at the senior center. One day, my mom called and said they didn't have enough men to partner all the women who showed up, so the next week, the guys and I put on our dancing shoes."

"Wait. You're telling me that Baz knows how to *waltz*?" she asked, her eyes wide with disbelief.

"Baz is better than I am. There's usually a fight over who gets to dance with him."

"That is not what I expected," Kyla said smiling. "You guys are incredible. The way you take care of people—of this town."

His chest warmed with her praise. "It's what anyone would do."

"No, Gav. It's not. Other people aren't spending their

Tuesday nights learning the mambo to make a bunch of old ladies happy."

"The mambo wasn't that hard."

"Other people don't sit in the dunk tank at the spring bazaar every year to raise money for the food pantry, or help build the new animal shelter, or spend hours of their time putting up with Norm and the Merchants' Association to try to help the local businesses."

"You do that last one," he said softly.

"Because you asked me to. You're a good man, Gavin West," she sighed, almost like his goodness was tiresome. "A good friend. A good father."

"I'm not a good father." He glanced away from her, fighting back the twisting guilt in his stomach.

"Yes, you are."

"A good father wouldn't be dancing with you right now."

A stormy look passed over her eyes, but he held her gaze, wanting her to see him. Not just the guy who loved his hometown, but *him*. A man who loved his son more than life itself but still couldn't make himself stay away from her.

"Even good fathers do things their children don't like sometimes," she said at last.

"Do you think he'll forgive me?" he asked, his voice barely a whisper.

"For dancing with me?"

His eyes dropped to her lips, to the way her chest rose and fell with each shaky breath, then back to meet her eyes. He wanted so much more than a dance.

Her eyes grew dark, as though she could hear his thoughts. As though maybe she shared them.

"I don't know," she said as the music faded away and he brought them to a stop in the middle of the dance floor.

No sooner had they stopped moving, than Ryan appeared at his side. "Gavin, it's time." He held a hand out towards the garden where Patrick and Zayne were waiting to go over Gavin's choice of who to send home.

But Gavin couldn't walk away yet, couldn't tear his eyes from Kyla's. The way she looked at him tore at his heart.

"Gavin," Ryan repeated.

He released a heavy breath and then leaned in, pressing a kiss to Kyla's temple. "Thanks for the dance," he whispered into her hair, before turning and leaving the ballroom.

"Who's it gonna be, champ?" Zayne asked when Gavin arrived at the designated spot in the garden, a bulletin board covered with each of the eligible ladies' headshots staring back at him.

He scanned the photos, lingering on Kyla's. It was so unlike the other photographs—all professional headshots and beauty pageant photos. Kyla's was dark, her face half in shadow, hands wrapped around a steaming mug and cheeks rosy beneath a knit winter hat. He stepped closer to the bulletin board, staring at the photograph in awe. It had clearly been taken at one of the bonfires during the Food and Wine Festival last winter, a festival they'd worked together to promote.

In the photo, her eyes danced with laughter, and a second, larger hand curled around her mug, offering her the red wine hot chocolate they'd been smelling for hours. He hadn't realized someone had captured that moment, the small window of time he'd stolen for himself that night to bring her a treat and watch her eyes glow in the firelight, to get too close to the woman who occupied his every thought, the woman who had chosen the wrong West.

Maybe this is our chance to get it right.

"Do you know who you want to send home?" Patrick asked.

He cleared his throat and blinked away thoughts of Kyla. "Lauren."

"Really? Are you sure?" Patrick asked.

He nodded.

Patrick exchanged an uneasy look with Zayne. "We thought you'd want to send Kyla home week one."

The hair on the back of Gavin's neck bristled. "Then why did you even cast her if you thought I'd just turn around and send her home?"

"To bring in viewers for the pilot," Zayne said as if it were obvious. "It's a scandal. You just have to give us a good sound bite about dating your son's ex-girlfriend and the first episode will practically sell itself."

"You want a sound bite," Gavin repeated, trying to keep himself calm at the implication that he would use Kyla—*humiliate* Kyla—for ratings.

"Let's be honest. You and I both know she's not winner material," Zayne said.

"What Zayne means is, she doesn't fit the mold of the typical contestant on a show like this," Patrick said.

Gavin glanced between them, a bitter taste on his tongue. "I'm not sending Kyla home. It's Lauren."

"The thing is, Gavin, our sponsors really like Lauren. She uses their products and promotes them on her social media channels. It would really help us out if you could keep her around for a while," Zayne said.

"Isn't it my choice?" Gavin glanced at Patrick.

"It is," Patrick said, shooting a dark look at Zayne.

"For now," Zayne agreed, unbothered by Patrick's glare. "But if there are other women that you've also been thinking about letting go, then you should send one of them home tonight instead. Or, you could stick to the script and send home Kyla."

Gavin glanced between the two producers. What the hell was happening?

"Just give it one more week. Get to know Lauren a little better. She might surprise you," Patrick said.

What did it matter who went first? In the end, he wasn't going to choose any of these women anyway. And he really didn't like that the producers were pushing so hard for Kyla to go home, that Zayne was already alluding to his veto power. Something told him he needed to keep the producers on his side.

"Alright. I'll send Mandy home." Gavin sighed. "Let's get this over with."

He followed Patrick and Zayne back through the garden towards Aster Place, only half listening to their advice for how to let Mandy down easy. They pushed through the double doors and his eyes immediately found Kyla. She stood to one side of the ballroom, talking with Roni. As he watched, she threw her head back and laughed, her eyes dancing. Then, as though she could sense him watching her, she turned her head and met his gaze, turning those sparkling eyes and that wide, bright smile towards him, knocking the air from his lungs. She was breathtaking—not just because of the gown or the tiara or the pretty pink lipstick someone had talked her into wearing, but because she was so *happy*, so luminous in her joy that he couldn't help but smile with her.

It didn't matter who he sent home tonight or what the hell Zayne was up to. The only thing that mattered was Kyla.

And your son.

The thought raced through his veins like ice water, chilling him where he stood. Kyla's laughter died away and her eyes narrowed slightly, posing a silent question across the ballroom.

What the hell was he going to do?

Brodie: Grandma says you've got a bunch of hotties fawning all over you. Must be nice.

Gavin: Your grandmother did not use the word "hotties."

Brodie: No, but Mrs. Kemp did when she told grandma about them.
Brodie: Did you bang any of them yet?

Gavin: First of all, that's inappropriate and disrespectful. Second of all, I will not be sleeping with anyone on national television.

Brodie: This opportunity's wasted on you.

Gavin: How are things in California?

Brodie: Expensive. And there's so much traffic.
Brodie: But it's alright. Nick has a friend here who showed us all the good spots for tacos.

Gavin: I'm glad you're having a good time.

Brodie: I am. So you better hurry up and find yourself a babe to keep you company. Don't want you getting all mopey about me being gone when you get home from filming.

Gavin: Let's just say, for argument's sake, that I did find someone. What if you don't think she's right for me?

Brodie: If you're happy, I'm happy.

Gavin: You mean that?

Brodie: Hell yeah. Do your thing. Bang the hottie.

Gavin: If a woman were important to me, I would want you to be okay with it.

Brodie: Dad, all my life, you've always done everything you can to make me happy. I appreciate it—really, I do. But I'm all grown up now. Maybe it's time you made yourself happy.

Chapter Sixteen

"Who needs another beer?" Ethan asked as he threw down his cards on the table in his living room and headed for the kitchen.

"Do you have any more of that summer ale?" Gavin called after him.

Ethan leaned his head back in the doorway to the living room, grinning. "Of course, your highness." He laughed and disappeared into the kitchen.

It was Gavin's one night off from filming this week and, while he was bummed it hadn't lined up with trivia night at The Rookery, his friends had pulled together a night of beer, cards, and junk food at Ethan's house. He had to keep reminding himself that he was off camera—no one would care if he slouched in his seat or took too big of a bite of his pizza. Funny how quickly he'd gotten used to being filmed around the clock.

"How *is* the show going?" Jamie gathered up the cards and shuffling again.

"It's fine, I guess. I don't know what I was expecting," Gavin hedged.

"And Kyla?" Baz asked as he refilled his Scotch from the drink cart in the corner of the room.

"She's definitely not what I was expecting."

Jamie paused in his shuffling, humming thoughtfully as he

exchanged a look with Baz. "I like Kyla," he said as he began dealing the cards.

Ethan set a beer down beside Gavin and retook his seat. "What's not to like? She's a nice kid. Makes a mean ginger scone."

Jamie and Baz exchanged another glance that raised alarm bells in Gavin's mind.

"What?" Gavin asked them.

"I'm just wondering if *you* like Kyla." Jamie grinned. "If you *like* like her."

"Jesus Christ, what are we twelve?" Baz set his glass down and picked up his cards, sorting them in his hand.

Only Baz knew the extent of Gavin's obsession with his son's ex-girlfriend and, while Gavin trusted Jamie and Ethan, the fewer people who knew, the better.

"Have you told Brodie that you're…dating? Is that the word we'd use in this scenario?" Ethan asked, glancing at his friends. "Is it still considered dating if it's contractually obligated?"

"According to Tessa it is," Jamie said. He turned to Ethan. "Any twos?"

"Go fish," Ethan said before taking a long pull from his beer.

"We're not dating," Gavin grumbled. "She only even signed up for the show to get the cash to open her photography studio."

"I don't know." Jamie drew a card and continued. "Tessa's been going on about the two of you since last fall."

"Last fall?" *God, had he been so obvious about his attraction to her that even Tessa had noticed?*

"She tried to convince me that you were secretly dating behind Brodie's back," Jamie said. "Which…I guess you kind of are now. Damn." He lowered his cards as he thought. "I guess that means it's her turn to pick where we—"

"Don't finish that sentence," Ethan said. "I told you. No talking about my daughter at guys' night." He turned to Baz. "Any queens?"

"Fuck you," Baz said, handing over a card.

Ethan laughed as he slapped his match down on the table.

"Tessa said you didn't stop by the bakery today. She set aside extra cupcakes for you. They're in the kitchen," Jamie said.

"I thought Kyla might be there," Gavin admitted.

"And that kept you from your cupcakes?" Jamie asked, surprise written across his face.

"We're not supposed to interact off camera." The excuse sounded lame even to Gavin.

Baz shook his head. "First, that's a bullshit rule and there's no way you're going to be able to abide by that for the whole time you're filming. Aster Bay is way too small. Second, give me all your fours."

Gavin handed over a card. "I should have sent her home last night."

Jamie barked out a laugh. "Please. Your face went all mopey just now at the mere thought of sending her home."

"She's half my age," Gavin protested.

Not that he gave a shit about the age difference, but he couldn't imagine that Kyla would be interested in a man his age. Maybe for a night at Olympus, but not for more than that. And while Gavin desperately wanted another chance at their night at Olympus, he also knew that one night, a secret fling that never saw the light of day, would never be enough. Not with her. Not when he already cared about her as much as he did.

"Tessa's sixteen years younger than me. It hasn't been a problem," Jamie said.

"Really? It was never a problem?" Ethan shot a glare at his best friend. "You falling for *my daughter* wasn't a problem?"

"Not because of the age difference," Jamie said. Then, with a wicked grin, "And I thought we weren't supposed to talk about *your daughter* at guys' night."

"All I'm saying is it's messy. Complicated," Ethan said.

"What modern family isn't complicated?" Jamie shot back.

"Will you all shut up and play cards?" Baz said. "Jesus Christ.

If I wanted to listen to gossip, I'd join Mrs. White's poker game."

"Except you don't know how to play poker," Gavin said, hoping to shift his friends' focus away from his love life.

"And you don't know shit about women," Baz grumbled.

"You do?" Ethan asked skeptically.

"I know Kyla sure as fuck doesn't care that Gav's old enough to be her father. If she did, she wouldn't have signed up to be on the show in the first place." Baz pointed at Jamie. "Sevens."

"Go fish," Jamie said.

"Son of a bitch." Baz turned his attention back to Gavin. "But even if that weren't the case, anyone with eyes can see the way you look at her. There's no way she hasn't noticed."

"That's not true. Is it?" Gavin asked, his voice high and tight.

Was his infatuation with her really that noticeable? Jamie and Ethan's overly intense focus on their cards made it clear that yes, he had in fact been that obvious.

"If she hasn't fucked off by now, I highly doubt she's going to. So enough with the half-assed excuses. No one's buying them anyway. Everyone—even Kyla—knows you want to fuck her. The real question is, do you want more than that?" Baz turned to meet Jamie's startled expression. "What's your problem?"

"I don't think I've ever heard you talk so much in one night," Jamie said.

"Don't get used to it." Baz threw back the rest of his Scotch.

"Everyone knows…" Gavin began, his mind reeling. Did Brodie know?

"Everyone," Ethan confirmed with a shrug. "We just figured it was a crush and you'd get over it."

"And you obviously weren't going to do anything about it while she was dating your son," Jamie said. "So, Baz is right. The question is, do you want more than a fling?"

He wanted so much more. He wanted late nights talking about their days and lazy mornings in bed, weekend trips to his family's cabin in New Hampshire and holiday meals with the extended family. But that's where the fantasy short circuited in his brain. Because how could he sit at a Thanksgiving table with both Kyla and Brodie? How could he ask that of her, or his son?

He couldn't, so that couldn't possibly be what he actually wanted.

After all, Gavin West didn't date. Everyone knew that. He'd had his chance at love and the happily-ever-after schtick and lord knew he was too old to start over now. And if he couldn't have forever, then all he could have were stolen moments, ephemeral affairs that meant nothing and didn't come anywhere near touching his heart.

Mornings spent lounging in bed and family get togethers were decidedly dating activities. They were the things he would do with a woman if she had the potential to be his forever, and that wasn't Kyla.

It was just the lust confusing him. That had to be it. Something about his attraction to Kyla was more potent, more powerful than the way he'd been attracted to other women before, and all those hormones were messing with his ability to think clearly. It was just about sex. Just two people looking to have a good time, that's what she'd said, right?

"No, that's not the question," Ethan said. "The question is, are you willing to jeopardize your relationship with Brodie for her?"

"Brodie's an adult—" Jamie protested.

"He's still his son," Ethan said. "And one that might not be as cool with Gavin and Kyla as I was about you and Tessa."

"If that was cool…" Jamie mumbled.

"What was that?" Ethan asked.

"He said, stop pretending you aren't happy for them or he'll tell you what they did in your kitchen when you were out of town," Baz said.

Ethan blanched as Jamie swore under his breath.

"Brodie would get over it," Baz said, turning back to Gavin. "He's young and their relationship had temporary written all over it from the start. Plus, you said yourself he's happy in California, so it's not about him. It's about you. You've always put yourself second to whatever he wanted. Can you handle not being the perfect parent?"

"I'm not a perfect parent," Gavin protested.

"But you try to be," Ethan said. "It's admirable, but at some point, you have to start doing things for you again."

"Shut up," Gavin grumbled, hating the sharpness in his tone. He wasn't angry with his friends, even if they had decided to completely abandon their card game in favor of ripping apart Gavin's personal life.

Jamie laughed. "Oh, man, you really do *like* like her."

I have to talk to her.

Maybe if they could speak without the cameras around, just the two of them, maybe then he could sort through the mess in his head. Could he really have a fling with his son's ex-girlfriend? He knew himself well enough to know sex with Kyla would never be meaningless—he already cared about her too much for that—but if there was a chance he could have something with her, even just sex, even just for a little while, wasn't that better than never having her at all?

He knew she was attracted to him, but that didn't mean she'd actually want to follow through on their flirtation. What if she just wanted the fantasy of the TV show, a night of forbidden touches at Olympus and nothing more?

Even as he thought the words, he couldn't bring himself to believe them. But how was he supposed to know for sure when he couldn't have this conversation with her on camera and if he tried to meet with her on their next night off, they were sure to be found out? Baz was right—Aster Bay was way too small to think he could avoid someone, and if the person he failed to avoid was one of the other eligible ladies, or a producer, then he'd be caught red-handed violating his contract.

He needed a way to talk to her, to see if this attraction between them was as mutual as he thought it was, without having to wonder what was real and what was for the cameras.

And if it was real, what then?

"I fold." Gavin threw his cards down on the table.

"You *fold*? It's Go Fish," Ethan protested.

"Sorry." Gavin pulled a twenty from his wallet to cover his share of the pizza and beer. "I'm gonna call it a night."

"Don't be like that, Gav," Jamie said. "We just want to help you figure out what you want."

"How am I supposed to do that when I can't even talk to her without five fucking cameras being shoved in our faces?" Gavin asked, surprised by his own outburst.

"Maybe it's time you find a way to talk to her without the cameras then," Jamie said, as if it were that simple.

"Don't do something that's going to get you sued for breach of contract," Baz cautioned as Gavin gathered his things.

He met his friend's too-knowing look and nodded.

Chapter Seventeen

Kyla stood in the empty storefront next door to Desire, Natalia's lingerie shop, with Molly and Jo. She'd tried to sneak away alone but Jo wasn't having any of that.

The space that would one day (soon—hopefully) house her boudoir photography studio had been a British tea shop and a fading Union Jack was still painted on one wall, a floor-to-ceiling homage to the previous business owner's homeland. Kyla, Jo, and Molly stood in the middle of the floor, their pile of supplies spilling out of hardware store bags around their feet, and Kyla realized she'd forgotten to bring a ladder. Not that she owned a ladder. What did a twenty-three-year-old bakery assistant need with a ladder?

"It'll be fine." Molly pulled her chestnut hair back into a ponytail. "We can start on the bottom half of the wall and we'll tackle the top half another day."

Kyla would have to buy a ladder and find a truck to transport it before then, but that was future-Kyla's problem.

"Kyla Luanne Mitchell—"

"Not my middle name," she said as she sifted through the supplies for the spray bottles of the vinegar mixture that would supposedly help loosen the paint.

"There will be no sulking, feeling sorry for yourself, or self-pity today," Jo said.

"Those all pretty much mean the same thing." Molly snagged the spray bottle and set to work spraying down a section of wall.

"We are going to scrape that flag off this wall and we are going to have fun doing it," Jo announced. She hit a few buttons on her phone and the unmistakable opening notes of *Spice Up Your Life* began playing from the small Bluetooth speaker she'd insisted on bringing. Jo danced across the room, retrieving the second spray bottle and Kyla couldn't help but smile. She had the best friends.

An hour and a half later and every muscle in Kyla's arms and back were screaming, but they'd only managed to clear a roughly three-square-foot section of wall. Apparently, the British flag had been painted over a layer of wallpaper in a neon green, black, and white floral pattern. At least that explained the odd raised lines running up and down the wall and the places where the paint had seemed to be bubbled away from the wall itself. But beneath the wallpaper was a layer of hot pink paint. Kyla was almost afraid to find out what was underneath that.

At this rate, it would take weeks just to scrape away the old paint and wallpaper. As it was, she wasn't sure she could do this again. Her neck was already getting stiffer by the minute, sharp flashes of pain shooting across her shoulders when she tried to turn her head. Jo and Molly were doing their best to stay positive, but even Molly was beginning to swear under her breath with every scrape.

To add insult to injury, Kyla's stomach growled. Loudly.

They weren't going to make any more progress today anyway. There had to be an easier way to remove the paint and wallpaper—one that wouldn't compromise her friendships or their ability to lift their arms.

With a sigh, she called an end to the day of manual labor, gathered their things, tidied up what they could, and locked up the storefront before heading home.

"I'll order pizza," Molly said as they dragged themselves into the apartment.

Kyla tossed her keys and phone on the coffee table before collapsing on the couch. "With extra pepperoni," Kyla called.

"And those garlic knot things!" Jo flopped down beside Kyla. "I can't feel my arms." She glanced at the offending limbs as though they had magically appeared.

"Consider yourself lucky," Kyla said, wincing as she shifted.

"I say we pool our money and hire a handyman to scrape the rest of the paint," Molly said as she came back into the living room, dropping into the armchair with a groan.

"I can't ask you guys to do that," Kyla said.

"You didn't. We're offering." Molly shifted so she could meet Kyla's eyes. "Jo and I have been talking. If you don't win this thing—"

"Which we both agree would one-hundred-percent be Prince Charming's loss and we're willing to cut off his balls to make that clear," Jo chimed in.

Molly rolled her eyes. "Yes, Jo is willing to castrate the poor ass for you. But the point is, if you don't win, then we're going to help you get the money."

"No," Kyla said, sitting up straighter. "Absolutely not."

"This is not up for debate," Molly said. "We will either help you find a co-signer—"

"I bet Mrs. White would do it," Jo mused. "She seems like she'd appreciate a good boudoir photograph."

"—or we will pool our resources. Either way, you are getting your studio," Molly finished.

"I can't let you do that." Kyla's voice was choked with the unbelievable love she had for these women. "And I can't even begin to tell you how much it means to me that you would offer. But if I don't win the money on *Once Upon A Town,* I've already decided what I have to do." She took a breath, her stomach souring even before she spoke the words. "I'll beg my parents to co-sign. They likely won't do it, but—"

"Absolutely not," Jo said. "You are not groveling to those motherfuckers."

"Jo," Molly chastised. "They're her parents."

"They're motherfuckers," Jo repeated. "I'm not about to let them shit all over your dreams. Not again. Especially not in the Year of Kyla. We're your family. We will figure it out. Together."

Kyla swallowed around the lump in her throat as tears welled in her eyes. "Have I told you two how much I love you?"

"Not lately," Molly said.

On the coffee table, Kyla's phone buzzed to life.

"Answer it." Molly waved to the phone. "I need to go change out of these clothes."

Molly and Jo disappeared down the hall, picking flecks of paint from each other's hair, as Kyla reached for her phone. The name on her screen sent an instant bolt of adrenaline through her veins, heat rushing through her body. Gavin was calling.

"Hello?" she answered, her voice a bit unsteady.

"I need to see you."

She closed her eyes as his rough tone washed over her, sending her pulse racing. "We're not supposed to see each other off camera."

What are you doing? You want *to see him!*

"Please, Kyla. Say you'll meet me."

She nodded for a moment before she remembered he couldn't see her. "Where?"

"Olympus."

Her heart fell even as heat curled around her spine. *You don't ask someone to meet you at a sex club if you don't want sex...but is that all he wants?*

"I only had a day pass," she said. "I'm not a member."

There was a pause, shuffling on the other end of the line.

"You are now. Confirmation number is in your email."

She exhaled, trying to calm her racing heart. How many

times had she fantasized about being back in Olympus with Gavin? About what might have been if they hadn't been interrupted that night? Maybe he did only want sex, but if that was all she could have from him, wasn't that better than nothing at all?

He said he can't stop looking at you. You don't say that to someone you just want to fuck.

Or you say it to someone when all you want to do is fuck.

How the hell was she supposed to know which one it was?

"Please, Kyla," he said, a hint of desperation creeping into his tone.

"I'll be there."

The half-hour cab ride to Olympus had felt both too long and too short. She stood on the sidewalk before the plain black door, the name of the club painted in faded letters that belied the luxury of the rooms beyond it.

"The Year of Kyla," she whispered to herself, her own kind of mantra.

What waited for her beyond those doors? Surely, if Gavin had wanted to warn her of her impending elimination from *Once Upon A Town* he wouldn't have chosen a sex club as the venue, right? He wouldn't have taken them back to the one place where they'd ever come close to giving in to the attraction between them, never mind buying her a membership.

With a final shake of her shoulders, she pushed through the door. The burly man behind the reception desk scanned the code that had been in her email and wished her a good night as he held open the door to the club, ushering her inside. And then there was no turning back.

She stood just beyond the front door, shifting awkwardly in her sneakers. Maybe she should have borrowed Jo's heels again, but she hadn't wanted to let on to her roommates where she'd been headed. So there she was, in the middle of a sex club, in jeans and sneakers. At least her silky top was low cut, her ample cleavage highlighted by the deep v of the neckline. She scanned the club, her eye flitting past the groups of two and three huddled clandestinely in booths around the perimeter, until her gaze landed on Gavin.

He sat at the bar, a glass of amber liquid between his hands, as he watched her. When their eyes met, he smiled, and the tension in the long line of his body receded, replaced by something she couldn't quite name. A quiet confidence, perhaps, a grace in even his smallest movements.

With a nod to the bartender, he unfolded himself from his seat and came to her, never releasing her gaze. She had the distinct impression of being hunted, of being caught in the gaze of a fearsome predator, but one who would lull her into submission with soft words and smiles. Her pulse quickened and heat pulled low in her belly at the thought.

God, why did he have to be so handsome?

When he reached her, he pressed a hand to her lower back, drawing her close with gentle pressure as he pressed a kiss to her temple. "You came." Something like relief washed over his eyes, making the gold flecks amongst the green glimmer in the low light.

"I said I would."

He led her to a booth at the edge of the club, and she marveled at the way he managed to make sliding across the cushioned bench look graceful. She picked at the edges of her fingers, knowing the makeup artists tomorrow would roll their eyes when they saw the state of her cuticles and it would mean getting a new manicure before filming began, but she couldn't help herself. Anxiety spun through her bloodstream, wrapping itself around bones and cartilage while he ordered her a bay breeze. How did he know that was her drink? The cocktail waitress, a leggy redhead in leather pants and a cropped sheer top over a glittery bra, left the fruity drink on a napkin on the table, the condensation soaking through the white paper as the awkwardness between she and Gavin grew.

She had intended to wait for him to talk first, to tell her why he'd asked her to meet him here, of all places, but screw that.

The Year of Kyla.

"You can't stop looking at me?" The question tumbled from her lips as soon as the waitress left them alone. He angled his head closer to her, confusion in the furrow of his brow even as his long limbs and broad torso remained relaxed against the bench. "The other day, you said—"

"Right," he said, nodding.

She tilted her chin up towards him. "Is that true?"

"Yes." The word sent a shiver down her spine.

"For how long?"

He lifted a hand, his fingers barely brushing her cheek as he tucked a loose strand of hair behind her ear. "Ever since I first saw you."

His words punched the air from her lungs, her breath escaping in a harsh huff. That couldn't possibly be true, could it? All this time, over a year, while she told herself that every conversation was just him being polite—all those times she thought she felt something between them, he felt it too?

He flashed an apologetic smile, his eyes sad and welcoming all at once. She wanted to trace the lines in his forehead with her thumb, smooth out the tension there until the sadness melted away.

"You never said anything," she said, trying to slot the Gavin she knew together with this new information, to press the pieces into place and make it make sense.

"You were my son's girlfriend. Call it self-preservation." His eyes danced between her own as though he wanted to read all their secrets.

She took a sip of her drink, her hand trembling slightly as she lifted the glass. He watched her, leaning back to give her more space. Those spare centimeters felt wrong, yet she didn't know how to close the distance. This was Brodie's *father.*

He folded his hands in his lap and set his gaze on the empty stage, as though he somehow knew she needed a minute to collect herself without him watching her.

"Did you know, the day you met Brodie, he wasn't supposed to be at the diner?" He gave her the briefest of glances before refocusing on the stage, his voice raw as he continued. "We were helping my mom set up her new bookcases and Brodie was doing more complaining than helping so everything was taking twice as long. I sent him to The Dockside before they closed to pick up the pie I'd ordered for us to have at dinner that night. Cherry. My mom's favorite. I never send Brodie on errands like that. I always go myself. Sometimes I wonder, if I had gone to the diner myself that day…if I'd met you first…"

"You wouldn't have even noticed me," she said.

"I would have noticed you." He turned towards her, his thigh pressing against her own. "I would have asked you to dinner."

She huffed out a laugh. "You don't ask women to dinner. Gavin West doesn't date."

"I would have asked you."

Her throat burned with longing. "I would have said yes."

His harsh exhale sent the hair around her face fluttering in a rush of hot breath as he took her hand where it lay in her lap and folded it into his own. "But he met you first." She could hardly hear him, but those words were a lance through her chest.

She nodded, the lump forming in her throat too great to speak past. What would have happened if she hadn't met his son first? What might the last year of her life have been like if Gavin hadn't sent Brodie to the Dockside instead of going himself?

"That day at the gallery, when I realized you were his girlfriend… I didn't know whether to be angry that he'd found you first or proud of him for recognizing how amazing you are. I'm not usually a jealous man, especially not of my own son, but I have never been so envious of someone in my entire life."

His eyes dropped to her lips and she felt herself drawn towards him, leaning into his heat, tilting her chin up as her eyes drifted closed. His hand in her hair, large and warm, guided her face towards him until his lips brushed against her temple.

"He's not here now," she said, her voice shaky even to her own ears.

He froze against her, his fingers in her hair tensing infinitesimally. "This past year has been torture, seeing him touch you. Kiss you." His voice was dark and rough, the jagged edges of his words settling against her as he dragged his nose along the curve of her jaw. "I thought it would go away, this craving for you. But it hasn't. If anything, the more I get to know you, the more I…" His thumb drew a line along her bottom lip, his eyes snagging there for a moment before he forced his gaze back to hers. "And then the other night, when I saw you here…I can't stop thinking about it, about what might have happened if we…"

"Were just two people?" He searched her eyes and nodded. She licked her lips, her mouth suddenly dry, and she grasped a fistful of the crisp fabric of his shirt. "We could be just two people tonight," she said, her words much bolder than she felt.

His eyes widened slightly as they snapped to hers before they went liquid and dark, the gold flecks in his irises melted into green. "What happens in Olympus stays in Olympus?"

Her tongue darted out, wetting her lips, and she nodded.

His hand in her hair flexed and he leaned forward, brushing his lips against the sensitive spot below her ear. He murmured against her skin, "I haven't felt like this about someone in a long time, Kyla."

"Like what?"

"Like you should be mine." The words vibrated through his chest with such ferocity they made her shiver.

His fingers tightened in her hair and he pulled her towards him, pressing his lips against hers with a softness that completely contradicted the sting in her scalp. A mere brushing of lips, hardly a kiss at all. She lifted her chin and kissed him again, learning the feel of his lips on hers, the expert slant of his mouth and the coiled tension in his grip.

Relief burst in her chest, like waves crashing on the shore. A fizzy, bubbling relief at finally kissing the man she'd dreamed about for so long, at knowing she hadn't imagined all those lingering looks and soft smiles.

She flicked her tongue against his upper lip and he groaned, opening to her, kissing her back in earnest. The slow slide of his tongue against hers, the desire coursing through her when his other hand reached up to cup the back of her neck, pulling her closer, angling her just so. She gripped his shirt with both hands, bunching the fabric in painfully tight fists as she gave herself over to him.

Kissing Gavin West wasn't like anything Kyla had ever experienced before. It was electricity and sizzle, dangerous and seductive, wrapped in a veneer of velvet. It made her want as she'd never wanted before. A chasm of yawning hunger that had opened within her and threatened to consume her whole, a delicious, aching fire that singed her lungs with a need that only he could satisfy.

She tried to scrabble closer to him, but she was caged in by the booth, unable to get close enough. With a frustrated humph she pulled away and he chuckled, leaning his forehead against hers. "We need to talk about the show," he said between peppering her face with soft brushes of his lips.

"Less talking. More kissing."

He chuckled, brushing his lips over hers. She hummed

happily, so he did it again, but the kiss was light, all of the urgency of a few moments ago gone. "There are things I need to tell you. Things you need to understand about my contract."

She kissed him again, cutting off his words. She didn't want to think about filming, or work, or anything outside of this room. If she started to think about those things, it would be too easy to think about all the reasons she shouldn't be there with him, kissing him. For once she didn't want to weigh the pros and cons; she just wanted to *feel.*

"I don't want to think about the show."

He hummed in agreement, flicking his tongue out to tease at the lips. "Tell me, little goddess, what do you want?"

"You."

Gavin gripped her hand and pulled her out of the booth after him. A firm hand on the small of her back urged her forward as he led her around the edge of the room to a long hall, each side lined with doors marked only with a single illuminated number. The private rooms. Jo had said these rooms were the three-hundred-level experience, but Kyla felt nothing but giddy anticipation as Gavin led her to a room about halfway down the hall. Room number seven.

He caged her in against the door and kissed her again, the long line of his body pressing against hers, the thick ridge of his erection against her belly.

"My God, you're beautiful." He captured her lips in a quick, bruising kiss that left her breathless. She fisted the shirt at his back and whimpered into his kiss, every part of her eager and ready for him. He ran a thumb over her bottom lip again, his eyes focused on the way the soft flesh moved beneath his finger.

This wasn't like Kyla. She didn't break the rules. She didn't sneak around. Getting involved with Gavin would be reckless, a stolen fantasy.

For the first time in her life, being reckless seemed like exactly what she needed.

She tilted her hips towards him and he slid a muscled thigh between her legs, pressing all that power against the apex of her thighs. She rocked against him, marveling at the delicious friction of him between her legs, the long line of his throat as he swallowed a groan, his eyes glued to the way she moved against him. He gripped her hips, large hands digging into her curves.

"I can't stop thinking about you either," she confessed.

His eyes snapped to hers. "Since we started filming?"

"Before."

He used his hold on her hips to move her against him in slow, deep arcs, the muscles and tendons in his neck standing out in sharp relief as he clenched his jaw.

"Since you broke up with Brodie?"

She watched him carefully, waiting for the mention of his son to break the spell. "Before," she said, delighting in the way his nostrils flared and jaw ticked in response to her words. An insistent pulse beat between her legs and she leaned into the movement. Could she come like this, just rocking against his thigh? She didn't think so, but now she wasn't so sure.

He drew her earlobe between his teeth, growling at her ear, "How long were you dating my son and thinking about me?"

She shivered, his voice harsher than she'd ever heard it before. Commanding and a little angry. Why did that turn her on so much? Her nipples pulled tight beneath her shirt and heat rushed between her legs.

"Since the night we met," she said.

He cut her off with a growl as he drank the words from her lips. He trailed hot kisses across her jaw, over her throat, burying his head in the crook of her neck. She gasped at the sharp bite of his teeth as he bit the curve where her shoulder met her neck.

"I shouldn't like hearing that so much," he said.

"Gavin, please," she groaned.

"What do you need, little goddess?" He nipped at her throat.

"Tell me and I'll take care of you."

"I need *more*." She dug her fingers into his muscular back.

She felt his smile against her skin, the quick flick of his tongue along her pulse point, then he pulled away, his chest rising and falling as he caught his breath.

"Get in the room, Kyla."

Chapter Eighteen

Gavin had only ever been in the private playrooms at Olympus a few times in all the years he'd been a member. He usually preferred to leave the club with the women he met there, go back to their apartments or hotels in the city. But he couldn't take Kyla home with him, and he certainly couldn't go back to her apartment with her roommates, not when someone in Aster Bay might see them, when members of the production crew might see them.

Besides, if he had her in his bed, he knew he wouldn't be able to stop. And he wanted to move slowly—well, as slowly as you can move when your secret meeting place is a sex club.

He flicked on the dim light in the playroom as the door fell shut behind him and turned the deadbolt that would dim the light of the number on the door, letting others know that the room was occupied and not open to additional guests. This particular room was sparsely decorated with dark, wide-plank hardwood floors, a curved leather couch of sorts in one corner, and a king bed with satiny sheets in another. At the far end of the room, a wide loveseat faced the wall, a mirror occupying most of the space above the chair rail.

Gavin caught her hand and led her into the room towards that loveseat, certain with each step they took that at any moment he was going to wake up and it would all have been a dream. At any moment, the guilt would creep in, the rational part of his brain would win out, telling him to stop this madness now before it went any further. But his heart pounded in his chest, blood rushing in his ears—she wanted *him*. She'd wanted him all this time.

Surely that meant something. Surely that meant that, regardless of what other circumstances might stand in their way, they were meant to end up here.

All his life, Gavin trusted his intuition. Every decision he'd ever made had been guided by a bone-deep knowledge that his gut would never lead him astray. He could count on one hand the number of times he'd ignored his gut instinct, and none of them had ended well—when he was in sixth grade and he and Baz snuck into an R-rated movie (they'd been promptly caught and their mothers had grounded them for the rest of the summer); when he was in high school and he kissed Missy Palmer at the homecoming dance even though he wasn't really interested in her (she'd cried and told the whole school he had bad breath); and one afternoon in an art gallery when he'd met the most beautiful woman he'd ever seen, a woman who made him laugh and saw things about the world he'd always overlooked, and he let her leave with his son.

Maybe this was his chance to do it over. Do it right.

He sat on the plush loveseat and pulled her into his lap, her knees straddling him and his hands tight on her thighs. She lay her hands on his shoulders, then frowned and moved them to his biceps. She drew her bottom lip between her teeth, a crease forming between her eyebrows as she moved her hands to his chest. The crease deepened.

He lifted one hand and traced his thumb over that crease. "You're nervous."

"I want to be good for you."

He took one of her hands in his, noting the slight tremble

in her fingers as he brought them to his lips and kissed each one. His chest constricted at the knowledge that, despite all her bravado, she was worried about being good enough.

"You already are," he assured her. She blew out a harsh breath through her nose like she didn't believe him, so he scraped his teeth against the fleshy part of her palm. "You don't need to try to be anything you aren't. You are already perfect."

"I've imagined this so many times," she murmured as her free hand stroked the stubble on his jaw.

"What did you imagine?" He set her other hand against his heart as he slid his fingers beneath her silky shirt, curling around her waist, and drew arcs beneath the curve of her breast with his thumb.

She bit her lip again and glanced away, as though she was trying to decide if she should answer, and that wouldn't do. He wanted to peel away the layers of distance he'd constructed between them over the last year, but he couldn't do that if she was uncomfortable.

He was moving too fast. They were in a playroom at a sex club, for Christ's sake. He was doing this all wrong.

He ran his thumb over her bottom lip, releasing the pouty flesh from her teeth.

"Kyla, do you want to stop?" he asked.

Her eyes went wide. "No!" Her fingers curled in his shirt, as if to punctuate the word.

He bit back a smile. "You'll tell me if you do?"

She nodded emphatically. "I just—I don't—I've never said those types of things to someone before. I don't know how."

"You don't know how to tell me what you want? What you've thought about?" He trailed a hand up her spine just to feel her shiver against him. She nodded. "What if I go first?"

"Yes, please," she said, wriggling against him.

His cock kicked beneath her as all the things he wanted to hear her say flooded through him at once. He brought his hands back to her thighs, using his thumbs to stroke along the seams of her jeans.

"I imagined how you'd feel in my arms," he said, starting off slowly, his voice pitched low and deep. "The way your skin would feel against my fingers." He dragged his hands up to her waist, pushing up the edge of her shirt just enough to let the pads of his fingers brush along the exposed skin above her waistband.

"I imagined that too." She rolled her hips lightly against the thick rod of his cock trapped between them.

He slid his hands higher, taking her shirt with him, his eyes locked on hers. He paused just beneath her bra, waiting for her nod of consent before he lifted her shirt over her head. She wore a plain black bra in some kind of shiny, soft material, and the sight nearly knocked him over. He let himself take her in, all that creamy, pale skin glowing in the dim light, and forced himself to go slow, to savor every new inch of herself she revealed to him.

Her confidence seemed to waver under his inspection, and she wrapped her arms around her stomach, concealing herself from view. He met her eyes, determined that she believe him when he said, "You're beautiful." He gently moved her arms away, replacing them with his hands as he skated them over her bare stomach. As the tension left her posture and her gaze heated again, he slid one hand around to her back, deftly unhooking the clasp of her bra and letting the material fall away.

He sucked in a breath as her breasts tumbled free—the most perfect, full breasts topped with large, pink nipples. He watched as they drew themselves into tighter furls beneath his gaze. He bracketed her ribs, gently lifting the weight of her breasts with his hands, and dragged his thumbs over those turgid peaks.

"You are so much better than I imagined," he said as he swiped his thumbs back and forth, thrilling at the way her breathing shuddered in response.

"What else did you imagine?" she asked, arching into his touch.

"I imagined what color these pretty nipples would be." He bent and took one straining tip into his mouth. She gasped and dug a hand into his hair, holding him against her chest as he worried her nipple with his teeth, sucking and nibbling.

Her answering moan went straight to his cock, making him somehow harder. "Pink like your lips, and just as sweet," he murmured against her skin before moving to the other nipple.

"What else?" she asked.

He slid a hand between her legs, stroking the heated place at the apex of her thighs through her jeans. "I imagined how hot and slick and soft you'd be."

She kissed him then, eager little noises falling from her lips as she pressed herself against his hand, the bare skin of her breasts sliding against his chest. He could live inside those noises.

He drew his tongue over the shell of her ear before whispering, "Are you wet for me, little goddess?"

"Yes," she panted.

"Will you show me?"

She climbed off his lap, never taking her eyes from him, until she stood between his thighs. He held her gaze as she unbuttoned her jeans and hooked her thumbs in the waistband. She pulled them down, kicking them off and to the side, her panties tangled in the denim. Her hands balled into fists at her sides, fingers fidgeting as his eyes raked over her naked skin, her curves smooth as polished marble. Reaching for her, he swept his thumb over the angry red indentation left by the elastic band of her panties on her hip. He pressed an open-mouthed kiss to the spot, as though he could kiss away the offending mark.

He could smell her arousal, and his mouth watered at the thought of pressing his tongue between her thighs, tasting her sweetness. But this was already going so much faster than he had planned, and he knew if he tasted her, he wouldn't be able to stop himself from sinking into her heat, from fucking her until neither one of them remembered their names. He dragged his tongue along the line on her hip, turning her in his arms, and sank his teeth lightly into her ass. She groaned as he bit her and it took everything in him not to drive into her right then.

But Kyla deserved more than a quick, hurried fuck. She deserved to be worshipped, to be petted and praised until she was limp with pleasure, until she was aching and desperate for him to fill her. Only then would he let himself discover how she'd feel when she came on his cock.

Above Kyla's head, mounted high on the wall, a small red light flickered to life. She followed the direction of his eyes, turning back to him with a puzzled expression. "What does that mean?"

He grinned. "Let me show you."

He pulled her back onto his lap, her back tight against his chest, her naked skin in stark contrast to his own fully-clothed form. Why was it so hot to hold her like this, completely naked when he hadn't even removed his shoes?

Gavin found the small keypad built into the arm of the loveseat and pressed a button. As he did, the mirror in front of them turned into a window looking out onto the main floor of the club with a stunning view of the stage. Kyla yelped, throwing her arms around her body to cover herself.

He chuckled and kissed the nape of her neck. "They can't see us, little goddess. To them, this is still a mirror."

She turned wary eyes his way, but she let her hands fall away from her breasts. "You're sure?"

"I'm sure." He kissed his way up her throat to the sensitive spot behind her ear that made her moan. "You like to watch, yes?"

"Yes," she said.

"Then watch."

She turned back towards the window where a petite woman with short dark hair had ascended the stage. She was naked save for a garter belt and thigh high stockings, and one of those corsets that curved beneath her breasts, offering no coverage at all but holding them high and on display. She was quickly joined by two tall men, each dressed only in black boxer briefs and already sporting massive erections.

Gavin lifted Kyla's knees, one at a time, and hooked her legs over his own thighs, holding her open as he dropped a hand between them and cupped her pussy. He groaned, letting his face fall into the crook of her neck, as her damp curls brushed against his fingers, the proof of her arousal slick beneath his touch.

On stage, the woman began sucking one man's cock while she pumped her fist over the other and Kyla wiggled in his lap, her breathing coming faster.

"Tell me what you see," he said.

"She's…with both of them. At once."

He hummed an acknowledgment against the nape of her neck as he used his free hand to tease her nipple into a stiff point. "With them how?" Kyla hesitated and he grazed her shoulder with his teeth. "Use your words, sweetheart."

"She's sucking his cock."

Pride bloomed in his chest as a blush rose in her cheeks. "Good girl. Does she look like she's enjoying it?"

"Yes," she whispered. "Oh, and now the other man…"

"Yes?"

"He's…fucking her."

"How?" He pinched her nipple.

"From behind."

He rewarded her with a slow drag of his finger through her slit, pleased to find her even wetter than before.

"I didn't know people did that outside of porn," she whispered. "Be with more than one person at once, I mean."

He bit down gently on the place where her shoulder curved into her neck and she shuddered in his arms, relaxing back against him. Later he wanted to find out more about what kinds of porn she'd been watching, what she turned to when she touched herself, but for now, he widened his thighs slightly, parting her legs even further.

"People do all kinds of things," he said. "Do you like it?"

She rocked in his lap, a slow movement that he wasn't sure she even knew she was doing. "I like watching it," she said and his cock pulsed against her as her ass moved against him.

"Watching what, little goddess?"

She took a shaky breath, her voice unsteady when she said, "I like watching them fuck."

Goddamn, she was even more perfect for him than he had known was possible. "Me too."

Leaning back against him and folding her own hand over his where it lay on her breast, urging him to touch her more roughly, she asked, "Do you have a condom?"

"I'm not fucking you tonight, Kyla."

"What?" She began to sit up, but he pulled her back down against himself. "Why?"

He held her tight enough that he was sure she could feel the unmistakable bulge of his erection pressing against her ass. "There's so much for us to do besides fucking." She harrumphed a frustrated sigh and he bit back his smile. "I'm not fucking you tonight, but that doesn't mean I can't make you come." He dragged a knuckle lazily through her slit. "Can I, little goddess?"

Kyla dropped her head back against his chest. "Gavin, I can't always—I mean, sometimes—It's not that easy. For me, I mean."

He deepened his stroke, letting his knuckle graze the tight bud at the apex of her thighs. She shivered in his arms, squirming against him.

"I'm in no rush." He pressed a kiss to her throat. "I'd like to try."

"You would?" she asked, surprise coloring her question.

He bit back the anger that flashed through him. That this woman should ever be surprised that her pleasure mattered, that she didn't believe that he would do whatever was required, spend his life with his hand between her thighs, give her his fingers, his tongue, his cock, anything she needed, *everything* she needed until she found her release—it was unacceptable.

"There is nothing I want more," he said. "Of all the things I've imagined, making you come is my favorite. Let me make you feel good."

Her assent was barely a whisper, but it was enough.

He slid a finger through her slit, pressing lightly against her clit. He stroked her in light, tight circles, petting the little bud until it swelled beneath his fingertip, growing plump and firm beneath his touch. He took her earlobe between his teeth as he worked in languid strokes. But he could feel the tension in her back and legs, the way she was trying to hold herself perfectly posed, like in one of her pictures.

"Relax, little goddess. I've got you." He dragged his lips over her neck. "Tell me what's happening on stage while I make you come."

She exhaled slowly, melting against him by degrees as he continued to stroke her. His touch was too gentle to get her off, but he wasn't ready—*she* wasn't ready—for that yet, anyway. Besides, he'd waited over a year to touch her like this. He wasn't about to hurry through it.

"One of the men is…in her mouth," she said, her cheeks turning a delicious shade of pink.

Funny that she could be riding his hand and yet this was what made her blush. He vowed to himself that one day he'd get her to tell him all her dirtiest fantasies, to speak the words aloud, and then he wouldn't rest until he'd made every last one come true.

"And the other?" he prompted.

"He's licking her," she whispered.

He groaned, flicking his eyes up to the show on stage to see for himself what she was seeing, the sights making her wetter by the moment. "Someday soon I'm going to kiss this pretty pussy," he said. "I want to know how you taste. I have a feeling it might be my new favorite meal." She moaned, her hips pressing up towards his fingers, so he increased his pressure. "Would you ride my tongue, sweetheart? Would you let me taste you when you come?"

"Yes," she breathed, her hips canting against him.

He pinched her nipple, twisting it until she whimpered and arched against him, each one of her little movements sliding against his cock.

"That's right, little goddess. Just like that," he praised. Keeping his thumb on her clit, he dipped a finger inside the tight clench of her heat. "You deserve to be worshipped. To have this pussy pet and stretched and licked and fucked until you beg me to stop." She sucked in a shaky, shocked breath. "That's what I've imagined."

He added a second finger, reveling in her groan, the way she rocked her hips up into his touch.

"I want that," she whimpered, grinding against his hand between her thighs and his cock beneath her ass. "God, Gavin, I want you."

"You have me." He curled his fingers and pressed them into the secret place behind her clit. "You've always had me."

She turned her head and caught his lips as he pumped between her legs. She moaned, her body pulling tight around his fingers, and he dropped his hand from her breast to work her clit in earnest as his fingers continued pressing and stroking inside her.

"I'm so close," she said, wonder and desperation warring in

her voice.

"I know, sweetheart," he crooned in her ear, sliding a third finger into her. She shuddered, dropping her head back against his shoulder.

"So close," she repeated, frustration tinging her words.

"I'll get you there. Trust me. I can't wait to see you come. To wring every last drop out of you. It's all I can think about."

She writhed in his arms, impaled on his fingers as he worked her, harder and faster. The harder he went, the more she moaned, and the idea that she needed it like this, hard and rough, nearly made him come on the spot.

"One day soon you'll come on my cock, and I'll be so deep inside you, you won't know where you end and I begin."

"Yes," she chanted, "Oh, God, yes."

"I'm going to learn all the ways to make you come, sweetheart. Do you know why?"

"Why?" she asked, breathless.

"Because your orgasms are mine now, little goddess. And I'm greedy. I want them all." He dragged her earlobe between his teeth, tugging gently. "Even when they weren't mine to have, I wanted them."

She sucked in a breath, her pussy fluttering around his fingers.

"You like knowing that I was dreaming of you when you were still dating my son?"

She dug her nails into his forearm. "Yes," she whispered, her inner muscles pulsing again.

"Even then I knew," he growled, unable to stop the words. "I knew you belonged with me. I knew I could fuck you better than he ever did."

Her back arched away from his chest as her breathing pitched higher, her thighs beginning to shake. "So much better."

The words lit a fuse in his chest and he worked her faster, pride and guilt and lust and shame and desperation all mixing together into a tangle of pure need.

"Let me hear you," he commanded as the strength of her contractions increased. "I want to know how a goddess sounds when she comes."

With a startled cry, as though her pleasure was a surprise, her inner muscles clamped down around his fingers. She rode his hand, sucking in tight breaths and shivering in his arms as her stomach contracted. "Oh, God, right there. Don't stop. Please don't stop. Oh, Gavin, I'm coming."

He caught her lips with his, wanting to taste her little cries of pleasure on his tongue. He didn't relent, pumping into her and rolling her clit between his fingers until she stopped shaking and pressed her thighs closed around his hands. He stilled his movements, but didn't withdraw his fingers, unwilling to stop touching her just yet, to relinquish the wet heat of her and the aftershocks of her orgasm around his fingers.

She curled up in his lap, turning into his chest, and he finally, reluctantly, withdrew his fingers from within her and banded his arms around her body, holding her close. He buried his head in the crook of her neck, swiping his tongue along her skin to taste the bead of sweat that had gathered there.

It wasn't until he'd kissed her goodnight and seen her safely slip into a cab to take her home, his chest aching at the idea of not sleeping curled next to her all night, not waking her with his mouth on her cunt, that he let himself acknowledge the truth: for him, this would never be just sex.

Brodie: Is my green hoodie in my room?

Gavin: I don't know. Your room is a black hole. I don't know how you ever found anything in there.

Brodie: I need a favor.

Gavin: I'm not digging through the garbage in your room for a hoodie. Buy a new one in CA.

Brodie: It's not that.

Gavin: Everything okay?

Brodie: I'm not sure I'm cut out for Los Angeles. I haven't met any industry people and none of the girls here want anything to do with me since I'm not an actor or someone who can get them a part in a movie.

Gavin: You've only been a few weeks. Give it time.

Brodie: Maybe I should just come home.
Brodie: Why should I bust my ass trying to meet new people in California when you know all these industry people from your show?

Gavin: What about Nick? I thought you wanted a new adventure.

Brodie: Nick doesn't need me. His internship will start at the end of the summer and then I'll just be stuck in this shitty apartment by myself all day. No car. No connections. No girlfriend.

Gavin: You said this was your dream. You can't give up on your dream after a few weeks.

Brodie: I'm not. I'm just thinking about it from another angle. I could come home and you could introduce me to the people from *Once Upon A Town*.

Gavin: That's not a good idea. These people are professionals and they're very busy during filming.

Brodie: Come on, Dad. I promise I won't embarrass you.

Gavin: I'm not worried about that. I'm worried about you bailing on things the second they get hard. Again.
Gavin: And I don't think you should give up on California so easily. Change is uncomfortable, B, but it's the only way you grow.

Brodie: Are you saying I can't come home?

Gavin: Of course that's not what I'm saying. You can always come home.
Gavin: I'm saying I think you should give it more time.

Brodie: Okay. But I'm not promising anything.

Chapter Nineteen

Once, in third grade, Kyla had tried to convince her parents that a squirrel in the neighborhood had eaten all of her mother's peanut brittle—she wasn't a convincing liar then and she suspected she wouldn't be a very convincing liar now. Kyla stood with the other eligible ladies at the edge of the Nuthatch Vineyard property, waiting for Ryan Harris to record his welcome monologue and pretending she wasn't so nervous she might be sick. What if everyone could tell what she and Gavin had done the other night?

But that wasn't the only thing turning her stomach into knots.

She was nervous about seeing Gavin.

Stupid. You've known Gavin for over a year. You see him all the time. This is no different.

But it was. This time she knew the little groaning sound he made when he kissed, the scrape of his stubble along her throat, the delicious fluttery feeling low in her belly when he told her all the dirty things he wanted to do to her in that low, growly voice, and the way her thighs shook when he pinched her clit and made her come all over his hands. Gavin West had a filthy mouth, and the skills to back it up, and she loved it. By all indications, he'd enjoyed their evening at Olympus as much as she had, even if he'd refused to let her take off his pants—so why was she so nervous?

Because now you know what you've been missing. Because now you wish you hadn't agreed to that stupid rule that what happens in Olympus stays in Olympus. Because now you want him so much more than you did before.

Before, the idea of being with Gavin was a fantasy, and one she had no expectation of ever coming true. But now, the idea of *not* being with Gavin, or worse, of someone else being with him, was enough to make her want to curl up in a ball, protecting her vital organs from the onslaught of pain. What if this was just about sex for Gavin when she, fool that she was, already couldn't separate the sex from the way he made her feel?

One night and she already knew she'd be devastated if he didn't choose her when this all ended. Because it wasn't just one night—it was over a year of little glances and jokes, soft smiles and his quiet belief in her. Over a year of falling for this man she should absolutely not be falling for. And now, to know the feeling of his lips on her skin, his growl in her ear? To know that all this time he'd been thinking about her, too, and yet still not know exactly what he wanted from her? How was a girl supposed to keep it together under those circumstances?

"Stop fidgeting," Erika whispered at her side, taking hold of Kyla's hand to still the motion of her fingers as they picked at her cuticles. "They're about to start."

The farmhouse-style main building that housed the winery and tasting room shone in the early summer sunshine, rays reflecting off the windows on the upper floors. One end of that building also housed Sugar Grapes, the now-closed bakery where Kyla had first worked for Tessa. The wood-shingled building blocked the view of the sprawling grounds with row after row of grapes, the property edged with tall pine trees acting like sentinels. She should have been comforted by the familiar surroundings, but instead all she could think about was how she was going to get through the next few days on camera before she and Gavin could be alone again.

"Welcome to *Robin Hood* week!" Ryan Harris exclaimed, clapping his hands together as his mouth spread into an oily grin.

"Is *Robin Hood* technically a fairy tale?" Roni, who stood on Kyla's other side, asked through a tight smile for the camera.

"There's an animated movie of it so…yes?" Kyla replied.

"That's right. With the fox." Roni nodded appreciatively.

"And what a fox he was," Erika said with a suggestive bob of her eyebrows.

As Ryan concluded his speech about the history of Nuthatch and the generations of Ethan's family who had owned the property, Gavin, Ethan, and Baz appeared in the doorway to the main building.

"What are they putting in the water around here?" Becca asked, fanning herself as she took in the men. "Is everyone in this town this gorgeous?"

Kyla couldn't answer, though. Not with her heart in her throat and her pulse racing. Gavin was so handsome it made her chest burn as her breath caught in her chest, his smile highlighting the barely-there creases at the corners of his eyes. With the sun glinting off his sandy-blonde hair, turning it golden in the reflected light, he'd never looked more perfect. He wore a heather gray t-shirt with Nuthatch's logo emblazoned across the back and dark jeans, the outfit drawing attention to his muscular biceps and thick thighs—thighs that she'd felt between her own as she straddled his lap only the night before.

"Are you ladies ready for some friendly competition?" Ryan asked.

On either side of her, the other women nodded and gave little whoops of excitement. *Shit. You were so busy ogling him, you didn't hear the instructions.*

"Then may the most eligible lady win!" Ryan stepped aside to let the women rush forward.

Kyla followed the pack around the back of the main building.

In the empty space between the rows of grapes, large targets had been set up, their bright red centers and outlines in stark contrast to all the greenery around them. At the edge of the field, sets of bows and quivers full of arrows waited for the women.

"Shit," Kyla said under her breath. "I don't know the first thing about archery."

"Pretty sure none of us do," Erika said as she chose a bow and quiver.

"I do," Lauren said, a smug smile tilting up her lips as she slung the quiver over her shoulder.

"You do?" Roni asked skeptically.

"Mmhmm," Lauren hummed, stepping away from the group and throwing a condescending "good luck" over her shoulder.

"Just go with it. Have fun," Becca said. "Gavin's going to care way more about you having a good time than about how many targets you hit."

"But don't forget that the first to hit five bullseyes gets a private dinner date with him tonight." Christina slid her hand up and down an arrow suggestively. "He can hit my target any day," she said before she, too, sauntered off to claim a target.

"What does that even mean?" Roni laughed.

But Kyla couldn't laugh. She was too busy picturing Gavin with one of these other women, laughing with them, touching them, kissing them.

Stop.

She blew out a frustrated breath and took up the last bow and quiver from the table. She had to win.

Kyla was going to lose.

Gavin, Ethan, and Baz watched from the edge of the field, behind the women, as they took shot after shot at the targets. The first woman to get five bullseyes would join him for a picnic dinner that night. He desperately wanted that woman to be Kyla.

And so far Lauren was in the lead, with Christina hot on her heels.

Fuck.

He raked his hands through his hair. At his side, Ethan laughed. "Man, you really can't stand her, can you?" He tilted his chin towards Lauren as she made a big show of bending over to select her next quiver, making sure the camera caught a shot of her round backside in the air.

"There's something off about her. I can't put my finger on it," Gavin said, measuring his response for the camera while never taking his eyes off Kyla.

"Doesn't look like Kyla stands a chance," Baz said.

Gavin watched as Kyla raised her bow once again, her hands unsteady as she tried to notch her arrow.

"Something's not right," Gavin muttered to himself.

"Or maybe she's just not good at archery," Baz said.

"I mean, really, who is?" Ethan asked.

"What?" Gavin glanced at his friends, having only half heard what they'd said. "Right."

He was already marching across the field before Ethan and Baz could say anything else. Kyla might be an awful archer, but that wasn't what had him worried. It was the way she clenched her jaw and her legs shook when she bent to retrieve an arrow from her quiver. The fact that she hadn't made eye contact with him since he'd arrived at the vineyard. The lines of tension in her neck and the high set of her shoulders.

What if she regrets last night? What if she's changed her mind?

He waited until she'd shot off the arrow currently notched

on her bow, the point finding a home in the ground a few feet from the target.

"Need a hand?"

She startled, pressing her hand to her chest. "I didn't see you there."

For the first time all day, she met his eyes and the tension in his chest uncoiled a bit. She didn't look like she regretted anything. In fact, she looked relieved to see him. He shuffled forward, intent on kissing her, when her eyes darted to the side towards the cameramen hovering nearby then back to meet his gaze and it hit him—he couldn't just kiss her now. Not on camera. Not without giving away that it wasn't their first kiss, that they'd broken their contract and he was already planning how soon he could break it again.

He smiled, loving the way her eyes softened in response. "May I?" He gestured to the bow in her hand.

She held the bow out to him, but he moved behind her, wrapping his own hand around hers where it gripped the bow. Maybe he couldn't grab her and kiss her the way he wanted to, smearing that pretty pink lipstick production had decided she'd wear each day, but like this, he could still touch her. Reassure her that they were in this together.

"Oh," she breathed as his fingers closed over hers.

She took a breath and he angled his hips away from her as that breathy sound shot down his spine. Reassuring her did not include getting hard on camera.

"Relax your grip." Her bicep trembled as he lifted the bow higher, and he pressed his arm against hers, supporting her with his body. "Now notch the arrow."

She did as he instructed, drawing her arm back, her elbow at nearly a ninety-degree angle to the ground. He bit back a grin and placed his other hand on her upper arm, pressing down gently. "Not so high." The new stance brought his body dangerously close to hers, his breath causing the wisps of hair around her face to flutter, her lavender and vanilla scent curling around him.

"Like this?" she asked, glancing over her shoulder at him.

If he leaned forward just the slightest bit, his lips would be on hers. She drew her bottom lip between her teeth and he stifled the groan that built in his chest. Christ, he wanted to kiss her. But not here. Not like this, surrounded by cameras and other people. No, he wanted to kiss her where he could take his time, where he could be certain that Zayne wouldn't see his desire for her and use it against him—or her.

"Just like that," he said, his voice rough. He tore his eyes away from her lips, turning to face the target. If he didn't look away, he was likely to kiss her, cameras be damned, especially now that he knew how those lips tasted, the way they moved against his own. "Sight your target," he instructed, waiting for her to comply and turn her head. "And release."

The arrow flew through the air and hit the outer edge of the target. She gasped, dropping her arms, and his hands tingled at the loss of her. "Holy shit," she whispered. She turned to him, dropping her bow and throwing her arms around his neck, pulling him into a hug, her eyes wide with disbelief "Holy shit! I hit the target!"

He chuckled and wrapped his arms around her, drawing her closer and resting his chin on the top of her head, breathing her in. "You did. My very own little Athena. Bright eyes and all."

She drew back, looking up at him with those blue eyes, and her gaze fell on his lips. His fingers curled in the thin cotton of her shirt, as much holding her close as holding her away, the tension in his arms keeping either of them from moving closer.

"Tell me," he said, his voice low enough that the others couldn't hear him. "What makes a goddess' legs shake like that?"

Her lips parted, as though she didn't know what to say. But she didn't have the chance to respond anyway.

Two rows over, Christina was jumping in the air, her breasts bouncing furiously in the tiny tank top that barely kept her contained. "I did it!" she screamed as she ran towards Gavin. Kyla barely stepped out of the way before Christina launched herself at him, jumping into his arms and going full spider monkey, wrapping her arms and legs around his torso as she continued to shout. "Five bullseyes! I won!"

"How?" Lauren demanded, throwing down her bow and marching off towards Zayne and Patrick who stood just off camera at the edge of the field.

Gavin was momentarily stunned, unable to process how he'd gone from nearly kissing Kyla to holding a half-dressed Christina. Catching sight of Patrick, who motioned urgently for Gavin to join in Christina's celebrations, Gavin smiled, the expression unnaturally stiff. "Congratulations," he said, glancing around for Kyla.

Where did she go? She was right here.

He set Christina down, doing his best not to let her body drag against his as he did, despite the way she clung to him. No sooner had her toes touched the ground than she dug a hand into the hair at the back of his head and pressed her lips against his. He froze, his brain short circuiting as the wrong set of lips kissed him. Gavin took hold of Christina's shoulders and gently pressed her away.

"That's just a preview." She winked as she reached up and wiped lipstick from the corner of his mouth.

Ryan appeared at their side, laughing and clapping as if they'd just put on a play. "Well, that was quite the kiss! Congratulations, Christina. You will be joining Gavin for a private dinner date tonight, a picnic on the beach." Ryan turned to address the assembled women and Gavin's friends at the edge of the field.

Gavin scanned the crowd, his eyes finally finding Kyla sandwiched between Erika and Roni. Her expression was blank and she focused her attention on a spot on the ground. *Fuck.*

"Ladies, thank you for joining us today," Ryan continued. "I'm going to take some time with Gavin and his friends here before tonight's date, and we'll see the rest of you tomorrow."

As soon as the cameramen lowered their equipment, Gavin brushed past the approaching producers, heading straight for Kyla. He had to talk to her, to make sure she was alright. Before he got two steps, Zayne intercepted him, his hand closing around Gavin's shoulder. Gavin stared at the offending grasp.

"No interacting off camera, remember," Zayne said.

"I just need five minutes."

Zayne laughed through a sneer. "Save it for the next group date, lover boy."

Gavin glared at Zayne until the producer faltered under his stare, dropping his hand and stepping back. But it was too late. When Gavin looked back, Kyla was gone.

Chapter Twenty

Hometown Helpers Interview
Official Transcript

Ryan Harris: Thank you so much for hosting us today at Nuthatch Vineyards, Ethan. You have a beautiful place here.

Ethan Hart: Thanks, Ryan. I'm pretty proud of it.

Ryan: I can see why. How long have you two known our Prince Charming?

Ethan: Gavin and I go all the way back. Our mothers were friends before we were born.

Baz: We all grew up together.

Ryan: And you two had some time to spend with our eligible ladies today. What did you think?

Ethan: Seems like a great group of girls.

Ryan: What did you think about Christina? Is she Gavin's type?

Baz: Not even a little bit.

Ethan: I think we can confidently say that Christina is not his type.

Ryan: Who do you think Gavin would say *is* his type?

Ethan: [light laughter] I don't think Gavin would know how to answer that question.

Ryan: But you do?

Ethan: [pause] Yeah, from where I'm sitting, Gavin definitely has a type.

Ryan: And that is? [long pause] It looked like he and Kyla were having a bit of a moment this afternoon. Did you know Kyla before coming here?

Ethan: I know Kyla very well. She works with my daughter.

Ryan: And what do you think of your friend dating his son's ex-girlfriend? Or, maybe more to the point, what do you think his *son* would say?

Baz: [pause] You know, I never understood the appeal of shows like this. Seems to me you're just trying to stir up trouble.

Ryan: We're just trying to help your friend find love.

Ethan: Then I'll tell you what I told him. Honesty is always the right answer.

Baz: He knows the person who's right for him.

Ryan: And do *you* know who that person is?

Ethan: I've got an idea.

Ryan: [light laughter] You Aster Bayers are a cryptic bunch.

Baz: Just loyal.

Ethan: Just looking out for each other.

"Bend your right knee a little more," Kyla instructed Erika as she peered through the viewfinder of her camera. "Perfect." *Click.* Kyla held the camera away to peek at the image on the screen. "Your legs are insane."

"You think?" Erika sat up on the bed and gestured for Kyla to turn the camera towards her.

Kyla obliged. "I know. Look at your calves."

Erika stared at her photograph, a look of unrestrained glee stealing across her face. "Damn. I look good," she whispered, almost like if she said it too loud, it wouldn't be true.

"This is what I'm saying!" Kyla glanced around the room before moving to the head of the bed and tossing the pillows on the floor. "I want to try something."

"Whatever you say, I'm in. I can't believe I'm doing this. If you would have asked me a few weeks ago if I would let someone take pictures of me in my underwear, I would have laughed in your face."

"And look at you now." Kyla gestured for Erika to scoot closer to the headboard. "Thanks for doing this."

"Are you kidding? This is the most fun I've had since we got here. This may have started as a way to get your mind off Gavin and Christina, but I am one hundred percent getting the most out of this."

Erika wore a simple bra and panty set in a bright orange that looked amazing against her dark skin and made the amber flecks in her eyes sparkle like flames. Neither she nor Kyla had packed any lingerie when they moved into their room in The Barclay, and Kyla certainly had never planned on photographing a boudoir session for one of her competitors when she brought her camera, but here they were.

Christina had left only an hour ago for her one-on-one picnic date with Gavin and Kyla had been going out of her mind remembering the way Christina had climbed him like a freaking tree and kissed him right there in the field at Nuthatch. If she was willing to maul him in broad daylight in front of all the other women, what might she do at night when they were alone?

Gavin would never go for Christina.

Why not? She's sexy and experienced. She *probably wouldn't have any difficulty telling him what her fantasies are. And she's closer to his age.*

He didn't care about age the other night.

But that was just about sex. That's what they'd agreed to, right? When it came time to choose someone to be with for more than one night at a sex club, he probably wasn't going to pick the woman who was twenty years younger than him.

Stop. You already decided you weren't going to think about it.

Erika had taken pity on Kyla's agitated state—or maybe her temporary roommate was just tired of the way Kyla was wearing a trench in the carpet with her pacing—and had asked what Kyla would usually do if she were at home and needed to clear her head. The answer was simple: photography. One thing led to another and here they were. Kyla would send Erika the pictures free of charge and, in exchange, she would select a handful that Kyla could use in her portfolio and hang on the walls in the lingerie shop and photography studio.

If you ever finish renovating it.

"Like this?" Erika asked, resting her feet on the headboard so her legs formed a ninety-degree angle.

"Not quite. Scoot your butt all the way up against the headboard and put your legs up straight on the wall. That's it. Now bend the knee closest to me, just a bit. There. Stay right there." Kyla snapped a few shots, moving around the bed as she did to make sure the light fell on Erika just right, shadows pooling in the defined line down the center of her abdomen and the hollow of her throat, light reflecting off her cheekbones and the sharp jut of her hips. "Now with one hand, hook your bra strap with your thumb, like you might drag it down. Perfect."

An hour later, they sat side by side on the bed, scrolling through the images on the camera screen. Each shot was better than the last as Kyla figured out the way the light moved in the hotel room and Erika got more comfortable being photographed.

"You are really good at this," Erika said.

"Thanks."

Erika took the camera from Kyla's hands to hold it closer to her face as she examined a shot that highlighted her ass. "My butt looks good!" Erika burst out laughing. "This is the weirdest thing I've ever done."

"But you had a good time?" Kyla asked nervously.

"Hell yeah! I had no idea that posing in my underwear would make me feel so…powerful. Is that weird to say?"

"Not weird at all. I know exactly what you mean."

"Are you feeling any better?"

"A little." Kyla shook out her shoulders and head. "I'm sorry. I shouldn't be moping. I knew what I signed up for when I joined this show. I knew he'd be dating multiple women at the same time."

"But you didn't know it'd be Gavin," Erika said.

"Yeah." Kyla's stomach twisted all over again.

"Would you have come if you knew?"

"Honestly, I'm not sure. I don't think I would have wanted to set myself up for the rejection, you know?"

"Isn't being on this show in the first place setting ourselves up for rejection?" Erika laughed.

"Rejection by *him*, I mean." Kyla bit her lip. When she spoke again it was quiet, more for herself than for Erika. "I just really want him to choose me."

Erika squeezed her hand where it lay between them on the comforter. "I saw the way he was looking at you and touching you at the archery competition. He sure as hell doesn't look at *me* that way. Or anyone else for that matter."

Kyla winced even as her heart swelled. "I'm sorry."

"Would you quit apologizing?" Erika nudged her shoulder with a smile. "You two seem like you'd be really good together." Kyla bit back her smile.

Someone knocked on the door to their room and Erika shot up, pulling a robe around herself as Kyla went to answer the door. Becca and Lauren stood on the other side.

"Get dressed. We're going out!" Becca said excitedly, looking like she was barely containing the urge to jump up and down and clap her hands.

"I thought we were supposed to stay in tonight." Kyla moved to block Lauren's curious perusal of her room.

"Zayne decided it would be good to show us out on the town. You know, check out the nightlife." Lauren ran an unimpressed glance over Kyla. "You do have nightlife in this backwater, don't you?"

Kyla leaned against the door frame and crossed her arms. "I think I'll pass."

Lauren barked out a laugh. "As if you have that choice. What Zayne wants, Zayne gets."

"It'll be fun, Kyla. All we have to do is shoot a couple promos for Pure Sexxy and we get to spend two whole hours kicking back in a local bar. Some place called the Bay Breeze," Becca said, practically pleading with Kyla to not ruin this for her.

If Jo kept her normal work schedule this week, she'd be behind the bar at the Bay Breeze tonight. "I'm in."

"Pure Sexxy is awful for you." Erika appeared at her side, now fully clothed. "I'm not promoting that stuff."

"It's a fun, great tasting aid to a healthy lifestyle," Lauren responded, the marketing line tumbling from her lips so automatically that Kyla was tempted to check behind her for cue cards.

"It's a caffeinated laxative," Erika responded.

"Just get dressed. We're leaving in twenty minutes." Lauren threw her hair over her shoulder as she turned to go, presumably to knock on the next door and notify Roni of their impending departure.

"Don't let her get under your skin, honey," Becca said, squeezing Kyla's hand. "This will be fun!"

"How did she get Zayne and Patrick to agree to this?" Erika asked.

"I don't think Patrick even knows. He's working Gavin and Christina's date. But Zayne thought it was a great idea. You know," Becca said, leaning in and whispering conspiratorially, "I think Lauren might be his favorite. And if I learned anything from beauty pageants, it's that you don't want to get on the bad side of the girl who the judges have picked as their favorite." She winked as though she'd just dispensed some invaluable life advice. At least Becca was sweet, even if she and Kyla didn't exactly click. "Shoot!" Becca glanced down at her empty hands. "I forgot my handbag. I'll see you ladies in the lobby in twenty minutes!" she called as she scurried down the hall towards her room.

"Do you really think Lauren is Zayne's favorite?" Kyla asked

Erika as she flipped up the edge of the duvet cover on her bed in search of her shoes.

Erika snorted. "I'm sure she is. How else do you think she got a private room?"

"There was an uneven number of us."

"Sure, and she was also the only one who didn't seem surprised by the fact that we were going to be competing in an archery competition today," Erika said, pulling on a little black dress.

"You think Zayne tipped her off? Why would he do that?" Erika just raised an eyebrow at her. "I can't see Patrick being okay with Zayne playing favorites."

"I don't think Patrick has the pull to override him. I heard that Patrick's only on this project as a courtesy because it was his idea and he has seniority at the network, but Zayne is the one who secured the sponsors. He's the one who has a history of getting ratings with reality TV. They might have equal billing, but Zayne's the one with the power. I'm telling you, befriend the makeup artists. They know everything." Erika turned to face Kyla, her hands held out to the side. "Does this look okay?"

Kyla reassured Erika that she looked beautiful, but she was only half paying attention to the rest of their conversation—something about hoping she could get a decent margarita and that they wouldn't have to dance because her heels were too thin for any sudden movements. Kyla was too busy thinking about what Erika had said about Patrick and Zayne.

"You aren't wearing that, are you?" Erika asked.

Kyla glanced down at her jeans and Gavin's holey sweatshirt. *Shit.*

Erika smiled. "Leave it to me." She threw open the door to their closet and flipped through the hangers of gowns. She pulled one out and turned, draping the hot pink and black color-blocked body con dress over her arm. "This is the one."

Jo had talked Kyla into buying that particular dress and the tags still hung from it. She had planned to return it after filming because there was no way Kyla was wearing a body con dress.

"Trust me," Erika said, holding the dress out to Kyla.

Kyla took the dress and shook off the uneasy feeling gnawing at the back of her mind. What did it matter if Zayne liked Lauren best or if Kyla wore a dress that did nothing to hide her belly? Gavin had already seen all of her, and he'd liked it well enough then. But it was one thing to want her in a private playroom at a sex club, and another entirely to choose her publicly. Even if she could manage to stay on the show long enough to help her business, even if she somehow won, when the cameras stopped rolling and they went back to their real lives, could she really have him?

Chapter Twenty-one

"Kyla Dorothea Mitchell!"

"Not my middle name," Kyla said with a smile.

"Get your smokin' hot ass over here!" Jo tossed down the towel she'd been using to wipe off the bar and leaned over the bar top to pull Kyla into an awkward hug. "I told you that dress would look amazing on you," she whispered into Kyla's ear.

Kyla blushed. "Yes, oh fashion guru. I will never doubt your styling advice again."

"You will and I pre-forgive you." Jo pulled back, already starting to mix a drink for Kyla.

"Where is everyone?"

The main room was nearly empty. The high-top tables had been pushed to the edges of the space, like clearing out a high school gymnasium for a middle school dance, and production had erected lighting and stationary cameras around the perimeter of the room. The wall of windows overlooking the bay remained unobstructed, however, and the rest of the girls had bypassed the bar completely in favor of taking in the stunning view. Kyla and her friends had been coming to The Bay Breeze since they turned twenty-one, but she vaguely remembered the first time she'd seen that view. It was even better at sunset, as they'd discovered when they became regulars at half-price appetizer happy hours.

"The network bought out the whole place for the rest of the night. But who cares about that? Spill. Since I'm going to find out now anyway, tell me!" Jo tried her best to look calm as she refilled the garnishes behind the bar.

"Tell you what?"

"Who's Prince Charming? I heard this rumor that it was Sam, the bartender over at The Rookery, but Molly went there for drinks the other night with some of the other teachers and she said he was there behind the bar. But that's not even the craziest rumor. Molly swears she overheard Dot Blumenthal and Judy Kemp talking about it being Gavin West." Jo threw her head back and laughed.

Kyla could feel the blush all the way down to her toes. "It *is* Gavin West."

"Kyla Hermione Mitchell!"

"Not my middle name."

Jo used her bar towel like a whip, throwing it out to strike against Kyla's arm. "I can't believe you didn't tell me!"

"I'm not supposed to tell anyone!"

Jo pouted but it quickly dissolved. She lowered her voice, leaning in conspiratorially. "Okay, but you have to tell me one thing. He's the reason you bailed on us on your one night off and were out until after midnight, right? You snuck out to see him? You two are totally—"

"Jo," Kyla said through a plastered-on smile, her eyes wide as she flicked them towards the bank of monitors in the corner where Patrick was watching them curiously.

Jo sighed. "Fine. I'm not supposed to talk to you while we're filming anyway, so get that hot ass out on the dance floor before you get us both in trouble. But next time you're home, I want details, lady."

Kyla laughed, squeezed Jo's hand for courage, and made her way across the room to where Erika and Roni were debating if the water would still be warm enough to swim. On the other side of the room, Lauren was giving a straight-to-camera testimonial about how Pure Sexxy Juice Enhancers were an essential part of her diet plan.

"Have either of you figured out the catch yet?" Roni asked before taking a sip of her beer.

"What catch?" Kyla asked.

"Production didn't shell out to shut down a bar for the night just so we could dance, or so we could film some bullshit promos for Pure Sexxy. There's going to be a twist," Roni said.

"How do you know?" Erika asked.

"Because I am a student of the art form," Roni said. "Meaning, I watch a lot of reality television. Especially dating shows. Trust me—there's always a twist."

Kyla glanced around the room and, sure enough, Ryan Harris pushed through the front door of the bar, two cameramen appearing from the hallway to capture his entrance and the girls' surprised reactions. Ryan stopped in the center of the room, adjusting the cuffs of his shirt and waiting for the women to gather around him. "Ladies," he said, when Becca finally took her place, "you all look lovely. There's been a change of plans."

"Told you," Roni whispered.

"The fairytale ball originally planned for tomorrow has been canceled." Ryan paused for dramatic effect as Becca and Lauren dutifully gasped. "Instead, in honor of Robin Hood's rebellious streak, tonight's dance party will be your last chance to spend time with Prince Charming before the elimination ceremony."

The front door of the bar swung open and Christina strutted through, practically dragging Gavin along behind her. She held up their clasped hands and let out a whoop, the shift in her posture raising the hem of her already perilously short dress. "Woo! We're here, bitches!"

At her side, Gavin winced and pulled his hand away, scraping it over his face. His eyes darted around the room until they landed on Kyla, the tension in his shoulders shifting subtly, becoming less beleaguered and more predatory. She bit her lower lip and adjusted her dress, loving the way his eyes roamed over her from across the room.

He wanted her, and that knowledge suffused her blood with a cool thread of power. He wanted *her*.

"Gavin," Ryan said, greeting him as though they hadn't seen each other only a few hours before, "your eligible ladies await."

Before he could even respond, Lauren stepped forward, holding out an expectant hand for Gavin. "Mind if I steal you?"

Kyla scanned the room, finally locating Zayne by the bar, whispering to Davis as they watched Lauren pull Gavin away. Erika appeared at Kyla's side, pressing a new drink into her hand. "Told you Lauren was his favorite. He probably set this whole thing up just to get her alone time with Gavin."

"Why would he do that though?" Kyla asked. "Why would he care who wins?"

Erika shrugged. "Pure Sexxy likes her. Maybe he gets some kind of kick back if she wins."

For the first time, as Kyla watched a reluctant Gavin escort Lauren to the back room of the bar, she wondered how important what Gavin wanted really was.

"I know people don't believe this because they see me on Instagram and I seem so confident," Lauren said, her eyes brimming with fake tears, "but I had a really hard time with my body image growing up."

"I'm sorry," Gavin said, though something about her delivery didn't ring true.

"I had really fat ankles," she whispered.

There it is.

"That must have been difficult," he replied, cycling through the canned responses Patrick had rehearsed with him for these types of conversations.

"It really was." She laid her hand on his knee, squeezing, and he fought the urge to push her away. "I knew you would understand."

Gavin glanced at Patrick in the corner of the room. He made a gesture with his hand that clearly indicated that he expected Gavin to continue the conversation, though what they were meant to talk about was beyond him.

"So you're a model," he said, grasping at straws.

She beamed. "I am! I love how you remember so much about me." He didn't. "And we have so much in common!" They didn't.

"How's that?"

"We're both in marketing, silly." She giggled, the sound hollow, before fixing him with a comically serious look. "But I don't just want to be a model. I have ambition."

"What do you want to do?"

She lowered her voice and leaned closely as though she were about to tell him some big secret. The hand on his knee slid up to his thigh, and he glared at it before shooting a pointed look at Patrick.

"I want to build my own reality TV empire." At his confused look, she continued. "Like the Kardashians, but better, because it'll be all about me and my friends and not some family that no one even knows why they're famous. Well," she said with a look that he'd come to learn meant she was about to say something unkind about someone, "aside from that sex tape, of course." Her hand slid higher. "Maybe we could make a tape of our own."

Gavin stood up, knocking Lauren back when he did. "If you'll excuse me."

"But I stole you." Lauren turned a disgruntled pout towards Patrick.

"And right now, I'm stealing myself. Patrick, a word." Gavin gave him his best professorial glare as he left the room.

Patrick followed him down the hall to the small office at the end. "Before you say anything," Patrick began as he closed the door behind him, "I want you to know, you handled that really well."

"What are you talking about? I practically ran away from her." Gavin ran a hand through his hair. "She needs to be the one eliminated tonight."

Patrick frowned. "I'll talk to Zayne, but I don't think he'll agree."

"But you agree with me."

Patrick shifted uneasily on his feet. "I can sympathize with your position."

"You can sympathize with my position," Gavin repeated, stunned. What the fuck was he talking about?

"Zayne has final sign off on eliminations. It's in his contract—and yours. And Zayne isn't going to want to send Lauren home yet."

"Why not? We're clearly not right for each other. The audience is going to know that as soon as they see us together."

"The audience isn't going to know who you like because you're being charming with *all* of the women," Patrick countered.

Gavin leaned against the desk, confusion furrowing his brow. "I don't understand what you want from me."

"Look, Pure Sexxy likes Lauren. What they'd like even more is for the person you choose to be someone who already publicly endorses their product."

"Who am I allowed to eliminate then?" Gavin asked, a weight sinking in his stomach.

"Erika, Roni, or Kyla."

"The only three women here that I actually get along with."

"You get along with all of the eligible ladies, Gavin," Patrick said. "It's part of what makes you such a good Prince Charming."

"But?"

Patrick pulled off his glasses and ran his fingers over his eyes, like he was exhausted by this conversation when he was the whole reason Gavin was in this mess.

"But if you aren't going to pick a frontrunner, then the show is going to have to do it for you. We need a narrative of you falling in love, and in the absence of you giving us that footage, Zayne is going to at least keep the sponsors happy."

"This is ridiculous." Gavin pushed off from the desk and began pacing around the room.

"I know it's not what you expected, but it's reality television. It's entertainment."

"No, don't do that. That's bullshit and you know it." He turned on Patrick. "I thought you were on my side. I thought this was *your* show."

Patrick lowered his voice and took a step closer. "If you want to make it harder for Zayne to send home the women you like, then start acting like they're important to you. This morning with Kyla at the archery competition was a start, but it's not enough."

"What do you mean?"

"That one moment is easy to edit out. A handful of moments is easy to edit out. But if you give us so many moments that we can't possibly tell this story without including them, then Zayne won't be able to spin that you're interested in the woman he's decided should be left standing when this is over. There has to be no doubt in anyone's mind that the audience will know who you're really interested in."

Someone knocked at the door and then it opened a crack, Kyla's roommate—*what was her name?*—peeking around the door. "Sorry to interrupt, but I need to get into the safe for a minute." She gestured to the large metal box bolted to the floor in the corner of the office.

"Of course," Patrick said, turning to leave.

Gavin followed him but, as soon as Patrick was gone, the blonde closed the door, leaning against it and blocking his exit. He raised an eyebrow at her, taking in her mischievous smile.

"You're Kyla's roommate, right?"

"Jo," she said, extending a hand towards him. "Nice to see you again, Daddy West."

"What did you just call me?"

"Your microphones aren't picking anything up back here. Something about signal interference," she said.

"How do you know that?"

She shrugged. "Bartenders are very good listeners. And that Zayne guy is really loud."

He watched her for a minute. "Why are you telling me this?"

Her smile widened as she reached behind her and turned the deadbolt on the office door. Gavin's stomach dropped. What was she doing?

Across the room, a section of the wall swung open and Kyla stepped out of the darkness into the room. Gavin glanced between the two women, Jo smiling from ear to ear and Kyla looking nervous, her eyes darting over her shoulder to the open passageway as though she expected one of the producers to pop out and reprimand her for breaking the rules.

"What's going on?" he asked.

Jo stepped away from the door to the hallway, passing an appraising eye over him as she crossed to the now-open secret door. "Did you know this building used to be the center of maritime trade in Aster Bay? Old man Aster himself had his office here. Rumor has it he was a paranoid motherfucker. There are secret passages all over this building, but this one's my favorite. Comes out behind the bar." She glanced at the darkened opening in the wall and squeezed Kyla's hand. "Don't take too long. They'll figure out you two are missing eventually." With a wink, she ducked into the passage, pulling the door shut behind her.

"I always heard there were secret passages in Aster Place, so I guess it makes sense that they'd be here, too," Gavin said.

Kyla took a halting step towards him, her fingers clenching the hem of her short pink dress. God, she looked good. He wanted to press her up against the wall and kiss her. He wanted to slide his hands under her skirt and remind himself—remind them both—how it felt when she came around his fingers. But for some reason he couldn't stop babbling about people who'd died over a hundred years ago.

"There's supposedly a secret passage in Aster Place that goes between the main house and the greenhouse. Underground. And—"

"Gavin," Kyla said, cutting him off, "I don't want to talk about secret passages."

He forced himself to take a breath. Why was he so nervous? This was Kyla.

Kyla who they want you to send home.

"You look beautiful." He clenched his fingers at his side to keep from reaching for her.

"You kissed Christina," she said, taking a halting step towards him.

Was she jealous? If she hadn't looked so nervous, it would have been laughable.

"*She* kissed *me*." He stepped closer, the toes of his dress shoes bumping against her sensible flats.

"Did you… Again? On your date?"

"Kiss her?" She nodded, her bottom lip pulled between her teeth. He ran his finger over her lip, releasing it from her bite. "No. There is only one woman here I want to kiss."

Her eyes sparkled, a smile tugging at the corners of her mouth, as he leaned in and brushed his lips over hers.

"There's no one else, Kyla," he said, cradling her face in his hands.

"Except the five other women who are competing for your attention."

"There are no other women. I thought I made myself clear the other night," he said, making his voice low and gritty the way she liked. "You're mine, little goddess."

Doubt swam in her eyes again and she reached up to grip his wrists. "I want to be."

"Is that why you arranged this little cloak and dagger meeting?" He smiled and brushed his thumbs along her jaw line.

She blushed. "It was Jo's idea."

"Oh, so Jo is the one who wanted to see me?" he asked with a grin, pulling his hands away.

Her grip on his wrists tightened and she held him to her. "No. That was me."

He rewarded her bravery with another kiss, his hand trailing down her spine to curve over her ass and pull her close. He wanted to feel her against him, even though he knew they were short on time, that soon someone would come looking for them. But for just a minute he didn't want to worry about the cameras and the producers—he just wanted to kiss this woman. He never wanted to stop kissing her.

"Let me prove to you that you're mine." He walked her back until her legs hit the edge of the desk. "You're the only one I want to be mine."

He helped her scoot up onto the desk, hiking her dress up and wedging his hips between her thighs as he kissed down her neck. "Gavin," she groaned, tilting her head to give him better access to her throat, "we don't have a lot of time."

He grinned against her skin, his tongue flicking over her pulse point. "I'll be quick."

He lowered himself to his knees in front of her and ran his hands up her thighs, his cock thickening in his pants. He slid his hands higher until he'd exposed her silky panties. Only then did he break eye contact, letting his eyes fall to the damp fabric between her legs.

"Are you wet for me, little goddess?"

"Yes," she whispered.

He lifted her feet, placing them on his shoulders, and pressed his palms to the inside of her thighs, opening her to his inspection.

"Gavin," she whined, "I thought you said you'd be quick."

He chuckled and pressed a kiss to the inside of her knee. "Let me look at you, Kyla. Let me see how beautiful you are." He hooked the gusset of her panties with his index finger and pulled it to the side, baring her completely to him. "I've been dying to taste you for months."

She whimpered, her hips tilting towards him, and he wondered if she was even aware she was doing it. But her eyes were tinged with hesitation, and that just wouldn't do. When he finally put his mouth between her legs, he needed her to want it as badly as he did.

"Can I taste you, little goddess?"

Her eyes darkened, blue swirling into black, and she licked her lips. "I think I'd like that." At the hesitation in her voice, he raised his eyes to meet hers. "No one's ever—"

He cursed under his breath and held her hips steady with strong hands. He pressed his mouth to the crease where her leg met her hip, inhaling her scent.

"Are you telling me no one has ever kissed you here, little goddess? No one has ever tasted this perfect pussy?" His voice was tight, as though he were in pain, as he nuzzled against her.

"No one," she said, breathing harder.

"Over a year and my son never licked your cunt?" he growled.

"He said he didn't like to..." She blushed. "It wasn't something he wanted to do."

"Is it something *you* want to do?"

She nodded, her eyes hooding.

"I need you to say the words, sweetheart." He dragged his

finger over her opening in lazy circles.

"Yes. Please, Gavin. I want you to."

Gavin gripped her panties in a fist and dragged them down her legs roughly, plunging his tongue between her folds. She gasped at the slick heat of his tongue against her clit. "I'm glad he never tasted you," he grunted as he used his thumbs to part her. "You don't know what it does to me to know I'm the first man to put my mouth on you."

"Oh, God." She dropped her head back between her shoulders as he ate her.

He should have gone slower, knowing this was the first time she'd had a man eat her cunt, but he couldn't stop himself. He needed to taste her release, to feel her clit pulse beneath his tongue.

"You taste so good, little goddess," he groaned. "I knew you would."

She moaned, the sound reverberating off the stone walls of the historic building. He sucked on her clit, hard, just to hear the sound again.

"You'll need to keep it down, Kyla, unless you want the whole crew to know you're having your pussy eaten."

She sucked in a breath, her hips canting against him, and he briefly wondered if he could make her scream loudly enough for the whole bar to hear. How many orgasms would it take for her to lose all control? Two? Five?

But he had no time to explore that particular thought. No matter how long he wanted to spend on his knees worshipping her, eventually someone would come looking for them. And as hot as the idea of someone hearing them was, he didn't actually want to share her like that. He wanted to be the only one who knew what she sounded like when she broke apart beneath his touch, the only one to hear her little cries as her sweetness flooded his mouth.

"Come for me, little goddess. Let me taste you."

She fell apart with a startled cry and a long, low moan, her hips rocking against his mouth of their own volition as her pleasure coated his tongue. His cock strained against his zipper and he fought the urge to take her right there, to take his own release in her welcoming heat.

But this was not the time or the place. He'd waited over a year to have Kyla and, when the time finally came, it wouldn't be a hurried fuck on a desk in the back office of a bar.

As she came down from her orgasm, he helped her back into her panties, pulled her dress back down over her hips, and got to his feet. He kissed her softly, loving the hungry way she licked herself off his lips.

Christ, this woman would be the end of him.

"That was..." Kyla sighed dreamily. "Thank you."

He kissed the curve of her jaw. "Believe me, the pleasure was all mine."

When he pulled back to look at her, the cloud of lust was clearing from her eyes, and in its place, storms were brewing, swirls of things she was holding back. It made his chest ache to know that even now, even moments after he'd had his head buried between her legs, she was still unsure of how to say what she needed from him.

"What is it?" He cradled her face in his hands and skated his thumbs over her cheeks.

She pressed her forehead to chest with a frustrated huff. "I'm scared," she whispered.

He pulled her closer, nestling her head under his chin and pressing a kiss to her hair. "Of what?"

"What happens when this is all over?"

"We go back to our lives."

She stiffened in his arms. "Right. I go back to being your son's ex-girlfriend, and you go back to being the guy who doesn't date," she said, pulling away.

His mouth went dry at the idea of them going back to how

things were. He wouldn't. He couldn't be in the same room with her without wanting to touch her, without *needing* her, and they'd only just begun.

But she was right. When the cameras left, they'd have to face Brodie, and everyone else in town who would never understand how Gavin West could be a good father and also be with his son's ex-girlfriend.

"Can't we just enjoy the time we have together now?" he asked.

Her eyes shuttered and he knew it had been the wrong thing to say, but he didn't have any answers. He wasn't ready to end this, doubted he'd ever be ready, but he also wasn't ready to face all the obstacles in their way. He was a coward and a horrible father and way too old for her. What kind of life could he offer her? Besides, she'd said it herself—she hadn't come on the show to find love; she'd come to help her business. *That* he could offer.

"Yeah, of course," she said, but her smile didn't reach her eyes.

By the time they emerged from the office, several minutes later than they probably should have—Gavin through the main door and Kyla back through the secret passageway—the party was clearly over. Zayne and Patrick stood in one corner speaking in heated whispers with Davis and Ryan, Becca sat on the floor in a heap of silk, crying as the other women huddled around her.

Patrick spotted Kyla first. "There you are. That was the longest bathroom break in the history of reality television."

"Sorry," Kyla said.

"Compression garments, am I right?" Jo offered from behind the bar.

"What?" Patrick asked, turning towards Jo.

"You know. Compression garments. The things women wear under their clothes to make them—" She made a sucking noise as she squeezed her waist.

Patrick sighed. "Right. Well, the important thing is you're

back now." Seeing Gavin lingering nearby, Patrick gestured to him. "Prince Charming, we need you over here." Gavin reluctantly followed Patrick across the room. "We have a situation," Patrick said when they'd joined the other men.

"It's not a fucking situation. It's a goddamn contract violation," Zayne bellowed.

Gavin froze, his blood turning to ice water in his veins. What was Zayne talking about—what Gavin and Kyla had done just now in the back office or their night at Olympus or the first night on the beach or—fuck, they might as well have set fire to their contracts.

"We're not going to sue the girl." Patrick glanced at Davis and Ryan as if he was seeking confirmation of that point.

"We can use this," Davis said. "This kind of thing happens on *The Bachelor* all the time. The audience will eat it up."

"Use what?" Gavin asked, already mentally dialing Baz to see if he knew of a good lawyer.

"Becca's been in contact with her ex-boyfriend on her day off—" Patrick began.

"Son of a bitch," Zayne swore.

"—and she wants to leave the show."

"Okay. Then let her leave the show," Gavin replied.

Zayne threw his hands in the air. "This isn't going to work."

Patrick cleared his throat and shot Zayne a frustrated look before refocusing his attention on Gavin. "You need to make it seem like you're sad to see her go. Like you saw a future with her."

"But I don't," Gavin said, confusion furrowing his brow.

"No, you're too busy making eyes at your son's ex and ruining my fucking show," Zayne spat.

The hair on the back of Gavin's neck prickled in warning.

"What Zayne is trying to say," Patrick continued, "is that you've been very reserved on camera. You're holding back. We need you to be more…demonstrative."

"What exactly do you need me to do?"

All eyes turned to Davis. The director thought for a minute. "We already have Becca's confessional telling us she wants to go home. Now we need her to tell you, and you have to act surprised—"

"And heartbroken," Patrick added.

"I'd settle for disappointed," Davis said. "Then you tell her you wish she would stay, but you understand, and you'll walk her out. Ryan will be waiting with a car to take her away."

It sounded so ominous. *Take her away.* Like he'd put Becca into that car and she'd just cease to exist. He supposed that for the men assembled before him that was basically true. Becca wanted to leave the show, so she was of no more use to them.

He played his part, sat beside her on a questionably clean bar floor while she sobbed that she was still in love with her college boyfriend and needed to go home. It was clear from the disjointed cadence of her speech that she'd had a few too many drinks, which was the likely cause of her abrupt decision to remove herself from the show. He hoped, for her sake, that she didn't regret her emotional confession once she sobered up. He thanked her for coming to meet him, told her she was a great woman who deserved to find her very own prince charming, and then escorted her outside to where Ryan waited to tuck Becca into a plain black car.

As Gavin watched the car drive away, his mind drifted back to the conversation with Zayne, to the disdain in his voice when he'd talked about Kyla, to how ready he was to invoke the steep fines in Becca's contract for misbehavior. If just talking to her ex-boyfriend had been a contract violation, what would Zayne do if he ever found out about what Gavin and Kyla had been doing off camera?

Something primal and possessive stirred in Gavin's chest, demanding that he protect Kyla from the nebulous threat. His hands clenched at this side as he tamped down the urge to find her, to pull her into his arms just to confirm for himself that she was still his.

But if Zayne got his wish and Kyla wasn't the last woman standing at the end of this, if she also got ushered into a black car and driven away along with her dreams of opening her own studio, no matter what Gavin wanted, would she still be his? It suddenly seemed vitally important that Kyla win, that he be able to give her that dream, and he could only do that if he could figure out how to keep Zayne from forcing him to send her home.

Patrick said he needed to be more demonstrative, to make sure the audience at home could tell who he liked. Maybe he'd been playing this wrong all along. Maybe instead of trying to downplay his attraction to Kyla in front of the cameras he should have been playing it up. And if the production captured hours of footage of Gavin and Kyla together, if he talked about her in all of his confessionals, if Davis and the rest of them made the story about *that*, then maybe, just maybe, Zayne wouldn't be able to send her home after all.

Chapter Twenty-two

Kyla hadn't realized how much she missed the smell of sugar and citrus that always hung in the air at The Corner Bakeshop until she and the other eligible ladies filed into the bakery the next morning. As PAs fussed with their hair and makeup and Davis oversaw the positioning of more lights in the corners of the room, Kyla caught sight of Tessa and her husband Jamie through the window of the doors to the kitchen. Tessa caught her eye and waved excitedly. Kyla smiled back and lifted her hand in acknowledgment.

"Who's that?" Christina asked.

"My boss," Kyla replied automatically. At the surprised expressions around her, she hesitantly continued. "Tessa owns the bakery, and her husband Jamie owns a restaurant in town. He's good friends with Gavin."

"I thought you were a photographer?" Roni asked, though she seemed more interested in eyeing the display of mini pavlovas in the glass case than in the conversation.

"I am. I'm still saving up to be able to open my own photography studio. In the meantime, I work here."

"In a bakery," Christina said in awe. "I could never. I'd eat my entire day's calories in raw cookie dough."

"Maybe she does," Lauren mused.

Kyla forced herself to breathe through the sting of the remark. *You've heard worse,* she reminded herself. *Her opinion doesn't matter. Your size does not define you.* She repeated the mantras she'd developed over years of therapy, letting each one wear away at Lauren's words until they were barely a scrape.

Ryan pushed through the bakery doors, followed closely by Tessa, Jamie, Gavin, and a slew of cameramen who fanned out around the room to capture the week's introduction from every possible angle.

"Ladies, welcome to *Sleeping Beauty* week!" The assembled women clapped on cue and waited for the rest of their instructions. Ryan introduced Tessa and Jamie, then turned to the women with a smile so wide it looked painful. "In one retelling of this classic fairytale, the three fairies attempt to make a towering birthday cake, with questionable success. This week, to determine who will get a one-on-one date with Gavin, you will work together in two teams to create your own towering birthday cakes. Gavin and this week's Hometown Helpers, Tessa and Jamie, will judge the cakes on both taste and height."

"But there's an uneven number of us," Christina protested.

"Our good friend Mrs. Kemp from *Cinderella* week will be joining us to even out the teams." Ryan held out a hand towards the kitchen. Nothing happened. "Mrs. Kemp!" he called. Still nothing. Ryan looked around, chuckling awkwardly.

"Aunt Judy!" Patrick bellowed from the side of the room.

A moment later, Judy Kemp's copper-colored hair peeked through the doors to the kitchen. "Sorry, dear, did you call for me? I was just whipping up a batch of my homemade chocolate frosting. Was I not supposed to do that?"

"I want to be on her team!" Lauren's hand shot in the air.

"Me too," Christina said, also raising her hand.

"Lovely!" Mrs. Kemp beamed. "Well, come along girls. This cake isn't going to bake itself."

Tessa and Jamie handed out aprons to the women—blue for Christina, Lauren, and Mrs. Kemp and pink for Kyla, Erika, and Roni—and then they were off.

The kitchen at The Corner Bakeshop had to be the most well-outfitted kitchen in all of Rhode Island. Kyla knew the giant mixers and endless row of ovens could be intimidating—hell, she'd been intimidated at first—but she knew this kitchen like the back of her hand. She knew that the last oven on the left ran about ten degrees hot, no matter what Tessa did to try to adjust it, and the air duct over the workstation on the far right could make finicky garnishes and gold leaf embellishments a challenge. She also knew most of Tessa's cake recipes by heart, so when Erika and Roni both expressed concern that they'd never baked anything that didn't come out of a box before, Kyla knew exactly what to do.

But most importantly, she knew Gavin's favorite cake.

She quickly jotted down the basics of the chocolate blackberry red wine cake, sending Erika off to gather wet ingredients while Roni began sifting together the dry and Kyla started a blackberry compote. In the back of the large walk in refrigerator, a container of blackberries sat on its usual shelf. She lifted the container and her eye caught a pink post-it note stuck to the shelf that had been hidden beneath the blackberries. There, in Tessa's neat handwriting, were the words "Don't forget the lemon zest." She smiled and added a bag of lemons to her haul.

Forty-five minutes later, Kyla, Erika, and Roni were pulling their first batch of cakes out of the oven and setting them in the blast chiller to cool, while Lauren and Christina argued over whether to decorate with fresh berries or sprinkles. As Kyla began teaching her team to level off the cooled cakes and cut them each into three even layers, Mrs. Kemp retrieved her team's cakes from the oven with an "Oh, dear." Their cakes were somehow both underbaked and burnt—a combination that was actually impressive in its awfulness.

"I suppose we could start again." Mrs. Kemp placed the disappointing cakes on the counter.

"We don't have time to start again." Christina pointed at the giant countdown clock that had been set up across the kitchen.

"It's fine. It's not like he's really going to eat it anyway. They never let us eat on camera. All that stuff about taste was just for the audience. It just has to be the tallest." Lauren glanced over at Kyla's team, who had moved on to crumb coating each layer while Roni checked to see if their last batch of cakes was ready.

"That's the spirit," Mrs. Kemp said. She took up the cake pans and brought them back to their station, shooting Kyla a wink as they passed.

That wink settled in Kyla's stomach like a lead balloon. She knew Mrs. Kemp to be a decent baker—her pies were always in the top three at the spring bazaar pie contest—and, as the only one of her teammates who actually ate cake, her team had used her recipe. It should have come out just fine. Unless of course Mrs. Kemp had altered her recipe, left out an egg or reduced the amount of baking soda…

Shit. Mrs. Kemp was throwing the competition, and she wasn't even being subtle about it. When she got caught, they'd all blame Kyla. If she was going to come out of this show with any hope of leveraging her fifteen minutes of fame to help her open the studio, she could not get a villain edit.

But what was she supposed to do? She'd been around Aster Bay long enough to know that no one stopped Mrs. Kemp or her friends once they decided to do something. She would just have to hope that no one else saw through Mrs. Kemp's thin attempts to conceal her sabotage.

Another hour later and Kyla's team's cake was assembled—a six tier tower made up of twelve cakes, blackberry compote, and buttercream frosting topped with a stack of cupcakes, multiple dowels placed strategically throughout the cake the way Tessa had taught Kyla over the last year, each layer meticulously decorated with dripping chocolate ganache. Just like Gavin liked.

Kyla stood back and wiped her forehead with the back of her hand, leaving behind a streak of powdered sugar. On the other side of the kitchen, Lauren and Christina were adding entire bowls of Mrs. Kemp's chocolate frosting in a semi-sculpted mound as a last-ditch effort to eke out a few more inches. But it wouldn't matter. Their cake was at least six inches shorter than Kyla's team's cake.

The buzzer on the countdown clock went off just as Ryan and Gavin pushed through the swinging kitchen doors, followed closely by Tessa and Jamie. Tessa caught Kyla's eye and mouthed "wow." Kyla couldn't help the burst of warmth in her chest, happiness at making Tessa proud sloughing away some of her exhaustion.

"Ladies, you've all done an incredible job," Ryan said, eyeing the two cakes. "Gavin, Jamie, and Tessa will now judge your cakes to pick a winning team. The first criteria is height."

Gavin chuckled. "There's no contest on that one. The pink team's cake is clearly taller than the blue team's." He flashed an apologetic smile at Lauren and Christina. "Sorry, ladies."

"Oh, heavens, don't fuss on our account." Mrs. Kemp looped an arm through Lauren's on one side and Christina's on the other, pulling them closer to her with a jolt and a smile. "We had so much darn fun, isn't that right, girls?"

Christina and Lauren muttered their agreement.

"Let's see how it tastes, shall we?" Ryan gestured towards the blue team's cake.

"Our cake is an homage to reality TV dating shows everywhere," Lauren said proudly.

"With homemade chocolate frosting," Christina added. "Lots."

Tessa carefully cut a piece from the bottom layer of the

cake, frosting squeezing out from all angles with every pass of the knife. Jamie's jaw clenched as he fought to keep his face neutral and they each took a tentative bite of the cake. Jamie immediately reeled back, going for the glass of water that had been preset for them. Tessa's eyebrows scrunched together as she slowly chewed and swallowed, but Gavin's eyes went wide and he fought back a cough.

"Interesting flavor," Gavin said as he clutched his own glass of water.

"Is that rosewater?" Tessa asked.

"It is," Lauren said through a smug smile. "That was my idea. Because there are always roses on reality dating shows."

"it's very…floral," Gavin offered.

"Soap like, even," Tessa said. "Too much rosewater and your entire bake will taste like you're eating Mrs. Kemp's potpourri."

"I do love my roses," Mrs. Kemp said, smiling.

"Thank you, ladies." Gavin struggled to smile between sips of water.

Next, they moved to Kyla's team's cake, Erika and Roni shifting their weight with excitement. Gavin's eyes swept over the cake before they landed on Kyla with a smile.

"Can you tell us about your cake?" Ryan asked.

"This is a blackberry red wine chocolate cake with blackberry compote and buttercream frosting," Kyla said.

"And chocolate ganache," Erika added, licking a bit of ganache off her finger.

"No flowers were harmed in the making of our cake," Roni said with a smirk.

Gavin chuckled while Tessa cut a slice of the bottom layer. Kyla held her breath as they each took a bite, not releasing it until Gavin groaned, his eyes dropping closed. "God, that's good."

Jamie went in for a second bite. "It's delicious. Great balance of flavors."

"I especially appreciate the lemon zest in the compote. Really enhances the flavor of the blackberry," Tessa said with a mischievous grin.

Gavin knocked Jamie's fork out of the way and scooped up the last bite of cake for himself. "I think we have a winning team."

Erika and Roni threw their arms out and pulled Kyla into a group hug, but Kyla never took her eyes off Gavin.

"This isn't fair!" Lauren cried from the other side of the kitchen. "This whole thing is rigged." She waited until all eyes—and cameras—were on her before continuing, pointing at Kyla with a fierce jab of the cake server. "She is a professional baker. This is where she works, and those are her friends. She's had an unfair advantage this whole time. I wouldn't be surprised if Mrs. Kemp sabotaged us just to make her look good."

"Heavens no! Why would I do such a thing?" Mrs. Kemp pressed a scandalized hand to her chest.

Ryan glanced uneasily at Zayne and Patrick.

"You're just pissed that your cake sucked," Roni said.

"She's manipulating the game!" Lauren protested.

"This isn't a game," Gavin said, his voice icy as it cut through the bickering. "This is my *life.*"

Lauren recoiled but she shot a look at Zayne. "Aren't you going to do something?" When he didn't respond, she threw her apron on the floor and stormed out of the kitchen. Zayne followed, cursing under his breath.

"Everyone take a break," Davis said. Gesturing to two cameramen, he pointed at the door through which Zayne and Lauren had disappeared. "Follow them."

In the confusion that followed, as the crew and the other women descended to get a slice of Kyla's cake, Tessa appeared at her side, tugging on her hand and pulling her into the walk-in refrigerator while no one else was watching.

"Spill. Tell me *everything.*" She leaned against the shelf that housed bricks of butter and cream cheese.

Kyla looked away, glancing around the walk in. "You know Gavin," she hedged.

"Yeah, but I don't *know* him." Tessa bobbed her eyebrows suggestively and Kyla nearly choked on her own tongue. She recovered quickly enough that Tessa didn't seem to notice as she barreled on with her questions. "Is it awkward? Dating him?"

"I thought it would be but—"

"I *knew* it!" she crowed. "I've been telling Jamie for *a year* that you two had chemistry."

"What? No, I mean we—before—It never occurred to me to—"

"Oh really? It never occurred to you that you might have more in common with Gavin than you do with his son? Not even when you were working together on the Food and Wine Festival, or the proposal for this show?"

Kyla swallowed hard and tried to ignore the strange sensation prickling down her spine. Did Tessa really think they had chemistry?

"I want details," Tessa said.

She hesitated, but only for a moment. She trusted Tessa implicitly and it would be so good to talk to someone about the show, someone who knew her and Gavin both.

"We hooked up." Tessa let out an excited squeak. "Off camera. But it's just sex."

Tessa's eyes went wide. "When? Where?"

"On our day off from filming. He asked me to meet him at this club in Providence and…" She blushed, remembering the way he'd touched her, the filthy things he'd growled in her ear as she came.

"Olympus?" Tessa asked with a knowing smile.

"You know about Olympus?"

"Don't act so shocked. But this isn't about me. Gavin's going to pick you and you're going to ride off into your reality-TV-fame-colored sunset."

"I don't know."

"But you said—"

"A couple of orgasms doesn't mean he's going to pick me," she said, fighting back the stinging in her nose. "Just the other day I asked him about what happens when this is over, and he didn't want to talk about it. And the fact that we've only hooked up at a sex club, or one time on a desk, I think it's pretty clear that he's only interested in sex. He's just keeping me on the show because he knows I need the money and exposure to open my studio."

"Gavin wouldn't do that. He wouldn't have crossed that line with you if he didn't want something more," Tessa said.

"How do you know? None of us have ever seen Gavin want something more than casual sex."

Tessa shook her head. "No, I don't believe that. I've seen the way he looks at you."

"How does he look at me?" Her mouth went dry as she pictured the heat in his eyes when he'd pinned her against that door at Olympus.

"Like you're the only person in the room." Tessa took her hand, squeezing it. "He's been looking at you that way for as long as I've known you."

Kyla wanted so badly to believe her, to think that she and Gavin could have a real future, not just stolen nights together. But he'd made it clear he didn't want to talk about the future. What would happen when the cameras left town and Brodie inevitably came home from California? When push came to shove, Brodie was his family and she was just his ex-girlfriend. This whole thing was doomed before it even began.

"I dated his son for *a year*. Brodie will never be okay with his dad and I being involved," she said miserably.

"It'll be a challenge to navigate at first, but that's what you have me for. I am a master of complicated relationships," Tessa said.

"That's different."

"Why? I married my father's best friend. Why can't you marry—"

"No one's talking about marriage," Kyla squeaked.

Tessa smirked. "Of course not. Why can't you *date* your ex-boyfriend's father? Unless you're still hung up on Brodie."

"Definitely not."

Tessa looked her in the eyes, taking both of her hands in hers the way she did when she had serious news to deliver. "Look, if I know Gavin at all—and I think I do—he always puts what he wants last. Always. He'll need to be one thousand percent certain that you want him, too, for more than sexy times at Olympus, before he'll ever let himself believe there's even a possibility for more. You have to tell him what you want."

"And if he can't give me what I want?" she asked, not sure she wanted an answer to that question.

"Then I guess you'll have a decision to make."

Confessional Interviews
Recorded individually, edited together into one clip

Christina: No, I don't think Kyla's right for Gavin.

Roni: I mean, it's a little weird that she dated his son and now she's here with him.

Lauren: Gavin's not going to want to bang the same chick his son used to bang. Who wants sloppy seconds?

Erika: I'm not really sure. I don't think they broke up that long ago.

Lauren: Is she even over the son yet? Or is she just rebounding with Gavin? And what happens when his son finds out? I know I wouldn't want to be a homewrecker.

Christina: I don't know that I'd say the baking competition was *rigged* but I also don't think it's a surprise that Kyla won. It doesn't really seem fair that the show picked baking as a competition when one of the girls is a professional baker.

Roni: I guess the rest of us are at a bit of a disadvantage. She knew him before the show. She knows this town and the people who have come to help advise him.

Lauren: She *works* for his friend's wife. Nothing about their advice is unbiased and I would hate to see Gavin miss out on a really wonderful woman because Kyla has somehow convinced everyone to help her win.

Zayne: [off-screen] Are you saying she's manipulating the Hometown Helpers?

Lauren: I would never accuse anyone of something so unethical. But when great girls like Mandy get sent home and Kyla continues to get alone time that the rest of us haven't had, it makes you start to wonder.

Erika: No, I'm not mad that Kyla got the one-on-one date. We used her recipe and her expertise to make that cake. She was the MVP so she deserved the date… Of course, I wish I had gotten some alone time with Gavin. I don't feel like he knows who I am yet.

Gavin: There are some women that I feel much more connected to than others. Part of that is just time and part of it is personality.

Patrick: [off-screen] Do you think Kyla has an unfair advantage?

Gavin: [pause] There's nothing unfair about it. Even if we hadn't known each other before this, she's the one I would be most interested in.

Lauren: They don't have anything in common.

Gavin: We have the most in common. Obviously we've worked together so we have a shared interest in marketing, a shared investment in our town. I like that she's more comfortable in a sweatshirt than a ballgown.

Christina: I do wonder if she's just trying to make the rest of us look bad by wearing that college sweatshirt all the time. Some of us didn't go to college and every time she wears that sweatshirt it's like she's trying to say she's better than us.

Patrick: [off-screen] So Kyla's a front runner?

Gavin: There isn't even a race. In my mind, Kyla's already the one standing with me at the end.

Chapter Twenty-three

The room was pitch black. A thin band of red lights lined the edge of the room, showing the way to the exit but not emitting enough light to illuminate anything else.

Gavin was led to a table in the center of the room by a PA wearing night vision goggles. He knew from the drive through Aster Bay that they were in the old carpet factory on the waterfront, but he'd never been inside. According to Patrick, the network had rented the room for this specific date, converting it into a restaurant of sorts, though he and Kyla had both been warned not to eat anything while filming as the chewing sounds would mess up the audio.

He thanked the PA as he lowered himself into the waiting chair, reaching out with his hand to feel for the edge of the table. It was covered in some kind of cottony floor length tablecloth, and his hand skimmed over the plate of cold pasta on the table. He wiped his hand on the tablecloth.

A few moments later, shuffling to his left indicated that Kyla was also being ushered into the room. As she lowered herself into her chair, the creaking of the wood seemed to echo in the concrete room. "Gavin?"

He reached out a hand, moving it slowly through the air until it connected with her arm. "I'm here."

Her fingers gripped his, clasping their hands together as he was hit with a wave of her lavender and vanilla scent. His cock thickened in his pants and he scooted his chair closer to the table, hoping the long tablecloth would conceal his poorly timed erection.

"I hate the dark," she said, her voice shaking slightly.

Gavin reached over until he found the bottom of her chair, gripping the wooden frame and pulling her closer to him. She squeaked at the sudden movement, her hand tightening in his, but now she was close enough for him to wrap his arm around her shoulder, to pull her against him. He brushed his lips over the crown of her head. "I've got you."

She scooted closer, leaning against him as his fingers stroked her shoulder. "Who the hell thinks of these dates?" she grumbled.

He laughed. "Apparently it's supposed to represent when the evil queen puts the entire castle to sleep after Sleeping Beauty pricks her finger."

"I never watched that movie. Sleeping Beauty or Snow White."

"Why's that?"

"Both of those women are unconscious, and a random prince kisses them, and we're supposed to think it's romantic and not assault. Patriarchy sucks."

"It does."

"Sorry, I just totally killed the mood. Let's talk about something else."

"Okay. What do you want to talk about?"

She shifted against him, the movement bringing their clasped hands to rest high on his thigh. If she stretched out her little finger, she'd brush against his erection. His cock kicked at the thought.

"Tell me about your parents," she said.

His fingers wandered over her shoulder to stroke her collar

bone as he spoke, a burst of masculine pride blooming in his chest when she sucked in a shaky breath at the teasing touch.

"I don't remember my father. For as long as I can remember it was just me, mom, and Caleb." He buried his nose in her hair, grounding himself with her scent as he waded through the story he'd been told but couldn't remember. "Dad worked construction. When we were little, mom stayed home with Caleb and me while Dad went all over the state, building bridges and high-rise apartment buildings and whatever else."

"What happened?" Her lips were pressed against his chest so he felt the question as much as he heard it.

"There was an accident. I was only four at the time, but the story goes that he was digging out the foundation of a new self-storage building and his excavator tipped over with him inside it. I don't know if anyone really knows why. But he didn't survive."

She wrapped her arm around him, burrowing into his chest. "I'm so sorry, Gav."

He held her close, accepting her comfort though the facts of his father's death had long ago ceased to hurt. "Thanks. I wish like hell that I remembered him, that he could see me, meet my son."

He trailed off. It was the first time he'd invoked Brodie since he'd taken her to Olympus, and he waited for the awkwardness to settle over them, but she only held him tighter, pressing her lips to his chest. He barreled ahead, feeling somehow lighter, like he'd shone a light in a dark corner to find there was nothing there.

"But mom was everything. She went to soccer games and school plays and packed lunches and taught us how to ride our bikes. She lost the love of her life and she poured all that love back into my brother and me."

"She sounds incredible," Kyla said.

"I think she'd like you." The words left his lips before he'd really thought them through.

He felt her shift against him, the slide of her cheek against his chest as she tilted her head up towards him. He wished he could see her face. Instead, he lifted his hand and cradled her cheek, sliding his thumb along her bottom lip to feel the curve of her smile.

"I'd like to meet her," she said.

Gavin's heart pounded in his chest as he pictured bringing Kyla home to meet his mother, sitting around the table in her kitchen while they ate cherry pie. His mother would want to know all about Kyla's photography, would rope her into teaching her how to use the different settings on her iPhone camera. He could see it so clearly, the two women he loved most learning to love each other.

Loved.

He let the word wash over him, let the truth of it knit itself into the marrow of his bones.

He loved Kyla.

He'd loved her for a long time, longer than he should admit. And that wasn't going to change, no matter what happened with the show.

He wanted to tell her, to pull her into his lap and kiss her until she couldn't possibly question the way he felt about her. But this was not the time or the place. Instead, he swallowed down the words and skated his thumb over her lip one more time.

"What about your parents?"

The smile fell from her lips. "My father is the chief financial officer of a shipping company in Manhattan. My mother is his trophy wife—the sister of a business partner."

"Do you have any siblings?"

"Nope, just me. Which made it so much worse when I wasn't what they wanted me to be."

He stiffened, his hold on her tightening. "What did they want you to be?"

She sighed. "Like them. I was supposed to get a degree in

something they deemed worthy—communications or political science or world economics if I was ambitious. And then I was supposed to move back to New Jersey and let them marry me off to whichever son of whichever business partner would be the most advantageous for dad's company."

"I didn't know people did things like that anymore." He struggled to wrap his brain around this alternate life Kyla could have been living, all the while he worked like hell to not be jealous of the nameless, faceless hypothetical man she was meant to marry.

"It's very common in my parents' social circles," she said. "My parents expected me to comply, to be polite and charming but never the center of attention, to be smart but not so smart that I'd show up the boys, to be a pretty little bargaining chip. Of course, they didn't tell me any of that. I found out when our housekeeper quit and she told me everything."

"They were planning your life without telling you?"

She barked out a bitter laugh. "Why would they tell me? I was just a chess piece; I was never important enough to have a voice in my own future. They haven't spoken to me since I decided to stay in Aster Bay after graduation and ruined their plans. But it wouldn't have happened the way they wanted anyway. I was never quiet enough, never obedient enough, never thin enough."

He growled, gathering her in his arms and pulling her into his lap. He took her face in his hands, pulling her down to him until their foreheads rested against each other so she could feel the heat of his words even if she couldn't see the sincerity on his face.

"You are enough. In all ways. Always." His voice was rough and gritty as he tried to slow his heartbeat and tamp down the primal urge to find her parents and tear them apart for making her question her value. "Say it."

"What?"

"'I am enough.' Say it."

Tears fell from her eyes, slipping between his fingers, and he wiped them away with his thumbs. "I am enough," she whispered.

He tilted her chin and brought her mouth to his, kissing her deeply. It was too rough for this moment, that primal beast in his chest clawing to get out as he slid his tongue between her lips, making her his with breath and lips and teeth. He was a man undone, lost to the taste of salt on her lips and the scent of vanilla in her hair and the little keening noises she made at the back of her throat as she melted against him.

He kissed down her throat, sucking on her pulse point and nipping at the place where her neck met her shoulder. "Little goddess," he murmured against her skin.

She dug her hands into his hair and pulled his mouth back to hers, kissing him back with as much urgency as he'd kissed her, grinding down against his cock, already aching for her. He slid his hands up her back, fumbling for the zipper at the back of her dress, when suddenly the room was flooded with red light and they pulled away from each other, dazed and blinking.

Patrick appeared at the edge of Gavin's line of sight and he instinctively tucked Kyla's head down against his shoulder. The producer cleared his throat and shifted on his feet uncomfortably. "I think we've got all we need."

Fuck. In the dark, Gavin had completely forgotten about the cameras, the microphones, the swarm of other people in the room now exchanging knowing smirks as they gathered their equipment. None of that had been meant for the cameras.

"Good work," Patrick said, tilting his head towards Gavin before he turned to go.

Kyla looked up at him, her eyes hooded with residual lust as the commotion around them broke into the little bubble they'd created. He cupped a hand over the microphone on his lapel and then did the same to hers, pressing his lips to her ear.

"Tonight," he whispered. "Come to my room."

A PA held a hand out to her. "Ms. Mitchell?" She waited for Kyla to accept her help to leave.

Kyla held his gaze for another minute, scratching her nails over his scalp as she removed her hand from his hair. She gave the smallest of nods and he thought he might break apart from the joy of it. He watched as the PA led her away, so entranced by the sight of her swaying slightly on unsteady legs that he hardly noticed Zayne had arrived at his other side.

With a sneer, the producer leaned close enough that no one else would hear him. "Well played."

Chapter Twenty-four

Gavin's stomach was in knots as he was driven back to The Barclay in the limo with Patrick and Zayne, the silence around them like a tangible thing. The two producers sat on one side of the car, Gavin on the other, and with each moment that passed, Gavin's anger grew.

"What the fuck did you mean?" he asked when he couldn't take it anymore.

Zayne glanced up from his phone where he was busy playing some match three game, then glanced at Patrick. "Do you know what he's talking about?"

"I'm right here," Gavin barked. "What the fuck did you mean 'well played'?"

Zayne lowered his phone, amusement pulling his mouth into a smug grin that Gavin wanted to punch off his face. "You've finally picked a girl. It's the wrong girl, but I think you know that or you wouldn't have gone to so much trouble to give us such a show tonight."

"None of that was for you," he said through gritted teeth.

"Wasn't it?"

"Zayne," Patrick said, a warning in his tone.

Zayne leaned forward, resting his elbows on his knees. "Let me lay it out for you, lover boy. This is my show, and all of our paychecks are cashed on Pure Sexxy's dime. They want a sex kitten with an Instagram following as their next spokesperson so that's what they're going to get. You want to fuck with my show, I'll make sure the whole goddamn country sees Kyla as the villain of the season, no matter how many heartfelt conversations you have or how often you stick your tongue down your son's girlfriend's throat."

"Ex-girlfriend," Gavin said, as if that was the part of Zayne's speech that mattered.

"We'll see." Zayne leaned back in his seat, effectively dismissing him.

Gavin wanted to ask what the hell that meant but the car pulled to a stop outside The Barclay and Zayne was out the door and gone before Gavin could say a word. He made to go after him when Patrick laid a hand on his arm.

"He's not worth it," Patrick said. "And the more you goad him, the more he's going to find ways to screw with you."

"And what the fuck are you doing about it?" Gavin demanded.

Patrick sighed. "I'm doing what I can."

"Do better," Gavin said as he stormed out of the car.

Thankfully, they were done filming for the night so he didn't have a cameraman dogging his every step, but when he entered his suite at The Barclay and his eyes fell on the cameras mounted in the corner of his bedroom, his brain short circuited. If they made Kyla seem like a villain, the bad press would destroy any chance she had to get her studio off the ground, even if he did manage to keep her on the show to the end. Before he knew what he was doing, he was standing on top of the dresser, ripping the cameras off the wall.

He caught his breath, his heart rate slowing and a destroyed camera still clasped in his hand, as he reached for his phone and fired off a text.

Gavin: I don't want a fling.

Gavin: I want what Jamie and Tessa have.
Gavin: I want Kyla.

Jamie: Halle-fuckin-luiah! He finally admits it!

Ethan: Did you really just type that out? Nerd.

Jamie: Excuse me, our friend is having a revelation. Focus, please.

Gavin: I know Brodie will be mad but he's an adult and maybe it's okay if he's mad.

Baz: It's about fucking time.

Jamie: Too bad you're not both on a reality show right now where your literal only objective is to date.
Jamie: Oh wait…

Gavin: One of the producers doesn't want me to choose her at the end. Something about the sponsor not wanting her.

Baz: Fuck the producers. It's your life.

Gavin: They have veto power. They can override my decision.

Ethan: Have you told Kyla?

Gavin: No. She has to win. She needs the money to open her studio.

Jamie: She's not going to care about the money. She cares about you.

Gavin: She deserves to open her studio. And I can give that to her if I can just figure out a way to get the producer to back off.

Ethan: You have to tell her.

Gavin: I ripped a camera off the wall.

Jamie: As one does.
Jamie: Though that hardly seems helpful.

Baz: Just get through the next few weeks without fucking it up and I can help her figure out the finances once this thing is over.

Gavin: I think I'm falling for her.

Jamie: You think?

Baz: We know.

Ethan: Tell her, not us.

It was just before midnight when Kyla tapped at the double doors that led from Gavin's balcony into his bathroom. The late June air, warm and thick with humidity, was tinged with salt from the ocean, leaving its taste on her tongue. It only took a moment for Gavin to throw open the doors. His eyes softened when he saw her standing there, still in the little black cocktail dress she'd worn for their date.

Her eyes raked over him in the warm glow of the room behind him. He'd changed into gray sweatpants, slung low on his hips, and a form fitting black t-shirt that clung to his biceps. His bare feet on the tiled floor somehow felt more intimate than anything else, though.

She stepped into the bathroom and he closed the door behind her, immediately backing her up against it until she was caged in between the cool glass and the heat of his body. He planted his hands on either side of her head and kissed her, hungrily, as though he hadn't just kissed her only a few hours earlier. As though she wouldn't let him kiss her any time he wanted.

"My little goddess," he said, lips moving over her throat, his stubble scraping against the sensitive skin.

He caught her hand and began pulling her after him towards the bedroom, but she dug in her heels to bring them to a stop. "Gavin, the cameras…"

He smiled wryly. "There are no cameras." He gestured to the trash bin tucket beneath the sink, to a mess of wires and metal. "Not anymore."

"What did you do?" she asked, laughing.

"They don't get any more of us than we want them to have." He bracketed her face with his hands. "Earlier, on our date, I forgot the cameras were there. I got carried away."

"Me too. I probably wouldn't have talked so much about my parents if I'd remembered."

He winced. "I'm sorry."

"It's not your fault."

"I asked you."

"I wanted you to know." She planted a kiss on his palm. "I want you to know me."

He kissed her again, softer this time but somehow more urgent, his tongue sweeping over the seam of her lips until she parted for him. With an arm around her lower back, he walked them back through the door into the bedroom, never taking his lips from hers.

"Tell me what else you want," he said between kisses.

Her mind felt fuzzy, words a vague concept when Gavin's lips were on her skin, his hands roaming over her body. He squeezed her ass and her cunt throbbed with need. How was she supposed to form words when he was touching her like he owned her? Why was it so hard to tell him what she wanted?

"Tell me how to make you feel good." His voice was like temptation itself.

"I—I'm not sure," she stammered as his thigh slid between her legs and pressed at the apex of her thighs.

"You liked my fingers?" He ghosted the digits in question over her cloth-covered mound.

"Yes," she confirmed as she ground against his thigh.

"And my mouth?"

"Yes."

He reached under her skirt and pulled her panties down as he dropped to his knees. "Hold that dress up, sweetheart, so you can see when I make you come on my tongue."

She hardly had time to process his command before he buried his face between her legs, licking and sucking like he'd never tasted anything sweeter than her. He held her open as he ate her, alternating between licking into her channel and flicking his tongue over her clit. It was so warm and wet, so filthy she thought she ought to be ashamed of the way she ground herself against his tongue, but it felt too good to stop.

As her orgasm grew closer, he moved a hand to her ass, using pressure there to hold her upright, locked between his hand and his face. "Tell me what you want," he demanded before grazing her clit with his teeth.

She gasped at the new sensation. "More of that."

She felt his smile between her thighs and he dragged his teeth over her again. She moaned, rocking against him, loving the roughness of his facial hair between her thighs. Then he sucked her clit into his mouth, drawing on it in long, hard pulls and she shuddered, her legs nearly giving way.

He pulled his face away, his chin glistening with her wetness, and with his hands on her hips, guided her to sit on the edge of the bed. He pressed his hands to her knees and spread her open for him.

"I wish you could see how beautiful this pussy is," he said, something like wonder in his tone. "So plump and pink and eager for me." He glanced up at her as he dragged his thumb over her swollen clit and she jolted in response. He grinned wickedly. "It's time to come, little goddess. I need you to come on my face and then, if you're a very good girl, I'll let you come on my cock."

He sucked her clit back into his mouth and she dug her hands into his hair, gasping and holding him to her as he drew her orgasm from her. Her release came as a surprise, her clit pulsing against his tongue as he drank down her pleasure with each long, hard pull on the swollen bud.

As her climax receded, he sat back on his heels, a look on his face like he already missed her taste. He ran the back of his hand over his mouth, then pulled her to her feet, gathering her into his arms for a bruising kiss that tasted like her pleasure. His erection pressed against her belly and she fumbled for the drawstrings on his sweatpants, eager to push them down his hips and finally see all of him.

He spun her in his arms and kissed the nape of her neck, pulling her back against his front so that she felt that solid ridge against the cleft of her ass. She wriggled against him and he huffed out a laugh, gathering her hair and lifting it over one shoulder.

"Patience, sweetheart."

"I don't want to be patient."

He drew down the zipper of her dress, kissing each inch of newly revealed skin as he went, until the dress fell away, leaving her in only her bra. Then he dispensed of that, too, and once again she was completely naked against his fully clothed form.

"I know what I want next," she said.

He spun her back around, his hand at her hip flexing. "Tell me."

She gripped the hem of his t-shirt and drew it over his head, tossing it aside. Amusement tugged at the corner of his lips as she hooked her thumbs in the waistband of his sweatpants and shoved them over his hips. He stepped out of the fabric pooled at his feet and wrapped his hand around the base of his cock. She covered his hand with her own and drew their palms up the length of him. He sucked in a breath as she traced the veins up the side with her thumb. When she ran that same thumb over the flared ridge of his crown, swiping it through the bead of precum pooling at his tip, he hissed.

"Tell me what you want," he said again, the words rough.

"I want you to fuck me."

He captured her lips, guiding her down onto the bed and crawling over her, his weight settling heavily between her thighs. As he kissed her, he rocked against her, the broad head of his cock sliding through her folds and nudging against her clit with each thrust.

He reached over to the bedside table and produced a condom. Sitting back on his heels, he ripped the foil packet open, but before he could slide the latex over himself, she sat up and leaned forward, taking his cock between her lips in one smooth motion that had him gripping her hair with a stinging hold and cursing. "Fuck, sweetheart."

She slowly drew back until only his tip remained in her mouth. She sucked lightly and he swore again before she lowered herself once more, taking as much of him as she could before he hit the back of her throat. She stayed there, savoring the stinging in her eyes and the musk of him on her tongue, savoring the fizzy feeling in her blood at how undone he seemed—because of her. This beautiful man, twenty years her senior and so much more experienced, was cursing and shuddering because of *her*. She'd never felt more powerful, more wanted.

Slowly she pulled off, taking the condom from his shaking hand and rolling the latex down over his cock. "I wanted to taste you too."

He gathered her in his arms, guiding her back down to the bed and hovering over her, resting on his elbows. "Such a good fucking girl," he said as he thrust into her, filling her with one smooth motion that drove the breath from her lungs.

She dug her nails into his back, crying out as he drove into her again and again, and she canted her hips up to meet him for each thrust.

"Fuck, you feel so good." He buried his head in her neck as he pistoned into her. "I want you to come on my cock, little goddess. I want to feel you squeeze me."

"Yes," she breathed, already feeling the tendrils of her orgasm gathering again as the head of his cock dragged against that hidden place behind her clit. "I want that."

"I'm going to make you come until I'm satisfied you've had enough. Until your pussy knows who it belongs to."

She wasn't sure if it was a promise or a warning.

"It belongs to you," she whimpered, her thighs beginning to shake.

He wound a hand between them and used his thumb to stroke her over-sensitive clit and she cried out as the orgasm ripped through her, clenching around his cock as he fucked her through it. As her orgasm receded, he redoubled his efforts.

"Again," he commanded.

She shook with the force of her second climax, her muscles bunching with the power of her pleasure as he tore another orgasm from her. He drank her cries from her lips.

"Again."

She sobbed into his kiss. "I can't."

"You can."

He fucked her harder, lifting her leg and resting her calf against his shoulder. At this new angle, he drove deeper inside her, stroking against parts of her that had never been touched, his pelvis dragging against her clit with each thrust.

"I knew that first day, that first moment, that you should be mine," he said.

Another orgasm gathered at the base of her spine and she nearly cried with the impending weight of it, fire tearing down her legs and burning the soles of her feet as he pushed her closer and closer to this unknown precipice.

"And you *are* mine now, Kyla," he grunted as he worked himself deeper. "And I'm yours." She sucked in a breath at the implication of his words, but she was too far gone to answer, her climax already bearing down on her. "My fingers, my tongue, my cock." Her back arched off the bed, her stomach contracting, her calf muscles straining against his shoulder. "They're yours now, little goddess. They've always been yours."

She cried out his name as her pleasure tore through her, a violent release that felt as though she'd shake apart if he weren't holding her so tightly, weren't filling her so completely. He dropped her leg and withdrew from her, discarding the condom, and pumping his hand over his cock.

She reached up and joined her hand with his, sliding over the slick length of his cock until he jolted in her grasp, hot streams of cum painting her stomach and pussy in thick ribbons of white. She felt each drop like a brand on her skin. His cock throbbed against her palm and she continued stroking, drawing every last bit from the angry red tip, until he twined his fingers with hers, both sticky with his cum, pressing their hands into the bed beside her head and kissed her.

He glanced down between them at the mess they'd made on her body, breathing hard. "I didn't think it was possible for you to look more beautiful, but you've never been prettier than you are now, covered in my cum."

She felt the blush down to her toes, and she watched as he dragged a finger through the stripes on her belly, gathering the proof of his release, and then pressed it to her lips. She opened eagerly for him, sucking the pad of his finger clean with swipes of her tongue. When he bent to kiss her, she knew he was tasting himself on her lips.

"I'm yours," he repeated, using his hand to smooth the hair back from her forehead, the words soft and full of wonder.

He'd promised her his body, every part, and that should be enough. It would have to be enough. So when she responded, she didn't say that she wanted to promise him more than her body, that she wanted more than just his body in return.

She simply said, "And I'm yours."

Chapter Twenty-five

"Gavin," Kyla whispered.

He wrapped his arm more tightly around her waist and pulled her back against him, nestling the soft curve of her ass against his groin. She giggled and squirmed in his arms.

"Gavin, I need to go."

"Five more minutes." He dragged his nose along the back of her neck. But even as he said it, he knew he was lying. His cock was already half hard just from the lavender and vanilla scent of her. Five more minutes would never be enough.

"I need to get back to my room before Erika wakes up." She pushed back against him, grinding her ass against his growing erection.

He grinned and scraped his teeth over her neck. "I'll be quick."

"You will not," she laughed, rolling onto her back.

He settled on top of her, his hips holding her thighs wide and his hands planted on either side of her head, caging her in. "I like having you in my bed," he said against her lips. "You should always be in my bed."

"You're not making it easy to leave," she groaned, nipping at his lower lip.

He smiled. "Good." He rolled off her, though, propping himself up on his elbow as she reluctantly sat up and pulled on her underwear.

"We should probably talk." She glanced nervously over her shoulder as she shimmied into her dress. "About what happens next, I mean."

He came up on his knees, lifting her hair over one shoulder and zipping up her dress. "What happens next is you go back to your room and I do my best to resist the urge to strip you bare and take you right there on the ballroom floor when I see you in a few hours." He loved the way she shivered at his gravelly words.

She turned in the circle of his arms, planting her hands on his chest. His heart pounded against her palm. "You know what I meant." Her eyes focused on her fingers as they swirled in his smattering of chest hair.

"I do." He caught her hand and brought it to his lips, pressing a kiss to her palm. "What are you concerned about exactly?"

She bit her lip, and he could practically see the wheels turning in her head.

"Tell me, Kyla."

"I don't want to come between you and Brodie." Her words tumbled out in a rush. She glanced at him with wide, achingly earnest eyes, and he gathered her into his arms, pressing kisses against her hair.

"You won't," he said with more confidence than he felt.

"You think he'll be okay with this?"

"I don't know." His heart twisted with that uncertainty, but he caught her chin and tilted her face up to his, wanting her to see his eyes when he said the next part. "I've waited over a decade to find someone that makes me feel the way I feel about you. I would do anything for my son, but his wounded pride isn't going to stop me from being with you."

She searched his eyes. "What if he asks you to?"

Just the idea of Brodie asking him to give Kyla up felt like a stab to his chest, a knife sliding between his ribs and twisting until the bone splintered, but he schooled his face into an expression of calm confidence. "I'm not giving you up that easily, little goddess."

She lifted up on her tiptoes and pressed a chaste kiss to his lips.

"Let me worry about Brodie," he continued, "and you focus on what color you're going to paint the walls of your new studio when the show is over."

She smiled, sliding her arms around to his back. "I already know. Thunderstorm. It's a dark charcoal gray with navy blue undertones. I've had the paint swatch on my bulletin board for months."

"Sounds perfect."

As though summoned by her mention of the paint color, he watched as her eyes bright blue eyes turned stormy, narrowing as she drew her bottom lip back between her teeth. He ran his thumb over her lip to release it.

"What is it?" he asked.

"Some of the girls were talking the other day. They think Zayne is playing favorites. That he's trying to make sure Lauren wins."

Tell her.

No, just take care of it. There's no need to worry her when you're going to handle it.

"You've talked to him more than we have," she continued, oblivious to the voices arguing in his head. "Do you think he's really manipulating the show?"

"You don't need to worry about that," he hedged.

"I don't think he likes me very much. Roni says there's always someone who the production makes look like a villain. If Zayne decided that was me, it could really mess things up for me, for opening the studio, I mean."

He brushed his lips against hers, silently promising himself that he would make sure that never happened. "It'll be fine, Ky. I promise."

She studied his eyes for a moment before shaking her head with a huffed laugh. "You're right. It's probably nothing. It's easy to get paranoid when you're filming all the time."

"We won't be filming the day after next." He slid his hands over her hips to cup her ass.

Her eyes sparkled as she pressed herself against him, the lace of her dress rough against his bare skin. "Whatever will I do with my day off?" she asked with a grin.

He chuckled, squeezing her curves. "Meet me at Olympus?"

"Always."

She kissed him, hard, her tongue demanding entrance to his mouth. Christ, she was perfect. He groaned as his cock stiffened against her belly, caught between the ecstasy of her kiss and the scratch of her lace dress. She pulled away suddenly, stepping back towards the balcony.

"See you at the ball, Prince Charming."

Another elimination day, another ball.

Gavin pulled at the knot in his tie to loosen it, just enough to let himself actually breathe, but he was quickly descended upon by a team of PAs, one adjusting the way his hair fell, another removing some invisible piece of lint from his forearm, and a third once again tightening his tie.

Across the room, Patrick and Davis were conferring with the cameramen, but Zayne had yet to make an appearance. His absence made Gavin uneasy. He much preferred to keep the snake in his line of sight rather than wonder what trouble he might be stirring up out of view.

The ballroom at Aster Place had been decorated with swags of greenery, wisteria dripping from the walls, and potted trees arranged around the edges of the room. Megan, the wardrobe consultant, as she held various ties up against his chest, had explained that the room was meant to look like the forest where the princess and prince first danced together in *Sleeping Beauty*. Ultimately, she'd settled on a hunter green tie to connect with the forest theme.

His mind was only half on the impending ball, however. The night before had been one of the best nights of his life, its luster only marred by the fact that he hadn't had the courage to tell Kyla what he really wanted, how he really felt. That he hadn't been able to wake up with her in his arms this morning. Thanks to their on-camera make-out session during the darkness date, he could now be physically affectionate with Kyla while filming, though he promised himself to keep it PG. He wanted to make it hard for Zayne to force his hand and send Kyla home, but he also needed to make sure Zayne didn't have anything he could twist to make her look like a villain. It was a balancing act, and Gavin didn't want to poke the bear too much.

The women arrived, followed by several cameramen, as Ryan approached Gavin. "You ready?"

"As I'll ever be."

Ryan shook his head. "I don't get you, man. You act like it's such a burden to have all these gorgeous women vying for your attention. You want my advice?"

"Not particularly," Gavin mumbled.

"Just relax and enjoy the ride." He grinned, raking his eyes over the assembled women. "Or, you know, let *them* enjoy the ride, if you catch my drift." Before Gavin could respond, Ryan stepped away from him and called the evening to order.

Within seconds, Christina had snaked an arm around him and pulled him onto the dance floor, claiming the first dance of the evening. She prattled on about how much she had enjoyed their picnic, filling in the gaps in their conversation with her musings on the price of real estate in Aster Bay and whether or not purchasing a condo on the bay would be a good investment.

As the first song ended, Erika approached them, her buttercup yellow silk gown moving like liquid gold as she walked. "Mind if I steal you?"

"Not at all," he said. He thanked Christina for the dance and placed his hand on the small of Erika's back to guide her away from the other woman. As they moved out of earshot, he sighed in relief. "Thanks for rescuing me."

She laughed. "Happy to be your eligible lady in shining armor."

He glanced down at the dress. "You look beautiful."

He meant it, and while Erika was an objectively beautiful woman, he found himself admiring her the way he imagined a big brother would admire his sister. There was no attraction there, even though they got along well.

"Thanks." Her eyes studied his as though she didn't really believe the compliment. "What do you say we go for a walk in the gardens instead of dancing?"

"Sure."

She looped her arm through his and he led her out of the ballroom. Erika guided them around the side of the mansion, out of view from the double doors that led into the ballroom, where Lauren and Christina were watching their every movement. "I think you and I need to have a little chat without the other ladies overhearing."

Gavin tensed as he glanced over his shoulder at the cameraman and Patrick following them. "Alright. Something on your mind?"

They stopped in a little copse of trees and Erika dropped his arm. "You're going to choose Kyla."

Apprehension clawed at his throat. Did Erika somehow know about the night before? She was Kyla's roommate—had Kyla told her?

No, Kyla wouldn't tell anyone.

Would she?

"It's okay," Erika continued with a sad smile. "You two are really cute together."

"I...don't know what to say." He scanned her face, searching for any hint that she knew more than she was letting on.

She arched an eyebrow. "You don't have to say anything. It's clear she's your favorite, and I can't say I blame you. She's pretty great."

"She is," he said, some of the tension melting from his shoulders.

"And, in case you didn't already know, she thinks you're pretty great too." Erika chuckled. "I thought she was going to lose her mind when you were on that date with Christina the other day."

He couldn't help but enjoy the fact that Kyla had been jealous, even if that jealousy was unfounded.

"So I think you should send me home tonight."

"Excuse me?" He hadn't expected that and, when he glanced over his shoulder at Patrick, it was clear the producer hadn't either.

She followed his line of sight, this time speaking directly to Patrick. "I've read the fine print in the contract a hundred times. If I choose to go home on my own, then the Network can seek damages. But if Gavin *sends* me home, even if I request it, then I'm still abiding by the rules of the show. There's nothing in the contract that says I can't ask Prince Charming to eliminate me. It's still his choice who he sends home. He could decide to be a jerk and ignore my request," she said with a cheeky smile.

Patrick glanced around uneasily before clearing his throat and frowning. "That's technically true, but—"

"Send me home." Erika turned back to Gavin. "You're not going to choose me. You're going to choose Kyla. And, since you are, I'd rather go home now and be with my daughter than ride it out another few weeks." Her eyes filled with tears, but she dashed them away before he could react. "I've been away from her long enough, and it's time I put her first again."

He pulled her into a hug, ignoring the way his stomach turned at the reminder that he wasn't putting his child first. "I'm sorry I'm not your prince charming."

"Me too. But if it wasn't going to be me, I'm really glad it's Kyla. Don't break her heart." Erika poked him square in the chest.

"I have no intention—"

"No one ever *intends* to break someone's heart. But our girl isn't as unflappable as she'd want us all to believe."

Confessional Interviews
Recorded individually, edited together into one clip

Gavin: Erika is a wonderful woman and I've really enjoyed getting to know her better. Ultimately, I just feel that I have a stronger connection with other women. I'm definitely going to miss her, but I also understand how hard it is to be away from your kid. I couldn't, in good conscience, keep Erika here knowing that doing so was keeping her away from her daughter.

Erika: No, no, there's no ill will towards Gavin. He's everything you'd want Prince Charming to be. But I think we both knew there wasn't really a spark. I hope we can still be friends when this is all over, but I'm glad to be going home to my daughter.

Roni: I don't think any of us expected Erika to go home. She's definitely one of the women in the house that I'll miss the most.

Kyla: I'm so sad to see Erika leave, but I think we'll stay in touch. I'm really grateful that we were on this journey together.

Lauren: I mean, no, I'm not really surprised. I think Gavin's looking for something specific and it's not her.

Zayne: [off-camera] What do you think he's looking for?

Lauren: Hopefully me!

Gavin: We're down to the last four women. Yeah, I'd say I'm starting to take this whole thing more seriously.

Patrick: [off-camera] Who do you feel you have the strongest connection with?

Gavin: I definitely have the strongest connection with Kyla. I think I can honestly say that neither one of us expected to find each other here, but I'm really glad we did.

Chapter Twenty-six

Gavin: Just checking in. Haven't heard from you in a few days. Making sure you're still alive.

Gavin: I suppose if you weren't still alive, Nick would have called your mom.
Gavin: Unless something happened to Nick too.
Gavin: Can you just text me back, please, B? Proof of life?

Gavin: I guess it's a Friday night and you're probably out. I hope you're having fun.
Gavin: Make good decisions.

Gavin: And text me when you get this. Put an old man out of his misery so I can stop worrying about you, yeah?

Brodie: I'm here. I'm fine. Just busy.

Gavin: He lives!
Gavin: Everything alright? It's not like you not to text me back. I was getting ready to call the LAPD to do a wellness check.

Brodie: I'm not a kid anymore, Dad. You don't need to check in on me all the time.

Gavin: I know you're not. I just worry. It's what parents do.

Brodie: I have to go. I'll catch you later.

Gavin: Yeah, any time you want. I'm here.
Gavin: I'm always here for you, Brodie.

"Mom?" Gavin called as he pushed through the screen door to his mother's kitchen.

"Just a minute!" his mother's voice called back.

He set the pie box down and leaned against the counter, surveying the room. It hadn't changed since he'd moved out over twenty years ago. It still had the same faux textured paint treatment on the walls—meant to mimic a Tuscan villa for some reason—the same cast iron roosters in a row on the shelf above the sink, the same stone tile backsplash.

"There you are, my Gav-a-loo," his mom said as she appeared in the arched doorway to the kitchen. Her hair was pulled up in a messy bun of brown and gray crowned with cobwebs.

"Were you in the attic again?" He pushed off from the counter and plucked the cobwebs from her hair, tossing them in the garbage.

"Oh, thank you, dear. Yes, I was just trying to find my old canning pot. Helen and Dot have arranged for Tessa to teach a jelly-making class at the senior center this week," she said as she washed the dirt and grime from her hands. "But for the life of me, I can't find that old pot."

"I'll get you a new one."

"Nonsense. I have a perfectly good pot somewhere in this house." She dried her hands on the rooster-themed dishtowel before turning to face Gavin. "Well. Enough of that. To what do I owe this unexpected pleasure?"

"I brought pie." Gavin gestured to the box on the counter, suddenly having cold feet. "Cherry."

"Uh oh." His mom planted her hands on her hips and arched a knowing eyebrow. "Something must really be bothering you. I'll get the milk; you serve the pie."

Gavin didn't argue, letting himself sink into the safety of his mother's kitchen as he served up two pieces of Tessa's cherry pie. Once they were settled at the little round table in the corner of the kitchen, his mother took a giant bite of her pie.

"Now tell me, what's troubling you? Aren't you supposed to be filming that little reality show?" she asked around a bite of cherry and crust.

"I am." He dragged his fork through the cherry-flavored gel that oozed out of the side of his piece of pie.

"So it's about a woman then." Gavin glanced at her and a look of glee stole across her face. "Gavin West, don't you dare get my hopes up if you don't mean it."

"I think I love her." Funny how saying it out loud made the words feel lighter.

His mother scoffed. "You don't *think* you love someone. You either love them or you don't. Does she love you too?"

He blew out a breath. "It's complicated."

"Love always is." His mother swapped her empty plate of pie for his full one and dug into his untouched slice. He smiled at the familiarity of it, the unspoken understanding that, of course, his mother was going to eat his slice of pie.

"It's Kyla."

His mother's fork stopped midway to her mouth and she lowered it slowly, her eyes locked on Gavin. "As in Brodie's Kyla?"

"They broke up months ago," he said, hating the defensiveness in his tone.

She set her fork down and leaned back in her chair, her forehead furrowed as she assessed her son. "I think we need something stronger than pie." She pushed away from the table and retrieved a bottle of wine from the rack on the counter.

"Mom, it's not even noon yet," Gavin protested.

She fumbled in the drawer for the wine opener, the metallic clanking of mismatched silverware filling the room. "It is somewhere," she said. "Ah ha! Success!" She jabbed the wine opener into the cork, popping the cork easily. "Now where are my wine glasses?" She opened a cabinet, frowned, and shut it again. "You know, when I'm by myself, I just drink straight from the bottle."

Gavin got up from the table with a resigned sigh and opened another cabinet, retrieving two wine glasses. "Don't drink from the bottle, mom."

"Why not? Who am I trying to impress?" she asked as she poured them each a glass. "Here. I think you need this more than me."

"I don't need alcohol," he said, though he took a sip anyway. His mom always had the best wine.

"I don't think I've met Kyla, but Brodie showed me a picture once," his mom said, squinting as though that would make her memory clearer. "Pretty little thing. Blonde."

He nodded. "That's her."

"Brodie said she wanted to work in pornography."

Gavin nearly spit his wine across the room. He set his glass down on the counter, coughing. "She does not work in pornography. She's a photographer."

"Hmm. Maybe she'd take my picture."

Gavin winced and did his best not to picture his mother posing for a boudoir shoot. He failed miserably.

"Alright, so she used to date your son but she's not anymore, and you think you're falling in love with her and she may or may not feel the same way. What's the problem exactly?"

He sagged against the counter, crossing his arms over his chest. "I'm worried Brodie won't like it."

"Of course he's not going to like it. You're boinking his ex-girlfriend," she said, gesturing to him with her wine glass.

"Mom, don't say boinking."

"Would you prefer I said fucking?"

Gavin pinched the bridge of his nose. Why had he thought this was a good idea?

"Listen," his mom said, setting her glass down on the counter with a clink. "Brodie is a big boy. I know he doesn't always act like it, but he's an adult now. Besides, he's all the way on the other side of the country. It may take him a while to get on board, but he's old enough to understand that sometimes these things happen. If she's important to you, he'll come around."

"What if he doesn't?"

"Then I'll knock some sense into him," she said, as if it would be that easy. "If he wants to behave like a child, he can be treated like a child."

"You don't think—" He broke off, swallowing the end of the sentence. He took a steadying breath and forced himself to say the thing he was most afraid of. "You don't think it makes me a terrible father?"

His mom stepped towards him and took his face in her hands. "You are an amazing father, Gav-a-loo. Your father would be so proud of you," she said, her voice catching on the last few words. Then she tapped his cheeks and went back to cut another piece of pie. "Even if you are boinking your son's ex-girlfriend."

Chapter Twenty-seven

"Well, that settles that. Shibari is definitely not my thing," Kyla said as she fished a cherry out of the bottom of her glass.

Gavin laughed and pulled her closer in their booth at Olympus as the Dom on stage finished untying the ropes that had bound his submissive only moments earlier. "That's good. I'm shit with knots."

Kyla smirked. "Oh yeah?"

He finished his beer and pushed the bottle away. "It's probably the only badge in Boy Scouts I never earned."

"Of course you were a Boy Scout," Kyla said with a playful roll of her eyes. She nestled herself against him, curling up beneath his arm like a contented cat, and his heart swelled. She fit him so perfectly. "Is there another show tonight?"

Gavin shook his head. "Not tonight. Sundays are slow at Olympus."

"Right. Because of the God thing."

"What God thing?"

"People feel extra guilty doing anything naughty on Sunday because of God. Because they think they should be in church." She glanced up at him with a smirk. "Seriously. Ask your brother about it. He's a priest. He'll know."

"I am not asking my brother about people having sex on

Sundays," he said, tickling her ribs.

She laughed, batting away his hand.

"Do you want to leave?" he asked.

She shot him a startled look. "Why would I want to leave?"

"Because there aren't any more shows tonight."

She smiled and dropped a chaste kiss on his lips. "Believe it or not, I didn't really come here for the shows." Her tongue slid along his lower lip before she pulled away, a glint of mischief in her eyes. "Though the shows don't hurt."

He wanted to give her everything, anything to see that smile on her face and know he put it there.

"I think I know where we can find another show." He took her hand and pulled her out of the booth after him. She giggled as she jogged to keep up with his long strides, happiness radiating off of her in intoxicating waves.

It felt so good to laugh with her, to hold her hand in a public place with no cameras to follow them, no producers whispering in their ear or orchestrating the next activity. Here, in their little oasis of sin, she practically glowed with confidence, no longer shrinking in the corner or afraid to tell him what she wanted.

He stroked his thumb over her wrist and wondered how she felt about him, if her feelings were even half as strong for him as his were for her. She'd said she was his, but was she really? Was she prepared to face the sideways glances they'd get outside of the confines of the show and the club, to correct the people who would assume he was her father rather than her lover? Did she really want to tie herself to a man twenty years her senior, a man with a grown child her own age?

Christ, he hoped so.

He led her to the back hallway where the private playrooms were, scanning the illuminated doors until he found what he was looking for. Room number eleven had a small red light glowing just below the number, and beside it, room ten stood empty.

Perfect.

Gavin led her into room ten, closing the door behind her and throwing the bolt. He leaned against the door and watched as Kyla wandered through the room, exploring. This playroom was much more elaborately furnished than the one they'd used last time. It still had the king-sized bed in one corner and a loveseat facing the two-way mirror on the wall opposite the stage in the main room, an identical set up facing the adjoining wall. But this room also featured a series of sturdy foam wedges and s-shaped loungers of various sizes, each covered in vinyl.

"What's in there?" She pointed to an armoire along one wall.

Gavin walked over, awareness of her eyes on him sending sparks along his skin, and opened the heavy wooden door to reveal the collection of glass and metal dildos and plugs, heavy leather floggers and paddles, fuzzy handcuffs and silicone vibrators. Kyla gasped, her eyes darting around the display.

He arched an eyebrow. "See something you want to try?"

She swallowed and took a halting step towards the case. "We can use these?"

He watched as her eyes moved over each item, noting the flare of interest when she examined the stainless-steel plug made from a stack of beads of increasing size. It was one of the narrower plugs on display, perfect for a beginner, and his cock stirred at her interest in the toy. "If you like. Everything is single use, replaced between customers."

"They throw them away?"

"No, little goddess. If you choose a toy to play with, you get to take it home with you."

She glanced at him, her eyes returning to the plug.

With a wolfish smile he plucked the plug from the display, tucking it into his pants pocket.

"Just in case," he said. Her cheeks heated to a pretty pink and he reminded himself to go slow, to enjoy the night they had together. He took her hand and led her over to one of the loveseats.

Gavin pointed at the wall facing the main room. "There's not another show on the stage tonight." He directed her attention to the other mirror-covered wall, to the red light glowing in the corner. "But there's a show in the other room."

"I don't understand." Her brow wrinkled in the most adorable way, and he couldn't stop himself from kissing her.

They sat on the loveseat, and he pulled her against his side, skating his fingers along her thigh until she shivered beneath his touch.

"On the other side of that wall is another room just like this one. And in that room, there are people who enjoy being watched, just as much as we enjoy watching."

"And they won't see us?" she asked, already squirming closer to his touch.

"Not unless you want them to." He pointed to the buttons in the arm of the chair. "This one lets us see them. They'll get a green light on their side letting them know we're watching, but they won't be able to see us." Kyla's breath was coming faster, in soft, needy pants that had his cock straining against his jeans. "And this button lets us see them *and* lets them see us."

Her eyes were already glazed with lust, her chest rising and falling rapidly. "The first one."

He bit her neck, dragging his teeth over the tender skin. "My perfect little goddess."

She climbed into his lap, thighs straddling his hips, and kissed him. Gavin gripped her thighs to pull her tight against him. He loved when she took charge like this, showing him what she wanted and how she wanted it, but he could only hold back so long before the need to control her pleasure took over. They fumbled to take off each other's shirts, an awkward series of tugs and lifting and laughing when the straps of her lacy shirt got twisted. A few more tugs and they were both shirtless, her breasts pert and topped with the most beautiful pink peaks that begged for his attention.

He sucked one tip into his mouth, worrying the nipple until she clasped his head to her chest, rocking her hips mindlessly against his growing erection.

"Tell me what you want," he growled against her skin.

"I want you to lick my pussy," she whispered.

Pride swelled in his chest. Could this be the same woman who could hardly ask for him to touch her only a few weeks ago, now demanding that he eat her cunt? He loved hearing the filthy words on her tongue, seeing the way they sent a blush across her skin.

He lifted her and spun her around so she was seated on the loveseat as he kneeled on the floor between her legs. He pushed her skirt up around her hips, not bothering to remove it, and dragged her lacy panties down her legs, letting his nails graze her skin on the way down.

"Do you want to watch the other room?" He reached for the buttons on the arm rest.

She stilled his hand. "I want to watch you."

He followed her eyes to the mirror on the opposite wall, to the reflection of himself kneeling between her spread legs, her hair disheveled and skirt hiked up around her waist. He wished he had a picture to capture how beautiful she looked with her lips swollen from his kisses and her eyes hungry for him.

She ran her fingers through his hair, a soft, affectionate touch, before she guided his head between her legs, spreading her thighs to accommodate him. He chuckled and pressed a kiss to the inside of her thigh. "That's right, beautiful girl. Take what you want from me."

He lifted each of her legs, setting her heels on the edge of the loveseat so she was spread open for him. He leaned back, allowing her a clear view of herself in the mirror.

Her breath caught at the sight, a blush climbing up her throat and across her cheeks. As she watched, he trailed a finger through her slit, circling at her entrance and then dragging her wetness back up to her clit, petting her like the treasure she was, letting her see the glistening evidence of her arousal.

She was the prettiest goddamn thing he'd ever seen, made all the more so for being his. "Look at how pretty you are, sweetheart. Look at how ready you are for me." He pressed lightly against her clit and she sucked in a breath. "Watch yourself come, little goddess."

He pressed his mouth to the apex of her thighs and she groaned, a long, primal sound low in her throat, her hand in his hair flexing and grasping. He took his time tasting her, dragging each lip into his mouth, scraping the swollen flesh lightly with his teeth. He wanted to live between her thighs, spend his days dropping to his knees and lapping up her sweetness and his nights sheathing himself in her tight, wet heat until neither of them could remember a time before they'd been together. He would wipe their slates clean with an overabundance of orgasms, pave the road to their future with kissing and sucking and fucking. He would build her the life she deserved, starting with bringing her more pleasure than she knew she was capable of receiving.

"Gavin," she whined, her hips rocking up to meet his mouth, "stop teasing me."

With one hand, he undid his belt, releasing his cock through the open fly of his pants. He stroked himself in long, languid strokes as he dragged the broad, flat edge of his tongue over her from opening to clit. She jolted beneath his touch, so he did it again and again, drinking her in with long laps of his tongue.

"More," she demanded, his little needy goddess. "Give me more."

He used his free hand to press two fingers into her opening as his tongue continued to flick and circle her clit. The room filled with the sounds of her soft moans and his hand flying over his cock, skin on skin.

She watched him in the mirror with wide eyes. "Are you

jerking off?"

He arched an eyebrow at her as he continued sucking her clit, unwilling to remove his mouth from her even long enough to answer.

"Fuck, that's hot," she groaned.

He grunted, the idea that she was turned on by him touching himself sending a thrill through him, and he reminded himself that he wanted to come when he was inside her this time and not a second before.

She rocked her hips restlessly, huffing out a frustrated breath.

"Tell me what you need." His lips moved against her pussy as he spoke.

"I don't know." The exasperation in her voice made it clear she wasn't just hedging—she really wasn't sure what she needed to help her fall over the edge of her orgasm.

Removing his hand from his cock, he retrieved the plug from his pocket. He pulled his fingers from inside her and replaced them with the plug, sliding it deeply into her slick channel. She gasped as the cool metal made contact with her skin. With a light suck on her clit, he pulled away from her pussy, replacing his tongue with his thumb as he continued to drive her towards her release.

"Would you like to try something different?" he asked as he slowly dragged the plug in and out of her, coating it in her wetness.

She swallowed. "What if I don't like it?" Anxiety pushed in at the edges of her eyes, clutching at his heart.

"Then we'll stop." He leaned forward and brushed his still-slick lips over hers. "I think you might like it, though. Very much." He let his pinky brush against her pleated rim and her eyes sparkled with liquid heat.

Slowly that heat melted into something else, mixing and mingling into a mesmerizing whirlpool of desire and something far more potent—trust. She trusted him. The knowledge nearly broke him, his fingers trembling as he gently swirled his finger against her back entrance again. She trusted him, and he silently promised himself that he would never betray that trust.

"Let's try it," she said.

He crushed his lips to hers, drinking in her little moans as he worked the toy in and out of her pussy and his cock pulsed in anticipation, beads of precum sliding down his shaft. When they were both out of breath and her eyes held no more trace of nerves, he rested back on his heels, focusing his attention on the way the metal glided in and out of her, the shine dulled by a coating of her pleasure.

Gavin shifted so she had a clear view of herself in the mirror. "Look at yourself, sweetheart." He pressed his pinky to her back entrance again, heat shooting down his spine at the way the muscles there contracted in anticipation. "See how greedy this little hole is already? It's begging to be fucked. It wants to be stretched and filled and used. Has anyone ever touched you here, Kyla?"

"No," she whispered, her eyes glued to the image of herself in the mirror.

A wave of feral possessiveness broke in his chest at the idea that he would be the first to play with her like this, to introduce her to all the pleasure there was to be had here. How many of her firsts had he already claimed? How many more could they explore together in the years that lay ahead?

He pressed just the tip of his finger inside her as she watched in the mirror, her breathing shallow and her mouth pulled into a tiny O of wonder. He slowly moved his finger deeper, allowing her to adjust to the feeling of him there.

"How do you feel?"

"Keep going." She tilted her hips up to allow herself a better view of his ministrations.

He scraped his teeth over the tender skin on the inside of her knee as he worked his finger deeper. "Look at yourself, Ky," he grated out, using his free hand to squeeze his cock in a vain attempt to stop it throbbing with need. "Christ, I thought your pussy was needy. Do you feel that? Feel yourself pulling me in, asking for more."

"Yes," she whimpered, her hips moving restlessly. "I want more."

"Someday when you're ready, I'm going to give you my cock here. I'm going to own your ass the same way I own your pussy." She groaned, her cunt glistening with a fresh wave of arousal that dripped down and onto his finger as he continued to move it inside her, her eyes glued to the spot. "Would you let me do that, little goddess? Would you let me fuck your ass and fill you up with my cum?"

"Yes." It was the most beautiful word he'd ever heard when it fell from her lips in the throws of pleasure.

"Someday soon. I swear it."

A vision darted across his eyes—Kyla in a white dress, clouds of chiffon and tulle rucked up around her waist, bent over for him as he sank his cock into her, claiming her body the way she'd claimed his heart, a ring on her finger marking her as his. Longing knocked the breath from his lungs and he pressed his lips to her thigh to ground himself with the feel of her.

Someday, he promised himself.

He pulled his finger from her and retrieved the toy. He couldn't think about someday, not if he was going to make sure she came before he did.

"Watch, little goddess."

He pressed the end of the toy against her puckered opening, the smallest ball with the slightest pressure, and it slid inside her easily. Her eyes went wide at the intrusion, at the touch of the cool metal, but all nervousness melted into heat within seconds.

"More." Her gaze focused on the filthy reflection of him between her legs, cock hard and twitching with each new knob of the toy that he slid inside her. And with each knob, she wriggled her hips, adjusting to the feel, then demanded more. By the time the toy was seated fully, she was flushed, her breasts heaving with the exertion of her breathing, and her cunt dripping.

"I'm going to fuck your ass now, sweetheart," he said, his voice gruff with need, "and while I do, you're going to come on my tongue. Do you think you can do that for me?"

"Yes," she whined, rocking her pelvis against the thumb strumming at her clit. "Gavin, please."

He fell on her like a man possessed, using one hand to work the plug in and out, alternating quick pumps with slow slides where she would feel each bead as it passed through the tight rings of muscle, while his mouth latched onto her pussy, his tongue flicking furiously against the hard bud above her opening. Her moans grew higher in pitch as her opening began to flutter, clutching at nothing.

"More," she demanded again.

With a grunt, he drove three fingers into her pussy, curling to press against the spot behind her clit, thumping in time to the thrusting of the toy. As her inner walls began to pulse around him, he drew her clit into his mouth, sucking in long, hard pulls until he'd sucked the orgasm directly from her, drinking down each drop of her release as she pulled his hair and screamed his name.

When her climax abated and she flopped back on the loveseat, he pressed the toy all the way inside her, seating it fully again, and got to his feet. He kicked off his shoes and divested of his jeans and boxer briefs, never taking his eyes off her. She was a goddess indeed, reclined and spent, exhausted by her own pleasure with a stunned look of satisfaction curling her lips, and he was the mere mortal who was lucky enough to worship her.

I'll worship her for the rest of my life.

He stroked himself slowly, using the precum at his tip as

lube, as he watched the aftershocks flutter through her thighs and pussy. He could come from that sight alone, knowing he'd put that glazed look on her face, that he'd been the one to plant that plug in her ass.

"Can you stand, sweetheart?" he asked.

She smiled lazily and lifted a hand for him to help her up. He grinned as he did so, pulling her into his arms and kissing her soundly. As they kissed, she trailed her fingers lightly, teasingly over his erection. "Will you fuck me now, please?" she asked.

He chuckled. "So polite. Yes, little goddess, I'll fuck you now."

He reached for a condom from the basket on the side table and she stilled his hand. "We've both been tested and I have an IUD." She drew his hand back between them, pressing it to her clit with a sharp inhale. He grinned, stroking her the way she was asking him to. "I want to ride you and I want to feel when you come inside me."

Fuck.

He kissed her roughly, plunging his tongue into her mouth, because how the fuck else was a man supposed to kiss her when she made a request like that? When she was gifting him with such trust?

He sat on the loveseat, but when she stepped towards him, he gripped her hips and spun her around so she was facing the mirror. He guided her down, lining his cock up with her entrance, and watched with rapt attention as she stretched around him, impaling herself in a slow glide, the end of the plug flashing between her cheeks as she did.

When he'd filled her completely, he hooked her legs over the outside of his, spreading his thighs to open her wide. "My perfect, little goddess," he growled at her ear as she began to move tentatively in his lap. "Look at how full you are with my cock in your pussy and a toy in your ass. Look at how you stretch so beautifully for me."

As she watched herself in the mirror, he watched her, pride

and some hazy, feral need to own her warring in his chest as he watched her expression change from surprise to lust to a confident sensuality, an awakening akin to the one he'd seen in her boudoir photograph so many months ago.

He reached around her hip and used his thumb to draw tight circles over her already-sensitive clit. She made a guttural sound in the back of her throat and began moving faster, bouncing herself on his cock.

"You're so fucking beautiful, Kyla," he rasped, his teeth grazing her shoulder. "I want you to watch when I make you come."

"I want you to watch when I make *you* come," she replied, circling her hips in challenge.

He grunted, wrapping his free arm around her waist and gripping her breast as he lost control and pistoned into her faster and harder, urging on those soft flutterings around his cock until they gathered strength and became an inescapable grip, pulling his orgasm from him as she shook above him, and he pumped her full of his release in rough bursts that knocked the air from his lungs.

They both watched, catching their breath, as he softened and slipped from inside her, their mingled pleasure dripping down their thighs. She turned in his arms, curling into him and kissing him as he dropped a hand to her ass and slowly removed the toy, tossing it aside. He framed her face with his hands, kissing her jaw and nose and eyelids. She laughed and redirected his wandering lips back to her mouth.

"Note to self: Gavin likes to fuck in front of mirrors," she giggled.

"That wasn't about the mirror; that was about you." He hesitated, but the ache in his chest demanded he say it all. "This thing we're doing… I don't want to leave it here. At Olympus." He scanned her eyes for any hit of her pulling away and, finding none, swallowed hard and barreled on. "I love you, Kyla."

Her mouth dropped open and she blinked as though she

thought she'd misunderstood.

"I probably shouldn't say that right after sex, but I promise you, this isn't the sex talking. I love you. I'm in love with you. I've known it for a long time and—"

"How long?"

His brain stuttered as he tried to process the question. That hadn't been the response he was expecting. "How long have I known I was in love with you?" She nodded. He rolled his lips through his teeth, weighing his answer. But he'd already come this far. No turning back now. "I think I've known for as long as I've known you. But I don't think I let myself really feel it until you showed up here that first night. And I didn't admit it to myself until a few nights ago."

"And you're only just saying something now?' she asked incredulously.

His brow furrowed. "Are you mad at me?"

"I'm furious!" She pushed his chest away so he fell back against the loveseat. She straddled his hips and pushed him again, this time harder. "All this time? We could have been together all this time?"

"Wait." He gripped her wrists so she had to stop shoving him. "What are you saying?"

"I'm in love with you, too, you dummy!"

Despite her exasperation, he couldn't help but smile. "You are?"

"Of course, I am!"

He pulled her face down to his, kissing her through his smile.

She pushed him away again, pouting. "No, I'm mad at you. When you love someone, you're supposed to tell them, Gavin."

"You didn't tell me either," he said, trying and failing not to smile. She loved him too. What else mattered?

She opened her mouth to respond, then closed it again. Biting back a smile of her own, she scraped her nails lightly against his chest.

"You really love me?" she asked.

"I do," he answered, his chest so full of happiness he thought his heart might burst. "I really love you. You really love me?"

"I do. I just wish we hadn't wasted so long dancing around each other."

He kissed her again. "Then I guess we better make up for lost time."

He tumbled her onto the loveseat, kissing his way down her body until her giggles turned to moans.

Gavin: I know you're busy living it up in LA but can we please find a time to talk? On the phone or video chat? Anything where we're both there having the same conversation at the same time.

Gavin: There have been some developments on my end and I really want to talk to you about them.

Gavin: That sounds ominous. I promise it's not.

Gavin: But it is important. To me.

Gavin: Brodie, please.

Brodie: Can't right now. We'll talk soon. I promise.

Chapter Twenty-eight

Kyla refused to get seasick.

No matter how long she'd lived in Aster Bay, she still hadn't mastered the art of being on a boat and not turning green.

The yacht that production had rented for this *Little Mermaid*-themed group date was larger than Kyla's apartment, with spacious on-deck seating and cocktail tables, and a below-deck room that looked more like a nightclub than a boat. The girls had all been instructed to wear their best beach wear, which Christina and Lauren had taken to mean fluorescent bikinis with thong bottoms and tops that were little more than two tiny triangles held together by string. Roni wore a tasteful turquoise bikini top with a full-coverage bottom beneath a gauzy wrap skirt, her golden skin taking on a deep tan as they sat on the white sofas on deck.

Kyla, on the other hand, had opted for a purple one-piece bathing suit, a shiny silver zipper running from the center of the neckline to just below her breasts, and a pair of flowy white palazzo pants. Megan, the wardrobe consultant, had begged her to consider a sarong instead, or to at least unzip the suit a few inches. In the end, Kyla had relented about the zipper, allowing Megan to pull it down just low enough to give a tease of cleavage, which Megan immediately dusted with some kind of shimmery bronzer.

But none of that would matter if she threw up before they even got to the competition part of the date. Gavin wasn't even on the yacht yet.

Each girl had been dropped off at one of Aster Bay's many antique shops earlier in the day with instructions to purchase two items that they thought represented who they were in some kind of nod to the little mermaid's cave of human treasures. Thankfully, Kyla had been dropped off at Third Times a Charm and had headed straight to the arrangement of antique cameras at the back of the shop.

Don't throw up, don't throw up, don't throw up.

"There he is!" Christina shrieked, getting up on her knees and holding on to the railing with one hand while she pointed at an approaching boat with her other.

Sure enough, Gavin sat high on the upper deck of a small cruiser that was rapidly approaching, his floppy hair blowing across his face and his partially open white shirt billowing in the breeze. As the boat drew nearer, she caught his eye and the corners of his mouth tipped up in a smile that made her forget all about the rocking of the boat or the fact that she ate too many clam cakes at lunch. She knew how that mouth felt on her skin, between her legs, the filthy things it said when he was inside her, and the sweet things it murmured against her ear when they lay sated and tangled in each other.

She loved him. And he loved her. They just needed to get through filming the rest of this show and then they could start their lives together.

She was so caught up in her own little private moment of happiness, reliving their last night at Olympus together, remembering the sincerity in his eyes when he'd told her he loved her, that she almost didn't hear Lauren commenting on how good his butt looked in his khakis as he boarded the yacht.

Almost.

"Ladies, you all look stunning." Ryan called the date to order as he appeared at Gavin's side and the cruiser that had carried Prince Charming to them was driven away. "Earlier today, you were each instructed to purchase two items from one of Aster Bay's many beautiful antique shops. You were all given the same amount of money and the same amount of time to curate your collection of treasures and now you'll present them to Gavin. The person he feels he connects with the most based on your finds will win tonight's private date. Roni, you're up first."

Roni approached the little table on the side of the deck where each of their purchases were displayed and picked up a tarnished, metal apple corer and a cloth doll.

"I chose the apple corer because of my work in food waste recovery and the doll because it reminds me of a doll my grandmother sewed for me when I was a child." She continued telling her story as Gavin listened attentively, asking follow-up questions that allowed her to talk more about her nonprofit work and her family.

When Ryan announced that Roni's time was up, Gavin hugged her and thanked her for sharing. Next up was Christina. She presented Gavin with a lobster trap to represent her hometown in Maine and a heavy, brass doorknocker to represent her work as a real estate agent. Again, Gavin was engaged, polite, and they parted with a friendly hug.

Next was Lauren. She held a pair of vintage high heels, the fabric fraying at the bottom of the heel and the toe encrusted with fake crystals.

"I only bought the shoes," she explained, "because there are two of them, and they have so many meanings for me. You already know I was Miss Los Angeles three years running, and obviously these shoes remind me of my beauty pageant days."

"I can see that. Sure," Gavin said.

"But they also stand for my philosophy on life." Lauren paused dramatically and Gavin glanced at Ryan, as though he thought he might be missing something.

"And what's that?" he finally asked.

"I'm so glad you asked. My philosophy is to never let anyone walk all over me. And the shoes are also a warning that no one should ever underestimate me just because I like a little glitz and glamour. I play to win, and I get what I want. Always."

The words landed like a weight across the group, Gavin's lips pressed together in a flat line as he took in her declaration. His eyes flitted over her shoulder to catch Kyla's before he returned his attention to Lauren.

"You are a fierce competitor, indeed," he said.

She giggled and flipped her blonde hair over her shoulder, the harshness of the previous moment wiped away by her effusive femininity. Ryan announced the end of her time and she set the shoes back on the table. If she'd been a bubbly caricature of flirtation moments before, her strut back to her seat was all business, and the look she pinned Kyla with was deadly.

Kyla was called forward and she gathered her items.

"Hi," she said as she set them down in front of Gavin.

"Hi." His voice was tinged with humor and his eyes soft.

She almost swayed forward to kiss him before she remembered herself. *Focus.*

She fiddled with the camera in her hands, training her eyes there as she took a deep breath and began. "I chose a vintage camera because I am hoping to make a career out of photography, but also because I've always loved old cameras. Shooting with film is a whole other art form. You can't retouch it. You can't see the image instantly. And I think I really fell in love with photography in the darkroom, developing black and white film in high school."

She glanced up and was momentarily stunned by the force of his attention on her, the way he was taking in every word. She held his gaze, swallowing, as she continued.

"I didn't have the best home life during my teenage years.

My parents were… Anyway, I joined the photography club at school. They hated that. My father said it was a waste of time and my mother insisted it took away from more important pursuits, like punishing myself on an exercise bike for hours on end for the crime of not being a size six."

Gavin reached out and took her hand, squeezing it lightly, as though he knew she needed the encouragement to continue.

"So, photography has always been my escape and the place I can best express myself. And when I open my studio, it will be the life I've built for myself. The one I chose."

She dropped her gaze to the second item in her hands, an old wire whisk with a jadeite handle. "And I guess that's why I chose this too." She held up the whisk with a small smile. "When I graduated from college, I thought I would have to go back to my parents and live the life they wanted me to lead. But it was my job in the bakeries here in town that gave me enough money to get a small apartment with my friends and stay in Aster Bay, and it was working for Tessa—and with you—on the Food and Wine Festival that made me start to believe that I was good enough to open my own studio. That festival and every opportunity you two have given me since changed my life. You changed my life."

Gavin's hand cupped her cheek, his thumb wiping away a tear at the corner of her eye.

"We changed each other," he whispered.

Ryan cut them off with an uneasy glance at Patrick and Zayne on the other side of the yacht. Within seconds, Patrick whisked Gavin away below deck, leaving Kyla swaying unsteadily in a way that had nothing to do with the waves.

"I don't give a fuck what you want," Zayne snarled through gritted teeth. "Roni or Lauren."

"They are the only two who haven't had a one-on-one date with you yet." Patrick tried to placate Gavin as he tugged—uselessly—on Gavin's arm in an attempt to pull he away from where he stood toe to toe with Zayne.

"I'm not choosing one of them in the end so why does that matter?" Gavin asked.

"It's not your fucking choice!" Zayne said with a barked laugh.

"Right, because you want Lauren to win. That's what her little speech was all about, right?" Gavin said. Zayne's eyes flashed with fire. "Why are you so invested in propping her up? What's in it for you?"

"The sponsor wants—"

"Try again," Gavin snapped.

"Lauren's a star. When she breaks up with you after the finale airs, she'll get her own show," Zayne said.

"Oh, you'll make sure of that."

"You signed the contract. That means I get to say who wins. So, there are two ways this can go, lover boy," Zayne said. "Either you can choose Roni for this one-on-one and let it be a pre-finale surprise when you realize you're madly in love with Lauren, or you can choose Lauren now and start laying the groundwork for her win. I don't give a fuck which way you want to play it. I will get my story."

Gavin clenched his teeth so hard his jaw cracked. He glanced at Patrick, who at least had the good graces to look sick over the conversation.

"Roni," Gavin spat as he pushed past Zayne and left the cramped cabin where he'd been unceremoniously hauled for that delightful little chat.

There was more to the story. He could feel it, but he couldn't see it, like he was trying to put together a puzzle and some of the pieces were missing. It didn't make sense that Zayne should be so invested in the winner of the show. Unless Lauren was cutting him in on her share of the prize money? That didn't seem right. There had to be something he was missing.

He tore around the corner, nearly barreling head on into Kyla, who yelped in surprise. He steadied her with an iron grip on her biceps and she pressed a hand to her chest.

"Are you okay?" Her too-watchful eye roamed over his face.

"What are you doing down here?" He glanced over his shoulder to be sure Zayne and Patrick weren't following him.

"I may have snuck away. I just wanted a few minutes of quiet," she confessed, the lightly mottled pink of her cheeks speaking to the emotion she'd displayed on deck while telling her story.

Gavin glanced over his shoulder again, then steered Kyla into another cabin at the back of the yacht. The room was empty save for a twin bed and a small desk.

"Gavin, what's wrong?"

He pressed her against the wall and dropped his forehead to hers, his hands running restlessly over her rib cage, her hips. *Tell her.*

"They're making me choose Roni for the date."

Coward.

"Okay." Kyla took his face in her hands, her nails lightly scratching at his stubble. "Then you'll go on a date with Roni."

He swallowed, squeezing his eyes shut. "It should be you."

"It'll be me at the end when it counts," she said, tipping his face up to hers.

Tell her.

"I can't thank you enough," she continued, her eyes sparkling. "Without you, I would never be able to renovate the studio, and once the show airs, hopefully I can leverage my fifteen minutes of fame into a full waiting list of clients. You know how I told you I wanted this year to be different? The Year of Kyla, I called it. And the top of that list was to open my studio. You know what else was on that list?"

"What?" His stomach twisted in knots—angry, coiling balls of tension in his gut with each word she spoke, each opportunity he let pass without telling her that she might not get the money for her studio. Hell, she might not even get the positive press for that waiting list of clients, and somehow, no matter how hard he tried to protect her, he just seemed to make it worse.

How was he going to fix this?

"Toe-curling, scream-your-lungs-out sex," she said with a grin. "I can thank you for checking that off my list too. But there was a secret additional item on my list that I didn't tell anyone about. I didn't even want to write it down because it felt like I'd jinx it." She took a deep breath, steadying herself to continue and his chest ached with the knowledge that he was failing her. "I wanted to know what it felt like to really be in love. That's something else you helped me with."

Tell her tell her tell her.

No. He could still fix this. He just had to figure out what kind of hold Lauren had over Zayne and then he could *fix* this. That's what he did. Kyla had basically just said as much—give him a task and he was the guy who made sure it got done. He was the guy who fixed things, who made everything alright for everyone else. If he couldn't do that for her, then what the hell did it matter if he couldn't go a second without needing to be near her, if he couldn't breathe without her? What the hell did anything matter if he couldn't give her all the things she deserved, the things she thought he'd given her already?

She brushed her lips against his. "I love you."

It was as though her words set fire to a fuse inside him, and suddenly he needed her, needed to be inside her, to reassure himself that he hadn't lost her. Not yet anyway. There was still time. He just had to *fix* it.

He kissed her back, harder, pressing her into the wall as he drew down the zipper on her swimsuit and ripped the straps down her shoulders, exposing her chest. He gripped her roughly, lifting one of her breasts to his mouth and drawing her nipple between his teeth.

"I fucking love you." He kissed her again, swallowing any response she might have.

He turned her and walked her to the bed until the back of her legs hit the mattress and he lay her down. As she moved up the bed to make room for him, he gripped the top of her swimsuit and pulled it down, cover-up pants and all, dropping them in a tangled mess on the floor.

"I need you, Ky," he grunted as he undid his belt with one hand, the other already pushing her thighs open.

"Yes." Her eyes hooded with lust as she watched him.

She dropped her knees to the side, revealing herself to him, and he swore under his breath, pushing his pants to the floor. He gripped her thighs and threw her legs over his shoulders as he dipped his head and feasted on her cunt, eating her with long strokes of his tongue and grazes of his teeth. It was hard and fast and not nearly as much as she deserved but he couldn't stop, couldn't slow down. He needed the taste of her on his lips, needed her to come more than he needed his next breath.

She arched her back and cupped her breasts, moaning, "God, right there."

He drove two fingers into her, pumping into her as he sucked on her clit until she shuddered beneath him, her sweetness coating his tongue.

As she came down from her orgasm, still panting and flushed, he got to his knees between her legs and lined up his cock with her entrance.

"Yes?" he asked.

"Yes." She tipped her hips up to him. "Please, Gavin. I need you too."

He drove into her with a single stroke that tore a cry from her lips. Hooking her knees with his forearms, he held her open for him, tilting her hips to exactly the right angle as he pistoned into her, losing himself in the tight clutch of her pussy and her increasingly urgent cries. He thrust into her as though he could fuck her hard enough to forget about the men in the other room playing God with their futures. As though he could make her come hard enough to erase how out of control he felt.

"Wish I had a camera, little goddess, so you could see yourself," he said, dropping one of her knees in favor of pressing his thumb to her clit.

"Describe it to me."

"You're so fucking wet. You're dripping all over my cock. You like when I fuck you like this, Ky? Rough and fast?"

"I like any way you fuck me," she said, pinching her nipples again.

He grunted, lifting her slightly to change the angle. As he drove into her again, she bit her lip, her eyes darkening with pleasure.

"Good. You take me so well, little goddess. You're so pretty like this, stretched around my cock, letting me fuck you so deep. I want to live between your legs, Ky, spend my life worshipping this cunt, keep you wet and ready for me always. Would you let me do that? Would you let me fuck this pussy until you can't remember a time it wasn't mine?"

"Yes! Oh, God, Gavin, don't stop," she panted, her eyes squeezed shut.

"Look at me. You look at me when I make you come so you know exactly whose cock is inside you."

She met his gaze as her orgasm ripped through her, her pussy contracting around him so hard it nearly pushed him out. He thrust into her again and came, pulsing inside her in time to the fluttering around his length.

He didn't want to leave this little room, where the air smelled of their sex and no one could come between them. But as the haze cleared from his mind, the sounds of the other cast members above deck and footsteps in the hall began to filter in, and he reluctantly withdrew, helping her clean up and get dressed.

"We better get going." Her grin was satisfied and sleepy and he wanted nothing more than to bundle her up in his arms and shut out the world, keep himself buried in her until everyone else forgot about them.

He caught her hand, pressing a kiss to her palm. "I really do love you, Kyla," he said, his voice too tight.

"I love you, too." She studied him with a confused wrinkle of her eyebrow. "I'll see you out there."

He watched her walk out of the cabin and tried to tell himself that everything was fine, that they would be fine, but even then he knew it wasn't true.

Chapter Twenty-nine

Kyla was practically floating as she walked down the hall towards her suite at The Barclay, her sandals hanging from her fingertips and her bare feet sinking into the carpet. She hummed some sappy love song from the Brozone as she dug in her bag for her keycard. Tessa liked to play the boy band's music in the kitchen at the bakery but Kyla had never learned all the words.

"My one and only," she sang to herself, filling in the blanks with humming, "…don't want to be lonely."

She let herself inside her suite, tossing her bag on the dresser. She lifted her eyes and stopped short, the song dying on her lips.

There, in the middle of her suite, stood Brodie surrounded by three cameramen. His hands were dug into the pockets of his jeans and he wore a crisp, short-sleeved button-up in a bright turquoise and neon orange pattern. Her eyes ran over him as she tried to process what she was seeing.

Brodie was supposed to be in California. Brodie was *not* supposed to be in her hotel room and he definitely wasn't supposed to be a part of *Once Upon A Town*.

"Hey, babe." He was grinning, but his eyes were cold. "Miss me?"

"What are you doing here?" she asked, her feet rooted to the ground where she stood.

"I'm here for you."

She barked out a laugh before she could catch herself, pressing a hand to her lips to smother the sound.

His eyes narrowed, his jaw clenched. "Is that any way to greet your boyfriend?"

Her mouth fell open, her eyes flitting to the cameras around her room. "You are *not* my boyfriend. We broke up months ago."

He rolled his eyes. "That's our thing. You and I both know that's what you do."

"What I do?"

"Yeah, babe. You get freaked out and you break things off and then after a few months, you come around and I take you back."

She must be going crazy. To hear their history described that way, like he hadn't been the one to show up on her doorstep and beg her to take him back all those times, to send late night booty call texts and dick pics. To act like it was a foregone conclusion that this break up was temporary, that they'd end up together. It was so preposterous she couldn't begin to formulate a response.

Brodie crossed the room towards her and reached for her hands. As soon as his skin made contact, she jerked her hand away, stepping back until she hit the wall behind her. His nostrils flared and he glanced over his shoulder at the camera that had followed him to her side.

"It's okay, babe. I forgive you. Weird as fuck that you've been dating my dad," he said, leaning on the last two words.

"Go again," Davis said from the corner of the room. It was the first time she'd noticed the director tucked away beside her nightstand. "No swearing."

Brodie turned towards the director with an affable smile. "Sorry, bro. I forgot." Then he turned back to Kyla, the smile now frozen on his face. "It's weird that you've been dating my dad, but we'll move past it. Together." He reached for her hand again.

"No," she said, pulling her hand away a second time. "Does Gavin know you're here?"

"Not yet. Figured we could tell him together."

"You should talk to your father—"

Brodie took a step back, dropped to one knee, and produced a small black box from his pants pocket. "Kyla Marie Mitchell—"

"What are you doing?" she hissed, eyes wide and panic racing through her blood. Her heartbeat thundered in her ears and the room tilted as she tried to make sense of the scene in front of her.

"You're kind of ruining my big moment, babe," he said with a huff and a shake of his head.

"Get up." Her voice crackled like dry leaves as she choked out the words. When he didn't move, she bent down and gripped his bicep, dragging him to his feet. "Get the fuck up!"

He rubbed the spot where she'd held his arm. "Damn, Ky. I didn't even ask you yet."

"You are not asking me anything." Angry tears gathered at the base of her throat, but she would not cry. Not here, surrounded by cameras and her asshole ex-boyfriend. "We are over, Brodie. We've *been* over. This is never happening."

"Babe—"

"We're over!" she shouted, her voice shrill and brittle. "Why are you doing this?" she asked, her voice cracking as those tears pushed forward.

Brodie glanced over his shoulder at Davis. "I think we should just tell her."

"Tell me what?"

Davis sighed and answered as though Kyla hadn't spoken at all. "Do what you want. We've got enough to piece it together anyway." He made a circling motion above his head and the cameramen followed him out of the room.

"Tell me what?" she demanded again.

Brodie waited until the door clicked shut before he turned back to her. All his charm and humor were gone, replaced by the tight set of his jaw and shoulders and a coldness in his eyes she'd never seen before.

"Is it true? Are you really fucking my dad?" Brodie asked, disgust etched into the lines of his face.

Kyla wrapped her arms around her middle as though she could protect herself from his scorn. *You always knew this day would come. You always knew you'd have to face him someday.*

But she'd assumed she'd have Gavin at her side. Instead, she felt his loss like a physical ache. She was facing Brodie's anger alone and he was off on a date with someone else.

"Seriously?" Brodie took a step away from her as though he'd be tainted by proximity to her. "What the fuck, Kyla?"

"My relationship with Gavin—"

"With *my dad.*"

"—has nothing to do with you."

He reeled back as though he'd been slapped. "You are fucking delusional, you know that?"

"You don't know anything," she said, clawing and scraping within herself to hold onto what she knew to be true. Gavin loved her. He'd told her so, over and over, with his words and his body and his private smiles. He *loved* her.

"You think just because my dad did this reality show—that *I* had to convince him to do in the first place, by the way— that he's going to suddenly settle down and, what? Be your boyfriend? He's twenty years older than us! And my dad doesn't fucking date! You know that."

She forced herself to take a beat, to breathe in and out slowly despite the way her hands shook. Brodie didn't know the way his father was with her. All those things he said might have been true of Gavin before, but not now.

Doubt pushed at the edges of her mind and she forced it

back. *Brodie's just mad. He's just trying to get under your skin.*

"We love each other."

Brodie snorted. "Please. Zayne told me all about how you've been photographing the other women for your portfolio, talking about your studio every chance you get. You just want the prize money."

"That's not true." Maybe it had started that way, but that wasn't why she was still there. It wasn't why Gavin had kept her there.

"No? Could've fooled me, babe. You never liked being in front of the camera before."

"Tell me what?" she asked again, her control fraying rapidly.

"He's not going to pick you," Brodie said, stone-faced.

She blinked and shook her head as though that would make his words untrue. "I'm sorry, I don't—"

"He was never going to pick you. He doesn't get to decide who wins."

"What are you talking about?"

"My dad doesn't get to choose which one of you wins in the end. That's up to Zayne, and Zayne doesn't want you."

His words landed like a blow, and no matter how much she wanted to deny them—because Gavin would have *told* her— she knew they were true. Deep in her gut. All the things Erika had said about Zayne having a favorite, about him having more power on set than anyone else, the way Gavin had said they were making him take Roni on a date…

Brodie continued, as though he hadn't just ripped apart her entire world with a few careless words. "But because you two can't keep your hands off each other—fucking *gross*, by the way—the show needs a reason for why you have to leave. They need the audience to think you betrayed Dad so they'll stop rooting for you."

He knew. All this time he knew, and he didn't say anything.

She stumbled backwards, leaning against the wall for

support. Why hadn't he said anything?

He'd let her make a fool of herself, let her believe he was helping her, that he *loved* her, when all this time he was setting her up to be humiliated on national television. And when he sent her home, it would confirm every awful thing her parents had ever said about her, every awful thing she'd ever thought about herself—*she wasn't enough.* Not enough to be worth fighting for and not even enough to be honest with. Why did she ever think she'd be enough for a man like Gavin to love?

It was too much. It hurt too much to think about the fact that she was losing him. No. Correction. She loved him and she'd already lost him.

And then, to add insult to injury, she realized that Gavin wasn't the only thing she'd lost in all this.

He'd let her prattle on and on about how much it meant to her to open the studio, made her think she'd be able to use her winnings to do just that, but there wouldn't be any winnings. There wouldn't be any studio. She'd be leaving without the man she loved and with her dreams well and truly shattered, and he'd known it was going to happen.

"They're going to make me the villain," she said. The final nail in the coffin of her business. Bad enough that she wouldn't have the cash, now she wouldn't even have her reputation.

Or Gavin.

She pressed her hands against the wall behind her to keep herself from doubling over as the pain sliced through her, lacerating vital organs as it twisted its way up her throat, pushing its way out as a sob she couldn't hold back.

"Can't have everyone wishing it was you at the end when Dad chooses someone else," Brodie said.

"So you thought I'd marry *you*?" She couldn't follow this absolutely batshit train of thought when her heart was shredding itself in her chest.

He scoffed. "Nah, babe. Zayne wanted me to come on and

confront you two while you were on a date, but I pitched him this instead."

"Why?"

He glanced away, swallowing thickly and, for the first time, she saw the hurt behind the anger in his eyes. "I'm fucking pissed, but he's still my dad. I'm not gonna air that shit on TV." He sniffed and then turned his attention back to her. "If I give Zayne a good story, he said he'll hook me up with his contacts in LA. Help me break into television."

"I'm not going to pretend to get engaged to you." Her voice shook and she curled her hands into fists, the bite of her nails in her palms grounding her.

You cannot fall apart. Not in front of him.

"Yeah, I thought you might say that." He sighed and flipped open the ring box. It was empty. "That's why I already filmed my side of the proposal, complete with sliding the ring onto the finger of some PA with the right size hands. The car is already on the way to pick you up and take you home. You're off the show and this is the story that's airing whether you play along or not."

"I don't understand."

"They'll cut it together, make it look like you said yes."

"But I didn't!"

He shrugged. "None of this is real, Kyla. It's all just for show. My dad knows that. How come you don't?"

Chapter Thirty

"You didn't say that to the UN Secretary General!" Gavin said as he and Roni walked back to her room, her arm linked through his.

"I did! I said, Mr. Secretary, you're full of shit," Roni said with a grin.

They both laughed.

"I would have paid money to see his face," Gavin said, shaking his head.

"It was pretty great." Roni nudged his shoulder with her own. "Just like this date." She smirked and pulled him into a hug. Her hand closed over his lapel mic and she whispered in his ear, "Kyla's a lucky girl."

As they separated, he scanned her eyes for any trace of disappointment or sadness, but all he found was the shared joy of a friend who was pleased to see him happy.

"Thank you." He squeezed her arm before she disappeared into her room.

He headed back to his suite, guilt souring in his stomach with every step. He needed to tell Kyla what was going on with Zayne, to warn her that this whole thing was beyond his control. Maybe he'd been fighting against the inevitable this whole time. It was time to admit defeat so he and Kyla could come up with a plan together.

He'd give her his half of the prize money so she could still open her studio, that much was obvious, but they'd need to find a way for her to have a graceful exit before Zayne came up with something on his own. He scrubbed his hand over his face. How was he supposed to tell the woman he loved that he couldn't save her from the public humiliation of him choosing another woman on national television?

Gavin rounded a corner, his steps slowing. There, seated on the floor outside his hotel suite, was Kyla. She still wore the outfit she'd worn earlier on the boat, but she was barefoot, her hair covering her face from his view.

"Hey, what are you doing here?" he asked with a chuckle as he approached.

She turned her face up to him and his steps faltered, his lungs forgetting how to function. She was pale, her expression harder than he'd ever seen it. There was no sparkle in her eyes, no softness in her lips. She got to her feet, unfurling herself and throwing her shoulders back like she was prepared for battle.

She knows.

"We need to talk." The hoarseness of her voice was like a thousand tiny papercuts across his skin.

He nodded, unable to speak as he unlocked his room and ushered her inside. It wasn't until the door closed behind him that he realized the conspicuous lack of cameras around them.

"Brodie's here," she began, the words rocking him back on his heels, "and he told me everything."

"Brodie's *here*?"

"He told me you don't actually get to choose the winner. Zayne does, but you already knew that. Three guesses who he's chosen, and the first two don't count." The lack of emotion in her voice was somehow so much worse than if she had been screaming at him.

"I can explain." He took a step towards her, but she stepped away from him, crossing her arms over her chest. She never shrank from him before.

"Since you and I were so convincing on camera, they need a reason to send me home. A way to make it look like I betrayed you, so the audience won't mind when you choose someone else in the end. They're going to air a story that I'm engaged to Brodie. For the record, I'm not."

"I didn't think you were."

She bobbed her head in the slightest of acknowledgments. "I thought you deserved to hear it from me. To have me look you in the eyes and tell you the truth about what games are being played with your life," she said, her voice breaking on the last word.

His stomach lurched. "Kyla." He reached for her, but she stepped away.

"Don't. You made a fool of me." Her eyes brimmed with tears and his nose stung with his own desire to cry. "The whole world is going to believe that I broke your heart and ran off with Brodie. They're going to hate me. This will destroy my business before I even get a chance to start it."

"Right." He stiffened, blinking back the moisture in his eyes as his heart sank further into his gut. "Because that's the only reason you were here at all. To start your business."

He knew it was an asshole thing to say, that he had no moral high ground here, but with panic closing in at the edges of his vision, he couldn't help it. He could feel her slipping away, or maybe that was just an illusion, a desperate hope that he still had time. Maybe he'd already lost her.

"That's not fair," she grated out.

"But it's true."

She threw her arms out to the side. "What do you want me to say, Gavin? Yes! I signed up to be on this show because I wanted to start my business. I never hid that from you. That doesn't mean—" She stopped herself, looking away from him.

"What? It doesn't mean what?"

"It doesn't mean I don't love you!"

Relief flooded through his veins and he reached for her again. "I love you too."

She shrugged him off and all the warmth fled his body. "You *lied* to me. Over and over again. You had so many opportunities to tell me what was going on and you chose not to. You had so many chances to send me home before the show decided to turn me into a villain, to put an end to this before it got this far, and you didn't. I would have waited for you. I would have—" She broke off on a sob and he physically ached with the need to hold her, his hands twitching at his sides. But she wouldn't let him touch her. Her voice broke when she asked, "Why couldn't you just tell me the truth?"

"I wanted to fix it. I'm going to fix it," he said, desperation making his voice tight.

"You can't fix it, Gavin. You signed a contract. All this time you've known…" She broke off, shaking her head and dashing away the rogue tear that fell down her cheek. "Was any of it real?"

"Yes," he growled. He cupped her face, his hands tangling in her hair and tilted her face up to his. "It was real. You know it was."

"I don't know anything," she said in a thready whisper.

"You know me." He gripped her hand and pressed it to his chest so she could feel his wild heartbeat. "I love you, Kyla. I didn't want to worry you when I could take care of it. I wanted to give you everything you deserved."

"I deserved the truth." She shoved him away. He fell back, stunned. "I deserve someone who sees me as an equal and not just a problem they have to solve. I deserve a partner who tells me things, especially when they impact my life."

"I wanted to fix it," he repeated helplessly.

"Who asked you to?" Tears slid down her cheeks. "We should have been trying to work it out together."

He pressed his forehead to hers. "Please, Kyla."

She took a shuddering breath. "I have to go."

His heart stopped. "Tell me this isn't over."

"I don't know what this is, Gavin, but right now, you have a show to do, and I need to leave."

She turned her back and headed towards the door. Every cell in his body screamed to go after her.

"When the show is done filming, I'm coming for you, little goddess. I will fight for you."

"I don't need someone to fight for me, Gavin. I need someone to be honest with me," she said sadly. "Talk to your son. He's angry, but he'll forgive you."

"Will you?" When she didn't answer right away, he exhaled harshly as though he'd been punched. "Kyla—" His voice broke and he tried again. "I love you."

Her face hardened as she dashed away the last of her tears. "Goodbye, Gavin."

It only took Gavin a few minutes to decide to go after Kyla, but it was too late. She was already gone.

"Get me Zayne!" he bellowed at the startled PA for the third time.

Instead, it was Patrick who rounded the corner, coming upon Gavin as his heartbreak morphed into anger. He pounced on the producer, gripping the front of his shirt and shoving him into the wall, Patrick's hands coming up defensively to keep some distance between the two of them.

"Did you know?" Gavin roared.

"Gavin, I—"

"Did you fucking know?"

"I was just told. I'm sorry. I really thought that if you gave him enough of a story, he'd back off."

"Where is he?" Gavin released Patrick's shirt and ran his hands through his hair, tugging on the ends until his scalp stung.

"I hear you're looking for me," Zayne said as he appeared in the hallway, flanked by cameramen and security guards.

Gavin chuckled bitterly and stumbled back until he was leaning against the wall. He recognized that taunting flash in the producer's eye, the way he was daring Gavin to lay a hand on him. He'd capture the whole thing on film and press charges, Gavin had no doubt. Zayne was just an overgrown schoolyard bully and Gavin was so tired of playing his game.

"You involved my son," Gavin said. "That wasn't in the agreement."

"Brodie's a legal adult. I entered into a contract with him the same as I did with you," Zayne said.

Gavin's fury mingled with panic. What had Brodie signed? What had he promised this asshole?

Zayne sneered. "Don't worry. He's fulfilled his end of the bargain, so his contract is no longer relevant."

Gavin took a step towards Zayne, jabbing a finger towards him. "I'm done. I quit."

Patrick sucked in a breath but it was Zayne's amused snort that held Gavin's attention. "Then you can expect to hear from our legal team. Tell me, lover boy, how much does a marketing professor make? Not enough to shoulder the six figure fines for quitting the show early, I'd wager." He clicked his tongue and shook his head. "And it's a shame your son won't get his payment for his part in this little play. That was always contingent on your continued cooperation." He cocked his head in mock confusion. "Or, wait, I'm sorry—I should say it's contingent on you starting to follow your contract to the fucking letter."

"What are you talking about?" Gavin asked.

"Tearing cameras off the wall of your hotel room. Meeting with Kyla off camera. You did that last one at least two times. How many more will I find if I review the footage more closely?" Gavin couldn't breath, couldn't think as ice flooded his veins. "That's a pretty clear violation of your contract. And hers. So how about I lay it out for you? This is *my* house. You play by *my* rules. You will choose Lauren as the winner and you will not have any more contact with Kyla until after the final episode airs. Not a phone call, not a text message, not a fucking carrier pigeon."

"Or what?" he asked, his voice sounding not at all like his own.

"Or I'll sue you both for breach of contract. And trust me, I'll enjoy destroying that bitch."

Gavin lunged at Zayne, cameras and security guards be damned, but Patrick stepped between them, holding him back.

"It's not worth it," Patrick said in a low voice. "I need you to trust me."

"Trusting you got me into this mess." Gavin shoved Patrick away.

Patrick nodded but didn't back down. "Your son is still in wardrobe. If you go now, you can probably catch him before he leaves for the airport."

Gavin's stomach twisted, guilt and anger and the urgent need to protect Kyla at all costs mixing with an overwhelming sense of loss into a tangled knot of pain that seared through him and made it hard to think. Still, he let Patrick guide him towards the suite that was being used by wardrobe and steadied himself at the door. Inside the room he could hear the light murmur of Megan's voice followed by Brodie's familiar laugh. That web of pain twisted in his gut, latching on to his vital organs, but he pushed the door open anyway.

Megan was laughing, a flirtatious smile on her face as she spoke with Brodie, who leaned against the vanity counter. They both turned at the sound of Gavin entering. Megan beamed at him.

"Gavin! I was just getting to know your son. He shares your sense of humor."

"Turns out there are a lot of things we share," Brodie said, turning to Gavin, "Isn't that right, old man?"

"Megan, would you mind giving us a minute?" Gavin asked.

Megan's eyes darted between the two men, the smile dropping from her lips as tension flooded the room. "Of course. Take all the time you need." She skirted out of the room, letting the door close behind her with a soft snick.

Gavin wasn't sure where to start. *I'm sorry*, and *how could you*, and *what the hell have you done*, all jockeying for position. He took a halting step towards Brodie, the wariness and distance in his son's eyes demanding that Gavin go to him, that he fix whatever was hurting him. But he couldn't, because *he* was hurting his son. He'd known all along that Brodie would be hurt by his relationship with Kyla and he'd done it anyway.

Just like you knew you should have told Kyla what was going on with Zayne and you didn't.

"What did you sign?" he asked, his voice calmer than he felt. Brodie looked startled by the question. "Your contract with Zayne. What did you sign?"

"You're worried about my *contract* right now?"

"I'm worried about you."

Brodie snorted, shaking his head and playing with a loose strand of faux pearls on the vanity beside him. "Yeah, right. You should've been worried about me when you were making moves on my girlfriend."

"Ex girlfriend," Gavin ground out. As if it mattered.

Brodie shook his head. "How long did you wait after we broke up? Or is that why she broke up with me? I knew it felt different this time, but it didn't occur to me that she might cheat—"

"She didn't cheat. Nothing happened while you were together," Gavin said, working like hell to keep his voice level.

"I guess at least there's that." Brodie pushed off from the vanity. "You know, when I told you to bang the hottie, I didn't mean her."

"I'm sorry I hurt you," Gavin said. "I'm sorry I let you down."

Brodie held up his hand to stop him and the apologies died in Gavin's throat. He meant it, every word, but he could never apologize for loving Kyla.

"I'm going back to California and your boy Zayne is gonna hook me up with all his contacts while you stay here and play out the rest of this midlife crisis, or whatever the fuck is going on with you."

"That's why you're doing this? That's why you hurt Kyla? To get ahead in Hollywood?"

"Pretty sure you're the one who hurt her."

He closed his eyes, letting the accusation sink into his skin. Brodie was right. Zayne and Brodie may have been the catalyst but Gavin was the one who set the whole thing in motion when he decided not to be honest with her.

"I love her," Gavin said, the words torn from his chest.

Brodie blinked and exhaled slowly. "I hope you're happy, Dad. But don't expect me to be happy for you."

"Tell me how to make it right." Desperation clawed at his throat. He'd never seen Brodie this cold before, this collected and calm. It terrified him. He couldn't lose the love of his life and his son in the same day. "You are the most important person in my life."

"Sure as fuck doesn't feel like it."

"Tell me what to do."

"You lied to me."

"I didn't. I never—"

"What did you always tell me growing up? A lie of omission is still a lie?" Brodie repeated the words Gavin had said over and over throughout the years, when Brodie didn't tell him about the lamp he'd broken playing soccer in the house when he was nine or his first failing grade on a paper when he was thirteen. "I never thought you'd lie to me," Brodie said, his brows drawn low and his voice soft as though he couldn't believe he even had to say it. "So how 'bout we start with no more lies, yeah, Dad?"

Gavin swallowed hard around the lump in his throat and nodded.

"I gotta go. I have a plane to catch."

Brodie stepped around Gavin.

"I'm sorry. I love you, son." Brodie froze, his back still to his father. When he didn't respond, Gavin tried again. "Do you hear me?"

"Yeah, I hear you, old man. Just don't know if I believe you."

Chapter Thirty-one

"That's it," Jo said as she and Kyla pushed through the door to their apartment, weighed down with bags of groceries. "Molly!"

Molly appeared in the hallway, her hair twisted into a bun held in place with a pencil and a pile of papers in her hand. "You bellowed?" She set the stack of to-be-graded essays on the coffee table.

"It's time," Jo said ominously, dropping the bags in the kitchen and shaking out her hands to restore circulation.

"Time for what?" Kyla asked as she kicked the front door closed behind her and deposited her own arsenal of bags beside Jo's.

"Time for Operation Get-Out-of-Dodge." Jo surveyed the grocery bags, selecting the few that contained perishables and stuffing the whole bags in the fridge. "There. We'll take the snacks with us and the rest will keep."

"What are you talking about?" Kyla asked, exhausted.

For the last week since she'd gotten home from The Barclay she'd been doing her best to fall back into her old routine, but she couldn't return to work at the bakery or really be seen out in public for more than quick errands without giving away that she'd been eliminated from the show.

You weren't eliminated. You left on your own.

If you call being manipulated by everyone around you until you end up looking like a total asshole 'leaving on your own.'

Her stomach turned at the thought, and she was momentarily surprised to find it was possible for her gut to wind itself into even tighter knots.

"Go pack a bag." Jo turned Kyla by her shoulders and walked her towards her bedroom. "We're going to my parents' cabin in the Berkshires for the weekend."

"I'll get the go bag," Molly said, turning towards her own bedroom.

"There's a go bag?" Kyla asked.

"A 'Prince Charming is an asshole and hurt my friend' go bag, yes. Chocolate, wine, romance novels, board games, a handful of DVDs—can you believe *John Tucker Must Die* isn't on streaming?—a voodoo doll kit—"

"I'm sorry, a *what*?" Kyla dug in her heels and brought them to a halt just inside her bedroom.

"A voodoo doll kit. In case you want to…voodoo…or something. I don't know how it works, but the lady at the store seemed to think it was a good idea," Jo said.

"For our go bag?" Kyla asked.

She felt like she was underwater, like she was hearing everything through a fuzzy speaker, the sound distorted just enough to make it difficult to follow Jo's train of thought. She knew it was just because she hadn't been sleeping, but how could she sleep when all she could think about was what she'd lost, what she'd probably never had in the first place.

None of this is real, Kyla. It's all just for show. My dad knows that. How come you don't?

Brodie's words haunted her day and night.

It had *felt* real. It had been real to her. And she could have sworn it was real for Gavin, but now she wasn't so sure.

Molly arrived in her bedroom, holding an overflowing raffia tote bag, a pack of graham crackers sticking out of the top. "The s'mores supplies were my idea. Do you need help packing?"

"I'm still not sure *why* I'm packing." Kyla flopped down on her bed and curled in on herself. "I just want to sleep."

"I know, hon, and you can do that at the cabin." Molly sat on the edge of the bed, combing her fingers through Kyla's hair like she was a child. If Kyla hadn't felt so numb, it would have been soothing. "What happened?"

"We ran into Mrs. Kemp," Jo said, her wince audible. "She went on and on about how surprised she was to see us because she didn't understand how Gavin could have eliminated Kyla when they were clearly—"

"Can we skip the recap?" Kyla asked.

She didn't want to hear it again. Couldn't handle hearing how even Mrs. Kemp thought she and Gavin were a perfect match, that she should be the one with him in the end. What did it matter what Mrs. Kemp or anyone else thought? The fact of the matter was it wasn't going to be her. Gavin had always known it wouldn't be and never bothered to tell her.

"Okay." Molly moved to Kyla's closet. She chose a handful of shirts from the hangers before moving to the dresser and methodically pulling out leggings, bras, and underwear. "Do you want your bathing suit?" Kyla could only blink at her. "I'll pack it just in case."

"We don't need to leave town," Kyla said, wrapping herself around her pillow.

"A change of scenery might do you good," Molly said. "Just for a few days. I have to teach on Monday."

There was a knock at the front door and Kyla groaned, turning her face into her pillow. Tessa had been on a campaign to cheer her up ever since she heard she was back home, but if Kyla ate one more cake pop she was going to explode. She appreciated the effort, but truth be told, she wasn't even sure she *wanted* to be cheered up. She wanted to wallow until she forgot what Gavin's hands felt like on her skin, the way his kiss tasted.

Then you'll be wallowing for eternity.

"I'll get it." She dragged herself into the living room, leaving her roommates behind to decide whether or not she needed a bathing suit for this ill-advised weekend getaway. As if a weekend away could make her forget.

When she pulled open the door, she was surprised to see Ethan.

"Hey, Kyla." He cupped the back of his neck and smiled sheepishly. "How's it going?"

"I've been better," she deadpanned.

He nodded and reached over to grab something on the floor just out of her view. When he straightened up again, he was holding a vase filled with the largest and most beautiful bouquet of flowers she'd ever seen. "Got a delivery for you."

Kyla stared at the flowers. "Didn't know you delivered flowers," she said, arching a skeptical eyebrow at him.

"They're from Gavin." At the sound of his name, her breath caught in her chest, stabbing her like a thousand shards of glass exploding behind her rib cage.

He'd sent her flowers.

What was she supposed to do with that?

Flowers didn't change the fact that he'd lied to her. They didn't change that he'd set her up to be humiliated on national television, or that he'd treated her like a problem to solve rather than a partner.

Still, her fingers itched with the need to reach for the flowers, to hold onto this tangible sign that he still cared for her.

None of this is real, Kyla. It's all just for show. My dad knows that. How come you don't?

"I'm sorry he made you come all the way here." Kyla clenched her hands into fists to keep herself from taking the flowers. "Tell him I don't want his flowers."

"He's trying, Kyla," Ethan said, his voice grim. "He's going out of his mind not being able to contact you. I've never heard him this distraught."

"Flowers don't fix anything."

"You're right." Ethan shifted the flowers to the side, his voice taking on that fatherly tone she'd heard him use with Tessa. "He messed up, and he knows it, but he also loves you. He's loved you for a long time, and I think you might love him too." Kyla blinked back the tears that pressed behind her eyes and looked away, crossing her arms to protect herself from Ethan's earnest words. "I guess if I were in your position I'd be asking myself if it's worth giving that up without a fight."

"He never gave us a chance to fight. He lied to me—"

"He's fighting now. He went about it the wrong way, but he's been fighting for you this whole time." Ethan set the flowers on the floor and stepped back. "Question is, do you want to fight for him?"

Kyla watched as Ethan walked away, waiting until he was gone from view before she took up the flowers and brought them into the apartment, setting them on the counter.

"Who was it?" Molly asked, eyeing the extravagant bouquet.

"Doesn't matter," Kyla said. "When do we leave?"

Chapter Thirty-two

"Are you sure about this?" Baz asked as he pulled his car into the departures lane at the airport.

"Yes," Gavin said, even though he wasn't sure about anything.

Filming had wrapped on *Once Upon A Town* the night before and it had taken every ounce of restraint he had not to go to Kyla's apartment and fall on his knees at her feet. Two weeks without her was already far too long.

But Zayne had been very clear: Gavin needed to follow his contract to the letter or he'd sue Kyla and he wouldn't set Brodie up with his contacts, hurting the two most important people in the world to Gavin in one blow.

Thankfully, the Travel Network would start airing the show in two weeks. Gavin did a few quick calculations in his head. Eight weeks until he could see her.

Fuck. He wasn't sure he'd survive it.

But if he couldn't beg for Kyla's forgiveness right now, at least he could try to repair his relationship with his son.

"How long will you be gone?" Baz asked.

"I'm not sure. It might be easier to stay out of town until the finale airs. I'm on sabbatical next term anyway."

Baz grunted an acknowledgement, pulling up to the curb and putting the car in park. Jamie had helped Gavin find a house rental just outside of LA, but Gavin knew his friends thought he was being rash. It didn't matter. He'd made a mess of things with both his son and Kyla, and in the end, Zayne had gotten his way anyway. Thankfully he'd at least allowed Gavin to film an ending where he chose Lauren but they mutually decided they were better off as friends. It was a crappy ending, but at least he didn't have to spend the next two months pretending to be in love with Lauren.

"Thanks for checking in on the house while I'm gone," Gavin said, "and for taking care of that other thing."

Baz arched an eyebrow. "Consider it taken care of. Text me when you land."

As Gavin waited for his flight, he couldn't help but continue to check his phone for any missed notifications. He knew there wouldn't be any. Ethan had told him Kyla refused his flowers, so he didn't know why he thought his friends might have any news to share.

He missed her. The words were so inadequate they were almost laughable. He didn't just miss her; he felt like he was missing a part of himself, an empty ache in his chest that had become his constant companion. He pressed the heel of his hand into his sternum as though he could touch that ache.

Eight weeks, he promised himself. *Eight weeks and then you're a free man. Eight weeks and then you can spend the rest of your life proving to her how much you love her.*

Not that he could wait eight weeks, but he wouldn't be in Aster Bay to see her reaction to the things he'd set in motion, the plans Baz would oversee for him in his stead. It wasn't enough to repair the trust he'd broken—he knew that would take much more than money—but he hoped it was at least enough to keep the door open.

Number one: Stop settling for happy enough. Break up with Brodie once and for all. Check.

Number two: Do something that pushes me outside of my comfort zone. She was pretty sure becoming a member at a sex club and being humiliated on national television both counted for that one. Double check.

Number three: Have amazing, toe-curling, life-changing, scream-your-lungs-out sex. So many checks.

Secret number three-and-a-half: Know what it feels like to really be in love. Giant, painful, stupid check.

New addition. Number three-and-three-quarters: Learn how to get through a day without thinking about the man responsible for the amazing sex and the falling in love.

Who was she kidding? She'd been in love with Gavin long before the orgasms and, if she was honest with herself, she knew she'd never go a day without thinking about him. Not now that she knew what it felt like to be loved by him, even if it had all fallen apart at the end.

She rolled her shoulders and refocused.

Number four: Open my own boudoir photography studio like the badass business babe I am so I can help other women feel like badass babes too. Lately she didn't feel badass, but maybe if she could open her studio anyway, she could at least help other women feel that way.

Outside the window of what would become Kyla's boudoir photography studio, the town of Aster Bay was practically buzzing. Tonight, Once Upon A Town would premiere on the Travel Network starring their very own Gavin West and the Merchants' Association had organized a watch party in the high school auditorium. Half the town would be there.

But not Kyla.

Despite the Association's best efforts (including recruiting Mrs. Kemp, Mrs. White, and their friends to launch a campaign to change her mind), Kyla had declined that particular invitation.

She wiped the sweat from her forehead with the back of her hand and cranked up the volume on her Bluetooth speaker, Destiny's Child blasting through the empty space and bouncing off the walls. Jo's playlist was exactly what she needed to get through another long day of scraping paint and wallpaper. The 90s and early 2000s mix had already helped her power through three days that week and, with any luck, by the end of the day, Kyla would have completely scraped clean one wall.

Only three more to go. Plus the bathroom. Fuck me.

The music was so loud she hardly heard the knock on the door. "Coming!" She turned down the volume as she dragged herself across the space to unlock the front door. "Oh, hi," she said, startled to see Baz.

He was tall and lean, his hair styled in a way designed to look like he hadn't done anything but roll out of bed despite his crisply tailored three-piece suit. "Can I come in?"

"Sure." Kyla stepped aside to let him through. "Don't mind the mess. And you're not going to convince me to go to the watch party."

"Wasn't going to try to." Baz surveyed the space before turning back to her. "It looks like the committee has chosen well."

"I'm sorry, chosen what?"

"The New Business Fund Committee of the Merchants' Association. Newly formed. Only came together about a week ago. You've been selected for a startup grant for…" He gestured vaguely to the chaotic space cluttered with tarps and peeling wallpaper. "…your startup."

"I didn't apply for a grant." Maybe she'd inhaled too many chemicals while she scraped paint for hours on end. "I didn't even know there was a grant."

"Like I said, it's newly formed." Baz reached into the inside pocket of his jacket and pulled out a bright white envelope, offering it to her. She tore it open to reveal a check for $50,000. "Should all be in order. Congratulations."

"This is from the New Business…"

"Fund Committee. Yes."

She swallowed, pain lancing through her chest. "Gavin wouldn't happen to be on that committee, would he?" She eyed Baz warily as his lips pressed into a flat line, his expression unreadable.

"Not technically, no."

Her hands shook as she stared at her name printed on the check. She didn't need Baz to confirm it to know this was Gavin's doing. He'd given her his entire portion of the prize money. He knew she'd never accept it from him directly, so he'd somehow arranged for this committee to act as a pass through. She didn't know whether to be elated or furious. Did he think he could buy her forgiveness?

Maybe he's trying to fulfill his promise that the prize money could help her open her business.

Maybe he shouldn't have made that promise to begin with if he wouldn't be able to keep it.

Except now he had kept it.

She wasn't sure how to feel about that.

Baz cleared his throat and indicated the envelope with a tilt of his chin. "The grant agreement stipulates that you'll repay twenty percent of the grant within the first five years of your business, allowing the funds to be used to support other startups."

Kyla pulled out a single sheet of paper on official town letterhead, skimming it as Baz explained its contents.

"Should you be unable to repay that amount within that time frame, you will be granted extensions in five-year periods.

If for some reason you have not paid back the twenty percent at the time that your business closes, the remaining balance is forgiven." He reached into the front pocket of his suit jacket and produced a pen, holding it out to her. "Sign at the bottom and the money's yours. If you'd prefer to have a lawyer look it over before you sign, that's fine," he said, his voice softening, "but it's a good deal, Kyla."

She blinked up at Baz, her throat thick with emotion as she reached for the pen. "It's a great deal."

She signed hastily, handing the agreement back to Baz. He nodded, folding the paper carefully and tucking it away in his jacket. "I'll forward you a copy of the fully executed agreement."

He turned to go, but Kyla called after him. "Why is he doing this?"

Baz turned slowly, his face inscrutable. "Because he loves you."

"He doesn't need to give me *money* to prove he loves me."

"He didn't. The town did," Baz said with a smirk. The smile fell from his face and he narrowed his eyes. He dug his hands into his pants pocket. "What would he need to do to prove it to you?"

She opened her mouth to reply, but closed it again. She wasn't sure what to say. She knew Gavin loved her. She didn't need him to prove that. And she loved him.

But she still wasn't sure how they could make it work. Being with her had caused a rift between him and his son, and the fact remained that he'd lied to her. He'd made decisions that directly affected her life without even consulting her, just like her parents had done. It didn't matter how much they loved each other if he wasn't going to treat her like a true partner.

As if Baz could hear her thoughts, he hummed to himself. "Gavin likes to fix things for the people he loves. He thinks that's why we love him. Because he smooths out the rough patches for us."

"He lied to me." Even she could tell her words lacked any real bite.

"He did. He's trying to apologize."

"*He's* not the one who's here."

Baz looked unimpressed. "That's to protect you too. Don't you get it? Gavin will always do whatever he needs to do to protect you. Including not talking to you until after the finale airs. He misses you so much it's obnoxious. Do you know how many times he's texted me today alone looking for any scrap of information about you?"

"How many?" she asked, her heart racing.

"Sixteen. It's not even noon, Kyla. So my question to you is, when I text him after I leave here, what am I going to be able to tell my friend?"

She swallowed hard, the envelope in her hand suddenly feeling heavy with the weight of their relationship. She didn't know how it was going to work, didn't know how she could trust that he wouldn't keep things from her again in the name of protecting her, but Baz was right. He was trying. That had to count for something, right?

"Tell him I said thank you. And that I miss him too."

Chapter Thirty-three

Gavin sat on the bench outside Brodie's apartment sipping his coffee for the fourth morning in a row. Brodie hadn't opened the door again this morning when Gavin knocked but that was okay, Gavin had time. *Five more weeks.* And he was familiar with Brodie's stubborn streak. When he was eight he decided that he wouldn't eat vegetables anymore so, in protest of the green beans on his plate at dinner, he'd shut himself in his room and refused to come out. Gavin had sat on the floor in the hallway, grading papers and talking to himself just loud enough to let Brodie know he was there, for three hours before Brodie's bladder finally proved stronger than his pride. This was just the twenty-three year-old version of that.

"You just gonna sit out here all day?"

Gavin glanced up from his phone—no new messages from his friends about Kyla—to see Brodie standing in the doorway to his apartment building, arms crossed over his chest.

"Good morning," Gavin said, smiling.

Brodie rolled his eyes. "Come on in." He yanked open the front door.

Gavin sprinted to grab the door before it slam-locked behind Brodie, just catching it in time. They walked in silence to the small, one-bedroom apartment at the back of the building that

Brodie shared with his stepbrother. A TV was propped up on a stack of cinder blocks in one corner, a couch that had seen better days along the far wall, stacks of unpacked boxes littered throughout the cramped space.

"It's nice," Gavin said.

Brodie snorted and headed into the kitchen, pulling out a frying pan. "I'm gonna make some eggs. You want some?"

"Sure." Gavin tried to tamp down his excitement that they were actually speaking. "I can help."

Brodie shot him a look. "Your eggs are shit. You always overcook 'em."

Gavin leaned against the counter, watching as Brodie cracked eggs into a bowl and whisked them into a frothy yellow liquid.

"So talk already," Brodie said, pouring the eggs into the pan. "I know you didn't come all the way across the country because you have nothing to say."

"I'm sorry." Gavin coughed lightly, surprised by the sudden pressure in his throat. "I should have talked to you about what was going on. That seems to be a theme for me lately. Not talking to the people I love about things that are important."

"I noticed." Brodie scraped down the sides of the pan with a rubber spatula as he scrambled the eggs. "So why didn't you?"

Gavin cupped the back of his neck. "Honestly? I'm not sure. I guess I was afraid you'd be upset."

"Afraid I'd think you weren't super-dad, more likely," Brodie muttered under his breath.

"What was that?"

Brodie shut the heat off and shoved the pan to the back of the stovetop, away from the hot burner, turning to look at Gavin directly. "You think you have to be super-dad all the time. You did it when I was a kid and you're doing it now. It's like you're afraid of me getting mad at you or something."

"That's not true." Gavin's stomach sank. It was. It was definitely true.

"Oh yeah?" Brodie arched an eyebrow and squared off his stance. "When I was thirteen, I got in trouble at school for teasing Jacky Leeburg and you had to come have a parent-teacher conference about it. Mom grounded me for the weekend, and you told her I could be grounded at your house, but then you let my friends come over and play ball with me in the backyard anyway."

"It was the first nice weekend of the year," Gavin said, grasping at straws.

"And when I was sixteen, you found porn on my computer, so you took away my internet privileges, but you let me choose what we ate for dinner every night until I got my laptop back."

"That's not such a—"

"We had buffalo wings and fries every night for two weeks. Ever since you and Mom got divorced, it's like you can't handle the idea that I might be mad at you."

"You're right," Gavin said, deflated. "I broke up our family when you were twelve and I saw how hard that was on you. I never wanted you to hurt like that again."

Brodie shook his head, reaching for a stack of paper plates on the counter and scooping eggs onto two of them. "Having your parents get divorced sucks, but that was eleven years ago, Dad. I'm not a fucking child. And sometimes I'm gonna be mad at you. Like right now."

"I'm sorry. I never expected to fall in love with Kyla."

"You think I'm mad about that?" Brodie shoved a floppy paper plate full of eggs at him.

"You're not?"

"Maybe at first," Brodie said, gesturing to the small table in the corner of the room. "It's weird as fuck that you're banging my ex-girlfriend, but whatever. She and I broke up and I'm not even on the same coast as her anymore. She can screw whoever she wants. Even if it's you."

Gavin's throat felt tight, warmth washing over him at his

son's grace.

"Just don't fuck it up," Brodie said between mouthfuls of eggs.

"I might have already done that." Gavin pushed his own eggs around with his fork.

"You lied to her the same way you lied to me."

"It didn't feel like lying. It felt like protecting her. Protecting you both."

"You were so busy trying to protect me—nah, not even that—you were so busy trying to protect the image you thought I had of you that you couldn't be honest with me. That's some shady shit, old man." Brodie dug into his eggs with a plastic fork, gesturing to Gavin's plate. "Eat. Cold eggs are disgusting."

Gavin bit back a smile as he took a bite of his eggs. "I'm sorry I lied to you. It won't happen again."

Brodie snorted. "No shit. I don't have any other exes who would be interested in hooking up with you."

"That's not what I meant."

"I know what you meant. I don't need you to protect my feelings, Dad. I need you to be real with me."

"Kyla said something similar," Gavin admitted.

"She's smart. You should listen to her." He grinned. "Though maybe not that smart if she wants to be with your old ass."

Gavin wanted to laugh at the joke but it twisted in his gut instead. Did she want to be with him? He wasn't sure anymore. Maybe he'd blown his one chance to be with her.

"Hey," Brodie said to get his attention. "Just talk to her. Not talking is how you got into this mess."

"When did you get so wise?" Gavin speared a bite of his breakfast.

One corner of Brodie's mouth tipped up. "Just eat your eggs."

Gavin groaned and dragged himself out of bed, the early morning sunshine streaming through the window of his rented bedroom far too bright. "Coming!" he called to whoever had decided this was a good time to lean against his doorbell.

He pulled the front door open, blinking until the fuzzy outline before him turned into the very clear shape of Patrick.

"I don't want to talk to you." Gavin stepped back and starting to close the door.

Patrick pressed a hand to the door to stop him. "I know. But you wouldn't answer any of my calls."

"Some people would take the hint."

"I need five minutes of your time. I think you'll want to hear what I have to say."

"The last time I gave you five minutes I wound up signing my life away to Zayne. I'll pass."

He tried to close the door again, but Patrick lunged forward, moving his slight frame into the opening just in time. "Zayne was fired this morning," he blurted.

Gavin paused, letting the door swing back open. "Good. Fuck him," he said, eying Patrick warily. "What happened?"

"Turns out he was sleeping with Lauren."

"I knew something was going on! His obsession with her winning didn't make sense."

"Five minutes, Gavin. I promise it'll be worth it."

Gavin nodded and stepped back, gesturing Patrick into the living room. "How'd you even know where to find me?"

Patrick glanced around the sparsely furnished rental as he took a seat at one end of the couch. "Aunt Judy. I swear, my aunt and her friends have a better information network than the FBI."

Gavin grunted in agreement, sitting on the opposite end of the couch.

Patrick cleared his throat, looking uneasy for the first time since he'd arrived. "I owe you an apology. I should have warned you when you signed on about how little control I would have over the production. But I never anticipated Zayne pulling the kind of stunts he did. He seemed like a normal enough guy when we'd worked together before, and he had such impressive reality show credentials." He shook his head. "Anyway, I'm sorry."

"I appreciate that. But you didn't track me down to apologize. What's going on, Patrick?"

"Like I said, Zayne was fired yesterday. And Lauren's prize money has been revoked. She'll need to pay it back, plus damages for violating the contract. But that's not the important part. As soon as Zayne was fired, I met with the network execs. I told them how much he'd manipulated the show, especially the final few episodes. And I got permission to re-edit those episodes."

Gavin leaned forward, resting his elbows on his knees. "What are you saying?"

"We can change the narrative, tell the story of what really happened, not this ridiculous hail Mary plot line about your son swooping in and proposing to Kyla. We can shine a light on the manipulation, the manufactured storylines that plague this genre. We're going to do something that's never been done in reality TV, Gavin, but I need your help."

"I'm not in any hurry to be involved in any more reality TV. No offense."

Patrick chuckled. "None taken. But if we do this right, it'll be a game changer for unscripted television. And I think it might just help you and Kyla get your happy ending."

Gavin narrowed his eyes. "Why would you care about that?"

"I'm a romantic. Don't forget, *Once Upon A Town* was my idea in the first place. I'd still like to see Prince Charming get his happily ever after. After all, if we strip away Zayne's script, the story we're left with is the story of you two falling in love. That's the story I'm interested in telling. And my Aunt Judy will have me strung up by my heels if I don't make this right."

Gavin scanned Patrick's face but found nothing to make him question the man's sincerity. And if Patrick was right, if they could re-edit the final episodes to remove the false narratives and tell the true story of how Gavin and Kyla had fallen in love, then maybe he could help Kyla see just how real their love had been all along.

Chapter Thirty-four

"Okay, I'm locking myself in my room with my wallpaper and tile samples for the next hour." Kyla gestured to the heavy bag of samples she'd picked up from the contractor earlier in the day. "I'll have my headphones on so you don't need to worry about keeping the volume down like last week."

Jo held up her glass of wine as if in a toast. "I'm not going to apologize for that. That date in the dark was hot."

Kyla rolled her eyes and pretended it didn't make her want to cry. Thinking about that date, about how close she'd felt to Gavin, about the night they'd spent together afterwards…it was too much. She'd resolved to shut away all of her feelings about Gavin in a box in the back of her mind until they were in the same time zone again, because no matter how many excuses he found to send his friends to talk to her, no matter how many bouquets of flowers and boxes of cupcakes he had delivered to her apartment, the fact of the matter remained: he was still in California and they still couldn't talk to each other without risking a lawsuit.

So she'd become intimately acquainted with the process of selecting fixtures and finishes, spending hours debating the merits of various kinds of drawer pulls and faucets just so she wouldn't think about the man she loved desperately and missed beyond reason choosing another woman on national television.

Just one more hour and it'll all be over.

"Are you sure you don't want to watch it with us?" Molly asked from where she sat cross-legged on the couch. Molly asked every week, and every week Kyla declined. "It's the finale. The teasers for this week said this is unlike any other episode they've done before."

"No, thanks. But I appreciate you two watching for me. I need to know what they air so I'm prepared for any social media backlash."

She'd researched all the advice she could find on handling these kinds of things, what comments to respond to, when to make a statement, so she was prepared for when the episode aired that would show her "engagement" to Brodie, but that didn't mean she wanted to watch it happen.

"Go pick out your tile," Jo said. "We've got this."

Kyla retreated to her bedroom, closing the door behind her. Her phone dinged with an incoming message as she set the bag of samples down at her feet. Which one of Gavin's friends was texting her now?

Jamie: Will you watch tonight?

Kyla: No. I don't need to see them try to convince the world that I got engaged to Brodie.

Jamie: I think you should watch tonight, Kyla. I had a preview of the episode. It's not going to be what you think.

What did that mean? She sighed and shoved the phone in her back pocket. She wasn't going to watch herself be portrayed as someone she wasn't. Besides, she had samples to choose.

She'd only just spread the heavy tile samples across her bed when Jo came bursting into her bedroom. "You have to see this. Come on, you're missing it." She grabbed Kyla's arm and pulled her into the living room.

"I told you, I don't want to—" Kyla broke off as they rounded the corner, Gavin's face on her television screen coming into view. Her throat was immediately choked with tears, the longing in her chest so heavy it pressed her down onto the couch, her eyes glued to the screen.

He wore a hunter green button-down, one curl of hair flopping into his eyes, as he spoke directly to the camera. "What you've seen up to this point is all true. It all happened." It felt like he was speaking just to her. "But what you didn't see is what was happening behind-the-scenes, when the cameras weren't supposed to be filming. Lucky for us all, on reality TV, someone is always filming," he said with a rueful smile.

The video cut to a far-away shot of Patrick, Zayne, and Gavin standing in the garden at Aster Place the night of the first ball. The video might have been hard to decipher in the dark but, thanks to Gavin's mic, the audio was clear, and just in case, they'd subtitled the scene unfolding on screen.

Patrick: *Do you know who you want to send home?*

Gavin: *Lauren*

Patrick: *Really? Are you sure? We thought you'd want to send Kyla home week one.*

Kyla's breathing hitched and Molly reached across the couch, squeezing her hand in solidarity.

Gavin: *Then why did you even cast her if you thought I'd just turn around and send her home?*

Zayne: *To bring in viewers for the pilot. It's a scandal. You just have to give us a good sound bite about dating your son's ex-girlfriend and the first episode will practically sell itself.*

Beside her, Jo muttered "motherfucker," under her breath.

Gavin: *You want a sound bite.*

Zayne: *Let's be honest. You and I both know she's not winner material.*

Patrick: *What Zayne means is, she doesn't fit the mold of the typical contestant on a show like this.*

Gavin: *I'm not sending Kyla home. It's Lauren.*

Zayne: *The thing is, Gavin, our sponsors really like Lauren. She uses their products and promotes them on her social media channels. It would really help us out if you could keep her around for a while.*

The screen cut back to Gavin, looking grim. He leaned forward, resting his elbows on his knees and looking up at the camera. Kyla felt like he was looking directly at her.

"I want to be very clear about something," he said. "From the first night, there was never a question in my mind that Kyla was it for me. I knew the production, specifically former Executive Producer Zayne Porter, wielded a great deal of influence and yes, I knew he even had the power to make decisions about eliminations, but I never expected him to exercise that power so cruelly for his own personal gain."

The screen cut to a montage of images of Zayne sneaking out of Lauren's room at The Barclay, each one time stamped with a pre-dawn hour, until it finally froze and zoomed in on a shot of him kissing her goodbye at the door. Kyla gasped, her eyes going wide and her heart pounding in her chest. The images continued, a barrage of bits of film—Zayne smacking Lauren's ass when she passed him in the hallway, Lauren emerging from a back room at Aster Place with her hair mussed and clothing disheveled followed closely by Zayne, lipstick all over his neck. The clips came faster and faster until they turned into a blur on the screen, dissolving back into Gavin.

"After we wrapped filming for the season, it came to light that Zayne Porter had a sexual relationship with Lauren, a contestant on the show, while he was serving as the show's Executive Producer. Not only is this unethical, but it is also a clear violation of both of their contracts and Zayne has been dismissed from the show and all future productions with The Travel Network."

Gavin leaned back in his seat and took a deep breath before continuing his speech to the camera. "We're not going to air the original cut of the final three episodes where Zayne manipulated us all so I would have to choose Lauren at the end. Instead, those episodes have been re-edited into this one, extended length episode, so we can show you what really happened."

The camera faded to black as the opening credit sequence began to roll and Kyla had the insane urge to reach for Gavin, as though she could touch him through the screen. In her pocket, her phone dinged, and she scrambled to get to it.

Jamie: Are you watching?

Kyla: I am. I don't know whether to laugh or cry or track down that asshole and punch him in the face.

Jamie: Keep watching.

If Jamie was telling her to watch, then Gavin wanted her to watch. So she did just that. She sat on the couch between her roommates and watched as she and the other girls presented their antiques to Gavin on a bay cruise, and she watched the shaky footage shot through a crack in the door as Zayne demanded he give the one-on-one date to Lauren or Roni.

She watched footage from a ceiling-mounted camera of she and Gavin sneaking into an empty cabin below deck, and more footage of them sneaking back out, her face flushed as he straightened her clothing.

She watched Gavin's date with Roni, where he asked her all about her charity and Roni told the story of growing up food insecure, of how much good her organization was doing in her community to make sure no child went to bed hungry. The website for her organization flashed across the bottom of the screen, encouraging viewers to donate to the cause.

She watched Davis directing a PA in a blonde wig to accept Brodie's proposal, followed by Brodie's actual proposal to her and then, to her surprise, she watched their argument captured on a wall mounted camera in her hotel room.

She watched herself leave Gavin's room in tears, watched him come after her only to be intercepted by Zayne, watched herself climb into a black SUV and be driven away from the hotel.

She watched as Gavin, face pale and eyes lifeless, went through the motions, taking Lauren on a date to a hot yoga class where she extolled the benefits of Pure Sexxy while wearing a sports bra and spandex shorts. She watched Roni consoling him in the garden of Aster Place as he confessed how much he missed Kyla, how much he loved her, how badly he'd messed things up. She watched Zayne bark at Gavin to get back inside,

Gavin sending Christina home before growling at the camera to get out of his face as he stormed off screen.

The camera panned out on an image of Lauren and Roni, the final two women, standing on the beach at The Barclay. Roni's multicolored ombre hair blew in the breeze as a voice over from one of her confessionals played.

"I don't think Gavin and I are a love match, no, but I hope we'll still be friends when this is all over," Roni said, the camera lingering over her flirty pale blue dress with ruffles along the plunging neckline and ending at her smiling face as she watched Gavin walk down the beach.

Gavin looked like a condemned man approaching the gallows, his face drawn, dark circles under his eyes.

Roni's voice over continued. "Anyone with eyes can see Gavin is in love with Kyla, and that she was in love with him too. I don't know what happened to make her leave, but I don't buy the story that she went back to his son. She was the one for Gavin from the start. All of us knew it."

The image on screen dissolved, replaced by a black screen with Gavin's voice over. "After we learned about the depth of Zayne's deception, the remaining producers and I discussed what should happen next. What ending we should show. I knew immediately that there was only one story I was interested in telling—the truth."

On screen, a montage of footage began to play of Kyla and Gavin, starting with that first night when she got out of the limo. She watched herself shuffle across the driveway, unsteady in her heels, her focus on her feet as his eyes drank her in, a smile stealing across his face. Flashes of footage captured all season filled her screen: them dancing in the ballroom at Aster Place and Gavin pressing his lips to her temple; Gavin helping her during the archery competition, the camera lingering on the way his hands skimmed over her skin; a stolen smile; a secret touch. A thousand little moments playing one after another.

The footage froze on an image of Kyla laughing while Gavin looked at her adoringly, and his voice reached out to her through the television. "This is real. It was always real. And the truth is, I'm not interested in a life without Kyla in it."

Just then, someone knocked on Kyla's front door.

Chapter Thirty-five

"Open the door!" Kyla's roommate screamed, loud enough that Gavin could hear it in the hallway.

He glanced nervously over his shoulder at the cameraman. What if she hadn't watched? What if he'd made a mistake doing this on camera? What if he was too late?

The door opened, Kyla slowly coming into view, and Gavin's knees nearly buckled. His eyes greedily drank her in, dancing over her silver-blonde hair, her red-rimmed eyes, her beautiful bottom lip pulled between her teeth. She wore his Williston sweatshirt and his heart pounded harder, knowing there was still hope.

"Hi," he said softly, reaching out to run his finger over her bottom lip, releasing it from her teeth. He dragged the back of his knuckles over her cheek. "Don't cry, little goddess."

Her eyes softened at his use of the nickname, but then they flicked over his shoulder to the cameraman and wariness seeped in.

"Can we come in?" he asked.

She hesitated a fraction of a second before nodding and stepping back to let them into her apartment. In one corner, Kyla's roommates huddled together, trying to get a look at the scene unfolding in front of them.

"Ladies." Gavin nodded his head in acknowledgement.

"Daddy West," Jo said with a smirk.

The other one—Molly, he thought—linked her arm through Jo's and began dragging her down the hall. "Don't mind her. We'll just be down here if you need us."

Kyla watched them go, waiting until they heard the click of a distant door before she turned back to him. "You brought company." She indicated the camera with a tilt of her head.

Gavin glanced at the camera. "I wanted to make sure everyone heard this part, because it's important that I make myself clear."

She arched an eyebrow at him and he steadied himself with a deep breath before he continued.

"I'm sorry." He held her gaze, focusing on the way the blue of her eyes shifted in the light, as he barreled on. "I didn't tell you what Zayne was trying to do because I thought I could take care of it on my own. I wanted to protect you."

"I didn't need you to protect me. I needed you to talk to me, to treat me like a partner, not an obligation."

"I know that now." He reached for her hand, his skin tingling as it brushed against hers for the first time in weeks. "I've been alone a long time. I'm used to being the guy who fixes things."

"You smooth the rough patches," she said. He narrowed his eyes at her. "Just something Baz said."

He smiled, ducking his head. He really had the best friends. "I smooth the rough patches," he confirmed. "And I'm used to having to do it on my own." He stepped closer to her, crowding her. When she didn't step back, when instead she tipped her head up to hold his gaze, a thrill shot down his spine. "I don't want to do it alone anymore, little goddess. I didn't think it was possible for me to fall in love again, and then you came into my life and I tried like hell not to fall for you. But how could I *not* love you?"

He slid his free hand over her cheek to cup her face, his

fingers drifting into her hair, and stepped even closer, until they were toe to toe.

"Loving you is the easiest thing I've ever done. And I want to love you the way you deserve—with my whole heart and my whole soul, with no secrets between us. I want to give you all of me because I want all of you." He pressed his forehead to hers, closing his eyes.

"I love you, Gavin West, with all I am and all I'll ever be."

She pressed her lips to his and he gathered her against him, crushing her to him to reassure himself it wasn't a dream. Kissing her was like coming home, like that first breath of air after swimming underwater. He'd been drowning before her; he just hadn't known it.

"This is real," she murmured against his lips, a hint of wonder in her voice.

"It's real, little goddess."

Epilogue

Six months later

"My money's on Tricia," Ethan said, tilting his head towards the group of women gathered around Kyla at the desk in the front cover.

"I'm betting on Natalia," Baz said.

The Eye of the Beholder, Kyla's high-end boudoir photography studio in downtown Aster Bay, was finally open for business. The last of the grand opening party guests were still lingering in the studio, appreciating the enlarged images that hung around the front half of the studio in what served as the reception area and admiring the vignettes arranged throughout the back half of the studio, the sets Kyla would use to photograph her clients. At one end of the room, Natalia, the owner of the lingerie shop next door, admired one of the photographs of Erika that Kyla had taken while they were filming. On another wall, Jo smirked at the camera as she pulled down the strap of her lace teddy, but it was the picture of Mrs. White wrapped in nothing but a silk sheet that had gathered the largest crowd, including the subject herself, her friends, and Gavin's mother.

They were all beautiful photographs, but they paled in

comparison to the photo of Kyla that hung behind the reception desk. It was the same one Gavin had caught a glimpse of in his kitchen over a year ago. Once, he knew, Kyla would have been embarrassed to display a photograph of herself, round belly, soft curves and all, alongside photos of Jo and Erika, and his heart swelled with pride as he watched her schedule yet another enthusiastic woman for a session while standing in front of her very own self portrait. An identical copy of that image hung in their bedroom above the dresser that now held her clothes alongside his.

"He's not even paying attention," Jamie said, elbowing Gavin.

"What?" Gavin asked.

"Who's next on the wall?" Ethan asked, tilting his chin towards the group gathered around Kyla.

"Tessa," Gavin said.

Ethan swore under his breath as Jamie burst out laughing. "You know, that's not a bad idea. I think I'll go see how soon we can fit my wife into the schedule." He sauntered off to join Tessa at the reception desk.

"You brought that on yourself, you know," Baz said.

Ethan rolled his eyes. "How's Brodie liking the new job?"

Gavin smirked but he let the subject change slide. He never tired of bragging about all Brodie had accomplished in the last few months. "He's loving it. Patrick says he's a natural."

After Zayne was unceremoniously ousted from the good graces of reality television execs everywhere, leaving Brodie without someone to introduce him to the more influential industry insiders, Patrick had offered to take Brodie under his wing. He was currently in a small town in Maine with the crew of *Once Upon A Town* filming season two starring Erika. Brodie was working directly with Patrick as his personal PA. Gavin had never heard him so excited about anything.

"Nothing like seeing your kid succeed." Ethan smiled knowingly as he glanced at the remains of the giant cupcake tower Tessa had provided for the party.

"I'm going to head out," Baz said. "Say goodbye to Kyla for me."

"Say goodbye yourself." Gavin tilted his chin towards the reception desk.

Baz glanced that way and shook his head, grimacing. "Not while Trisha's still over there. She keeps texting me suggestive gifs."

"I didn't know that was a thing," said Ethan at the same time Gavin asked, "Suggestive how?"

Baz rolled his eyes. "See you both tomorrow at trivia."

"I have a good feeling about this week," Gavin said. "I think we're going to win this one."

"You say that every week," Ethan said.

"And eventually I'll be right."

Kyla caught Gavin's eye from across the room, an easy smile sliding across her lips. She arched an eyebrow and blew him a kiss before turning her attention back to helping Tessa schedule a session.

"Baz told me about the ring," Ethan said softly. Gavin nodded. "Are you asking her tonight?"

"No. Tonight's all about her. She's worked too hard for this for me to pull any attention away from what she's accomplished here."

He and Baz, with significant guidance from Tessa over video chat, had picked up the engagement ring from the jeweler last week. Since then, it had been safely hidden away in Gavin's sock drawer. He wasn't sure when he'd actually propose, but he'd know when the time was right. Besides, he didn't need a ring on her finger to prove they'd be together forever.

An hour later, Kyla closed and locked the door behind the last guests, waving goodbye. As she turned the deadbolt, Gavin came up behind her, wrapping his arms around her waist and resting his chin on her shoulder.

"Congratulations. You were amazing tonight."

She melted back against him, pulling his arms tighter around her waist. "Thank you. This was incredible."

He brushed his lips over her ear. "Are you ready for one more surprise?"

She turned to look at him, her eyes dancing as a slow smile spread across her lips. "What are you up to?"

"Come and see."

He took her hand in his and led her through the studio to the little office in the back. Just before he opened the door, he moved behind her, using his hands to cover her eyes. She giggled as he slowly walked her through the door into the room. He led her to a spot in the center of the small office, turning her slightly until she was positioned exactly as he wanted her.

"Ready?" he asked.

"Mmhmm." She wiggled her hips against him, the suggestive slide of her curves over his groin making his cock twitch in interest.

He chuckled. "Later, little goddess." He nipped at her ear. "I reserved your favorite room at Olympus to celebrate the grand opening."

"Ooh, let's go!" she said, pressing back against him harder.

"You're a menace." He dragged his teeth over the curve of her neck. "I'm trying to give you a gift."

"Well, if there's a gift involved, I suppose I can wait," she teased.

"Open your eyes." He dropped his hands to her hips, squeezing her curves lightly as he held her against him.

She gasped, her hand flying to her mouth. Behind her desk hung the painting of the little red dinghy from the art gallery.

"How did you do this?" She spun around to face him, pressing her hands to his chest. "The curator told me it wasn't for sale."

He gripped her hips and walked her backwards towards her

desk. "It wasn't. But it turns out the curator's wife is a huge fan of reality television." The back of her legs hit the desk and she leaned against it, her ass resting on the edge. "I told him I'd be happy to stop by her birthday party and pose for some photographs and suddenly he was more than happy to sell it to me."

"I don't know whether to be impressed by your ingenuity or jealous," she said with a smirk as he dragged his hand over her knee, up her thigh, his fingers slipping beneath the edge of her skirt.

"Don't you know by now? You have nothing to be jealous of."

As his fingers drifted higher, she parted her thighs, wrapping her feet around his calves and pulling him closer. "I thought you said we were going to Olympus later."

"We are," he said, smiling. He traced the line of her panties beneath her skirt, skipping over her cloth-covered mound to repeat the move on the other side, and she huffed in disappointment. Her pout was adorable and he couldn't resist kissing her until it melted back into a smile. "I've been watching you all night. I've been watching you *glow* like the star you are." She blushed and he traced her slit through her panties, the fabric already deliciously damp. "I need you to tell me something, sweetheart."

"What's that?"

"Do you taste different when you glow like that?"

Her eyes sparked to life as she dropped her thighs to the side, her skirt sliding up to her hips as she did. "You tell me."

He kissed her again until she was soft and pliant in his arms, his finger continuing its slow exploration of her through her panties. "Go get your camera, little goddess."

She reached behind her and retrieved a small remote from the top drawer of her desk. Aiming it over his shoulder, she pressed a button and the unmistakable sound of a shutter filled the room. Gavin glanced over his shoulder to where her camera was already arranged on a tripod, aimed perfectly at the desk. The shutter sounded again.

"It's on a timer." She set the remote aside and the shutter sounded another time. "Every few seconds it will take a picture until I turn it off again."

Christ, she was the perfect woman. "How did you know I'd need to fuck you on this desk before the night was through?"

She giggled, the sound dancing across his skin. "Let's just say I was hopeful."

He dropped to his knees between her spread thighs as the camera continued to click in the corner. She lifted herself up just enough to help him pull her panties down her legs. Once her legs were free, he held the wet fabric to his nose, inhaling her scent, and then tucked them into his pocket. His cock jolted as the smell of her flooded his senses, earthy and sweet and so very her.

"You're so wet already." He dragged a finger through her slit, gathering wetness as he went. The camera shutter sounded again and more moisture pooled at her opening. "You like the idea of having your pussy eaten on camera, Ky? You like knowing it'll be captured forever, how greedy your little cunt is?"

She whimpered, wiggling her hips towards him. "I like knowing we can see ourselves whenever we want."

"That's right," he purred against her. "My little goddess likes to watch. So, watch, goddess. Watch while you ride my tongue. Watch how beautiful you are when you come."

He buried his face between her thighs, licking up her dripping sweetness with ravenous laps of his tongue, and teasing her clit until it was ripe and swollen and pulsing with need.

"Tell me what you need," he growled.

"I need to come." She drove her hips up against his face, riding his mouth as a hand fisted in his hair. "Oh, God, please make me come."

Who was he to deny his goddess? He plunged two fingers

into her opening and sucked on her clit, dragging his teeth over the sensitive bud, until she screamed his name, her thighs shaking against his ears.

When her knees fell back away, he stood up, wiping his mouth with the back of his hand as he undid his belt with the other. "Fucking delicious."

She pulled him to her, kissing the taste of herself from his lips as she released his cock. They both breathed a sigh of relief when she wrapped her hand around his straining erection, dragging her thumb along the thick vein running down his length. A few slow pumps, and then she guided his tip to her opening. He pushed through the tight ring of her fingers into her pussy, enveloping himself in her slickness and heat.

"I'm so goddamn proud of you, Kyla," he growled at her ear, loving the way she shivered when he let that gravel into his tone.

He fucked her in slow strokes, drawing out their pleasure to be sure every second would be captured by the camera. Later, he'd print the best photographs, the obscene ones that showed her swollen and stretched around him, and the glorious ones that immortalized the pleasure etched on their faces and the shape of her mouth when she cried out her pleasure, and he'd keep them in a little box by their bed. Their own private show any time they wanted to remember this moment. And he wanted to remember forever, the intense heat and the tight grip of her around his cock, the way she moved against him, but also the way she'd taken up residence in his heart, how she'd cracked him open and stitched him together anew, how this joining of their bodies was all the more incandescent for the joining of their souls.

He came with a roar, pumping his release deep within her, writing his love inside her body. As they came down from their orgasms, he pressed his lips to her temple, her eyelids, her jaw, caressing her with his kiss as he murmured his praise for how beautiful and brilliant she was, how perfect she was for him, how she'd been made just for him.

"I love you, little goddess," he said against her lips.

She smiled through their kiss. "And I love you, Prince Charming."

352

The End

Also by Cara Dion

Love Song Series
Irreplaceable

Indiscreet

Undeniable

Aster Bay Series
Whisking It All

Just For Show

Visit my website to learn more and
download free bonus content:

<h1 style="text-align:center">Acknowledgments</h1>

About a year ago, my aunt Ann invited me to a Facebook group for a local boudoir photographer. I was skeptical (what business did I have joining a boudoir group??) but I accepted the invitation anyway.

Over the next year, I was awed by the relentless positivity of the group, by the way bodies of all sizes and shapes were celebrated, with an entire group of women—most of whom did not know each other—cheering each other on for their bravery and their beauty.

And at the center of it all, boudoir photographer Kerry Callahan.

An idea began to form. I reached out to Kerry and asked if I could interview her as research for this book, and she generously and enthusiastically gave of her time and knowledge (romance readers are the best!). At the end of that interview, she invited me to come to her studio and have my own boudoir session, something I never thought I'd be comfortable doing.

But the seed was planted, and I'll admit, I was intrigued. I couldn't shake the feeling that doing this could be a powerful part of my own journey of recovery from disordered eating and negative body image. I had no idea how true that would be.

It has been an honor to try to put on page a fraction of the magic that Kerry (and other boudoir photographers like her) works when she helps women see how beautiful and powerful they are, when she helps us view our bodies as works of art and not liabilities.

Kerry—I cannot thank you enough for your generosity and your support, and for the amazing work you do helping women believe in their own beauty and worth. I only hope I have done you justice on the page.

As I've said before, no book is created in a vacuum, and there are so many people I need to thank for helping to bring Kyla and Gavin's story to life.

My husband—thank you for always supporting me, for reminding me to give myself grace, for not-so-subtly encouraging me to rest.

My son—thank you for being so proud of Mama, even when you don't know all the ins and outs of what I do. Having you march into the library and proudly tell the librarian that your Mama writes books made me happier than you'll ever know.

Mom and John—I know I say it every book, but I do not know where I'd be without you. Thank you for always believing in me, for always being my biggest champions and cheerleaders, for all the big and little ways you support me. I am the luckiest person around to call you my parents.

To my amazing author friends, Ginny B. Moore and Sophie Snow—without these women to read early drafts of my work, and brainstorm plot points, my books would not be what they are. Thank you both. And Ginny, thank you for being the person I can text at any time of day or night with unhinged half ideas and for helping me make sense of them.

Brittany (@caffeine_and_spice) and Nicole (@ thesmuttykindle)—thank you for being my informal focus group when I need a second (or third) opinion, for polling your own followers to help me zero in on specific elements, for always being quick with a book recommendation for any mood, and for the countless hours of reality TV discussion.

Finally, thank you to each and every one of my readers. You have no idea what it means to me that you continue to read my stories. I am grateful every day for your support.

About the Author

Cara Dion writes steamy, contemporary romance, often with a forbidden or age gap relationship.

Cara has always had an overactive imagination and spent much of her teenage years watching 80s and 90s romcoms with her aunt. She read her first romance when a friend snuck one of their mother's Harlequins into their Catholic school and passed it around like contraband, but she didn't return to romancelandia until the pandemic.

She has been an English teacher, professional musician, and nonprofit administrator. When she's not reading or writing romance, Cara loves cooking, Broadway musicals, and all things Disney.

Cara lives in a small town in New England with her husband, son, and two very demanding cats.

Follow Cara on Instagram at caradion.author and contact her at cara@caradion.com. Visit the website and join Cara's newsletter to get insider information on upcoming books and exclusive content.